The Altered Moon II

The Tyrant of Unity

By
James Alan McGettigan

Copyright © 2023 James Alan McGettigan
All Rights Reserved

No part of this publication may be reproduced, distributed, or transmitted in any form, or by any means, including photocopying, recording, or other electronic or mechanical, methods without the prior written permission of the author, except in the case of brief quotations embodied in reviews and certain other non-commercial uses permitted by copyright law.

This book is dedicated specifically to my father. He is the reason why I write the way I do. He assisted me in the creation of the series' name and inspired the arc of the story, which begins here, in book two.

The Author would like to add a trigger warning for all readers of this novel. As there are graphic and complex fight scenes between male and female characters. There are also tropes of toxic relationships between some of the characters and drug addiction in this novel.

Contents

Prologue 1
I A New World, Awakened 10
II Bumpy Ride 13
III Skiv 18
IV Quantum Fade 25
V Void Sight 37
VI Compromised 41
VII Drakkar 47
VIII Alternate Interrogation 50
IX Diazep 59
X Nano Brain 66
XI The Diramal's Cho'Zai 73
XII Dark Wave 78
XIII Honor Between Rivals 86
XIV Relapse 90
XV Shadow Scar 97
XVI Returning Home 100
XVII Dreaming Into The Past 104
XVIII Inspection 108
XIX Kalbrook And Vykin 116
XX Neuro-chip Free 119
XXI Cracks In My Wall 128
XXII Promotions 133
XXIII Recollection 137
XXIV Broken Promise 142

XXV Ion City	145
XXVI Warv	160
XXVII A City Submerged	171
XXVIII Marks Of Sanctuary	179
XXIX 9247-Nacilag	194
XXX Shadows In the Blacklight	198
XXXI Unforgettable Faces	206
XXXII Sphike	214
XXXIII Orphaned	226
XXXIV Anua's Hidden Child	240
XXXV Breaking The Unbreaking	245
XXXVI Exile	260
XXXVII Shine	268
XXXVIII Artificial Organism	272
XXXIX First Date	280
XL Hide And Strike	288
XLI Buried Fortune	294
XLII Warter	302
XLIII The Důlabega Quadrant Incident	311
About the Author	316
Author's Social Media	317
Glossary	319

Prologue
(Olson)

For two years, this war between humanity and alien has waged on. Neither side ever seems to have the upper hand over the other. In the first month, after the invaders darkened our skies, we stood no chance of countering the incredible speeds at which their vessels and they themselves move. Fortunately, that obstacle faltered shortly after M.I.S.T. conducted studies on the body Amat brought back from Anua. As the lead scientists in the study, Doctors Hanker and Rogen discovered how the aliens move so quickly and adapted it into a technology we can use. From my understanding of the subject, the aliens produce a natural source of atoms that have been labeled "Merceuros." These atoms are found throughout the bodies of the aliens—in their skin, blood, and flesh. Much like how our mass, as humans, is predominantly composed of water, Merceuro makes up most of the mass found in the aliens. Through further examination, they discovered that the atoms split and expand, proceeding to collide and bounce off one another frenetically. This activity creates an energy field around the bodies of the aliens, propels them, and allows them to move at great velocities. Rogen and Hanker built armored suits that allowed our armies to alter time by stocking them with alien blood. After some time, the suits need to be replenished, of course, but a few drops can last over a week if the suit is used sparingly.

After having spent a week on the surface of Galiza fighting off the alien forces without relief, Log, our cousin Lara, and I went to the Y'Gůtsa Base cafeteria to alleviate our appetites. Though exhausted, we longed to eat a decent meal and drink fresh water. Out on the surface of Galiza, food is rationed and just enough is supplied to give us the strength to fight for a few days at a time, a week tops.

Only a handful of others were present within the cafeteria. It was open all day round, but everyone's meals were monitored and limited to just two a day. We all ordered our food separately and regrouped at one of the tables. No words were exchanged until after we finished.

"Do you know how long we have 'til we're due back out?" Log asked, scraping up the last clusters of food off his tray.

"Two days, I think," Lara replied.

"Olson, do you think you'd want to spend the day with Mom and Dad tomorrow?" Log asked.

"If I feel up to it, sure. It's been a while since they've seen us; I'm sure they'd appreciate you stopping by, even if you're on your own," I replied.

Log and I gave each other worn smiles.

Log stared at his left hand as its index fingernail agitatedly tapped the table.

"What's on your mind?" Lara asked.

"Well . . . I was wondering if either of you'd heard any update on when Amat would be coming back?" Log replied.

Lara shifted her attention to the table, uncomfortable with the subject matter.

I sighed and shook my head.

"Log—"

"I know that we can't reach out to him, any more than he can to us, but that doesn't mean we shouldn't be concerned for his safety. He's still family," said Log.

I stared into Log's sympathetic eyes. I pitied him, for how highly he continued to praise Amat, in spite of what our cousin had become.

"Yes, he is," Lara butted in. Both Log and I looked over at her. "And you shouldn't be ashamed for being so concerned for him, Log. Ever. I think Olson and I just . . . struggle to hold an open mind as you do. But to answer your question, I haven't heard anything."

It's been weeks since any of us last saw Amat. Normally, it's consecutive months before we catch any sighting of him. A year into the war, Log, Lara, and I joined the ranks of the Alphas, hoping it might allow us to get closer to Amat, since it's the only rank he'll take under his command. It was Lara who encouraged us to pursue the rank; she was more determined than either of us at the time to find a way to reclaim her brother. Her speeches managed to seep so deeply into Log's head that they left him with a false sense of hope. A part of me resented Lara for having created such a desperate mindset within my brother, after all he himself had been through.

In the end, our efforts proved to be for naught. Right out of the program, we found ourselves under the command of a Jinn who wasn't too dissimilar from the Diramal's persona: Jinn Ch'Guart. At times I find myself having a similar dynamic that I imagine Amat must have had with the Diramal, after Uncle Bod was killed.

Neither Log nor I blamed Amat for how he behaved toward us in our last engagement with him when he returned from Anua. Looking back on it, we can acknowledge that he was only trying to keep us safe from his enemies, the Diramal in particular. A man who has long since been a threat to the Criptous family.

Where Log seems to have forgiven Amat for what he did, I myself wonder how much of our cousin we'd already lost before he became who he is now. I do worry about him; I just don't see how our cousin could ever be returned to us. Sickens me when I think about it too much.

"I've heard that Amat and his men should be returning sometime next month," I said.

"Thank you, Olson," replied Log.

I nodded.

"Say, *um*, hasn't it been almost a year since you've been clean?" I asked, trying to change the subject.

Lara widened her eyes as she shifted her attention to Log.

"It will be, next week," Log replied.

Lara and I smiled.

"That's great; I'm proud of you," I said and patted him on the shoulder.

"In that case, perhaps we should all meet sometime tomorrow or the day after. To celebrate you and your recovery," said Lara, raising her cup to Log.

"Perhaps we should," I added.

A few months into the war, Log had become overwhelmed by . . . a multitude of things. Losing our cousin, being forced to fight in a war against an alien species, and practically losing our father to faulty programming in the nano-regenerators. Our father wasn't killed, but around four months into the war, he came down with something awful, and after being treated with the nanotech . . . he just hasn't been the same since. That was the blow that finally broke him, I think. And Log got himself involved with . . . the wrong kind of coping mechanism, as a result.

Log gave me a weary smile and yawned. His eyes were red with exhaustion.

"Yeah, I feel much the same way," I said, gesturing to my brother's open mouth. "We should all get some rest while we can."

"I second that. My back's probably gonna be stiff in the morning from the sudden shift, but I can't wait to just drop my back onto a soft mattress," Lara said.

"I'll raise my cup to that," said Log.

Log and I stood and shook hands.

"See you tomorrow," Log continued.

As I turned to Lara, the base trembled, the alarms went off, and blue lights flickered from the walls. A voice shouted on the intercoms.

"Attention, all recruits of base Y'Gůtsa! This is Jinn-hid Criptous. I am being pursued by an overwhelming alien aeronautical threat and we're running extremely low on ammunition. My squadron has taken heavy losses, I need immediate—" The feed suddenly cut out.

The ground shook again as dust fell from the roof. We all looked at each other and ran straight for the base's hangar. Swiftly, we strapped into separate Dailagons, an upgrade from its predecessor, the Krogen fighter jet. Equipped with antigravity tech, which allows us to keep up with the alien craft in a scrap, barely. All was dark once the canopy locked down; then a clear display of everything outside the Dailagon was visible before me and several holographic interfaces displayed within reach. The engine hummed, gradually rising in pitch as I zoomed outside the base. Molecular scanners activated across the interior of the canopy.

The alien crafts moved as fast as the aliens themselves. Thus, a pilot's reflexes in this war must be keen, and the slightest hint of hesitation truly means the difference between life or death. However, Dailagons are equipped with high-grade tracking and automated targeting systems to keep the pilot aware of his or her surroundings. Providing the pilot with the most assured aim.

At times, aspects of the alien crafts were clear, but their details were blurred as they swooped and stretched past. The body was oval-shaped and there were two small forward curving wings at either side.

Almost immediately after the molecular display was activated, I saw an alien craft closing in on me, head-on. The craft burst into flame and fell apart as I flew past it. The next instant, I witnessed the Peroma dive ahead of me amid the explosion. *Amat,* I thought.

"Alpha Olson Criptous, are you receiving me?" Amat asked over comms.

"Y-y-yes, Jinn-hid," I replied.

I saw another alien craft looping toward me, so I spun around, evading its shot, and fired back. It didn't land, but I bought myself a moment's rest.

"Over half of my Fades have been taken out. I need you to help me create a distraction, to lure the majority of the hostile forces from them so that they can dock safely," said Amat.

"What do you have in mind, sir?" I asked.

"How many Dailagons do you have available to you, Alpha?" asked Amat.

"About forty, Jinn-hid," I replied.

"Six of my Fades are still airborne, Alpha; assign your Dailagons to form in groups of six or seven around each Fade and see them all home. Leave the rest to me," Amat replied.

"Yessir!"

I relayed the orders from Amat. Log, Lara, and I oversaw that each of the carriers were well protected and assisted in the fight if the aliens focused too closely on any particular Fade. Amat flew the Peroma almost as wickedly as the aliens themselves, firing her weapons so precisely he scarcely missed his targets. No more than a few seconds passed between each craft he shot down. However, it wasn't long before several alien fighters started to converge onto Amat. I assumed this was his plan all along. No matter; Amat weaved through every shot the alien forces took at him. Dancing in the air, blasting the alien forces out of the sky.

After we had successfully moved all six of the Fades into Y'Gûtsa, Log, Lara and I flew out to help Amat fend against the large force that surrounded him. We pushed our Dailagons to their maximum speed and gradually shot down one alien craft after another. Before we could hope to take all of them out, the Peroma started to take a heavy beating, but Amat kept her airborne as long as he could.

When only four of the alien craft remained, one of them landed a critical shot at the center of the Peroma. The shot hit just to the rear of the pilot's seat and the Peroma started to plummet. I cursed. Lara immediately shot the same craft down. I fired at two more, flying beside one another and landed a shot on one of them. The force of the explosion threw the second off balance. Log swooped down and blew it out of the sky before it could recover. The fourth craft fell back before anyone could get a lock on it.

Amat's ship crashed through several floors of multiple buildings; the crash seemed anything but survivable. I had shut everything else out of my head, denying the high probability that Amat had been killed. Though, a part of me couldn't be so sure, considering all Amat had survived in the entirety of this war.

"AMAT!" Log and Lara yelled over comms, snapping my attention back to the present.

"Olson, Lara?! Do either of you see any movement by the Peroma?!" Log continued.

I looped around over the crash site.

"Negative," I replied.

"I'm passing over the crash now..." Lara said. She sighed with regret. "Negative."

"No . . . no, no, no! We have to get down there!" Log said.

"Log, nobody could have survived that kind of crash. Not to mention the hit that brought her down was right behind the pilot's seat," I said.

"Well, I don't have to take your word for it. I'm going down after him," Log replied.

"I'm going too," Lara added.

"I'll go down with you guys. I never said we shouldn't collect him . . . just don't be surprised by what we find, Log," I said.

We landed on a road next to the house that had halted the Peroma and rushed in through the opening. None of us could get any of the hatches to open, so we came to the front of the ship and breached the cockpit.

"Amat?!" Log yelled.

We saw his body still strapped into his chair. But to my surprise, completely unscathed. The loose straps were the only things keeping Amat's body from falling onto the control panel. He hung there limply. Log looked back at me, panting. I examined Amat's body closely and observed tiny droplets of blood dripping from the seeps of his helm. Lara covered her mouth as she burst into tears. It broke my heart to see it, but I knew it would only be a matter of time before that code nine neuro-chip sent Amat to his death. I placed my hands on Lara's and Log's shoulders as I walked past them.

"He's gone. Will you help me take him out of the ship?" I asked.

Log nodded as tears welled in his eyes. We walked back up to Amat's body and unstrapped him when—

"AHHHH!" Lara screamed and stumbled back. Amat clenched his fingers around Log's and my arms as he caught his breath.

"Jinn-hid?" I asked as we stumbled out of the Peroma.

"Amat, you're alive!" Log blurted out, overjoyed.

"How?" Lara asked, her tone reinvigorating as she collected herself.

"Wait, both of you, stay back, stay back," I said, placing Amat on the ground and creating some space between him and the others.

Coughing, Amat unveiled his head as the metallic constructs shifted over the armaments around his shoulders, neck, and back. Amat looked up at us, puzzled.

"*Huh,* Lara, is that you?" Amat asked.

My cousin's tone had changed. He sounded . . . like himself. He hadn't asked the question like he normally would in the form of a demand, nor did he refer to Lara by her rank.

Lara's breath caught.

"Amat? You referred to me by name, how could—"

I stopped Lara's approach. She shifted her head toward me to protest.

"Wait, Log, Olson, did I hear your voices too?" Amat asked.

I slowly advanced toward Amat, knelt, and retracted my own helm; the light coming off the flickering flames from the crash was enough to illuminate the details of our faces. Amat smiled—an expression I hadn't seen him wear in years.

"Olson, it is you," said Amat.

"And . . . it's you," I replied in awe.

"It is him?" Lara rushed to my side and took one look into Amat's eyes with her own as she retracted her helm. Amat's jaw dropped as he took in Lara, stretching his fingers out to her hair. He mouthed her name. "Oh, Goddess, it's a miracle!" Lara wrapped her arms around Amat, ignoring the fact that her grasp knocked the air out of him.

As Amat stroked his hand against Lara's back, he studied the area, trying to recollect what had happened. He paused when he looked back at the Peroma.

"What's happened? Where are we? Is our family safe?" Amat asked.

Lara studied Amat's eyes. Log and I looked at one another uncertainly.

"You were just in an accident. You crashed over a neighborhood in Dath'Jagol, and our family is safe, within the confines of base Y'Gůtsa," said Lara.

"Dath'Jagol? Base Y'Gůtsa? But . . . how did—"

"Amat, who are we to you?" I asked, interrupting my cousin's contemplation.

Amat was thrown off by the question.

"You're my cousins and Lara, my sister; my family. You mean everything to me," Amat replied.

Amat coughed and raised his hand to the cut on his head.

"How does that feel?" Lara asked, as she held Amat's face in her hands and examined the wound.

"It stings," Amat replied, turning back toward his ship. "What happened to the Peroma?"

"You were in an accident, Amat, shot down by the invaders. You don't remember?" Asked Log.

"Invaders? You mean the aliens; they've invaded?" Amat asked.

"The wound doesn't seem lethal, but we should get him back to base," Lara said, ignoring Amat's previous question as she picked him up off the ground.

"Hey, easy, Lara, we don't know how bad he's—"

"Base? What, the S.E.F. base? I just got out of the infirmary over there . . ." Amat said, speaking over me.

Lara, Log, and I paused, glancing at one another.

"Amat, what year do you think it is?" I asked.

"It's still twenty-five forty-eight, isn't it?" Amat replied.

A quizzical silence fell between us all.

"Amat, it's twenty-five fifty," Log said.

"You've had a code nine neuro-chip in control of your psyche for two years," I added.

Amat seemed taken aback. His legs trembled and gave out under him. He was about to bring Lara down with him, but I rushed to Amat's side and helped him back up.

"Whoa, whoa, Amat. Take it easy." I took a closer look at Amat's injury for myself. "Something tells me that blow to the head is worse than it looks. He shouldn't be moving too much on his own."

Amat growled as we dragged him toward Lara's Dailagon.

"Log, open up my Dailagon's canopy," Lara said.

Log moved to do just that.

"I'm fine, just need a moment to process . . ." Amat's words faded.

"Rest is what you need," Lara said.

I could see Amat fighting the drowsiness hanging over him.

"It's alright, Amat, you can rest. We'll take you home," I said.

"Home . . . No, wait!" Amat lifted his legs and pressed against the concrete as he twisted back toward his ship. "Don't leave the Peroma; come back for her. Make sure she's salvaged, Olson."

We paused.

"I promise you; we'll come back and retrieve the ship," I said.

"Thank you . . ."

Amat drifted off to sleep. I wanted to smile at the idea that I finally had my cousin back, but I wouldn't know for sure until after his wounds had been mended. For all I knew, that could turn him back into the lifeless machine he'd been for the past two years.

I
A New World, Awakened
(Amat)

Time has gone by so slowly ever since I started to regain control over my consciousness compared to the washed-out blur of events that followed the implantation of my code nine neuro-chip. Subsequent to my crash in Peroma, a year back, I started having gaps of time where I would regain my own self-awareness. During said gaps, my cousins helped me to preserve a substance of my own making. When finished, I used it to melt away the neuro-chip in my head, permanently deactivating it, using what I call nano-magmic reanimation.

The substance was adopted through the new and enhanced technology of the regenerators. A mechanism that is now recognized and used by all members of our species. Prior to the invasion of our world, the old regenerators functioned off a highly concentrated form of solar energy. Even after M.I.S.T.'s development of the quantum suits that allow the rest of my species to move like the aliens . . . like me, it was decided that every fighting man and woman played a crucial role in this war. Thus, it was imperative that all had access to the nano regenerators, which has proven to be a far more effective source of revival. Unlike the solar regenerators, men and women who have been dead as long as an hour have come back. Though, there are very few. None who return from the dead can recall where they went to next; if they went anywhere at all. Nevertheless, I've heard it said there are notable changes in their character after their return to life. Once marked with this trait, these soldiers are referred to as a Dövar.

The nanites in the regenerators are, in a way, live organisms, programmed by the mechanism to revive any damaged tissue. Hence how, in some cases, they can bring some back from the dead, as the nanites themselves are filled with life. Similarly, in the making of my substance, I programmed the nanites to attack any non-organic appliances in my body. However, the way they carried out their programming was not a pleasant experience in the slightest. When the day finally came to administer the adapted substance, my cousins, and especially Lara, monitored the activity around my brain. They noted that the nanites were using high temperatures, in bursts, melting away my tissue as well as the chip little by little and then immediately repairing the tissue. I suppose you could say the process is like the nanites fighting themselves. Hence the name nano-molecular, and magmic, reanimation. Upon completion, the nanites dispersed and died off.

Not a day goes by when I don't still feel the pain, the anger, and the drive to kill every last one of the savages that have terrorized and ravaged my world. All thanks to a triangle of men—myself, my father, and the Diramal—our world has been overrun by an otherworldly presence. Our skies are still darkened by the formation of the alien ships, and no one has dared to face them head-on. This begs the question of how much longer the aliens can persist in their invasion of our world as we run their numbers down, on the surface.

    Credit to the scars that mark my body from the early days of this war, I am constantly reminded of what I endured when the Diramal broke my body and used a mark-one model regenerator to restore it. I'd recently discovered it did more than that. Besides the vigorous incisions, several solutions were injected throughout my anatomy. I can't begin to think what they contained, but I have reason to believe they may have made me more adept at my time-altering abilities, as I've noted they're much easier to activate and control. This, of course, raises more questions: How would the Diramal know about such a serum and in using it, why would he seek to amplify my abilities, even as a slave?

    Thanks to the researchers and engineers of M.I.S.T., much of our weapons, power, and technology now run off ice. A technology they back-engineered from the data that Doctors Rogen and Hanker retrieved on that second mission to Anua. It has recently come to my attention that they are both dead, unfortunately. After reading the reports on their deaths, I concluded both occurred too close in time to each other for it to be a coincidence. Perhaps when they spoke about challenging the Diramal's authority, they weren't just saying what I wanted to hear after all. My guess is the Diramal saw the knowledgeable partnership between the two doctors as valuable but as a means to an end.

Later, I asked Olson about Rogen and Hanker, and whether he knew specifically what either one of them had done to draw attention to themselves. Olson didn't know much about Hanker, but he heard rumors of Rogen openly speaking out against certain regulations and procedures regarding the 'Skivs.' The majority of humanity who are starving, weak, and helpless. Shunned to the chaos of this great conflict. In some situations, I've heard it said that Skivs are shot on sight should they come near the grounds of any military base. Had I the authority, I would never condone such a distasteful action and the gunmen would meet with *serious* consequences.

Among the Skivs are also the 'Warvs.' Various bands of humans out in the scrap of the world scavenging for anything they can get their hands on, to survive and provide their own resistance against the invading forces. Unsupported by the military and are, in fact, in retaliation against it. In many circumstances, it is hard to discern Skiv from Warv, and in some ways, they are but the same. To my eyes, no labels discern the fact that we are all human, enduring the same fight.

Rumors had also spread about Hanker—how he became superstitious in the last few months of his life. He hardly left his lab, not even to eat, and Rogen had apparently been taking care of him when he could. Makes me wonder what must have been on both the good doctors' minds, whether spoken aloud or not. Death hardly seems a reasonable punishment for either man.

One other thing that strikes me as strange is how there have been no ramifications to Galiza's natural environment. Since this arrival of prodigious craft and their numbers, there has been no shift in the tides, no tremors, and no violent volcanic activity. As if Anua continued to maintain the balance of nature, even in death. Considering the technology the first of these invaders displayed, amplifying the gravitational field between Anua and Galiza, I'd consider the possibility that these other ships cluttering our skies may also be compensating for what we lost in Anua's gravitational field. The question is . . . why?

II
Bumpy Ride
(Amat)

Septica 26, 2551, 6:42 a.m., strapped down in a Fade, flying over Ornvike City. A large concentration of invaders has been detected, taking positions to the east of this city. I've been tasked to command a squadron of Alphas to track and wipe out the converging alien presence. I, however, have a priority of my own that only my troops and I know of. To seek out and rescue as many Skivs as possible, for the purpose of returning them to Y'Gûtsa. There, I have trusted connections that smuggle the Skivs into various bases around the world—an underground process I've been overseeing for the past seven months. Civilians aren't rapidly dropping dead, but there's a lot more space and rations to be spared than the Diramal will admit. And as far as he's concerned, I'm still his puppet.

Since the Peroma's crash, I haven't been flying much on my own. Ironically, with a name like "Fade," you would think the ship flies a smooth course, when in fact it was quite rigid. Doesn't take me long to be reminded of how different it feels to be the passenger of a craft, rather than its pilot. I'm not sure if it was the lack of control or the scenario itself, but on numerous occasions, I felt sick while aboard a Fade. Though, I wasn't the only one staining the plated floors with vomit at times.

I got up from my seat and walked over to the pilot.
"Koyût Sarak." I called her by rank.
"Jinn-hid Criptous," she replied.
After several short encounters with her, I learned that I could trust Sarak Almeida. She was from Afeikita, a moderately sized tropical country near the equator of my world. Her skin was as dark as the fur that covered her neck and scalp. Her eyes looked as pure as silver. It was she who had proposed the idea of recovering Skivs.
"What brings you up here to the main deck?" Sarak asked.
I sighed.

"You know how my men get sick on these rides—" I paused as the Fade rocked vigorously. "At a certain point, the stench gets to be too much."

"*Hm*, I can only imagine." Sarak chuckled.

"How fortunate you are, sitting where you are as opposed to myself." I shifted uncomfortably.

"Oh, don't count me as so advantageous, sir. I've still had my fair share of combat. I know what it's like to be in the back of a rocking truck, driving through thick wilds. With the fear of not knowing who might be hiding in the muggy woods of my country. Made me anxious at times," said Sarak.

"You said you were driven out in trucks. You didn't start out in the Air Guard?" I asked.

"No, when I fought in my own country, I was a Reganga, a rank equivalent to your Gromrolls. The kind of soldier you put on the front line—cannon fodder," Sarak said.

That's a bit harsh, I was once demoted to Gromroll, I thought.

"But I stayed alive, worked my way through the ranks, and shortly after the invasion, I was recruited to fight here, in Utopion, trained in the Air Guard."

"That's a peculiar transition," I noted. "It sounds like you amounted to a highly valued soldier. How did you get transferred to a different branch of the military?"

"I was brought here to train as an Alpha, but I didn't do so well in the program. I couldn't handle the training for the Marine Fleet. The only thing I learned from that was my phobia for the ocean," Sarak said with a smile. "I failed my artillery trials, but when it came to my aerospace training, it seemed I'd found a new talent to excel in and acquired a much more precise aim. Thus, I spent the second year of the war piloting Dailagons at the rank of Jŭtŭk, then worked my way up once again."

"Sounds admirable," I replied.

"I understand your father got you involved in the Alpha training program when you were still very young. Did you ever find out why he was so insistent on enlisting you?" asked Sarak.

I hadn't really thought of my father in years. Even as I regained control over my conscience and abilities, I'd never really noticed his presence again. I sighed as I tried to bring my thoughts back to center.

"*Uh*, my father, he didn't put me in Alpha training. I enlisted and he despised me for that. He ended up pulling me out of the program, right after I graduated, taking me under his wing and command. I hated him for it, at first. But now I see he was only trying to get me to understand what I do now. That war and division among people were being used to keep us distracted from something. He never had a chance to tell me what it was, exactly."

"I should hope you find it someday, sir," said Sarak.

"I should hope so too," I replied.

We shared a smile.

"We're about to pass over the target area, sir. Time to arrival is five minutes."

"Very good. I'll ready the troops then," I said, as I stepped away from Almeida.

My team dressed in their quantum suits: QS-25s. QS stood for "Quantum System," and the number 25 referred to the depth of the quantum level in which time could be altered. In the three years of this war, there have been two predecessors of this technology: the QS-75 and QS-50. The lower the number, the slower you can safely make the outside world move around you. This is to say, in a QS-75, you could push the suit to the same depths as a QS-50, but at the risk of succumbing to quantum fade.

Quantum fade is a hazard that comes with the utilization of the quantum suits, in which one pushes the limits of his or her suit too far, too long. Moving at speeds that exhaust the oxygen throughout one's anatomy, regardless of how deep and or hard they breathe. Push through that for too long and your organs could implode. Often, it's the heart.

Of course, I didn't require one of these suits myself. All the same, I wore one as it provided me with armor and helped to enhance my control over the ability. My eyes, on the other hand, are a different story. In the helm of the suit, there is an interface that lights up the world with a digital reflection of the land's layout, amplified through sensors used to create augmented realities in matrix platforms. This is paired with a concentrated molecular sensor that tracks and distinguishes the movements of our enemies and allies. I seldom used this feature of the suit; my eyes still had their own way of illuminating my surroundings and distinguishing entities.

We all equipped ourselves with a weapon of choice and stocked up on ammo. Along with one additional piece of equipment developed by M.I.S.T. in the second year of the war when they studied alien P.O.W.s. The device was called a cryptic, fitted to be placed over the laryngeal prominence of our throats. It makes dialogue shared over comms sound identical to the alien language. To us, we hear each spoken message in our native tongues. But should any outside source, physical or virtual, overhear our conversations, it would sound alien.

Soon after the QS-75's development, it was discovered that the aliens have a heightened sense of hearing and, at the right range, could even hear a group of soldiers whispering amongst themselves out in the open. Compromising their position, entire squadrons would be ambushed within a matter of seconds. Since its making, the cryptic has greatly helped to hide our presence on the battlefield.

After I'd gotten myself fully geared up, I returned to Sarak.

"How close are we to the other allied Fades?" I asked.

"Not far off, Jinn-hid. Fades two through six are around half a mile out from our position. Seven through twelve are about an extra mile out from us," Koyût Sarak replied.

"Contact seven through twelve and tell them to pull east of our route to minimize the cluster of our fall," I commanded.

"Yessir!"

Sarak relayed my orders as I marched back to the rear to meet with my troops.

"ALRIGHT, FORM UP! TIME TO JUMP IS EXACTLY ONE MINUTE!" I shouted.

The troops made way and formed up behind me as I passed them, until I reached the front, where we awaited the opening of the hatch.

"Shutting off interior lights," Koyût Sarak said over comms.

"Activate molecular sensors!" I ordered.

The lights switched off and the hatch of the carrier slowly opened. The wind came gushing in as the hatch opened fully.

"Activate quantum Suits and fall out!" I barked.

My troops and I raced out of the opening and fell to the chaos of our world.

III
Skiv
(Amat)

When you fall from 30,000 feet in the air, wind blows more harshly as it passes you in altered time. Like a whirling hurricane. Moving faster than the speed of sound, yet everything around you moves slower than an old man on crutches. You're tranquil . . . until you have to move. I shifted my head to my left, instinctively, and observed the alien fighter swooping in. Quickly, I tucked my arms in and extended my legs closely, spinning with so much turbulence in the seeps of my armor that it allowed me to arch over the craft. Granting myself more control over my fall, I activated the suit's nano-fabric, which formed between the legs, inner arms, and ribcage, to serve as a wingsuit. A little further down, I pulled my chute and landed safely on the ground.

I opened a channel that was linked to all members under my command.

"Squads two through twelve, do you read me?" I asked.

The obnoxious gibberish of the alien language, translated by the cryptic, could dimly be heard outside my helm. There was no reply.

"Squads two through twelve, this is the Jinn-hid. Do you read? Over."

"On your right, Jinn-hid," Lara said, walking to my side. I turned to look at my sister. "No answer?"

"No," I replied.

"There must be some interference, sir. At this rate, most of the troops should be on the ground, standing by for orders," Log said, as he followed in behind Lara.

"Thank you, Alpha, for stating the obvious. That's always helpful," I said.

I felt Lara's glowering gaze on me, despite the cover of her helm. I shrugged and furiously began pressing buttons on my fizer—a multipurpose device that all Utopian militia had been issued during the start of the war, built into the tops of our forearms. It helped us better communicate and navigate our surroundings, among other things. Our suits retract an opening so that we may access the device while armored.

"Sorry, sir—"

"*Sh!*" I silenced Log. "Did you hear that?"

"What, sir?" Lara asked.

"*Listen!*" I stressed.

We all stood in silence. A few moments passed and we all heard it. A woman's voice screaming in the distance. I pointed in the direction of the noise.

"That."

I returned to my fizer and dragged a nav point over a holographic map of the area, pinned it, and sent it out to my troops.

"That should help get everyone in order. Let's fall out," I said, as I altered time.

"See you at the rendezvous point, sir," said Log, just before I raced off.

Everyone ran through the streets in altered time, hurdling over obstacles. Executing advanced parkour at high velocities in order to maneuver past the debris that cluttered the streets and within the buildings. Galiza, our home, had become a ruined wasteland.

I stopped as I noticed a faint particle signature. Something that looked like a small group of Skivs . . . or Warvs. I unveiled my fizer and remotely sent out a static surge. A means of communication while we were all in altered time. Sound, especially communicated over comms, is useless in altered time, as it can't be registered in the same instance it is uttered. So, we send out surge signals—a subtle jolt of electricity, nothing so extreme as to impose harm, but powerful enough to draw attention.

"Sir? Is there a problem?" asked Olson over comms.

Olson, glad to see you made it safely down with the rest of us.

"None that I've seen directly. I detected a particle signature back a ways: human. I'm going back to investigate. Alphas Olson and Log Criptous, you have command over the troops," I said.

"Yes, sir," replied Log.

"I'll catch up with you once I've assessed the signature. Carry on," I added.

"Yes, sir," said Olson.

"I'm going with you, Jinn-hid," Lara said.

"Very well, find me in the street, heading back the way we came."

"Roger that," she responded.

I altered time and backtracked with caution. Before long, Lara moved in beside me and we continued the rest of the way within the ruins that filled the streets.

I never discriminated against Skiv or Warv, but that didn't mean they did the same, especially the Warvs. Lara and I entered the remains of the ruined home through a gaping hole near the entrance, with our guard up.

We found the family at the other end of the house, and they hardly seemed to notice us or cared to acknowledge our presence as we approached. Still, Lara and I trod lightly. For all we knew, this could have been a Warv trap. Reaching the Skivs, Lara and I eased down to their level. The Skivs all had the same expressions, the same longing shared amongst their eyes. There were four of them: the oldest I took for the mother, an older boy, who lay on the ground before them, and two younger girls. Each of them trembled and though the boy lay very still, I could see his chest rise and fall inconsistently. I slid my fingers across the side of my helmet and scanned the boy. I received an analysis that the boy was in critical condition. They were all dressed in robes, but the mother's was the most detailed. It gave her the resemblance of a Rella, a figure of our faith.

Lara's helmet reshaped itself into an extra layer of armor over her shoulders, revealing her face. She proceeded to emanate a dim light from her fizer, removed the cryptic at her throat, and introduced herself.

"Hello," Lara said courteously.

No one replied. I heard a deep thud in the distance and suddenly the air filled with echoes of explosions and gunfire. Lara and I looked over at one another.

"That's too much gunfire," I said.

"Should we go?" Lara asked.

I considered that for a moment. My troops had been ambushed, but I had every confidence in Olson and Log's ability to handle the situation. Still, I wanted to get this family to safety as quickly as possible. I looked back and caught one of the younger girls glancing at me.

"No. We'll stay," I said, removing my helm and shining my own light from my fizer. "Hey, it's alright."

The girl glanced around, avoiding my eyes.

"Do you have a name?" I asked.

"L-Lúvi," she replied.

"Lúvi, it's a pretty name," Lara said with a smile.

"It's nice to meet you, Lúvi. I'm Amat, and this is my sister Lara." Lúvi went back to ignoring us.

"Lúvi, is he your brother?" Lara asked, pointing at the boy.

Lúvi nodded her head, her eyes filling with tears.

"He's sick, isn't he?" Lara asked. Lúvi took a moment to respond.

"He's dying. My mother and sister are in a state of Änga. We are praying that Anua will ascend his soul to the Luminous Paradise. Even in her passing," Lúvi replied curtly. Her tone had Lara taken aback.

Änga, so the mother is a Rella.

"He may not have to," I said. Lúvi slowly raised her head. "We can take him and the rest of you somewhere safe. Somewhere we can get him help—"

"*No.* They'll kill us at your military bases." Lúvi cut me off.

"Were it any other circumstance, that would be true. But I can ensure your safety," I said.

"Anua ensures our safety," said Lúvi.

Lúvi looked away from me and back at her brother. I looked at Lúvi's mother, whose eyes stared blankly down at her son.

"Lúvi, your mother, can she hear us? Or maybe, is your father around? Could we talk—"

"My father is dead." Lúvi spoke so calmly, it was like she was talking about an everyday thing. I sighed impatiently. Lara remained silent for a moment as she attempted to place a sympathetic hand over Lúvi's.

"Words can't describe how sorry I am to hear that, Lúvi," Lara said.

Lúvi tugged her hand away before Lara could touch her. Lara respectfully pulled her arm back.

"You know, I lost my father to the invaders as well—"

"My father wasn't killed by the invaders," Lúvi said abruptly, cutting Lara short.

I almost didn't hear her. Lara and I shared uncertain looks.

"What was that?" Lara asked.

"Something worse than the invaders killed my father," replied Lúvi.

Worse than the invaders? What could she be talking about?

"I can still hear their screeches," Lúvi said desolately.

I concluded that Lúvi's state of mind clearly wasn't sound, and that trauma was doing most of the talking. The thunderous noises of the battle waged on, intensifying. If Lara and I were going to safely move Lúvi and her family, we needed to do it quickly.

"Lúvi, your brother, as we've established, is dying. The rest of your family will suffer the same fate, if not worse, and if we meant you any harm, it would have already happened. We can and will save your brother if you'll let us. As much as we will leave you here to die . . . if you let us," I said.

Lúvi stared at me for a moment, then turned back toward her mother and awakened her from her deep state of Änga. The mother's eyes widened with a primal fury as she observed Lara and I. Whispers were shared between mother and daughter, the mother's eyes holding a stare with my own. Lúvi faced us once again after her mother nodded.

"We will go with you, Amat. But should you trick us, mark my words, Anua will forever curse you and your family," said Lúvi.

"Your words are marked well, Lúvi. I wouldn't take such words lightly, especially from a daughter of a Rella, as I see your mother is."

Lara and I enveloped our helms around our heads, and we led the family outside. Lara carried the young boy while the others followed.

"Stay behind me and keep quiet," I said, peeking outside around the house to make sure there were no signs of hostiles in the area.

"Okay, here," Lara said, walking back toward them. "We should be alright, but in the event we are separated, take these." Lara handed each of the Skivs a light source to help guide their way, which Lúvi and the others refused to accept.

"We would see better without these," Lúvi said.

I nodded.

"Alright, then at least take this. It's a fizer. If we are separated, press this button"—I pressed the button, and it revealed a route—"and it'll lead you to a Fade piloted by a trusted friend of mine. Her name is Sarak. She will see to it your brother is nurtured back to health and your family is given shelter."

Lúvi nodded as she took the device from me.

As I turned to exit the house, a pair of razor-sharp claws latched into the seeps of my armor, grazing my shoulders, and flung me out onto the street. My sister's shouts slowed and shifted in tone as I altered time, just long enough to keep from tumbling across the pavement. When I came to a stop, I stabilized time and commanded Lara to take the family and run. The next moment, something scraped and sparked across my armor, knocking me to the ground. I altered time again and turned my head in the direction of the alien, but it was gone. The next moment, the alien scraped its claws across my back, almost forcing me flat on my chest. I growled as I pushed myself off the ground and whipped out the claws at the tips of my suit's fingers.

I glanced frantically in every direction for this tactical foe, but by the time I'd spotted it, the alien rammed its two horns against my gut, knocking the air out of me and slamming me against a wall. I dug and scraped my claws into the back of the alien's ribs. The alien screeched as I grabbed it by the horns and flung it into the air, landing on its back. Pouncing atop the alien, I pressed my hands around its hairy, frail neck, my claws slowly drawing blood as they pressed deeper and deeper. The alien hissed as it placed two of its hands on my elbows and the others on my waist, pushing me off.

The alien rolled over and raised its right two claws for another swing. I unsheathed my knife and pierced one of the alien's palms as the second arm scraped and sparked across my armor, the seeps of my suit clenching. The alien shrieked as I stood, picked it up off the ground, and threw it into the wall. Its body shriveled up, and its limbs were crooked. I regulated time, observing as the alien lived out its final moments in anguish. It emanated a weak, lisped trill as I approached it. Thrusting and twisting my blade into one of the alien's hearts, I heard the invader let out its final cries.

I turned away to catch up with Lara and the Skiv family. Running up the road, I found them, regulating my altered time ahead of their path. They were startled to see me, but I settled them down.

"Are you alright?" I asked.

"Yes, we're all safe," Lara said.

"Good, we'll show you the rest of the way to the Fade."

We ran as fast as we could to the Fade, located inside an old building with no roof.

I walked up to the hatch and opened a channel.

"Almeida, this is the Jinn-hid. Open the door," I commanded.

"Yes, sir," she replied over comms.

The hatch opened. Lara and I escorted the family into the Fade and introduced them to Almeida.

"Almeida, this is Lúvi and her family. Her brother is in critical condition, and he needs a regenerator asap," I said, as Lara set the boy down in a seat and strapped him in.

"Of course, sir. I'll give them clearance along the way," said Sarak.

"Good." I took one final look at Lúvi.

"We must go now, Lúvi. I wish you and your family a safe journey," I said and started to walk toward the exit.

"Wait," Lúvi cried. I stopped and turned around toward her. She walked up to me. "Thank you, Amat, and you, Lara."

I nodded my head and acknowledged Lúvi's thanks with a smile. Lara knelt at Lúvi's level.

"Keep looking after your family, Lúvi," Lara said.

My sister and I promptly turned back around, altered time, and regrouped with the troops.

IV
Quantum Fade
(Amat)

Pushing the power of our QS-25s to their limits, Lara was hardly able to keep up in our race against time to rendezvous with the troops. When we finally reached my squadron, just under half the troops were still alive. A considerable loss, but compared to the number of fallen enemies, my losses seemed minimal.

"Did you locate the Skivs, sir?" Olson asked.

I slowly shifted my attention to him.

"We did. They're with Sarak," I replied.

"Is Sarak still holding her position, sir?" asked Olson.

"No, one of the Skivs was terminally ill. I ordered Sarak to get him medical attention."

"I suppose that doesn't leave very much hope for all our fallen brothers and sisters here then," said Log. His tone suggested passive aggression.

I whipped my attention to my younger cousin.

"The boy was still alive, Log, he'll have a greater chance at life from the regenerators than most of these men and women combined. Y'Gůtsa is more than an hour out from this city," I asserted.

"That doesn't justify the fact that we lost more than half of our troops in this battle," Log interjected.

My helmet reshaped and revealed my face as I gave Log a soft but piercing stare.

"Perhaps I should have trusted my command to someone *else* among your rank then." I spoke sternly. "Each of these men and women, both on the ground and still breathing, is the best in our army. I have no doubt the ones who fell here today fought with every bit of strength they had. Their sacrifice will not go unnoticed by Anua."

"Anua has been long lost to us, Jinn-hid," Log growled.

I walked up to Log until only a few inches separated us.

"No, dear cousin. Merely her physical form is obstructed and lost to us. But her essence lives on"—I spoke louder, addressing each of the troops that stood there—"and continues to surround us, even in this dark segment of history we find ourselves in. Of that, I am quite certain. As should each of you be."

I dropped to a knee beside one of my fallen soldiers, placed a hand over her heart, and lowered my head. I whispered a silent prayer for her and all the others that would join her in the Luminous Paradise.

Leaving the fallen soldier to rest in peace, I asked what remained of my team to gather around and form our next move.

"What's the play, sir?" Olson asked.

I stood with my arms crossed as I contemplated my next strategy.

"I need everyone to fall into three columns," I replied.

With the exception of Olson, Log, and Lara, who stood at my side, the others did as they were instructed. I beckoned for three specific Alphas to stand at the head of each column. There were roughly sixty men and women to a column.

"Each Alpha standing within your column is who you will be scouting with. Your priority will be to seek out and escort as many Skivs as you can find. You will be guiding them back to this exact location in three days' time. Fight only when you need. Alphas Jiu-Gok, Waikü, and Kravon, who are at the head of your columns, have been deemed worthy of leading each column. Be on your guard and may Anua illumine us all," I said.

I raised my hand to my team, presenting the back and then the palm. They responded with the same gesture.

During the first day, as my sister, cousins, and I hiked out into the ruins of Ornvike, we found no sign of Skivs, Warvs, or the invaders. As we grew tired, we took refuge inside a building that had somehow hardly been touched by war. We each rested six hours and took a two-hour watch in between. Log, not being much of an early riser, was hesitant to get up as quickly as the rest of us. But he carried out his watch without complaint.

***

On the second day, we came across a section of town where the roads were cracked and so badly rifted that they would have served as good cover if we were ever attacked. Most of the buildings had been reduced to piles of rubble and those that still stood hardly remained intact. We followed the road for miles and in all that time, much of the scenery hadn't changed. Barely a word was uttered between the four of us, except for when we'd occasionally reach out to one another, asking if anyone had spotted something worth mentioning.

Finally, Log decided to start a conversation worth building off.

"Jinn-hid, I'm sorry if I might have been a bit outspoken towards you back at the remnants of the ambush," Log said.

I reflected on that for a moment.

"That's alright, Log. I understood where you were coming from and, in some respect, you were right. I should have been there fighting alongside you and the others. However, sacrifice is a part of war and sometimes the costs are greater than we'd like to bear. What truly matters is that we do not allow the sacrifice of our fallen kin to pass in vain. That we honor their sacrifice by continuing our own fight and protecting what remains of our race," I replied.

"I know and I support you fully in that objective," said Log.

I turned toward Log and nodded my head.

"I know you do," I replied.

Olson sighed. "I wonder if we'll find anything out here at this rate."

"I have a feeling we might, good or bad," I replied.

"I don't know, Jinn-hid. How long ago did Sarak report to you after her surveillance over the area?" Lara asked.

"Less than a week ago," I replied.

"Hopefully, whatever we find turns out to be good," Log said. "I think I must have rolled over or rested my back on some rubble last night—it's really *stiff*."

"It's not going to hinder your ability to fight, is it?" I asked.

"Wouldn't be my preference in this condition, but I have no doubt I could. I don't see any reason to worry, however, there's been no sign of hostiles for over a day," said Log.

"That could change at any moment," said Lara.

"Stop and see if you can stretch it out. It's better to be prepared for the worst than walk into a combat zone handicapped," I said.

We stopped by a rift in the road that had been formed by a crashed Dailagon and was big enough to provide cover for the four of us if we were attacked. Log bent forward and back, twisted his spine, and leaned this way and that in an attempt to loosen it up.

"Jinn-hid?" Log asked.

"Yes?" I replied.

"Do you still blame Uncle Bod's death on the invaders?"

An unspoken gloom was suddenly shared between us all. A flash flood of unnerving memories sprang to mind.

"Still?" I chuckled and shook my head. "Always. There's not a day that goes by when I don't miss Dad. I despise these savages for it." I looked up at the black sky. "They've caged us up like rodents. I never forgot who *really* killed him, though."

"Do you mean the Diramal?" Log asked.

Prrrrrr! Shots were fired at us before I could answer Log's question. Log blurted a curse.

"TAKE COVER!" I yelled.

"Log, get down!" Olson shouted.

Beams of orange and purple lights flew past us. We all crawled to the rift and armed ourselves. It was a tight squeeze between the four of us.

I tried to peek my head over the rift, but the incoming fire was too heavy. I turned over to my cousins and sister. "All of you, stay right here!" I yelled at them over the seemingly endless volley of gunfire.

They nodded their heads and yelled back: "Yessir!"

I altered time and turned back. Springing up, I dashed for the nearest building where I found shelter. Beams of light flew past me as I pushed my altered time ability to such a level that the shots moved slow enough for me to evade them. I scaled up a few stories and broke into one of the levels of the building. Taking cover, I tried to count as many windows that emanated enemy gun-fire.

I returned to my sister and cousins.

"How many are there?!" Log asked.

"I counted up to sixty, plus!" I replied.

Log cursed, jerking forward.

"There seem to be more sources of fire coming from the right side of the street rather than the left. If you two cover the left side, Lara and I can take the right," I said.

"Are we so sure we can take on that many, just between the four of us?" Olson yelled over the crossfire.

"I know we can," I yelled back.

"How do we know there aren't more invaders headed this way, to reinforce this front, and if that happens, what then?" Lara butted in. "We'd already be pushing our luck with these numbers. We should fall back and—"

"We fall back, and we risk being overrun in their pursuit of us. This is an abnormal cluster of the enemy; they could be defending something. Or worse yet, there could be Skivs stuck in the crossfire. Should we just abandon them?!" I argued.

"And what if the rest of the world loses you? Do you think anyone else will take on the Diramal and his tyranny in your place?" pressed Olson.

"That won't happen," I responded.

"You can't know that for sure," said Olson.

"Alpha Olson Criptous, I am your commanding officer. My say outweighs your own and I say we fight! That is final," I barked.

Olson growled and looked away.

"We'll stay in contact over comms. If any one of you is harmed, we will fall back. Are you ready?!" I asked.

"Yes, sir!" Log replied.

We all hugged each other tightly and got ready to initiate our attack.

"Alright, on my mark…"

I heard something land just on the other side of the bunker that made a high-pitched noise. Then I saw it, a few feet away from our positions. I was about to blurt out, *"Grenade!"* but it had already gone off before I could warn my cousins and sister. I was close enough to the blast that a powerful wave pushed me sideways, knocking me off balance. I couldn't feel or hear anything except for a ringing in my ears. Lara came to my side and tried to get my attention, her yells muffled, but I was fixated on Log. I watched as Olson examined his younger brother. Log nodded his head as Lara proceeded to shake me. I raised my arm to her and fell back.

"Go!" I blurted, waving my hand at them.

I altered time and forced myself up, despite my disorientation. I ran so fast that I scaled the walls of a nearby building on the right side of the street. Making my way up to the top of the building, I felt wearier and wearier by the second, so I took cover behind a chimney to catch my breath. I could hear my heartbeat pulsing in my ears and feel the blood pumping in my head. A painful nausea filled my chest that seemed to get worse the faster my heart pumped. My legs were shaky, and my eyelids were heavy.

I shut my eyes tight as my head rang like a bell. Lara found me and came to my side; her voice was still distorted. Feeling well enough to proceed, I ignored my sister and ran to the edge of the roof toward the next building containing hostiles. Lara remained close to my side. Smashing through separate windows, Lara and I rolled up to a desk and knocked it over for cover. A few invaders turned toward us right when we entered. We gunned them down without hesitation. Pulling the clip off a grenade, I dragged Lara down by her shoulder to take cover. I held the grenade for four seconds, then threw it as far as I could. The moment I ducked down, it detonated. I took out my electric shock-put 101 and charged the alien forces in the room, killing any and all that got in my way. I stopped in the center of the room to hold my ground against a charging hostile, and Lara swooped in behind me to cover my rear.

Once we cleared the building of invaders, we launched ourselves into the next one over. I pulled out the crystal magazine in my E.S.P. 101 and threw it toward a door flooding with enemies. The moment the crystal cracked against the floor, it emitted a short burst of static light and evaporated several enemies near it. Lara gave me cover fire as I swiftly loaded my E.S.P. 101 with another crystal. Together, we stood our ground as the alien force continued to grow, edging closer and closer to our position. Overwhelmed by the sight of their numbers, I felt I could barely stand. I was losing control, and sooner or later I was going to have to snap out of my quantum field before my body gave out. Distracted, I allowed a lone alien to catch me off guard, ready to swipe two blades at me. I cracked the bottom of my gun against the alien's chin, grabbed my own knife, and sliced its chest.

As I ran by, I looked out of the windows to the right of me and saw my cousins struggling across the way, in the other building. *I must keep going!* I told myself. *For them. For my sister. They need my help!* Lara and I reached the end of the level of the building we were in and jumped out of a window. I moved from my cover, spraying my fire across the alien formation. Dancing from one to another, not spending more than two moves on each to take them down. Before long, Lara came close to my side and joined me.

One launched right at me and I stabbed it in the throat, forcing it to the ground before its dead weight could pin me down. As I pried the knife out, another dashed beside me, and its lower right claws scraped across my arm. Growling, I swiped my blade at it, barely scraping the back of its scalp. The next, coming within inches of me. I had no choice but to kneel down and unsheathe my second blade, driving it into the charging invader's gut. Using its momentum to lift it above me. The fourth I stabbed in the foot, flicked open my claws, and swiped them across the alien's gut. A knee, from my left, *launched* against my chin and jolted my head back. Another, from my right, scraped across my shoulder armor. I howled and bent my ears back as part of the armor was scraped off before the seeps could clench.

It was then that the sounds of Lara's own struggle reached my ears. Out of the corner of my eye, I glimpsed a pair of aliens overwhelm her. Her cries echoed to me and the moment I redirected my attention, I saw one was about to land a lethal blow.

"No!" I howled, stretching my arm out to the creature. Its movements froze, and suddenly I reached a depth to altered time, causing the surrounding bodies to move very gradually. Filled with a moment's relief, I tried to piece together just how I did that. I lowered and twisted my wrist subtly, and the being's motion steadily reversed. I held my hand stiff, noting that its movement determined that of the alien's. Then I stood, twisted my wrist as far as it would go, and realized the creature had moved back a few paces. I stepped close to the alien, took one final glance at my hand, back at the creature, and lowered my wrist. Everyone's movements picked up immediately after. Hardly ready, I swiped my blade up along its body, turned back around, and saw that Lara had managed to take down the second invader on her own.

I stared at the alien I had just slain, still processing what had happened, before a very slight movement on the wall distracted me. It was another alien, staring at me with curiosity. I tightened my grip on my knife. It was the most subtle twitch of the head, and while the aliens had no irises, I knew this one was looking past me. Something had drawn its attention there. I swiftly turned and met with one of the remaining aliens. Lara quickly reached her claws around its face and tore them across its flesh. I twirled back around and threw my knife, expecting the alien pinned on the wall to still be there. The blade penetrated only the wall, as I caught a faint glimpse of the final creature escaping the room. I took a step to pursue it, but then Lara placed her hand on my shoulder and halted me. She directed my attention across the street, reminding me. *Right, our cousins... there's no time.*

Reluctantly, I collected my weapons, and we charged into one final building where the aliens had taken positions. Upon entry, Lara and I were separated, landing at different levels of the building. I immediately took out two of the aliens beside one another on my own. Not stopping to take cover, knowing it would kill my adrenaline rush. I took out my pistol and fired one, two, three times. Killed one, wounded one, killed another, pushing further into the room.

I glanced over to my side, catching movement out of the corner of my eye. An alien had gotten the jump on me and pinned me to the ground. It buried its claws into the seeps of my helm, their tips barely scratching at my scalp. Growling, I launched my elbow into its face and rolled over on my back, punching the alien with my fist. As I motioned to strike a killing blow, the surrounding enemies piled themselves atop me. My right arm had been held down firmly, but I could still wiggle my left—barely. The alien directly atop me squealed as it squeezed its pincers against the steel of my helm. I slammed the back of my head into its mouth; the blow granted me enough wiggle room to lift my left hand and slice my blade across the alien's neck. The alien above extended one of its arms to try to restrain my left. In the struggle, I lifted my left arm as I shifted my legs into a tuck, planted my toes against the ground, and pushed myself out. Shots were fired as my sister moved in to assist. Sliding across the ground, I felt woozy as I found my feet. A punch landed across my jaw, then a second swing, but I raised my arm and blocked it. Lara killed the alien that tried to pin me down and came to my side, helping me off the ground.

Stumbling to my feet, I pushed Lara forward, directing her to the nearest window. I pulled a pin off a grenade but did not remove it from my belt. Holding Lara's grasp tightly with one hand so as not to let her slip away, and held the belt in the other for four seconds. I dropped the belt on the ground. The invaders clutched at our heels with their speed. In normal time, the grenade would have gone off almost immediately after I pulled the pin. But in altered time, weaponry is impacted by the phenomena. Still in altered time, Lara and I had a few extra seconds before the detonation.

Lara jumped out of the building and *boom!* The grenade had set itself and the handful of others attached to the belt off in a grand explosion. I was steps away from the window frame when the blast sent a shock wave through the room. I leaped, and the shock wave propelled me forward, through the window. Tucking my limbs, I closed my eyes, and readied myself for the impact. The fall toward the paved road seemed so gradual. The ringing in my ears dissipated . . . just before the impact. All movements quickened—in sight and in my physical body—as I tumbled like a barrel until I finally slowed and expanded my limbs. Regulating time.

Lying on my back, I rested, motionless, with the echo of the battle waging in the near distance. The pain didn't settle in right away. At first, it was only numbness. It crept in on me, and with every beat of my heart, the ache grew sharper and sharper. So tempted to allow my conscience to escape into the depths of my mind . . . if it hadn't been for a familiar voice.

"*Amat . . .*" a voice said, as a cold chill came over my heart.

"Dad? Is that you? Oh, goddess, I pray it is. If you can hear me . . . please, speak to me. Give me strength."

I waited patiently for a response. I rolled over to my side with a growl as I slowly pried my upper body off the ground.

"*Father!*" I barked in my head.

"*Amat . . .*" my father replied almost instantly. "*Get up.*"

I eased my knees under me, grunting.

"*Come on, Jinn-hid, move!*" said my father.

I sniffed and shook a trailing tear off my cheek from inside my helm.

"*Yes, sir!*" I replied.

"Amat!" Lara shouted as she grabbed my arms and took in my appearance. I planted my hand on her shoulder.

"I'll be alright." Slowly, I nodded. A thunderous collage of explosions drew our attention up to the other side of the street. "This is almost over. We need to get to Olson and Log."

Lara nodded her head. "I'll follow your lead, Jinn-hid."

Lara and I launched ourselves forward, altered time, and I armed myself with my E.S.P. 101, peering up to determine where the enemies held their ground. Once I caught wind of their position, Lara and I moved in to flank the enemy.

We rushed up the side of a building and I rolled into an opening behind enemy lines, where I proceeded to fight with an unhinged ferocity. Sliding across the floor, I shot down my passing foes. Rushing forward, I holstered my gun and got out two knives, one in each hand, taking on several aliens at a time. In unexpected instances, Lara and I would converge on the same target. Meanwhile, down the way, Olson and Log were still pinned down. I stopped to scavenge a few alien grenades off a corpse before pushing further. Olson and Log were just in the next building.

Lara and I sprinted through an opening and dove into the next building over. Lara was immediately met by two aliens on either side of her. On her knees, Lara ducked, extended her leg out, and swung it around so hard she tripped and shattered the legs of the first alien, then stopped beside the second. The alien swung two blades at my sister as she leaned back and then shifted forward, stabbing the alien in the gut.

I crashed atop an alien, digging my suit's claws into its throat and ripping it out. I stood and threw a grenade to a side of the room occupied by a large cluster of the invaders. Their attention shifted to me as I ran all around the room, annihilating every hostile that persisted.

One caught sight of my berserk charge and took aim at me, but I thwarted it with a push of my hand and punched it in the waist. The alien shoved its gun into my face. I swiped my left leg under the alien's feet and as it fell, I stabbed it in the chest. Two more came to me from the side, with three others following behind it. I ran up and stopped behind them, sheathing my right-hand knife, got out my pistol, and shot the three at the rear. I tossed the gun aside and replaced it with a knife. One of the aliens

The Tyrant of Unity

had blades of their own; curving and arching over their knuckles. The other had a wrist attachment with blades extending forty-five degrees at either side of their forearms.

As I spun, I swung each of my knives at both foes, steel sparking steel. One of the curved blades on the alien's lower extremity scraped against the waist of my armor. I planted my feet just after I passed them and swiped at the shoulder of the one bearing the curved blades. Lara swooped in and met with the angled blades. It sensed her rushing from behind and swiped its blades toward Lara's face; she dropped to her knees, slid, and scraped the claws of her suit against the alien's lower armpit. Lara stood at my side and faced our remaining foes. Panting, we stood still for a moment. Taking in their armaments, I considered: *Ya know . . . I wonder . . .*

I proceeded to holster my right-hand blade and flicked out my claws. My sister and I charged the aliens, and moments before we made contact, I aimed my palm at Curved Blades, took a deep breath, and twisted my wrist. Its movements were 'versed, just like the one before. The act made Angled Blades turn their head back. One more step and I lunged low, swiping my blade across the alien's side. Lara proceeded to finish it off. I moved my focus to Curved Blades. It too seemed taken aback, as it witnessed its ally fall. Wasting no time, I spun around, leaned forward, and swiped my blade deep across the alien's guts.

I whipped my leg around the alien's back and knocked it to the ground, almost splitting it in two. I regulated time and turned to meet my cousins' stares, limping toward them as I let my blade escape my grasp. Out of breath, I removed my helmet to get some fresh air in my lungs. Still, I couldn't escape the light-headedness. I stumbled toward the ground, but Lara rushed to my side before I could collapse.

"Are you alright?" I asked my cousins. The next instance, my eyes rolled up in my head.

I was in a regenerator, lying flat on my back, with Lara, Olson, and Log standing right beside me. We were in a med bay with a single bright spotlight illuminating the regenerator. I woke up startled, but Lara calmed me down.

"Easy, Amat, you've just recovered from quantum fade," said Lara.

I couldn't see much of my surroundings, as most of the room was extremely dark.

"Where . . . where are we, and the road, what did we find beyond the road?" I asked wearily.

Olson and Log shared smirks. Lara gave a silent chuckle.

"Should we show him?" Log asked.

"Yes, I think we should," Olson answered.

"What . . . what did we find?" I asked anxiously.

"See for yourself, brother," said Lara.

Olson propped up my bed so that I could see what rested beyond it. What I saw was . . . grotesque. So many women, children, men—civilian and soldier alike—dead. The floor and the people were drenched in blood, as they all lay there motionless. All life was sucked from their eyes. They looked as though they had died from savagery. My tongue was stilled. The more mesmerizing the scenery became, the more a dark outline immersed itself over the people. I shed a tear, just one. As it dripped, I heard an intruding voice.

"Aren't you proud of yourself, Amat?" the voice asked.

I turned my head toward the spokesman aggressively and saw the Diramal. He stood between my cousins, as if they were working together. The Diramal wore an evil grin on his face. My heart raced as my breath escaped me. The betrayal and the loss I felt in that moment. The Diramal put a gun to my head and pulled the trigger.

I woke up, yelling, tormented by my vision, and thrust myself into an upright position, coated in sweat.

V
Void Sight
(Amat)

As I collected myself, someone moaned beside me. I turned and saw Olson resting there.

"Ohhhh," Olson sighed as he stretched.

"Olson?" I asked.

"Yeah, Amat, it's me," he replied.

"Where's Log?" I asked.

"He's on your left," replied Olson.

I turned my head and met with Log's waking glance.

"Amat," Log yawned my name.

I acknowledged Log with a nod.

"Somebody pour a bucket of water on you?" asked Log.

I glanced down at my clothes and wiped at my cheek, noting how sweaty I was.

"Yeah, are you alright?" asked Olson, resting his hand on my shoulder.

I cleared my throat.

"Head hurts," I replied, gently retracting Olson's hand.

"You're not the only one," said Log.

"Where's Lara?" I asked.

"She's with Aunt Judi," Log replied.

"Ah, of course," I answered.

"Amat, do you remember much of what happened?" Olson asked.

"Uh, a little, not much. I remember feeling overwhelmed, like I could barely keep it together. My altered time state," I said.

"Do you remember . . . reversing the movements of that one invader?" asked Olson.

"Reversing?" I took a moment to process what Olson meant by that. "Wait, yes, vaguely. There were two. I did it for the first time in one of the other buildings. I extended an open hand out toward them in both instances, twisted my wrist . . . I'm not sure how I did it."

"You had no control?" asked Olson.

"Not particularly. Like when I first started altering time on my own, it just happened. I will say, being able to do it twice consistently suggests I have more control over this ability than I did—altering time by itself."

Olson shook his head.

"You should have called it off, Amat. Quantum fade is not something to be taken lightly. We were lucky Sarak brought us back to the base when she did," Olson said.

"Did Sarak say if she got the girl and her family to safety?" I asked, ignoring Olson's concern.

"Yes," Olson replied, irked.

"And is the boy safe?" I asked.

"Yes, they're all fine and well. They've taken up quarters here until Sarak can find them a safer base to reside in," said Olson.

"Good," I replied.

"Sarak said that she overheard the little girl, Lúvi, discussing a strange entity with her mother. Something that plagued them in the waste. Sarak later asked Lúvi about it; the girl referred to it as a 'shadow scar.' Some kind of cursed figure," said Log.

Log's mention of the word "shadow scar," echoed the word within my ears. At first as a series of overlapped whispers that progressively grew louder. I shook my head and sealed my eyes. A flash of light exploded over my own sight and I found myself standing in a dark hallway. My surroundings estranged me, as I had never experienced anything like this before. My eyes adjusted gradually to the dimness. Every step I took echoed and splashed in a thin layer of black water that flooded the floors.

I continued to walk down the hall until it led me to columns: endless columns of humans, asleep in capsules. Being experimented on, tortured, and mutated into some sort of creature. I was drawn to one in particular, a woman whose body hadn't been scathed yet.

What little light illuminated my surroundings dimmed, and I sensed an ominous presence fill the atmosphere. The woman looked so tranquil, and her breath was steady, shoulders rising and falling with her chest. Slowly, her brows tensed, and her mouth frowned. Head twitched, then her shoulder, and wild spasms contorted her body. Her eyes whipped open as she pressed her hands against the glass and screamed. I wanted to turn away from the horror, but I couldn't. Even if I wanted to help her, my free will was somehow held back. But what disturbed me the most was that a part of me *wanted* to look. A part of my character that had been deeply suppressed. It felt familiar, in a sense, like the *hate* that burned within me every time I fought in battle against the invaders.

I watched as the woman's skin grew dark, as it decayed and was infected with some sort of . . . virus. I felt a smirk grow on my face and, in that moment, I disgusted myself. An unseen presence inhaled deeply.

"What a magnificent creation!" the presence said, wickedly. "Superb strength and accomplishment will come from this new breed of your species. They will prove to be the perfect soldiers among their brethren. Once we've recovered the rest of the human race scattered across Galiza, I will finally exact my revenge upon the humans," the presence boasted.

At last, I was allowed to turn away and looked all around me. The capsules had vanished and there was nothing but darkness. *Whoosh!* A figure, hardly visible, hovered swiftly before me. I fell back as I looked up at the faceless entity—its body twisted, ever molding and immense. Thousands of dark figures marched into view behind it.

"This will be your doing, Amat," the dark figure said.

"No," I gasped.

"You will be the downfall of your own kin."

"No!" I yelled.

I snapped out of the vision, shouting in fear.

Log cursed.

"Whoa-whoa-whoa, what's wrong, Amat, what happened?" Olson asked, concerned.

He tried to calm me down before anyone came by and noticed how disturbed I was. Panting and desperate for breath, I answered slowly.

"Nu-nothing, I'm okay. I just . . . zoned out into an unpleasant daydream," I replied, shivering.

"What did you see?" Olson asked.

I massaged my forehead as I tried to get a grip on myself. My breath was shaky.

"I don't know," I said, finally.

Olson and Log shared a glance and leaned in close.

"It was like—it was like I was shown something. A warning maybe."

"Has this happened before?" Olson asked.

"Only once." I closed my eyes to gather my thoughts. "I'm starting to experience things like I did before. Remember how I told you, after my father died, he'd talk to me?"

"Yes, of course," Olson said.

"Yeah," Log said.

"I heard him again for the first time in . . . years. And—I saw our kin, abandoned in the darkness, consumed by something evil," I said.

Log gulped.

"What do you think that means?" Log asked.

I shrugged.

"Maybe the Skivs and Warvs will come to haunt me if I don't work faster to save them from the shadow of the outside world. Maybe that our kin are in danger from something greater than just the invaders, like Lúvi said," I said.

Log sat back in his seat and exhaled heavily. Olson sat still, deep in thought.

"What should we do?" Olson asked.

"I don't know that there's anything that *can* presently be done about it," I replied.

Footsteps marched toward us. I saw, by the look of her uniform, she was a Duka.

"Alphas Olson, Log, and Jinn-hid Criptous," the Duka said. "By order of the Diramal, you are all to report to his office."

"How soon?" I asked, in as dry a tone as I could muster.

"Now," the Duka replied.

VI
Compromised
(Amat)

As we made our way to the Diramal's office, I felt so weary I could hardly walk in a straight line. My cousins aided me most of the way there, when we could avoid militant eyes. Just before we reached the door to the Diramal's office, I released myself from Olson and Log's assistance. I regretted it immediately after, feeling as though I would collapse without their strength. Even with the revival of the nano-regenerator, the effects of quantum fade are not easily overcome. But I couldn't show any sign of struggle here. The code nine neuro-chip, which the Diramal still thought dominated my psyche, also shuts down one's nerve endings. So, to maintain that non-suspicion, I would have to suck up my pain.

Perhaps if I keep my replies short, it'll be enough to fool him.

I had difficulty breathing. My lungs felt weighed down. Olson looked at me to see if I was doing alright. I nodded, signifying that I had the strength to face what was about to happen.

"Don't worry about me," I whispered as the Cho'Zai guards opened the doors to us.

We walked in, and there he was, the Diramal, with Blick at his side. Decorated as the Reikag, Y'Gŭtsa's head of security.

"Evening, gentlemen," the Diramal said.

"Evening, sir," Olson and Log replied.

The only reason I didn't respond was that the neuro-chip only allowed me to respond to commands and questions.

The longer I stood up straight, the thinner the atmosphere became. My eyes were heavy with fatigue, but I had to keep them sharp and aimed forward. Every moment that I maintained my stiff stature my strength faded. My fist tightened so much that the edges of my claws pierced the skin of my palms. I felt that no matter how cleverly I tried to hide it, the Diramal would see through my strain.

"I'm sure you're all wondering why you were summoned, so I'll get straight to the point," said the Diramal. "I would like to know exactly how we lost 362 of our country's best men within the span of one day. I want to know why you didn't wait for backup after the ambush. I would also like to know whose idea it was to split up what remained of the squadron after the ambush. And I want to know how fighting on a 185-yard stretch of road, filled with an overwhelming force of invaders with just four of you against them, seemed like a good idea."

The Diramal sat in silence for a moment, tapping his knuckles on his desk.

"You can answer now," the Diramal said.

Olson cleared his throat.

"Well, sir," Olson began. "Jinn-hid Criptous insisted that we press our attack despite our disadvantages. He felt that the unusual cluster of enemy forces must have meant the invaders were hiding something. They seemed so driven to defend that stretch of road and he was confident in our abilities to carry out said task. As we are among the fiercest warriors in this conflict."

"Hm, I see. Is this true, Jinn-hid?" the Diramal asked.

"Yes, sir," I replied immediately.

The sudden shout seemed to exhaust me further as I took long, fading blinks. The Diramal paused to scan my body language. He observed the blood that dripped from my fists and smirked.

"So, you're the one who gave the order to fight, Amat?" the Diramal asked.

"Yes, sir," I replied.

"Hm, you must have been rather confident in your abilities to succeed," noted the Diramal.

"That I was, sir," I replied.

"And knowing what you do now, in terms of how it panned out, you nearly dying by overstraining your heart, depleting your body of oxygen, and not to mention the fact the invaders were hiding nothing at all, would you take that risk again?" the Diramal asked.

"Yes, sir, I would," I said.

"Makes me wonder. What drives you so, Jinn-hid?" The Diramal got out of his seat and looked out of a window that showed only the darkness. The same darkness that had covered the surface of Galiza for three years.

"You know the appearance of the modern outside world disturbs many people," the Diramal continued. "The select group calling themselves the Warvs have succumbed to madness from all its terrors and chaos. I, on the other hand, find it calming . . . somewhat beautiful."

The Diramal poured some water into a couple of glasses.

"What do you find it to be, Amat?" the Diramal asked, offering me the glass of water.

I stared into the Diramal's eyes, as acknowledging the water would suggest a fault in the robotic programming of my code nine neuro-chip.

"I find it to be a reminder of what we've all lost, sir," I replied.

The Diramal stretched his arm out, continuing to offer me one of the glasses. It was a test to see how vulnerable I was, or if I was vulnerable at all. A code nine suppresses the body's necessities to eat and drink by conserving the body's amino acids. It also reduces the body's tendency to shed water, be it sweating or crying, to conserve the body's hydration.

"So, you think of it as a punishment, rather than a gift?" The Diramal retracted his arm, after I hadn't even flinched at his gesture. He proceeded to drink out of both glasses.

"Something like that, sir," I replied.

The Diramal finished his drink and set the glasses on the desk.

The Diramal looked down at my fists again and watched as my blood stained the carpet. He slapped his grasp around my fist and squeezed, not so much that it hurt, but enough to drench his palm.

"Hm, it's a funny thing, bloodshed." The Diramal retracted his hand and wiped it across his mouth. "Necessary, when life is in jeopardy. And lives are most certainly in jeopardy. I think if your father were here, Amat, the war would be over by now. Not that you haven't done a good job leading our army against these invaders, Criptous. I appreciate all that you've done, and I'm sure your father would be proud of you. It's just that I'm sure none of this would have been necessary if your father hadn't… shot first. I honestly don't know what he was thinking at the time."

My jaw tightened as I clenched my teeth, and my claws buried deeper into the palms of my hands.

"But we cannot dwell on the past. We must concentrate on what is happening now, in the present," continued the Diramal.

The Diramal looked back out into the darkness of our dying world and took a deep breath in and out.

"I sense you have an urge to express something, Amat. Would you care to tell me what that may be?" the Diramal asked.

He knows.

At this rate, there was no point in holding back any further.

"Would I have permission to speak freely, sir?" I asked.

The Diramal slowly turned toward me, scrutinizing me carefully.

"If you'd like to, you may," the Diramal replied.

"Very well, let's see. Ah, I suspect I should start by enlightening you about where you've led our people—to rot," I barked.

The Diramal looked up at me with awe in his eyes. The Reikag, Log, and Olson too had shocked looks. I suppose everyone in that room did.

"People are dying all around our world, and only a few places still hold civilization," I continued. "Like Zeta, Borthalon, Rafik, Tarconous, Varkaten, and us, Utopion. Within another two years' time, we'll all be dead."

"What would you have me do then, Amat Luciph Criptous?" asked the Diramal. Addressing me by my full name suggested his suspicions had been confirmed. He knew he was no longer dealing with just the Jinn-hid, but my mind as well.

"There is a habitable planet six light years away, orbiting our second closest star Anobose. And if you would just see beyond your insanity, you could comprehend that a global evacuation is the only chance our species has. To survive this war. To take one last stand against these invaders and flee to a new salvation!"

There was no denying it, then, the Diramal saw. I was once again beyond his grasp. I analyzed the look in his eyes, processed his suppressed fury, and noted the gentle footsteps closing behind me. So I backed off for my own safety. The Diramal raised his hand to the Cho'Zai.

"Amat, come over to me," the Diramal finally said.

I approached the Diramal confidently. When just a step away, he gently reached his hand toward my neck. Once within reach, he gripped the back of my neck firmly and pulled my face toward his own.

The Tyrant of Unity

"I know your secret now. Be careful, boy," the Diramal whispered.

"Is that a threat?" I asked.

"That will depend on how you proceed with your regained freedom. But I want you to remember something, Amat. I drove your father to his own death, and I can do the same to you." The Diramal continued to speak softly.

"You already broke me once, Diramal. You should note where I stand now, and mark well that I am much stronger than my father in mind and body," I replied.

The Diramal smirked and let go of my neck, gently. I stood up straight.

"You three are dismissed," the Diramal said.

Before I left, I looked at Blick eye to eye. Both of us seeing right through one another. Then I took my leave, exhausted. Olson and Log opened the doors for me, and we all walked down a hall. As soon as we rounded a corner, I dropped to my knees and collapsed onto my chest.

"Amat, are you alright?" asked Log.

As I lay there, my chest was so tight that I couldn't breathe against the floor. And I didn't have the strength to turn onto my side.

"Here, Log, help me lift Amat up against the wall," said Olson.

Olson flipped me over and grabbed me by the right arm while Log took me by the left and sat me up. Pain shot through my anatomy as my conscience suddenly drifted elsewhere. I witnessed flashes of distorted sceneries and felt the presence of two spirits who I had never met before, and yet, at the same time, there was a familiarity about them. One male and one female, one ancient and one . . . something else. I heard their voices mesh over one another, processing only pieces of what they said.

"I pride myself in you, Reinosso," the male presence said.

"The Hanu were left vulnerable—" the female presence uttered.

"You are different from the others, no doubt," said the male presence.

"—to the workings of Drakkar," the female presence hissed.

"There shan't be another," said the male presence.

I shook my head, feeling dizzy as I refocused my attention. Taking time to make sense of what I had just encountered as it faded further away every second, I tried to recall it. Catching my breath, I turned to Olson.

Both he and Log didn't seem to notice my blackout, if it was a blackout. Perhaps it didn't last as long as I felt.

"Ol-Olson," I said panting.

"What do you need?" Olson asked.

"I don't . . . think I'll be moving for a while . . ."

"That's alright, you should rest," Olson said.

Feeling faint, I closed my eyes and shook my head. I grabbed onto Olson's collar and gently pulled him close.

"I'm sorry, I don't know what came over me. I put everything at risk, our family, our operations. Everything."

Olson placed his hand over my own.

"It will be alright, Amat. Yes, you have made a grave mistake. But now is not the time to let the unknown get the best of us. Pick yourself up. Now is the time to clear your mind and gather strength."

I nodded and tried to stand, pressing my hand against the wall for support. I took a deep breath and limped forward. After a few steps, my legs started to wobble and gave out.

"Log!" Olson blurted as he and Log lifted me up.

"I'm sorry," I said as my cousins dragged my feet across the floor, all the way back to the med bay. "We'll have to inform Lara of this as well."

VII
Drakkar
(The Diramal)

How? How could Amat have resisted the control of the code nine neurochip? For how long now has his mind escaped my grasp? I thought, as I rode the central elevator of Y'Gůtsa down to a restricted area. *I just hope he won't be too furious with me.*

When the elevator finally came to a stop, the doors revealed a long plain hallway with a single door at the end, guarded by two Cho'Zai women. Green lights dimly lit the path. The Cho'Zai saluted me in the way of our kin by crossing one arm over their chest and another across their abdomen.
"Sir," the two Cho'Zai said, and I returned the salute.
"I must speak with him," I said.
"Of course, sir. We heard about the circumstances with Jinn-hid Criptous," the Cho'Zai to the right of the door said.
"You'd be wise not to remind me of it," I said sternly.
The Cho'Zai cleared her throat and shifted in her stance.
"Yes, apologies, sir—"
"As you were," I said, walking through the door.
The room was small. A tall table, reaching chest level, stood at its center. On the table sat two ancient and highly powerful items. One, a large scale, grand enough to fill my arms. The scale was teal in color, with shades of black and small sparkles that moved as I shifted my perspective about the object. The second object was a gaseous, glowing embodiment of stardust. Its outside layer was crystalized in a rigid shape. The object sat suspended above the table, pulsing, like a heart, shifting colors. Though this dust emanated twinkles of light, there was a time when it shone far brighter . . . before we took it from the humans.
I massaged the palm of my left hand with my right thumb before hesitantly reaching it over the large scale. When close, my hand was pulled

onto the scale as if the two were magnetically drawn to one another. I shut my eyes and grunted as I was taken to another plane of existence.

It was dark, and the ground was thick with a layer of water that covered my boots. I was surprised he was not there to greet me, as I expected he would be furious. There was a faint sound of something like a flag flapping in the wind. The flapping grew nearer, followed by the sound of overlapping whispers converting into one voice.

"*Ah*, Diramal." The voice came from behind, so abruptly, so thunderously.

I turned around swiftly and saw him. I hurriedly bowed my head.

"Drakkar, I'm afraid I bring unfortunate news."

"Unfortunate?!" Drakkar stretched the word in a low-pitched rumble.

"Yes," I replied.

"What news is this, then?" Drakkar asked.

His form twisted, twirled, and stretched like a wild shadow as he moved around me.

"I'm afraid Amat Luciph Criptous has escaped our grasp. I don't know how long his mind has been free, but it became apparent to me in our meeting today. Forgive me, I could not sense it sooner."

"I am *unimpressed* you are just now aware of this. But that is hardly a concern of mine." Drakkar shifted around me, then stopped. "Fear not, Diramal. This is of little consequence to our operations. I have known about this for some time now."

"And you did not inform me?"

"I assumed you *knew*." Drakkar's tone sounded irritated. "The boy has gained a knack for visions," said Drakkar.

"How can you know this?" I asked.

"I have entered them myself. He's seen what we're doing to the ones regarded as 'Skivs' and 'Warvs.' Though, I don't think he's quite put all the pieces together yet. I sense his judgment is uncertain," said Drakkar.

"What shall we do with him, then?" I asked.

"*Hm*, we will keep a close eye on him. But we will not exert our control over him. Through the eyes of the Varx, I have seen that Amat has deceived you in more ways than one. For many months now, he's been harboring Skivs, giving them shelter among your bases. He intends to go on with this and take his people to the planet that revolves around the star he calls Anobose. Both you and I know what that planet is, Diramal," Drakkar continued, hovering around me. "I say we lead him on into executing this ambition of his, as it would come to work in our favor."

"How's that?" I asked.

Drakkar chuckled sinisterly as he came up close to me.

"Diramal, it almost seems to me, in the time you have spent blinding the humans to their place in the universe, you've in turn dulled your own vision. Tell the boy you'll give him what he wants, on the condition one of your best accompanies him. Tell this informant to befriend Amat and gain his trust, thus maximizing our intel on him. Do you think you can do that?"

I cleared my throat.

"Yes, Drakkar."

"Good. Now go!" Drakkar bellowed.

I almost fell back as I re-entered my body. Before exiting I caught my breath and composed myself. I would not have the Cho'Zai see me so uneasy after a meeting with Drakkar.

As I left, I contemplated who among my ranks I would choose to befriend Amat. *Not Blick; that feels too risky. Perhaps . . . ah, I know who.*

VIII
Alternate Interrogation
(Log)

By the time Olson and I had brought Amat back to the infirmary, he passed out, his feet dragging across the floor. My neck was cramped, and my shoulder was sore from having to lift him up most of the way there.

"What time is it?" I asked.

"Probably somewhere in the afternoon," my brother replied.

"Are you hungry at all?" Log asked.

"I'm starved, but we should probably find Lara first and tell her about what happened today," said Olson.

"I'm afraid lunch will have to wait, Alphas Olson and Log Criptous," a voice said from behind us. My brother and I turned around to find two men walking toward us.

They were hard to make out in the dim lighting, but as they approached, I noted both pairs of blood-red eyes. I took in the rest of their appearances and identified them as Cho'Zai Voruke and Xaizar, two of the Diramal's personal bodyguards. These and the other two, Quavek and especially Zothra, were said to be the greatest warriors in the world. Though many of their mission details were kept classified, they were well renowned for their participation in various wars, prior to Galiza's invasion.

Both Olson and I stiffened, saluting the Cho'Zai.

"Cho'Zai Xaizar, Cho'Zai Voruke. How may we serve you?" I asked, almost forgetting that it was two Cho'Zai who cornered Amat in a bathroom at Vivothar three years ago.

"We will need both of you to come with us for interrogation. As you must be aware, *by now,* Amat Luciph Criptous has somehow resisted the programming of his code nine neuro-chip," Xaizar said.

"Seeing as how you are among his closest relatives and have recently been placed under his command, we have orders to ask you both a series of questions regarding your knowledge of these circumstances. To see if you were aware of them at any earlier time frame," Voruke added.

Olson cleared his throat.

"Of course, Cho'Zai. We will cooperate," Olson said.

"We could care less if you'll cooperate. What most concerns us is the truth and before the day is over, we will uncover it," Xaizar said.

"Now, now, Xaizar there's no need to be harsh. We don't want Alphas Olson and Log Criptous to get the wrong idea here. All we want is some questions answered and until then, we should have no reason to suspect the worst of them . . . *yet,*" Voruke said. Voruke turned to the side and gestured toward the exit. "If you would please accompany us."

Voruke's tone was like that of the Diramal's—soft, yet menacing. As if to say there'd be worse in store for us if we didn't comply.

***

Olson and I were separated. He had gone off with Voruke and I had been left with Xaizar. There'd be no telling who got sent off with the better Cho'Zai. Personally, I feared the worst for myself, noting how easily Olson enraged Xaizar earlier. The room I entered was painted black, from the walls to the ceiling to the floor, with a faint light that hovered over a small table. The room had a symmetrical box shape to it. It was spacious, but something about how dark the room was gave a sense of claustrophobia. While a good four feet separated me from Xaizar, our faces felt inches away from one another, somehow. And the illusion took my breath away.

Xaizar swiftly pulled one of the chairs from the table; the legs scraping loudly across the floor.

"Sit," Xaizar said sternly.

My breath shuddered as I stepped forward. The moment I sat down, Xaizar vigorously lifted the chair and pushed me close to the edge of the table. My ribs flared with pain as they scraped across the table's thin edge.

My eyes tracked the Cho'Zai as he slowly walked around the table to the other seat. He kicked it to the side slightly, dropped in his seat, scooted up, and slammed his arms onto mine. I growled as the Cho'Zai's claws dug just deep enough into my skin to give me a stinging pain but not to make me bleed. I tried to wiggle free, but the more I moved, the harder the Cho'Zai pressed his claws.

"How long have you known of Amat Luciph Criptous' immunity to the programming of his code nine neuro-chip?" Xaizar asked.

"Just today; he never showed any such sign before," I replied, grunting.

"So, when the Jinn-hid added you and your brother to his command, after showing no interest in either of you for two straight years, that didn't suggest maybe he was trying to reach out and tell you both something? Frankly, I'm a little surprised we didn't notice it sooner," said Xaizar.

He then dug the tips of his claws into my arms, releasing tiny trails of blood. I clenched my fists and tucked my chin to my chest, shutting my eyes briefly.

"If it was . . . he never made it clear . . . never spoke to me or Olson as if we were anything to him… but ordinary Alphas under his command. We had our own reasons . . . not to suspect . . . he was anything more than the same insensitive machine the Diramal programmed him to be." I looked the Cho'Zai dead in the eye as I spoke.

Xaizar threw my arms to the side, and one of his claws left a long, bleeding gash across my right forearm. I cursed and covered the wound with my left hand. The Cho'Zai stood in a frenzy, kicking back his chair so hard it flew against the wall. If not for a lack of better lighting, I'd say the chair dented the wall.

Composing himself, the Cho'Zai started walking slowly around the table. *He's not convinced. Anua, protect me. Give me strength where I have none, so that I may not fail my cousin or my brother.*

"I *almost* believe you, Alpha Log Criptous," Xaizar said, covered in shadow.

The Cho'Zai made a peculiar sound; the only way I could think to describe it was "inhuman." Then another sound emanated from his figure, as if something was being peeled off a surface.

"But there's only one way that I can be sure," Xaizar said, stepping toward the light.

And then I saw it, or him? I didn't know at the time what I was looking at, as the Cho'Zai's appearance had completely changed. His skin was totally black and slimy. His face was what appeared to be a wide mouth, with dozens of tiny tentacles wiggling out. The overall shape of his head was narrow and there were no specific points that defined a nose or eyes except for two small holes at either side of his head that were possibly his ears. His hands were tentacle-like as well. My heart skipped a beat and I almost fell back in my chair, but the Cho'Zai kept the seat from tipping. He leaned in, close enough that I could smell his horrible stench and hear every sludgy movement of his anatomy.

"Hold still," commanded the Cho'Zai.

I could barely make out the words; they sounded meshed with another language entirely. His voice was deep and gurgling. With his free hand, the Cho'Zai lifted one of his tentacles beside my right ear, and it slowly reached inside. I'm not quite sure what the Cho'Zai did, but it made my eyes roll back and my body squirm and tense. The next moment I was confronted by, not images or sounds, but an overwhelming sense of fear, such that I had never felt before. Soon after, my mind started playing tricks on me, filling in the gaps of what I was so afraid of. Glimpses of one graphic, disturbing image followed by another.

In one instance, I saw something that appeared to be a drooling mouth, illuminated by a burning light, with shifting curved teeth rolling forward and back toward me, revealing its bloody gums. The next, a pale, bald humanoid crawled across a floor and with every reach and pull of its body, its skin drew tighter and tighter to its bones. When the skin reached its bones, it melted away, and the thing cried out to me for help. This was followed by a pair of glowing yellow eyes staring back at me. The eyes caved in as if something had crushed them and the color melted out of the sockets, revealing a face without a nose and a wide split in the upper lip of this creature . . .

The terrible visions went on and all I could do was shake and scream uncontrollably.

Finally, the Cho'Zai pulled away, but my body continued to spasm.

"Now, are you sure there aren't any details you're forgetting? Any encounters with Amat during these past three years where he seemed more like himself than not?" Xaizar asked.

I remained in my chair, not even wanting to change the direction I was looking. Tears fell from my eyes and I couldn't will myself to wipe them away. I opened my mouth and my jaw twitched as I tried to speak the words: "W-w-what are . . . y-you?"

The Cho'Zai stepped forward.

"You wouldn't be allowed to leave this room with that knowledge. I'll have to wipe your memory either way before we're done here. Now, tell me. How long has Amat Luciph Criptous been operating as his own person?"

I managed to shift my gaze onto that horrifying face, trembling where I sat. *Anua, save me,* I prayed.

"I . . . I don't know."

The Cho'Zai swiftly pulled my chair closer to him and stretched his tentacles back into my ear. The smaller ones on his face extended out as well and made a high-pitched noise that added to the intensity of what I felt and saw. I couldn't help but *howl* at the top of my voice.

(Olson)

After he led me into the dimly lit interrogation room, Cho'Zai Voruke took a seat at a table at the room's center. The Cho'Zai gestured to the other chair across the way.

"Please, have a seat, Alpha Olson Criptous," said Voruke.

I took a deep breath and sat myself down across the way from him.

"Thank you, my hope is that this won't take long. I'll just be asking you a set of specific questions. Answer them truthfully and we'll be done here," Voruke continued.

"Understood, sir," I replied.

"Are you ready?" Voruke asked.

"Yessir," I replied.

"Very well, then."

The Cho'Zai blinked, and I couldn't be certain with such little light between us, but I could have sworn his irises changed shape and color.

"How long have you known the Jinn-hid?" asked Voruke.

"All my life, sir," I said, trying to ignore what I thought was my mind playing tricks on me.

The Cho'Zai blinked and his eyes seemed to change once again. They hadn't shifted in shape, but they seemed to shift in texture. They were like nets.

"Over three years ago, you were reunited with the Jinn-hid after a five-year gap since he'd been sent to Alpha training at Gallethol. Tell me, how would you describe his state of mind after the events of the second mission to the moon? Was he any different from when you spent time with him prior to his training?" asked Voruke.

The Cho'Zai finished his question with a disturbing grin on his face. I struggled to find the words to reply. I closed my eyes, shook my head, and looked away briefly.

"Keep your eyes on me, Alpha," Voruke said.

I looked back at the Cho'Zai, whose stare hadn't shifted in the slightest.

"Um . . . yes, my cousin did seem different after the events of the second mission to Anua. In comparison to how he was when we were younger, I'd say he was—"

"Unhinged?" Voruke broke in.

"Uh, yes, sir," I replied.

I began to feel a strange tickle passing through my head, followed by a quiet but high-pitched ring.

"Alpha Olson Criptous, I have a report here that states you and your brother came to the aid of Jinn-hid Amat Criptous on Pocto seventh, Twenty-five fifty. On this date, the Jinn-hid was overwhelmed by aerial invader forces. You, your brother, and cousin, Lara Criptous, were reported to have brought him back to base. It was said that the Jinn-hid received a serious head injury to the back of his scalp—the general location of his code nine neuro-chip." The Cho'Zai leaned in close over the table and blinked once again. His eyes no longer looked insect-like, but they'd somehow grown, and their color had shifted to a glowing pink. "Tell me, was there anything strange in the Jinn-hid's behavior when you recovered him?" asked Voruke.

The ringing in my ears got more intense, and the tickle seemed to spread all throughout my mind. It felt like something was moving in there. I breathed heavily.

"He-um, no, sir," I replied.

The Cho'Zai's pupils suddenly expanded, squeezing almost all the color from his irises, and I sank deep into their darkness, leaving my body behind. I felt like I'd forgotten how to breathe. I *had* left my body, but somehow I could still the cold atmosphere of the interrogation room; pricking up the hairs at my forearms. For a long moment, I was surrounded by darkness. I don't recall closing my eyes, but after some time, I'd opened them. I witnessed Voruke walking with a child, asleep in his arms, a girl, down a long hallway. The Cho'Zai walked right past me as if I was not there. He placed the child down on a device, something that at first glance I took for a regenerator. But then I saw the design was very different.

I pressed my hand to my head as I felt the tickle in my head intensify, briefly making me dizzy as a buzzing noise filled my ears. But it wasn't enough to distract me from what was going on.

Voruke stroked the child's hair and smirked. He then looked over to an interface and started pressing buttons. Arms emerged from beneath the device and arched themselves over the child. Each arm had a syringe attached to the end of it, filled with a cloudy serum. I wasn't quite sure what was going on, nor what to expect, until I observed the arms inject the child with the serum at several points across her body. Almost immediately after, she jerked and arched her back. One moment the girl was uncomfortably moaning the next she was *screaming* as her skin turned as black as the shadows that darken the outside world.

I stepped back and stumbled onto the ground. It appeared I was now outside and could barely see anything, but eventually my eyes adjusted, and I could make out shapes and figures. I stood in the middle of a plaza, where a burning Dailagon rested near me. A skid trail ran behind it and at its front, a cluster of dirt and debris plowed over it.

I examined the area around me further and saw several ruined buildings surrounding the plaza. A slight movement within an opening drew my eyes to one of the buildings. As I moved to investigate, something swiftly chased after the small figure, stopping before them. It was . . . *an alien?!* What amazed me even more was how the young human reacted so calmly to the invader's presence. I watched as the alien slowly lifted its arms and serenely led the child back into the ruined building.

Footsteps sounded beside me, so looked to my right and saw Voruke, along with several other Cho'Zai, overlooking the plaza. I couldn't quite make out all their faces, but none of them looked to be wearing QS-25s and some of them had very distinct outlines.

"*Ah*, finally, we've discovered where the Zeltons are harboring a group of Skivs," Voruke said. Voruke turned his attention to his troops. "Ready yourselves."

The Tyrant of Unity

The Cho'Zai *dashed* across the Plaza. They moved too quickly to note where they'd gone specifically, but moments later there were screeches from the aliens, overlapped with human screams that echoed across the air. A collage of gunshots were exchanged, accompanied with the sounds of sharp blades tearing flesh. I rushed towards the chaos, to the opening where I saw a human emerge. By the time I reached it, the sounds of battle had ended and the tingling sensation within my head returned, stopping me in my tracks. Footsteps came toward me, and I looked up to see Voruke emerge with the same girl in his arms from before. I backed away in horror. *No!*

"You're safe now," I heard Voruke whisper to the girl.

"No!" I yelled.

My voice echoed and a deep *thrump* filled the air. The ground cracked like shallow ice and broke beneath me. I fell through a place filled with meshing voices. The surroundings were red and dark. I had no idea where I was and it felt like a hundred parasites were wriggling through my mind, eating through it, dividing it. Falling further and further until I shut my eyes and covered my ears, praying for it all to end.

Opening my eyes to the interrogation room, I wondered how I got there, as Voruke finished injecting something into my arm.

"*Ah*, perfect, and we're done here," the Cho'Zai said enthusiastically.

"Whu-done with what?" I asked in a tired tone.

"Well, the interrogation, of course, Alpha Olson Criptous. I'm unable to disclose to you the results at this time, as I must report my findings back to the Diramal before coming to a decision," said Voruke.

"Uh . . . a decision about what?" I asked.

"Don't trouble yourself with that now. Go on to your quarters and get some rest. I will inform you of any potential consequences from my findings in this interrogation."

He lifted me from my seat and began to escort me from the room. I stumbled and before I knew it, I was outside the room.

"You are dismissed, Alpha Olson Criptous," Voruke said.

The door to the interrogation room closed.

"Wait, wait!" I barked.

I stumbled up to the door and banged on it.

James Alan McG

"What was I being interrogated for?!"
There was no answer.

IX
Diazep
(Log)

I awoke, panting, my breath echoed in my head, and everything else was dimmed over a slight ringing in my ear. My vision was dark and blurred as I cracked my eyes open. A few moments passed and I could see clearly, though my thoughts were still scrambled. I couldn't recall what I felt so anxious about; all I knew was that I was scared stiff and paranoid.

There was a sting in my arm. I swung my head and saw Cho'Zai Xaizar injecting me with some sort of serum. My heart started beating faster and my eyes widened; the Cho'Zai said something that I couldn't make out despite him standing right beside me. With all the strength I had available, I jumped back in my seat and flailed my arms. The pain in my arm surged as the needle wiggled around and flew out of my vein. The syringe shattered against the floor as I rolled away and scurried to my feet, growling. Xaizar was yelling at me, reaching out with his arms in a way that indicated a calming gesture. The Cho'Zai continued speaking, rather sternly I think, but I still couldn't make out what he said.

I glanced around the room, assessing for any nearby threats. The Cho'Zai stepped toward me slowly, but I backed away from him until I came up to the door. The interface was close to my hand. I looked back at him as I pounded the interface and the door slid open. Spinning around, I dashed out of there as fast as I could. The path ahead slowed me down, as it seemed to twist in a spiral, I stumbled against a wall. A broad body collapsed into me, pinning me to the wall as two shouting voices escalated in their outbursts. The sound of my breath filled my ears, still, but the voices were more transparent now.

Suddenly, I was turned around and met face to face with Xaizar.

"Alpha!" the Cho'Zai barked, bashing me against the wall. "Control yourself."

"Cho'Zai Xaizar, what is the meaning of this?!" another voice close by blurted.

James Alan McG

I looked over and saw my brother. Xaizar raised a hand to him.

"Step back, Alpha Olson Criptous. Your brother is in a frenzy; he's responding poorly to the truth serum I administered."

I was still shaking and overwhelmed with anxiety. I hardly understood what was going on.

"Pull yourself together, soldier," Xaizar said. "You're alright, it's over, we're done."

As the Cho'Zai attempted to calm me, I saw, deep in the pupils of his eyes, tiny squirming tentacles that grew in number and in size until they encompassed his face and stretched out toward me. Unable to believe my own eyes, I blinked so fast and frequently trying to escape the illusion, but it wouldn't go away. A third hand rested itself on my shoulder, belonging to my brother. The moment's distraction he provided was enough to end the disturbing image. I trembled as I nodded my head, staring deep into those red eyes.

The Cho'Zai let me go and I stumbled over to Olson, falling into his arms.

"Anua's light, Log! What happened?!" Olson blurted.

"Just as I said," Xaizar said sternly. "He's reacting poorly to the truth serum I administered. At times it can make individuals paranoid. He'll be fine."

"What was all this even for?"

Xaizar slowly walked up to Olson, towering over him. I stood on my feet, leaning on my brother.

"That you don't remember is why I can't disclose it to you. You and your brother will be notified of the next steps in this investigation once we have received further orders from the Diramal. Take my advice, Alpha Olson Criptous. Sleep it off and forget about it while you can."

Olson and Xaizar gave each other hard stares as the Cho'Zai walked away. When he felt the Cho'Zai had ventured far enough away, Olson turned his attention back to me.

"Log? Log?!" Olson shook me. "Are you alright?"

I looked into my brother's eyes, fearful of seeing those horrifying tentacles sprout from his pupils as well. A simple head nod was all I could manage. Olson frowned as he noted the gash on my arm.

"You're bleeding! I'm taking you to the infirmary," Olson said.

"No," I blurted, clutching at my brother's uniform. "Take me to my quarters; I have bandages and wrappings there. It's the only place that'll give me some peace of mind at this present moment."

"What about Mom and Dad? Would you feel safer with them?" Olson asked.

"No. My quarters, Olson, please," I pleaded.

I don't intend to stay there very long, I thought.

"Alright. Can you walk?" Olson asked.

"I can try," I replied.

Olson assisted me all the way to my quarters, set me on my bed, and tended to the gash on my forearm. I sighed with relief as my back felt the soft cushion of the mattress under me.

"Feeling better?" Olson asked.

"A little," I said, with my eyes closed.

"I think I'll stay," Olson said.

"You don't have to. I'll be fine, just need to rest, you should too," I said, rolling on my side.

"I'll just sleep on the sofa in the other room—"

"Olson, please. I-I can't have anyone around me right now. I just want to be alone," I broke in, over my brother.

Olson sighed as he placed a gentle hand on my shoulder.

"You're sure you'll be alright?" Olson asked.

"What part of *leave* don't you understand?!" I barked, as I abruptly sat up and faced my brother.

I could tell by his expression; I had alienated my brother. Olson took a few steps back and turned away with his head down.

I waited a while after I heard the door close behind him before standing from my bed. A silence filled my room that disturbed me. I breathed so quietly that even I couldn't hear it. I dared not, for fear that something or someone would emerge from the shadows. Someone with a face of tentacles. My hands shook as I stood and slowly exited my quarters, minding my every step. On my way out, I grabbed some ration cards, a coat, and my unit card.

I peeked my head out of my quarters before fully exiting to make sure Olson was no longer in sight. With the coast clear, I walked down the hall and started heading for the cafeteria. Along the way, I activated my fizer and contacted someone—a woman I used to be in close communication with who went by the name Kaia. I opened a channel and called her. Before long, she picked up, but she didn't respond right away.

"Hello?" I asked.

"Log. This is a surprise. I never expected to hear from you again," Kaia said.

"How much longer are you gonna be there today?" I asked.

"Not much longer. In five minutes, my operation is shut down for the day. If you want to meet, let's set something up for tomorrow," said Kaia.

"That won't work. I need something now."

Kaia laughed.

"Ho, man, you sound desperate. What's changed?" she asked.

"That is not your concern. I need it now, or I'll report you," I pressed.

Kaia held a silence before finally sighing.

"Alright, for old time's sake. Same place. I'll hold out for you, just this once. But hurry, soon patrols are gonna start coming by," Kaia said.

"I'll be there; just don't move," I replied.

I closed the channel and moved as quickly as I could the rest of the way to the cafeteria.

When I got there, I scanned the area and found Kaia at our normal meeting place. I also saw a couple of guards walking down the same route I came in. I subtly made my way to Kaia, swiftly enough before she would have noticed the guards, slow enough not to draw attention. Kaia seemed impatient, bouncing her leg, her chin resting on her fist. She whipped her head toward me as I slowly sat down and looked at me like she'd seen a ghost with those yellow eyes of hers. She almost looked like one herself, with all the white fur that enveloped her scalp and neck. Her cheeks sparkled blue and pink from make-up. She had a pink snout, and she wore several baggy coats with leather pants and a gray shirt.

"Don't freak out. There are two guards coming in. If you cooperate, we can make the exchange before they notice us together," I said. Kaia looked over to one of the entrances and saw the guards emerge. "*Don't look;* they won't pay us any immediate attention if we don't them."

Kaia dropped a fist on the table; she bared her fangs and narrowed her eyes, leaning close to me.

"What are you thinking?!" she growled.

"Don't. Fret," I growled back.

"I'm not taking this risk; I've been doing this for almost three years with no inspections because I keep to rules. I'm not about to break them now," Kaia said.

Kaia stood to leave, but I grasped her arm, firmly.

"You go, and I'll give you your first inspection on your record. I don't know what you have on you, but it may be enough for them to evict you from the base. Wouldn't do either of us any good."

Kaia looked over to the guards, who were still ordering their food, and sat down reluctantly.

"How much do you need?" Kaia asked, infuriated.

"Diazep, four grams," I replied.

"What makes you think I would carry that much, especially at this time of day?" Kaia scoffed.

"Last I remember, it's one of your less popular products."

"You were my top client for it. I'll give you that," said Kaia.

"And with all those pockets, I would guess you have at least two grams spread between them." Kaia glanced over at the guards. "Stop looking at them. Check your supply."

Kaia gave me an irritated look and then checked her pockets.

"I've got it. Eight hundred units," said Kaia.

"Four. It's two hundred a gram," I replied.

"Circumstance brought the price up."

"Six hundred or I bring the guards over. I'll add two ration cards, and tomorrow you'll come to my quarters with another six grams. I'll pay you fourteen hundred. Consider the extra two a convenience fee."

Kaia shook her head and smirked as she pulled out the two grams of Diazep.

"Time off this stuff has upped your negotiation skills. Shame to hook yourself back on it."

I yanked the doses from Kaia's hand under the table and exchanged the ration cards. I hid the doses and brought out my unit card, pressing it against Kaia's fizer. Once the funds were transferred, we stood. "Have fun with that." Kaia smiled.

"Six more grams tomorrow," I replied.

Kaia and I went our separate ways after that. She went out the nearest exit, and I went out the same way I came in. I passed by the guards as they walked toward a table with their trays of food, but they paid me no mind.

***

When I got back to my quarters, I examined the doses: two tiny bags, each holding a gram. Ideally, one was all you needed, as a little Diazep went a long way. But I needed a big hit to get rid of whatever was eating at me.

I went to my room and fetched my old pinch gun. A small device with three needles on its face, able to inject liquid substances into various places such as the palms of your hands or the bottoms of your feet, as those places are more easily concealed. But the one place Diazep hits the best is the neck. Inject it into the back of your neck, however, where the spine connects to your cerebellum, and you'd permanently paralyze yourself, or worse.

I went into my kitchen and filled a glass with some water, poured a gram, mixed it, and loaded it into my pinch gun. I stared at the needles, took a deep breath, and injected the substance into my neck. The gun *zinged* as the needles twisted into my neck. The sensation is a lot like stapling yourself.

I tensed and put the gun aside as I prepared another dose. The injection didn't hurt as badly the second time around. I almost wished I had a third dose on me at that moment.

Let's not get carried away, I told myself. *It's bad enough I'm back on this crap. I'll micro-dose the six grams I'll receive tomorrow and ease myself off this stuff.*

Didn't take long before I started feeling the effects of the Diazep. In its raw form, it serves as an anxiety suppressor. But in liquid form, the effects are amplified. It increases dopamine levels and makes you serene. With a standard dose, it's somewhat stimulating, but taking more than the average would show me something new.

The Tyrant of Unity

The initial sensation was ecstasy. I'd forgotten everything that happened earlier that day, and the disturbing images in my head vanished. Normally, this was the limit to the experience. But sometime later, I started to feel like I could do anything; superhuman in a sense. I proceeded to test how many reps I could do in each of my routines. Over the course of each one, I felt like I could go on forever, even as my body shook and slowed from fatigue. It got to the point where I'd get so tense I forgot to breathe, and my body would give out. Despite repetitively wearing myself out, I couldn't help but laugh hysterically every time. Even after I found myself numbly resting on the ground, I still felt invincible. I threw whatever was around, as hard as I could against the walls and floor. I even hit the walls with all my strength until my knuckles were bruised and bleeding. A few times I tried tipping over my furniture, failing at each attempt, and bursting into hysteria every time after. Next, I got so hungry I ate what little leftovers I had saved from my rations. I'm almost certain some of it had gone bad, but I didn't care. I was practically starving.

Finally, I went into my room and took out my pistol, loaded it, turned the safety off, and cocked the barrel back. After being mesmerized by the weapon for some time, I looked across my room at a mirror. I didn't realize I was looking at my own reflection. I pointed the gun at myself and laughed.

"You gonna shoot?" I asked my reflection. "No, you won't, you don't have it in you. Come on. I'm standing right here. Do it. Do it!"

I pulled the trigger . . . the glass shattered into pieces and the bullet dented the metal wall.

X
Nano Brain
(Olson)

I walked down the halls of Y'Gůtsa with my head hanging low. The voices of passing strangers were dimmed to the sound of my own inner voice. *I shouldn't have left my little brother alone. I should have just slept on the furniture regardless of his outburst. Makes me wonder if he remembers something from the interrogation. If I asked him about it, anytime soon at least, he'd probably just lash out again. I just hope he doesn't do anything rash.*

I arrived at my parents' quarters, hoping my mother had some sage advice on this. A moment's hesitation stayed my hand before knocking on the door, as I tried to think of a way to bring up the situation without making my parents worried. Finally, I knocked.

"Who is it?" my mother's voice sounded on the interface.

"It's me, Olson," I replied.

The door slid open, and my mother greeted me with a warm smile on her face. She came up to me and we embraced one another.

"Olson," she said with a laugh. "It's so good to see you."

"Come on, Mom, it's only been a few weeks," I replied.

My mother pulled back and looked me in the eye.

"Any time between visits feels like a lifetime, knowing what parts us. Come in, make yourself comfortable," my mother said.

I walked in and racked my coat by the door while she walked into the kitchen.

"Is Dad up?" I asked.

"He's in the family room. I tried to get him to read, but I think he just ended up falling asleep," she replied.

"Has he gotten any better?" I asked.

My mother wiped her hands dry after washing them. She gave me a half smile and shook her head. I nodded in reply.

Walking into the family room, I found my father sitting on the couch. An open book rested on his chest, his head was leaning forward, and his arms were at his side as he snored. I placed my hand on his shoulder and gently shook him. He snorted and blinked his eyes up at me.

"Hey, Dad," I said.

A smile grew on his face.

"Old Didron, when did you get in?!" he exclaimed and laughed. "Oh, how long has it been now? Almost fifteen years since we saw each other at I.I.D.?"

"No, Dad, I'm Olson, your oldest son," I said.

"Didron, you comic, what are you joking about? Sally's hardly one month pregnant with our firstborn," replied my father.

"Oh, wouldn't I love that to be true. How old would that make me nineteen years ago—about twenty-seven. I kept it pretty good back then, though I think I looked my best in my late teens," my mother said.

My father leaned in close and looked me straight in the eye.

"This crazy woman that's been staying here persists in claiming the identity of my wife. But she's not! You've got what, Torúga, say, twenty years on her?" my father asked.

"Ah, a moment ago I was in labor with you, Olson, and now I've jumped forward twenty years to my real age. Every mother in labor would want to hear that," my mother replied sarcastically.

"You look fine, Mom. Come on, Dad, let me help you to the table," I said.

"Stop calling me that, Didron, I'm young enough to be your brother," my father replied.

My father grunted as he set aside his book and tried to stand, pushing off the ground with a cane. He barely lifted his rear from the cushion. I refused to let him persist on his own and helped my father to his feet.

He suffered from a rare disease caused by the nano-regenerators. Four months into the invasion, my father's liver had started to fail. At the time, the nanotech in the regenerators was just starting and certain kinks hadn't been worked out, but with all things considered, it was his best chance of survival. Our worries became grim when the doctors informed us that the nano treatment hadn't taken immediate effect, as it normally would. After a thorough examination, it was discovered that my father's biology saw the nanites as a virus and refused their care. By that time, the nanites had reprogrammed themselves to shut down certain parts of my father's brain so that his body wouldn't retaliate against them. The problem was, once this was done, the nanites did not dissipate like they normally would after healing a person of their ailments. Instead, they gradually started seeping into his mind, shutting down other parts of it.

From then on, we sent him to get monthly treatments of additional nanites administered to counteract the ones that had gone rogue. But that only does so much for him. The disease has been labeled as nano-disassociation; very few suffer from it and fewer have lasted as long as my father.

I sat my father down at the table and my mother set some trays of food down on the table for us.

"I'm sorry, Olson, I only got two rations for myself and your father. If I'd known you were coming, I would have used a third," my mom said.

"It's alright, I'm not hungry anyway." That was a lie—I still didn't have anything to eat from earlier.

My stomach grumbled.

"*Mm*, your stomach doesn't seem to think so. If you want, I'll share some of mine with you," my mother offered.

"What is this?!" my father cut in.

"It's our rations, dear," my mother said with a smile.

My father picked up a spoon and poked at the glop that sat in one of the tray pockets. It was blue in color, filled with nutrients, and tasted horrible. Log and I called it oat pudding to make it go down a little easier. Its texture was thick, like pudding with tiny crunchy grains. But it has a sour taste and a goopy texture.

"Surely we have a nice cut of sterf somewhere in the fridge that we can cook, Torúga," my father complained.

"No, this is all we have, and you need to eat it. Now come on, have at it," my mother replied.

My father looked down at his tray, staring at it for a moment, and then, in a swift movement, *whacked* it off the table, spilling some of the goop on my mother.

"I want a sterf, Torúga!" he yelled.

I stood and marched to my father's side.

"Alright, you've done enough. Let's go," I said, lifting my father to his feet.

"Get your hands off me, Didron!" my father yelled.

He jerked his hand free of my grasp and swung his cane at my leg. The blow, however, was light enough not to hurt me.

"Gordon!" my mother yelled.

"It's alright, Mom, just stay back," I replied.

My father swung his cane at me once again, but I caught it and pulled it away from him. He was about to fall over before I caught him. I hoisted him over my shoulder and took him to the bedroom.

"Put me down, Didron!" he yelled.

"That's not my name, Dad," I replied.

"And I'm not your father! You are not my son!" my father barked.

"No, you're right, my father wouldn't hit me with a cane and act like a child," I replied, sternly.

I set my father down on his bed and locked the door from the outside. I returned to my mother, who was wiping herself clean of all the goop that covered her face and clothes.

"Are you alright?" I asked.

My mother turned back toward me and continued washing her face.

"Ah, I'm fine, Olson. It's your father who's not alright," she replied.

"Are his episodes more frequent when Log and I aren't around?"

My mother turned off the sink and dried her hands.

"It's nothing I can't handle. At this rate, I keep my distance and whenever he needs anything urgently, I tend to him. It works just fine that way, for both of us."

"If you need more help or if he's getting more violent, Log and I can work something out—"

"Judi and the girls come by often enough to help," my mother cut in, passively. "We keep Lia away from him except on the rare occasions when he's himself again. But their help is more than enough."

I sighed as my mother started cleaning the floor where the tray fell.

"I'll get that; you go ahead and eat," I said.

My mother smiled at me as she handed me the rag.

"Thank you. Call it a mother's intuition, but I don't think you came here just to check up on me and see your father," she said.

I paused my wiping of the floor and looked at her.

"No, it wasn't."

"Well, I'm here when you're ready to talk. Sooner would be better; it would help take my mind off the taste of this glop." My mother smiled at her own joke.

I waited a moment, trying to find the right words on how to bring it up.

"Log and I were interrogated today by two members of the Diramal's Cho'Zai—his best."

I heard my mother drop her spoon.

"What for?!" she burst out.

I looked back over to her.

"We can't remember, or at least I can't. Voruke wiped my memory clean of the interrogation," I replied.

"Well, what did he say?!" my mother asked impatiently.

"Voruke said he would have to consult with the Diramal before making a decision. I do have an idea of what the interrogation might have concerned. The Diramal found out that Amat freed himself of his code nine neuro-chip."

"You say that as if you already knew it for yourself."

"I did, I have. Log too," I replied.

My mother's eyes went wide as she slowly shook her head.

"Well, for how long? Do Judi and the girls know? Why didn't you tell us—"

"For reasons concerning your safety. No, Aunt Judi and Lia do not know, as far as I understand. Lara does, given that we all fight together in the field. Amat wanted it that way to minimize the risk of the Diramal discovering his secret. Though now that the word is out, I suspect he'll tell them soon enough. Anyway, that's all beside the point I'm trying to get to here. Which is, I think maybe Log knows for certain what the interrogation was all about and more importantly *how* it was carried out. Afterward, I caught up with him and he seemed . . . paranoid. He pushed me away when I tried to offer him comfort and I'm scared of what that might make him do."

The Tyrant of Unity

"Anua's light, Olson! Why didn't you stay with your brother? Or better yet, why didn't you call one of us? Even Amat since he's himself again?" My mother's voice was heavy with disappointment.

"Amat is in the infirmary. On our last mission, he pushed his quantum suit so harshly his heart nearly gave out. And quantum fade is not something one easily recovers from, even with the assistance of nano-tech. Aunt Judi has Lia to look after and is in mourning for the loss of her son. Who, as far as she is concerned, is dead to her. *You* are already busy with Dad, and you don't need more on your plate," I said.

"When something this urgent is raised, Olson, I would bend over backward for your father and both my sons. Even if it cost my sanity or worse, my life. I would give both to see you all well." My mother spoke a little more sympathetically.

I avoided my mother's eyes as I recollected myself.

"Well, what do you think I should do then, about Log?" I asked.

"Stay by his side, even when he pushes you away." My mother leaned in close. "That's what makes the difference between siblings and family."

"What do you mean by that?" I asked.

My mother shifted as she considered her reply.

"You don't know this, but I had an older sister growing up. Your Grandpa Quam and your Grandma Gisha told me she was a lot sweeter before I came along. She was confident in herself, very outspoken. I suppose some of those qualities rubbed off on me. When I was finally born, however, she'd changed. She didn't like that I would get more attention from our parents than she did. So, she'd abuse me as a toddler. She'd pinch me, throw things at me, knock me over. When I got older, her resentment only persisted, and she found new ways to hurt and get me into trouble. So, we were always siblings, but I never saw her as family, because she didn't treat me as such."

"What happened to her?" I asked.

"She joined the militia and died in Afeikita," my mother replied in a dry tone.

"How did that make you feel?" I asked.

My mother shook her head.

"I didn't feel anything. There was never any love between us. I had nothing to mourn. But then I met your father, who introduced me to your aunt, and I found the sister I never had. She helped me to peel back the layers of my suppressed insecurities through art; she welcomed me into her life with no judgments; she's always ecstatic when we see each other. She's family to me, as I am to her. That is what I mean when I talk about a difference between siblings and family."

My mother stood and took her tray over to the sink and cleaned it frustratedly.

XI
The Diramal's Cho'Zai
(The Diramal)

I walked into my office, saluting the Cho'Zai that stood there, in the way of the human's kin. I activated my fizer and called upon my greatest warrior. He answered before the first buzz ended.

"Sir." Though the hour was late, his voice was unfatigued.

"Zothra, I request your presence urgently. Attend my office in fifteen," I ordered.

"I'll be there in ten, sir," said Zothra.

I nodded and closed the channel. Within ten minutes, Zothra marched into my office, stopped at its center, and saluted me.

"At grace, Vorüm'Qij Zothra."

Zothra placed his hands behind his back and widened his stance.

"What do you require of me, sir?" Zothra asked.

I sighed, tapping my finger against my desk, staring at it.

"It has come to my attention that Amat Luciph Criptous has escaped my grasp, and I spoke with . . . *him*."

Zothra slowly dropped his jaw and nodded, brows raised.

"*Him*, sir?" Zothra replied.

I nodded.

"*He* told me that we are to comply with Amat. Since the boy has grown aware of Serakis, which has recently jumped to the star Quaron, or as the humans call it, Anobose. Amat intends to rally what remains of the humans and push a final front against the Zeltons to reach Serakis. I am to allow this, as it will only assist us in our motives."

"Very good, sir," Zothra replied.

I stood and approached Zothra.

"There is a matter, however, that will need tending in this scenario. Amat *is* free of our control and even if I offered a truce, as part of a condition in giving him the forces needed to find what little remains of his race, he would continue to plot against me. He holds too great a grudge against me, for what I did to the former Jinn-hid, clouding his mind with fear. Eyes will have to be set on him."

Zothra nodded.

"I understand, sir," said Zothra.

"Understand this as well, you are not to alienate Amat. Your mission will be to befriend him, gain his trust, and if he opens up to you about *anything* regarding his opinions or intentions toward me, listen and report back. I imagine there'll be much he'll see that may change his perception of the Zeltons if he hasn't already. Do what you can to preserve his poor reflection on them. And lastly, as far as Amat will be concerned, when occupying the base, he will be free of your surveillance, but you are to continue your work until the boy lays his head to rest. Only then will you report back to me," I commanded.

"Yes, sir," said Zothra.

"You are dismissed."

Zothra saluted me and turned to leave. As he walked through the doors, he was met by Voruke and Xaizar. They greeted one another kindly and the two entered my office.

"Sir," Voruke said.

"Report," I commanded.

"We've discovered quite a bit about Amat's cousins," said Voruke.

"They knew all along of his recovery from the code nine neuro-chip," Xaizar broke in, with a crude tone.

He sounded eager to get to the point. I gestured at Xaizar to calm himself.

"Cause?" I asked.

"Log and Olson Criptous were there for that, too. Amat had been overwhelmed and shot down by a fleet of Zeltonian Sphikes," Voruke said.

I nodded.

"I remember the day his precious Peroma ship was finally taken down," said Xaizar.

"During the crash, it would seem Amat received a number of traumas to his head, somehow damaging the neuro-chip. For a time, the neuro-chip proceeded to operate normally, but there were frequent glitches that allowed Amat to walk freely as himself. In that time, he and his cousins created a code to repurpose a portion of nanites, extracted from the regenerators, to attack any non-biological bodies within his own. For a little less than a year now, Amat has been operating as a total loose cannon."

"In other words, his cousins were withholding information, sir. And the sister is a likely accomplice. They're a threat, same as him. The boy may be valuable to us, but these loosely connected members of his family are nothing more than liabilities to our operations. I, for one, am in favor of excluding them from the equation, sir," proposed Xaizar.

I turned an intense gaze onto Xaizar. My stare seemed to cut him short of saying anything else.

"Xaizar, I counted you among my Qi'val for your skill at war and ability to make others fall in line, not your opinionated speech," I said.

Xaizar stepped back and lowered his head.

"Yes, sir, forgive—"

"Just keep quiet for the remainder of the debriefing and let Voruke take it from here. Understood?" I cut Xaizar short.

Xaizar said nothing in reply.

Good, I thought. I turned my attention back to Voruke.

"Is there anything else to report, Qi'val Voruke?" I asked.

"No, sir," said Voruke.

"Very well. Given that Amat's cousins knew of his secret, I think it's safe to assume his sister, Lara, does as well. As upsetting as this news is, I will not have Alphas Lara, Olson, or Log Criptous punished by any means at this time. I have spoken to *him.*" Xaizar raised his head and Voruke lifted an eyebrow as he shifted his head. "*He* has relayed to me that he would have us comply with Amat in rescuing what remains of his kin. Offing his cousins and sister would only raise more trouble on all sides of the table. With that said"—I shifted my attention back onto Xaizar—"can I count on you to restrain yourself, Qi'val Xaizar?" I asked rhetorically.

Xaizar tightened his lips and growled.

"Yes, sir," Xaizar replied.

"Good; in the meantime, I want you to keep tabs on Log and Olson Criptous. Voruke, you will be charged with Olson and Xaizar with Log. You are to merely follow and observe their activities as indirectly as possible. That means no contact whatsoever," I said.

"Yes, sir," Xaizar and Voruke responded.

"Dismissed," I said.

I saluted my Cho'Zai, and they exited the room. I sat back in my chair, deep in thought. *It won't be long before the base, perhaps even the world, knows that Amat Luciph Criptous has freed himself of a code nine neuro-chip. And if he doesn't know about it already, Gordon Criptous may seek to help his nephew and sons conspire against me. That is, if he is capable of helping them with that nano glitch that plagues his mind. But given the Criptous reputation, I wouldn't put it past the old man and there's still one more Qi'val at my disposal.*

I activated my fizer and opened a channel to Quavek. Before long, she answered.

"*Mm*, sir, how may I be of service?" Quavek asked. I could hear her stiff body, joints popping, bones contorting as her voice wheezed.

"I have a mission for you, Quavek. Attend to my office, promptly," I said.

"Yes, sir. I'll be there shortly," Quavek replied.

I closed the channel and waited patiently for Quavek. When she arrived, Quavek burst the doors open, stumbling in a crooked stature. Her pace was slow as she approached my desk, only when she stopped did she stand up straight, as much as she could. Her spine cracked as she stiffened and sighed. Her shoulders were tugged forward, and her elbows remained tucked. Despite these appearances, she was stronger than most would have believed at first glance. Her race was known as the Korthodon, before we added them among the Varx. Insect-like beings, tall and skinny, and it was clear that Quavek struggled to move comfortably within her skinsuit. Nevertheless, she was one of my Qi'val.

Quavek saluted me and added a subtle bow, dragging one of her legs back and lowering her head.

"I have come to serve, Diramal. What would you require of me?" asked Quavek.

Quavek spoke very softly, like a whisper, emphasizing "S's" and "I's."

"Quavek, as I'm sure you've heard, Amat Luciph Criptous has freed himself of his neuro-chip," I said.

"I regret to inform you, sir, that I have not heard this. Given my disliking for this . . . disguise, I don't get out much. But it pains me to hear it so." Quavek stood and looked me in the eye. "Would you like me to deal with the boy?"

"No," I replied. Quavek twitched her head down and tucked her arms as she briefly looked away. "I've already charged Zothra to monitor Amat."

"Of course, sir. Excuse my presumptions." Quavek slowly nodded her head in a bowing gesture.

"What I had in mind for you is a task of greater importance," I said.

Quavek peeked at me with a curious interest.

"It is a matter of Amat's uncle, Gordon Criptous," I said.

"Ah, yes, the simpleton," said Quavek.

"He wasn't always so. As a matter of fact, there were times that Gordon Criptous was just as troublesome as his brother when he worked for I.I.D.," I said.

"Yes, sir."

"I want you to monitor Gordon Criptous. I'll allow you to use whatever tactics you prefer, but don't interact with him or Sally; this is a covert operation," I said.

"Thank you, sir. Understood. What will I be searching for, in my observations of Gordon Criptous?" asked Quavek.

"Anything that would suggest he is attempting to assist or inform his sons and nephew about our operations. The man worked for I.I.D. and had access to all kinds of files and data. If he can recall any of it, or worse, if he still has access to something we don't know about that could be used against me, I want to know about it."

"Of course, sir. You can trust that I will catch any threat there is to be found about Gordon Criptous," said Quavek.

"Good, dismissed," I said.

Quavek saluted and bowed as she did before.

"Always a pleasure to serve you, Diramal," said Quavek.

Quavek turned around and walked awkwardly out of my office, twitching her head and flicking at her nose with her hands.

XII
Dark Wave
(Amat)

I couldn't help but pass out from exhaustion before reaching the med bay. In that time, I had a dream, one where I had been tortured and traumatized by the Diramal. My wrists were chained and held up. My lungs felt sore and my head light. Watching helplessly as the Diramal killed my family. I woke up drenched in sweat, scared to death. I looked around my room and noted a dark figure in the shadows.

"Who are you?" I asked, shifting uncomfortably in my bed.

"An old friend," the figure replied.

"I have no friends. My family is all I need."

The figure slowly stepped forward, revealing himself in the light.

"Well then, if you don't remember me as a friend, perhaps you would remember me as a brother in arms," said the figure.

"Blick?" I queried.

"Amat," Blick replied.

"What do you want?" I asked, sternly.

"The same thing you want," said Blick.

"And what might that be?" I asked.

"To take the Diramal down," he replied.

Hm, not likely.

"How do I know I can trust you?" I asked.

"You can't, but that doesn't mean I'm a threat to you, or anyone else you care for," Blick said.

"That doesn't mean anything to me," I responded.

"Would knowing that it wasn't me who attacked you on the Peroma during the second mission on the moon mean anything to you?" I gave Blick a quizzical look. "My neuro-chip had been overwritten. Someone forced me to attack you. I faced a court martial and was sentenced back into the service of the Diramal. Seems a bit contradictory to what I would have wanted, wouldn't you say?" asked Blick. I still didn't buy it. "Look,

The Tyrant of Unity

I would have explained all this to you if I'd known you hadn't been under the Diramal's control all this time. And now that I have, you can look at it this way: I'm a world of information. As the Reikag, I have access to everything he sees, everything he hears, everything he hides. If you want to bring him down and I know you do, you'll find that easier to execute with me at your side."

I considered all Blick had said.

"Fine," I finally said. "But first, before I can allow you back into my trust, you must earn it."

"Yes, sir. What do you need?" Blick asked promptly.

"See if you can find me any files on secret experiments the Diramal may be running. I've . . . received certain information that the Diramal or someone he's in league with might be up to something. Bring me back what you find before the end of tomorrow. Then I will determine if you're worthy of regaining my trust."

"Understood," replied Blick.

"Dismissed."

Blick turned around and disappeared into the dark, as his footsteps echoed throughout the med bay.

***

The next morning, I woke up early and left the infirmary to attend my office. Before leaving, I extracted some nanites from a nearby regenerator and carefully poured them into a large flask while the medical personnel weren't around. On my way out, I subtly stole a syringe as well.

I sat at my desk, logged onto my computer, and opened a program. A window with a line of code was displayed. A long, cylindrical frame rose from my desk with a pair of adjustable arms at either side of its center. I placed the syringe in a drawer and the flask in the frame as the arms wrapped around it. A purple light faintly illuminated the interior of the flask. I typed in a code that would repurpose the nanites to attack and destroy any devices found within a human's anatomy.

I sat back in my chair as the code processed and contemplated the existence of these so-called "Shadow Scar." *Do they really exist? If so, are they linked to the people whose bodies turned to shadow in my dreams?*

Hopefully, Blick's intel can shed some light on that dilemma. Suddenly, someone knocked on the door of my office. I minimized the coding window on my screen and hid the vial within my desk. I slowly opened a drawer to my right, concealing a pistol.

"Enter," I said, placing my hand on the weapon.

My grip on the pistol tightened, and the door slid open, only to reveal Blick.

"Ah, I wondered if I'd find you here," he said.

I took my hand off the pistol and subtly closed the drawer before the Reikag could notice it.

"You've been here before?" I asked.

"Not really, but it's a part of my job to stay updated on whose quarters are where throughout the base. Which is in part why the Diramal never discovered someone had been smuggling in newcomers from outside the base, who I now assume was you?" asked Blick.

I tilted my head.

"Yes . . . I'm curious; since you mentioned that, who did you suspect brought in all those names on file?" I asked.

The Reikag shrugged.

"To be frank, I had my suspicions it could have been you, but I saw no evidence to confirm this suspicion. I went on to assume it was your cousins or even some rogue smuggler in the ranks," Blick said.

"And you never saw any reason to report it?" I asked.

"Someone who was giving innocents safety and shelter from the chaos of the world? No."

I gave the Reikag a blank stare as I considered that.

"Do you have something for me?" I asked.

"Yes, sir," Blick replied. He reached down into one of his velcro-type-sealed pockets and pulled out a small data crystal. "It's not much, but it's what I could manage to find on such short notice."

I reached out my hand and the Reikag placed the crystal in my palm. I placed the crystal in front of the light that displayed my computer screen, and the information was revealed. Eight files that I read swiftly and thoroughly. They all had two things in common in their reports. Missing persons and they'd been selected for a classified project titled "Dark Wave."

"What's project Dark Wave?" I asked.

"Yeah, I couldn't find that out. Like I said, it isn't much," Blick replied.

"Can you dig deeper into this?" I asked.

"I tried, but the files on project Dark Wave are scrambled and guarded by a high-security clearance protocol," replied Blick.

"Higher than the clearance granted to a Reikag?" I mocked as I sat back in my chair.

"If I had more time I could—"

I reeled forward, plucked the data crystal, and tossed it back to Blick. He barely caught it.

"You have it, if you think you can do better. All that does is raise more questions. It doesn't help me," I said.

The coding window popped up and the frame holding the vial of nanites rose from my desk. Before the Reikag could say anything, there was another knock at my door.

"Enter," I said, minimizing my coding window, and the frame sank into the desk. A Duka stood in the doorway.

"Jinn-hid," she said.

The Duka saluted me and I, her.

"Sir, the Diramal wishes to speak with you, urgently," the Duka said.

"Tell him I'll tend to his office shortly," I replied.

"Yes, sir," replied the Duka.

The Duka left and the door shut behind her. I stood from my seat.

"Reikag Vykin, while what you've brought me here demonstrates something of interest to me, it clarifies nothing. If you wish to earn my trust back, I encourage you to strengthen your efforts at finding out what this project Dark Wave is," I said.

The Reikag stood straight and took a deep breath.

"I'll do my best, sir," Blick said.

"No, do better. Dismissed," I replied.

"Sir." Blick saluted me.

I returned the salute and we both left to go our separate ways… for the time being.

***

As I walked through the halls of Y'Gůtsa, I opened a secure channel between myself and Sarak. Before my meeting with the Diramal, there was something I wanted to set in motion.

"Sarak," I said, once she answered.

"Jinn-hid," she replied.

"The family that you helped the other day, the one with the little girl, Lúvi, are they still in Y'Gůtsa?" I asked.

Though the channel was secure, I chose my words cautiously. I wouldn't think it likely, but if someone overheard this conversation, I wouldn't want them knowing that a Skiv family had been smuggled into the base.

"Yes, sir, they are. I was going to . . . attend to them later today," Sarak said, catching onto my subtle speech. "See if they were adjusting well with their new quarters."

"That's kind of you, Sarak. But I'm afraid I'm going to have to ask you to delay that task for now and run some reconnaissance for our next run."

"Yes, sir, understood," Sarak said.

"In the meantime, forward me their current quarters, I might be able to help the family with any potential accommodations they may need," I said.

"Yes, sir," said Sarak.

"Criptous out."

I walked to Log's quarters and knocked on the door.

"Who is it?" Log asked, his voice amplified over the interface beside the door.

"Amat," I replied.

Log's response was delayed.

"Come in," Log said, as the door slid open.

I entered Log's quarters. Everything looked out of place, and the main room was a complete mess. I would have cracked a joke about how tidy Log was, but there wasn't any time for pleasantries.

"I need you to do something for me," I said.

"Hello to you too," Log said, scratching his head.

Log's hair was mangy, and his odor was foul. He wore no shirt and stumbled on his trash-covered floor as he approached me.

"That's close enough," I said.

I rose my hand to Log and quite literally froze him in place. It threw me off, then I remembered my new ability. I lowered my hand and Log's movements proceeded naturally. He gestured to his furniture as he rubbed the side of his neck, seemingly oblivious to what had just happened.

"You didn't notice that?" I asked.

"Notice what?" Log winced.

I gave Log a quizzical stare.

"It's not important," I replied, taking my seat.

I suppose I've got to be mindful of that, I thought.

Log took a seat across from me; it was then I noticed the whites of his eyes showed signs of strain and drowsiness.

"Wait," I said.

As much as I disliked it, I approached Log, and his reeking aroma made my nostrils flare. Log held a woozy expression on his face as I removed his hand from his neck, revealing a triangular needle formation with a fourth in the middle. I trailed my claw across the markings.

"Log," I growled. "Have you been using again?"

Log frowned.

"No," he said, pulling his arm away from my grasp.

"That better be the truth. By the looks of your quarters alone, one could speculate otherwise," I replied.

"Screw you, Amat," Log barked. "You might have been able to just pass out after that meeting with the Diramal, but Olson and I were pulled aside shortly after we returned you to the infirmary. Brutally interrogated by members of the Cho'Zai for reasons we can't recall. I hardly slept last night and for your information, that's an old scar from a while back."

I crossed my arms abruptly, disturbed by Log's new information.

"You and Olson were interrogated by Cho'Zai?" I inquired.

"Yes," replied Log.

"Is that what it's from then? Or did something happen that would cause you to—"

"I'm *not* using," Log barked.

I sighed and nodded.

"I'll take your word for it, just this once. But if I find so much as one more mark that resembles any kind of shot, I'll inform Olson and you'll be temporarily discharged from duty. Understood?" I asked.

Log stared at me, slouched over. Something shifted in his eyes suddenly. He was about to be cocky.

"That sounds very reminiscent—"

"Am I understood?" I voiced.

"—of a scenario you were prompted with, not very long ago," Log said.

"Am I understood!" I barked.

Log held me in his gaze.

"Yes, sir," replied Log.

I glared at my younger cousin, silently asking him why he was acting the way he was. Log shrugged, throwing his arm up as he glanced away.

"Is there any other reason you came here, beyond sharing suspicions?" asked Log.

I held my gaze just a moment longer.

"I need you to run a quick mission for me. It's subtle; I just need you to go to these quarters"—I said, sending the address from my fizer—"and talk to Lúvi. Ask her more about these Shadow Scar. How does she know about them? What do they look like? Are they a new faction of the outside world? What are their motives and goals? Even if you don't think she'll know all the answers, ask the questions anyway, find out everything she knows."

"Understood, sir," Log said, squinting his eyes at the display of the address on his fizer.

"Clean yourself up before you go and dress in uniform. I doubt Lúvi's mother will let you see her otherwise," I said.

"Yes, sir," said Log.

"And while you're at it, when you get back, tidy up some of this crap. You're an Alpha, Log, set some standards for yourself, be responsible," I said sternly.

Log glanced up at me, curling his lips mockingly.

"Yes, sir," Log replied.

I turned briskly to march out.

"You're more like him every day, you know? Uncle Bod," he blurted out.

"That meant to be a compliment?" I asked.

"If you don't know, how would I?" replied Log.

"I suppose we'll have to make that assessment when we see how I fare once my feud with the Diramal ceases."

I headed straight to the Diramal's office to attend my meeting with him.

XIII
Honor Between Rivals
(Amat)

I reached the Diramal's office, ready for anything. I walked in slowly; it was uncomfortably quiet. The Diramal paid me no mind at first, as he was preoccupied with making his marks on some documents. I could barely hear my own steps pressing against the carpet. I stopped in the center of the room, put my hands behind my back, and cleared my throat.

"Diramal, you called for me?" I asked.

"Yes, Amat, I believe I did. I'm just finishing up some contracts here. It shouldn't take much longer . . . and there we are," the Diramal replied.

The Diramal shuffled and sorted the paperwork into separate folders, which he then handed over to a member of his Cho'Zai. I passed my gaze over them, trying to catch a glimpse of the contents, seeing if there might have been any reference to the project Dark Wave. I couldn't determine whether it did.

"See to it that these get sent out to their corresponding officers," the Diramal said.

"Yes, sir," replied the Cho'Zai.

The Cho'Zai made eye contact with me as he walked past—it was Xaizar. He gave me a sly smile as he passed; I found it strange how the expression held a resemblance to Log's, from earlier. The Diramal gestured to the rest of the Cho'Zai in the room.

"Leave us," said the Diramal.

I found this strange, too. The Diramal had never held a private audience before, not since he spoke to my father before the mission to the first of the invader craft.

"I imagine that was unexpected," he said.

I turned my attention back to him and stiffened.

"Yes," I replied.

"Does it disturb you, being isolated with me?" The Diramal stood from his seat and slowly stepped toward me. "You afraid I might . . . manipulate your mind, as I did your father's?"

"No," I replied once we were face to face.

The Diramal looked me up and down.

"*Hm*, curious, you're not lying." The Diramal turned away and admired the contents of his office. "I imagined you would be, after our last private encounter."

"Should I anticipate another quarrel like the one we had three years ago?" I asked.

"Certain arrangements would not have it so," replied the Diramal. I wasn't quite sure what he meant by that, but I didn't bother prying. "For reasons beyond me, Amat, you have discovered a way to decrypt the most advanced neural suppressive software that's ever been created. And I never thought to inspect your feed because I was so sure I had you under my thumb all this time. Given your resiliency, I have decided to *temporarily* cooperate in your mandate to seek out and rescue the surviving members of our race and attempt to reach this seemingly habitable planet that revolves around the star Anobose. But there is one condition."

I couldn't believe the words that came out of the Diramal's mouth. *"Cooperate?" With me? Why would he do this?* What made me refocus was the Diramal's mention of a "condition."

The Diramal leaned over his desk.

"During this operation that you'll be commanding, given your past rebellious behavior, you will be accompanied by an informant of mine. Cho'Zai Zothra. The Cho'Zai will be operating on behalf of both our interests, ensuring you do all that you can to protect the Skivs and Warvs, if they'll let you. And that you don't plot against me," he said.

Cho'Zai Zothra. There was a time when I admired him almost as much as the Diramal. Though, ever since my quarrels with the Diramal and not to mention my incident with the two Cho'Zai at Vīvothar three years ago, my views on him have changed as well.

"A fair condition, Diramal. I do, however, wonder, should I expect him to jump me in a rest stop at some point down the line?" I asked.

"While within base Y'Gůtsa, Zothra will have other duties to attend, and you can expect he won't be anywhere near you. So long as you do not plot against me," said the Diramal.

"Can I expect you to leave my family alone, then, as well?" I asked.

The Diramal stood tall and sighed.

"Yes. Call it a temporary truce between ourselves. For a greater . . . purpose," he replied.

"And what purpose might that be?" I asked.

"The survival of the human race."

"*Hm*, strange to find out that you truly care about it at all," I said.

"I never said I did. My priority is winning the war. That can't be done if all those at my disposal have dropped dead, whether it be in battle or of starvation," said the Diramal.

"The other countries that haven't gone dark, have they also agreed to this?" I asked.

"I haven't spoken to all of them yet, but Afeikita, Rafik, Borthalon, and Druteika have all agreed to it, since they are all our allies. It's the other countries like Zeta, Varkaten, Tarconous, the Dronomen Islands, and others that will be challenging to convince. But I'm certain they'll come round to the idea."

"I thought the Dronomen Islands had already gone dark," I queried.

"Not entirely. Their militia is no longer operational, but a fight still wages there, carried out by a band of Warvs."

"I see. How many troops will I have under my command for this operation?" I asked.

"Well, I'd imagine, for a mission of this scale, you'd need the force of the whole base. Over fifty-five hundred men and women, not including my Cho'Zai, with the exception of Zothra. All one hundred thirty Fades, and thirteen hundred Dailagons all at your disposal, Jinn-hid."

"You would give me command over the entire force of the base? Why?" I asked.

"It's as I said, Amat, for a greater purpose. Do you have any other questions?"

I shifted in my stance as I considered.

"Two. How soon will the troops be ready?" I asked.

"All troops were recalled yesterday afternoon to give them two days' rest from the chaos of their most recent runs. Preparations for the next mission will start tomorrow morning," said the Diramal.

"I thought you found that chaos calming and beautiful?" I replied.

The Diramal gave a half smile and blinked, vexed.

"What is your other question?" he asked.

"When should I expect Zothra to report to me?" I asked.

"Tomorrow, when you inspect the troops."

I nodded.

"Is there anything else, Diramal?" I asked.

The Diramal shook his head.

"Am I dismissed then?" I asked.

"You are," the Diramal replied.

I paused, then stepped forward and brought forth my hand to the Diramal. He looked at me, almost shocked, but it was more than that. In his eyes I could see, for whatever reason, my offering my hand to him, in peace, meant something monumental to him. For the first time, I felt I'd seen genuine gratitude in the Diramal. He shifted his gaze to my hand as he slowly joined his own with mine. We exchanged nods and I left.

XIV
Relapse
(Log)

I felt better, in a way, as fear no longer plagued my mind. But now I was ailed with a new kind of suffering, a deep necessity for another hit and if I didn't get it, in time the fear would surely return once again. My arms and legs were so sore I could hardly dress myself and my back prickled with a thousand invisible razor-sharp blades any time I stood too tall.

As I finished dressing in my uniform, there was a knock on my door. I cleared my throat and wiped the sweat from my face.

"Come in," I said.

The door opened and Kaia stood in its frame with a confident smirk on her face.

"Well, well, look at you," said Kaia. She glanced around the room as I approached her. "Love what you've done with the place."

"Shut it. Do you have what we agreed to?" I asked.

Kaia flicked the bags clenched tightly between her fingers with that same fake smile, squinting those yellow eyes at me.

"As requested."

I reached for them, and she swiftly tucked them away.

"Uh-uh, where's my payment?" Kaia demanded.

I scoffed, stepping back as I raised my fizer. Kaia stepped forward and the door slid shut behind her. I paused to look her in the eye. Kaia moved elegantly as she closed the space between us to just a few inches. Her gaze looked past me, taking in the mess I'd made.

"Make yourself at home, why don't you?" I said unenthusiastically.

Kaia shifted her eyes to me, lowering her chin as she grinned.

"I will."

She wandered over to the table that held up my glass-screen television and picked up a frame. Then jumped as shattered glass fell from it. Finally, my fizer was set for transfer.

"Alright, let's do this," I said, stepping up to her.

"Is this your family?" Kaia asked.

I paused and glanced over at the image in the frame. The picture was of me, my brother, and our parents standing outside our old home, from a time that seemed a lifetime ago.

"Yeah, that's them. So?" I asked, impatiently.

"You never told me you were cute as a kid," Kaia replied.

"Right, 'cause I've such an ugly mug now? I appreciate the compliment."

I yanked Kaia's fizer arm close so I could make the transfer.

"I didn't say that," said Kaia.

My eyes met Kaia's. She moved in, pausing close enough for me to feel her breath.

"How old are you now, Log?" Kaia asked, brushing her hand along my arm.

"Fifteen," I replied.

Kaia looked up at me and pressed her lips against mine. We looked at one another. My heart jumped beats as I licked my snout and shifted in place.

"Why did you do that?" I asked.

"That's the wrong question," Kaia replied.

Kaia kissed me once again, this time longer and more passionately. She pulled away and continued looking at me.

"What's the right one, then?" I asked.

Kaia laughed lightly, took my hand, and lead me to my bedroom.

**

I wandered down the halls feeling drained and hungry as I located the quarters of this Skiv family Amat picked up from our previous mission. All the while thinking back to what I'd just experienced. Something unexpected and that I'd surely look forward to happening again. *But not too frequently. I'm not made of ration cards. I needed to reserve my energy for the battlefield anyway.*

I arrived at the Skiv's quarters and knocked on their door.

"Who is it?" a woman's voice sounded on the interface.

"My name is Log Criptous. I'm related to the man who brought you here, Amat. He sent me here to talk to Lúvi," I replied.

The door did not slide open immediately. Eventually, the woman who was revealed behind it stood armed with a gun, aimed at me. I raised an eyebrow. *Must be the mother.* The woman twitched the gun toward the inside of her quarters. It was dimly lit, almost to the point of complete darkness. I suppose it was easier on their eyes, after having spent three years in darkness.

"No sudden movements. Come on," she said.

"This day just keeps getting more and more interesting," I remarked, as I slowly entered the quarters.

I kept my body facing the lady, even though I didn't think she'd shoot me without reason. But then again, this was a Skiv I was dealing with.

"You know how to use that thing?" I asked. The mother pulled the hammer back on the pistol. I pouted and nodded. "I'll take that as a yes."

The woman flicked the gun forward, pressing me deeper into the quarters, and led me to one of the bedrooms. Inside was a little girl. She turned her attention to me calmly and looked at me as if she expected me.

"Sit down, please," the woman said.

"Can't say 'no' to commands given to me so kindly," I replied.

I took a seat across from Lúvi and the woman sat beside her child on the bed. I smiled awkwardly, shrugged with my palms up, and then clasped my hands together.

"I take it you're Lúvi?" I said to the little girl.

"You look sick," Lúvi replied promptly.

I let out an uncomfortable laugh.

"I'm actually keeping in good health, but I appreciate—"

"You look sick," Lúvi said again.

The woman shifted in her seat.

"Is he—"

"No. He's just a young man, in pain," Lúvi said, cutting her mother short.

Do I really look that bad? I wondered. I glanced beyond the girl and took in my reflection. My color was a little pink, but there were no bags under my eyes, nor sweat that trickled down from my brow.

"I, *um,* I'm afraid I don't know what you're talking about," I said.

"Deny all you want, but the Goddess sees and knows all. She tells me things," said Lúvi.

The Tyrant of Unity

I was shocked at how observant the child was. I'd heard of the wisdom within Rellas, but I never imagined they had superstitious ways about them, especially at this girl's age.

"The Goddess tells me you wish to know something," Lúvi continued.

"Yes," I replied.

"What is it?" asked Lúvi.

I cleared my throat.

"My, *uh*, cousin, Amat, the man who brought you and your family here. He wanted me to ask you more about the ones you call the Shadow Scar," I replied.

"He wishes to know what they are," said Lúvi.

"Yes," I replied.

"On the matter of their origin, I cannot say. I can only tell you that they are an outside threat to our kin. They are not aligned with the ones who encompass our skies," Lúvi said.

I nodded and considered this.

"You sound so certain, but I'm having a little trouble understanding this for myself," I replied.

"You desire an explanation," said Lúvi.

"Please."

"Very well. But I will only tell it once, so listen close," she said.

I chuckled.

"I'm all ears," I replied, leaning in.

"A few weeks ago, my family and I were running low on resources, food, water, and such. My brother had started falling ill and my younger sister had similar symptoms. Normally, my father would take my brother out with him to scavenge for what we lacked. Since that was not an option at the time, my father chose me to accompany him."

"Why would a father put one of his daughters at risk in such a chaotic environment?" I asked.

"It was not my first time. And out there an extra pair of hands to carry what you find, can mean the difference between survival for another week or another month," replied Lúvi.

"Right, sorry. Continue, Lúvi," I said.

"My father and I had been scavenging for over a day and found some food, but no amount worth bringing back home. So, we traveled a little further than we normally would, into territory my father was unfamiliar with. We entered a ruined building and found what we needed. While we were rummaging through the kitchens of various apartments, my father and I heard clanks and swift footsteps. My father thought it could have been Warvs, and given that some have a reputation for cannibalism, we didn't draw any attention to ourselves. We trod lightly on our way out, peeking around every corner before walking down each hall. As we came down the final flight of stairs, my father paused and looked around the corner. The abrupt stop caused me to slip and fall on the dusty steps. He only checked on me briefly to see that I was alright, and then swiftly peeked back around the corner, as if he expected something to attack within the shadows. Screeches echoed throughout the higher levels, but each one was distinctive from the other, and it was unlike any sound we'd heard the invaders make. We made a swift escape from the building, but the screeches pursued.

"Back out in the open waste, the screeches became more numerous, and we could not escape them. My father hid me in a large pile of garbage and rubble. He said he would attempt to outrun the screeches himself. Told me to stay there until he returned. Not long had gone by before I heard his own screams. His silence marked his passing. One of these... entities that we've named the Shadow Scar, had doubled back and somehow it knew I was there. Smelling the air as it tracked me. When I least expected it, the Shadow Scar stood over me, mindlessly tearing and pounding at the mound that hid me. I never got a good look at its overall appearance, but its face was covered in tentacles," said Lúvi.

I stiffened my back and raised my eyebrows.

"Something about being around this creature filled my ears with a ringing," Lúvi continued.

I rubbed the tips of my fingers against my forehead as I was confronted with a vivid image in my mind, a face like the one Lúvi described. "I wouldn't have screamed if I didn't feel so scared, more than I had ever been in my whole life. But the fear did not feel like it was my own. It felt . . . inflicted somehow."

I covered my ear as I felt a strange sensation, like something was stretching and squirming inside it. Horrid noises and imagery filled my head. I heard what sounded like screaming . . . my own screams. "I remember this Shadow Scar had several tentacles that made up its arm as well. It reached for me with them," Lúvi continued. "But something saved me, something fast. I didn't remain where I was, long enough to see who or what it was. All I know is that a conflict broke out and there wasn't a single scream on that field that sounded human in the slightest."

A drop of sweat trickled down the side of my head onto my uniform. I wiped my scalp to find that I was drenched. My chest rose and fell rapidly, and my heart pulsed in my ears. Lúvi, too, seemed agitated. But in my reflection, I saw that I looked far worse off than she did.

"I see my story upsets you, gives rise to a memory. Perhaps a suppressed one?" she said. I gulped and blinked. "You *are* sick, Log Criptous. You will not mend until you face your ailment."

"You can't cure a disease by acknowledging it," I replied.

"For some, that is the only way they can be healed," Lúvi replied.

I stood, as did Lúvi's mother, her pistol still aimed at me.

"No, it is alright, Mother. He's no threat to us, but he may be, to himself," Lúvi said. I tilted my head at Lúvi. "I will pray the Goddess blesses you with sight to see your fears and courage to smite them, Log Criptous."

I turned around and left the Skiv's quarters promptly. *I'm not sick,* I told myself. *I don't know what I saw back there. That little Rella probably cast some sort of spell to help me envision what she saw. Curse my tongue for asking explicitly to make me understand what she knew.*

All the while during the walk back to my quarters, the image of that strange face kept popping back into my head, engulfing my vision. Slowly, the overwhelming paranoia seeped back into my heart. As people passed me in the halls, I walked as far from them as I could, especially if they were guards. *What if they know? I can't get caught using again. I won't let it happen.* "I won't!" I blurted. Hurriedly, I kept my head down as I realized my thoughts had come right out of my mouth. I wasn't sure if anyone cared, but there were a few people that I had just passed and surely, they heard me.

I entered an elevator, alone, fortunately. But then again, perhaps not. As soon as the doors closed, I felt small, like the dimensions of the container were expanding. I breathed heavily and pressed my hand against one of the walls. The face flashed in my head again, and the strange feeling in my ear returned. I squeezed my eyes shut and raised my hand beside my ear, twirling my fingers intensely. *What are you? Stop it!* "Get out of my head!" The doors opened and there was a small family of civilian occupants waiting on the other side of the door. They didn't seem all that disturbed by me. In fact, they nodded and saluted me, showing me the fronts and backs of their hands.

"Alpha," the mother said.

It's a trick. They're not civilians. They must be spies, secret operatives. Do they know? I'm sure they suspect! I sprung forward and pushed past them, almost pushing the father flat onto the ground. I didn't stop to see if he was alright. I just ran and continued to do so until I reached my quarters, whereupon I marched to my room; my bed still a mess. I found a note on my nightstand, picked it up, and unfolded it. I could barely read the scribbles: "Let me know when you need your next hit." Underneath was a very detailed drawing of Kaia, winking and puckering her lips. I crumpled the note and tossed it aside as I rummaged through my drawer to find a gram of Diazep and my pinch gun. Then I turned around to set it all out in the kitchen, but I stopped when I heard a knock at my door. I cursed as I threw everything back in its place and wiped my brow of sweat as I answered the door.

XV
Shadow Scar
(Amat)

Before long, Log opened the door. I could tell something was off about him. My face bore a puzzled expression as I observed my younger cousin. He leaned against the door frame, wiping sweat off his brow, glancing at me, and avoiding eye contact.

"Hey," Log said.

"Hey," I replied.

"Come in," Log said.

His quarters didn't seem any cleaner from when I visited earlier, but that was hardly something that concerned me. Log walked around his apartment tidying up little things here and there, massaging his head with the tips of his fingers.

"Log, tell me the truth. Is everything alright?" I asked.

Log stood up straight with his back facing me and sighed. He walked past me and chucked the trash he picked up off the ground into a bin.

"Log—"

"Everything's fine, Amat. Nothing's changed. I imagine you want to debrief me on the intel I gathered from Lúvi," Log cut me short.

I crossed my arms.

"Yes, but if you're in some kind of trouble—"

"She told me she was attacked," Log blurted, walking over to his sofa, taking a seat. "Her father was killed by one of the Shadow Scar. She was attacked by one, herself. The description she gave of it. . . it was so vivid, Amat. A face and arms of tentacles. She said it had this ability to inflict fear into her mind, to such an extreme she had never felt before. She said she was saved by something that was likely moving in a quantum field. She isn't sure who or what it was, but as she escaped the area, she heard all kinds of cries . . . and none of which sounded human."

I nodded as I considered all of this. *These Shadow Scar may very well be real. But what does it mean if they're no friends to the invaders?*

Assuming that's how it played out in the scenario Lúvi described. Whose side are they on? Where do they come from?

"What do you think?" I asked.

"About what?" Log replied.

"Lúvi's story. Do you believe her?" I clarified.

Log exhaled heavily and rubbed his hands together.

"I do," Log said.

His tone suggests he could somehow validate Lúvi's story.

"As do I," I said.

"But there's still too much we don't know," noted Log.

"That may be, but we know more than we did before. These Shadow Scar are an outside threat, a potential *common* threat to our kin and the invaders. Who knows what it could all mean?" I asked.

"Are you saying you'd be willing to put aside your differences with the invaders?" asked Log.

I had a sudden shift in my mood; a dark cloud crept over my conscience, one that I had seldom felt since my incident with the Peroma, but had encountered several times before,

"Could you, Amat? Could you consider peace *with the invaders?"* A sinister voice from within my mind spoke.

I inhaled deeply and sat straight as I took a moment to acknowledge the pressing thought in my mind.

Could I ever allow myself to forgive or be forgiven for all the wrong I've contributed to in this world, if I can't even bring myself to consider the possibility? No, I will *consider it. But I need more to go on than a whim,* I replied to the voice.

I leaned in to acknowledge my cousin.

"I'm not sure I could ever fully forgive them for what they took from me, what they took from us all. But if peace with the invaders meant our people would be safe and the Diramal would see justice, I would," I replied. Log shifted uncomfortably in his seat, looking at me. "Is there anything else you wish to tell me, Log?"

Log shook his head. I glanced around and sighed.

"Alright, I'll leave you then."

"Are you going to see Olson?" Log asked as I walked for the exit.

"I wasn't planning on it."

"If you do, tell him I'm sorry. Don't ask why, just tell him for me, alright?" Log pleaded.

"Alright."

I opened the door and paused.

"If you ever feel the need to talk, Log, I'll listen," I said.

I left Log's quarters and opened a channel to Lara.

"Hello?" Lara's response was cagey, as though trying to hide that it was the real me calling her.

That must mean she's home.

"Lara, it's me . . . I'm coming home."

"Home?! W-why? Won't that—"

"My status has been compromised. The Diramal knows," I interjected.

Lara paused.

"I suppose we have a lot to discuss then," my sister replied.

"Much. Don't tell Mom or Lia. Just let them have their own reaction when I arrive," I said.

XVI
Returning Home
(Amat)

I took a deep breath as I walked up to my family's quarters and knocked on the door. A few moments later, the door slid open, revealing Lara. She greeted me with a half-smile.

"Are you ready?" Lara asked.

"Whether we are or aren't doesn't matter. There's no more time for secrets," I replied.

Lara nodded as we turned to enter the quarters.

"Lara?" My ears pricked up at the sound of my mother's voice, and my heart nearly skipped a beat. "Who was at the door?"

Lara cleared her throat as we came into our mother's view.

"Mom, we have a visitor," Lara said.

"Oh, is it your friend Joycill again—" My mother stopped herself short as she peered up from what she was doing in the kitchen.

Her stare froze me in place. She looked as though she knew me, or at least a ghost of me. The next thing I heard was my name being exclaimed. I turned my head and my sister Lia had run into my side, enveloping her arms around my waist.

"We missed you," Lia said.

"I missed you as well, Lia. So much," I replied, wrapping my arms around my little sister's head.

My mother lifted my chin with the tips of her fingers. Her eyes still filled with awe, and her hands trembled as she plowed her fingers through my hair.

"Amat?" my mother asked.

My eyes suddenly swelled up with tears and I took a moment to hold them back.

"Yeah, Mom, it's me," I replied.

"Amat . . . are . . . are you, you?" my mother asked.

"I am."

"My son . . ." My mother wrapped her arms around me. "Oh, Goddess, thank you for returning my boy to me."

I took in my mother's scent as I closed my eyes and leaned my head over hers as she wept. I heard Lara sniff behind us. When my mother was finally ready to look at me once again, she held my face in her hands and smiled.

"You've grown taller," she said. "You're turning out to look more like me. But I sense you've grown to behave more like your father. Some essence of him resides in your eyes." As we stared at one another, I failed to hold back my tears any longer. "Can . . . can you stay for dinner?"

My mother, Lara, and I gave a half laugh, half cry.

"If you'll have me," I said, wiping away a tear.

"I'll get lunch ready then."

"You'll get it ready? As in, you'll prepare it?" I asked.

"Well, yes, that goop may be what most people have to eat in today's world. But being the widow of a Jinn-hid has its perks when it comes to obtaining *rare* ingredients, like those in Argetti," my mother replied.

My eyes widened as I gasped, "No!"

"Yes, I was saving it for a special occasion. Now couldn't be a better time for it. But I'll take care of it. The rest of you go ahead and talk amongst yourselves. You all have a lot of catching up to do."

The rest of the afternoon was filled with pleasantries and laughs between us. Sometimes my mom would chime in something that had relevance to what we were discussing. And my little sister showed me some of her projects. I was amazed she was still so creative.

At dinner I was relatively quiet, as it was the first proper cooked meal I'd had in years. They all laughed every time I moaned with pleasure at the taste. Before long, my mother noticed that Lara didn't seem as amazed by the turn of events as she and Lia were. I put down my utensils and sighed.

"It's not that Lara isn't happy to see me home, Mom," I said, "As I'm sure you're aware, Lara is an Alpha and she's been following my command for over a year, since I freed myself of my code nine neuro-chip."

My mother tilted her head at me, then shifted her gaze to Lara.

"Wait, so you mean to tell me you've been yourself for over a year, Lara knew"—my mother shifted her attention to my sister—"and you didn't tell me or Lia about it?" My mother spoke deeply, with a sheer sense of disappointment. Lara lowered her head.

"It was *my* decision . . ." My mother flicked her head back toward me. "And Lara shouldn't be blamed for it. It was a precaution to keep you, Lia, Uncle Gordon, and Aunt Sally safe from the Diramal. The only reason that's changed is that he's finally figured it out. During our last mission, I'd met with quantum fade, and just after I awoke, I was called to a meeting with the Diramal. Still fatigued from my recovery, I couldn't keep my composure and I let him get the better of me."

My mother and I stared at one another in silence.

"Does that mean Mommy and I are going to end up like Daddy?" asked Lia.

I leaned over and took Lia's hands into my own.

"So long as I live and breathe, I will never allow it. I promise, Lia," I replied.

"What does it mean, then?" asked my mother.

"I don't know yet," I replied. "I saw the Diramal again today and to my surprise, it went well, too well. I suspect that means the Diramal is plotting something new—another game, likely—and something I still won't take lightly is your safety. Thus, I'm working on something that will better ensure your safety and security."

"Do you think we're in danger now?" my mother asked.

"I hope not, but what I have in mind would be used more as a precaution rather than a necessity."

"Do you think the Diramal would try to trick you into feeling you can trust him?" Lara asked.

"I don't trust him and if he feels I do, perhaps I can use that to my advantage," I replied.

"An advantage for what?"

I looked directly into my mother's eyes.

"Taking him down," I replied.

"And are you sure that wouldn't put us at an even greater risk?" my mother asked. I could tell by her tone she expected a particular answer.

"It may, but then there's the flip side to that question: are you all at greater risk if I do nothing? More importantly . . . is the whole world at greater risk if he's not dealt with?" I asked.

"It's hard to imagine the world in a worse position than where it currently stands. Perhaps that's not the true reason you seek to remove the Diramal. Perhaps it relates to something more personal," my mother proposed.

"I'm not trying to hide the fact, that part of my obligation in discharging the Diramal falls back greatly on what he did to Dad."

"Is it truly an obligation then, or a vendetta?"

"Are you defending him? After all he's done to us, to *me*?" I tightened my fist.

"I would never defend a man who stripped me of both my husband and, for a time, my only son. But I am questioning your approach to permanently resolving those issues and the risks involved. I'm questioning whether you've thought everything through," she replied.

"I'm confident that I have. But if I find that I haven't, then I will figure it out. I wouldn't dabble in these kinds of risks if I wasn't sure I had a thorough plan in mind," I asserted.

I put my napkin on the table and stood.

"Where are you going?" Lia asked.

"I'm sorry, Lia. As much as I'd love to stay, I can see there are some tensions rising within this conversation. I'd rather leave and let them douse than stay and see them burst. Thank you for the meal, Mom, it was refreshing. It was good catching up with you both. Lara, report to the launch bay tomorrow morning for inspection. I will return when I can."

I started walking for the door.

"Amat!" Lia barked.

I turned around and she ran into me, wrapping her arms around me.

"Come back soon," Lia said.

I kneeled to her level and smiled reassuringly.

"I promise, I will. Perhaps by tomorrow, if certain arrangements are ready to begin. If not, before too long," I replied.

I turned around, exited, and headed to my own quarters to retire for the night.

XVII
Dreaming into the past
(Amat)

When I arrived at my quarters, I didn't bother changing out of my uniform. I just fell flat on my bed. The soft cushion put me to sleep almost instantly.

I dreamt of the past, back to my first mission on Anua with my father, aboard that first invader craft. Everything played out as it happened to a T. It was like I was seeing it all for the first time again.

I suddenly found myself isolated from the rest of the team. The atmosphere felt colder, and I could see my breath leave my mouth in a faint misty cloud. Chirping screeches echoed deep within the ship; they didn't frighten me, as a matter of fact, they intrigued me. I followed them cautiously, trying to locate their origin. A loud *crack* sounded, like a snapping bone, followed by a sinister chuckle. I paused, unsure of what to do next, and suddenly someone jerked my shoulder.

"Amat!" my father whispered furiously, out of breath.

My father was covered in sweat; small trails of blood coated his Laquar suit. Whether it was his own or someone else's I couldn't say.

"Dad? What's wrong, where's the rest of—"

My father shushed me and grunted, clutching at his blood-drenched hip.

"You're hurt?" I asked.

"Keep your voice down, boy. Listen, we don't have much time. We have to leave before he gets back," my father whispered harshly.

"Who?" I asked, in a whisper.

"*Ah*! There's no time to explain. Come on, Amat, we need to get back to the Peroma," he replied.

My father grabbed my arm and lead the way back to the entrance, limping. With his other hand, he kept pressure on his wound. Along the way, my father slowed and hid us behind a wall. Around the corner, I could hear voices, human voices. My father gestured for me to keep quiet. I nodded in reply. He peeked his head around the corner and pulled back.

"Okay, there are three Cho'Zai blocking the exit," he whispered.

"Cho'Zai?" I asked, shocked.

"Yes, and I can take one out with this," he said as he loaded a magazine into his pistol. "Do you have a couple knives on you still?"

I looked down at my waist, not expecting anything to be there. Yet to my surprise, I found a belt; at the front of my waist was a pistol in a holster, and at either side of my waist hung some knives.

"I do," I said, as I armed both my hands.

"Good. Now, one of them is facing more toward us. I'll take him out so that he won't alert the others immediately. You stay low, run as fast as you can, and take down the other two. Make sure you stab them somewhere they won't recover from."

"Yes, sir," I said.

"Alright, ready?"

I nodded.

"Three, two, one, go."

My father took a deep breath, stood, and walked out from cover. He aimed right at the Cho'Zai's head furthest from us and shot her dead. I ran and crouched with all my speed, knives raised, and pounded them into the skulls of the other two Cho'Zai.

As I pried my blades from the Cho'Zai's brains, another sinister chuckle filled the ship. My father looked ahead to the exit. I was still trying to pry one of my knives when my father limped up to me.

"Come on, son, leave it!" he ordered as he grabbed my arm and led us to the elevator.

Steps away from entering, my father shouted in pain as three shots were fired.

"Dad!" I yelled.

He squeezed my arm tight as he dragged me down onto the floor with him. I quickly pulled out my pistol and turned around, but couldn't see anyone there. I looked over my father—all life had left his eyes.

"Dad? Dad!" I cried.

I flipped him over and listened to his heart; there was no beat. My jaw dropped as I pulled away and stared down at him. Shock emptied my mind as tears started to trail down my face. Once again, that chuckle filled the ship. A dark wind encircled me, and I heard footsteps from behind, followed by a pistol's hammer clicking back. I whirled to look behind me. The figure's features were all dark, from his clothes to his shoes, to his skin and hair. He embodied the Diramal, though I felt he was someone else entirely. He stood not ten paces away from me, lording over a being of radiant blue light. The way it seated itself on the ground seemed to mirror me.

"Having fun in these dreams yet, Reinosso? I, for one, am!" it said.

I rushed to my feet to stop the dark figure, but by then he had already pulled the trigger. I awoke yelling, springing up from my bed. I was covered in sweat, as were the sheets. Slowly, I sat up on the edge of the bed and slouched over, pressing the palms of my hands into my forehead.

After a moment's reflection on the dream, I thought to myself: *Reinosso. Where have I heard that name before? What does it mean?*

Grumbling to myself, I stood and walked to my AI computer. Everyone's quarters came equipped with one.

"Computer, what time is it?" I asked.

"Current time is 5:42 a.m.," the AI replied.

"And when did I start sleeping?" I asked.

"Jinn-hid Amat Luciph Criptous started sleeping at 10:47 p.m.," said the AI.

"Were there any entries into my quarters while I was asleep, unauthorized or otherwise?" I asked.

"Negative, there were no entries made into your quarters while you slept, Jinn-hid," said the AI.

"Scan me for any traces of intoxication."

I took a few steps back, widened my legs, and lifted my arms. The computer emitted a narrow, orange light that went up and down my body. It condensed and analyzed the results. I walked back up to the terminal.

"Report," I said.

"No sign of intoxication, Jinn-hid. However, your heart rate is spiking and there is an increase in beta wave activity within your brain, sir. I would recommend some meditation to help with this condition."

"I'll take that under advisement."

"Shall I play some harmonic music—"

"No," I replied.

"Confirmed, powering down," replied the AI.

I stepped into my bathroom and undressed. I paused when I caught sight of my reflection, where I could more clearly see the scars over my body. On either side of my rib cage were four long scars from the deep cut one of the invaders marked me with in the last fight on Anua. Along my arms, across my chest, and down the sides of my legs were fine-cut incisions from the mark-one regenerator. I reached over my shoulder and traced my fingers along one of the scars that stretched from my shoulder blade, curving up my neck and around my skull. It was then I squinted at the sudden remembrance of the final and most painful incision from the device when the code nine neuro-chip was placed inside my brain. I *punched* and cracked the mirror to silence the echo of my own screams in my mind. My hand trembled as I studied my bloodied knuckles. I exhaled as I took one last glance at myself, disgusted with my appearance. Only one word came to mind. *Weapon.*

While that may be all that I am, a weapon is meant to protect as much as it is to destroy, I reminded myself.

With that, I heated up the shower head, cleaned and mended my wound, and got ready for the day.

XVIII
Inspection
(Amat)

I got dressed and made my way to the hangar where I arrived to the sight of over fifty-five hundred men and women, loading a hundred thirty Fades with weapons and supplies, docking thirteen hundred Dailagons within the Fades. I stepped forward and found Olson, Log, Lara, and the Reikag speaking with someone I couldn't see.

"Good morning," I said as I approached them.

"Good morning, Jinn-hid," Blick replied.

"Morning, sir," my family added.

"Good morning, Amat," the fifth member of the group said.

I paused my walk and tilted my head at the sound of her voice. The Reikag, Olson, and Log stepped aside for me to see her. I almost couldn't believe my eyes, but I held back from showing my surprise.

"Mae?" I asked.

"Amat, it's been a while," Mae said.

"Over three years." I nodded. "How do you come to be here?"

"I've been transferred to serve under your command," Mae replied.

She handed me a folder with documents containing her orders, references, and experience. Lara gave me a knowing smile. I frowned at my sister as I took the documents from Mae.

"You're an Io-Pac now?" I asked, after having glossed over the contents of Mae's documents.

"Yes, promoted after the first year into the war," said Mae.

"I see. Looks like you served across the east coast for most of it," I observed.

"Yes, they flew me out to Zeta before the war with the invaders broke out. I only spent a couple months there before receiving orders to return home and serve in the same squadron as my sister at base Bajethor, in Yútheta," said Mae.

"I didn't know you had a sister," I replied.

"I did, an older one," said Mae.

"My sympathies," I said as I passed the folder back to Mae.

"Thank you," she said.

Part of me was overjoyed to see Mae once again. A part that I wouldn't allow her to see. Another part of me questioned it, not her, but the situation.

"It seems a bit of a coincidence seeing you here again after so long. May I enquire as to who ordered your transfer?" I asked.

"That would be the Diramal, sir," said Mae.

There it was . . . my suspicion confirmed. Had she been sent as a distraction for me? Was the Diramal hoping she would lower my guard? Make me soft, so that he could pull strings in the background without me noticing?

But if that were true, how would the Diramal know my feelings for Mae? I've hardly ever expressed them openly to anyone.

"I see. Well, happy to have you on board the operation, Io-Pac Kalbrook. I'll get you up to speed later. For now, I'm going to have to take these four with me."

"Of course, sir," Mae replied.

Mae saluted me and I, her.

"Reikag, Alphas," I called.

I turned and gestured for Vykin and my family to follow me.

"What happened to your hand?" Olson asked, before I could speak.

I stopped and glanced at my bandaged hand. I'd almost forgotten that I'd shattered my bathroom mirror a couple hours prior. Shaking my head as I recollected myself, I waved my hand at Olson.

"I've suffered worse. On a more important note, I have questions for each of you that I need answered. Let's get the most obvious out of the way. Reikag Vykin, what are you doing here? Why aren't you tending to your duties as Reikag?" I asked.

"Those duties do not start until later today, sir. I'd heard about the arrangement you made with the Diramal, and I wanted to see the fleet for myself," Blick replied.

"Did it not occur to you, Reikag, that your interest in my operation might raise some questions about the stance on our relationship to one another?" I asked.

"No, sir, it did not," Blick said with a sigh.

"Clearly, or else you wouldn't be here." I glanced back at the others. "None of you seem shocked by the notion that Reikag Vykin and I are working together again."

"He told us about it earlier," Log said.

"Of course he did," I growled.

"Not that that grants him our trust," Lara said, crossing her arms as she stared at Blick.

"I never said whether or not he had mine in full, either," I said to my sister. "But the Reikag here has brought to light something of interest to me. Speaking of which, did you at least come with an update on your findings, Vykin?"

"As a matter of fact, I did, sir," Blick said.

"Then why am I still waiting?" I asked.

The Reikag gave me an irked glance.

"The names of the people that went missing resurfaced in secret classified operations issued by the Diramal," said Blick.

I slowly stopped my stride and turned toward the Reikag.

"How do you know this?" I asked.

"From here." Blick pried a folder from his coat and handed it to me.

I swiped it from him and opened it up. A lot of the writing was redacted, but as I scanned through the papers, I caught sight of some names and the Reikag helped to point them out.

"There 'Klyva' is the same name that belonged to 'Klyva Strogue' on this data crystal." The Reikag held up the crystal to his fizer, and a light pierced through it, displaying the crystal's contents. The Reikag found the name again. "She went missing on Janak seventeenth, twenty-five forty-nine. Hold this up to the light"—the Reikag pinched the paper I was looking at and held it to the light—"and you can see the rest of her name is there."

"And a peculiar acronym before it. HV four-two-seven. Any idea what that means?" I asked.

"No. But there're half a dozen brief reports in there, bearing names that these two sources have in common," said Blick.

I gave the Reikag a sidelong look and considered all he told me. I was satisfied, I had to admit. What he brought didn't completely unveil the mystery I was confronted with, but it did prove something of interest. People, civilians, were going missing and being issued secret missions. Whether they were being forced to do so remained to be seen. But that would be discovered in due time.

I took both folder and crystal from the Reikag, concealing them in my coat.

"Reikag Vykin, what you've brought me here today has proven fruitful. Attend my office and I will meet you there shortly."

"But what about my duties as the Reikag?" asked Blick.

"I'll take care of that. Now go."

"Yes, sir," Blick said, with a trusting smile.

The Reikag saluted me and I, him.

"What are you going to do with him?" Lara asked when Blick was out of earshot.

"That doesn't matter, at present . . ." Lara tilted her head. "What does, is Io-Pac Kalbrook. What did you all discuss with her?" I asked.

"Nothing in particular. We introduced ourselves and we all got to talking about how we knew you," Lara said.

"That's it?" I asked.

"Yeah, she's nice," Olson said.

"I know she is," I replied, my thoughts drifting for a moment.

"I remember you said you liked her," Olson said.

I looked directly at Olson, my gaze intense.

"You didn't tell her that," I said, sternly.

"No, I didn't," Olson said, almost as equally stern.

"Wise choice. Don't ever mention it to her," I said.

"I wouldn't, ever. That's not my place," Olson replied.

"Good. Now, back to what I was saying about Mae. I find it extremely odd that she's here and that the Diramal assigned her to me specifically. Other than the records of our squadron at Gallethol, I can't begin to understand how he would know my correlation to her. I think it's a ploy to distract me from something he may be scheming."

"What do you intend to do about it, then?" Log asked.

"I'm going to confront him. See if this is what I think it is. In the meantime, just lie low until the mission launches. And not that I don't trust her, but, Lara, I'm going to pair you closely with Mae on this mission. See if you can find out why she's here," I said.

Lara chortled.

"Something funny?" I asked.

Lara blinked and the smile faded from her face.

"No, sir," Lara replied.

"Then your orders are clear?" I asked.

"Yes, sir."

"Good—"

"Jinn-hid," a voice sounded from behind.

I turned around and saw the Cho'Zai Zothra standing before me.

"I am Cho'Zai Zothra, and I've been assigned to you as the Diramal's liaison on this mission of yours."

"Right, hang back a second. I'll be with you shortly," I said.

"Of course, sir," Zothra replied.

I twisted my head at that. It wasn't standard for a Cho'Zai to call anyone other than the Diramal "sir." I turned back around, and both my cousins had shocked looks on their faces. Lara held a mildly concerned expression on her face, but the look in her eyes suggested she did not feel betrayed by me.

"When were you planning on telling us about this? Or did we find out as you had planned, abruptly and on our own?" Log asked.

"He is a condition, as part of my agreement with the Diramal, to make this mission a reality. Now's not the best time to discuss it, but we will later."

Log marched away. Lara followed and called after him. Olson nodded and took his own path from me.

I turned around and walked up to Zothra.

"Family trouble, sir?" Zothra asked.

I squinted at the Cho'Zai.

"That's hardly any concern of yours," I replied.

"Of course, apologies, sir, only trying to lighten the mood," replied Zothra.

Zothra reached out his file to me. I glanced down at it.

"There's no need for that. I am well aware of your reputation already," I said.

"Very well then, sir," Zothra said, pulling back his file.

The Cho'Zai maintained a mocking grin on his face.

Already, a game has begun with this one.

"Why do you refer to me as 'sir'? We both know there's a peculiar gray area between our ranks. Even though I am technically an officer, and a superior, and you are a soldier bred for war since birth, you take your commands solely from the Diramal," I clarified.

"True, sir, but as you said, you *are* an officer and *my* superior in this scenario. Though I may still report and carry out demands from the Diramal, I have been placed under your command as far as this operation is concerned. I'd like to think that I am working for the benefit of both you and the Diramal." Zothra smiled, almost too pleasantly.

"How noble of you," I said, unimpressed.

Zothra nodded.

"I get the sense that you don't trust me, sir," said Zothra.

"Really? What gave that away?" I asked, sarcastically.

Zothra sighed.

"I know about your history with two members among my rank, sir. An incident that occurred over three years ago. But I assure you, not all of us are like that," he said.

"What, obedient to the Diramal?" I asked.

"We are all that much, but we still have a say in what assignments we choose to partake in."

I could sense the lie in his voice.

"And I wonder how often you all speak your mind," I said.

"You might be surprised, sir," said Zothra.

I ground my teeth and *tsked* as I shook my head. Zothra and I stared in silence at one another.

This one's sharp at being elusive.

"Is there anything else?" I finally asked.

"No, sir," Zothra replied.

"Good, you are dismissed."

Zothra took one step, stopped, and looked back at me.

"I suppose I do have one question, sir. When will we be departing?"

"Noon, now that you mention it. Why don't you go around and make sure the men, women, and Fades are ready to leave by then."

"Of course, sir. Right away."

My nostrils flared as Zothra finally left my sight. I didn't trust him one bit. *For all the trouble it would get me in, if he puts one foot out of line, I will kill him.*

***

I left the launch bay and headed to my office to meet with the Reikag. I found him pacing back and forth in front of my door. His face drooped with boredom. Once he caught sight of me, he approached.

"Sure took your time, didn't you?" Blick said.

"In a rush? I already told you, don't worry about getting to the Diramal," I said, punching in the code to unlock my office door. "Your new position starts today."

The door opened. I logged onto my computer and opened my coding program. The circular frame rose from my desk with the flask of nanites. As the two arms unraveled themselves from the flask, I grabbed it and took out the syringe from my drawer. I opened the flask and filled the syringe to the brim with the nanites.

"What's that?" asked Blick.

"This?" I asked, referring to the syringe. "This is your initiation into my command, my condition to regain your place in my good graces. In bringing me these sources"—I said, removing them from my coat and placing them in one of my drawers—"you have proven to me where your priorities lie. But to completely earn my trust"—I stood and walked up to the Reikag—"I need to get rid of any and all neuro-chips planted in your brain."

"So, this is how you did it, then. This is how you freed yourself from your code nine?" Blick asked.

"Yes," I replied.

"Reprogramming nanotech. What inspired that idea?" he asked.

"A hunch," I replied.

"I see. Well, let's not waste any more time." Blick's voice was deep and direct.

"Tilt your head to the side," I said, walking to Blick's side.

The Reikag did as I instructed and I injected the nanites into his neck.

"In a few minutes, you're going to feel your worst," I said. "Your head is going to feel hot; you're going to get consistent episodes of vertigo in short bursts. You'll also likely slur your speech and potentially worse."

"I can hardly wait." Blick's tone shifted from confident to sarcastic.

"Head over to the cafeteria; *don't* eat anything. Just wait for me there and I'll come as soon as I can. If you start feeling sick early on, just take a breather, don't push yourself. But try to reach the cafeteria," I said.

"Got it," Blick said.

"I'll try to meet you there in thirty."

The Reikag left my office, and I headed over to the Diramal's office to discuss a few things.

XIX
Kalbrook And Vykin
(Amat)

I marched through the doors of the Diramal's office. He looked up at me, hardly fazed by my unannounced appearance.

"Ah, Amat, what an unexpected surprise. How does this morning treat you?" the Diramal asked.

"Full of surprises, sir," I replied.

"Surprises? Anything I should concern myself with?"

I paused only for a moment before answering.

"No, sir. Not at all. Though there is one thing you would have knowledge of already," I said, leaning over the Diramal's desk. The Diramal glanced down at my clenched fists as he waved his hand.

"And what might that be?" The Diramal stared intently back at me.

"Io-Pac Kalbrook, sir."

The Diramal squinted at me, thrown off.

"Who?" the Diramal asked.

"Mae Kalbrook, you assigned her to me from Bajethor," I said.

"Ah, that one, yes. She put in a request to be placed under your command a few nights past," said the Diramal.

"She requested it?" I asked, thrown off myself now.

"Yes," said the Diramal.

The Diramal held a puzzled expression. Then he sat back and smiled sinisterly.

"Why are you so concerned with this Io-Pac, Amat? Could it be that you know her?" he asked.

He didn't know?! I silently cursed. *Now I've exposed him to another variable that can be used against me!* I held my silence and took a deep breath.

"Ah, you do. But I sense, there's more to it, isn't there—"

"That's enough," I broke in.

The Diramal raised his hands and lowered his head.

"Forgive me, I don't mean to pry. I'm merely intrigued. I never knew you had feelings for someone," the Diramal admitted. Giving the Diramal a hard stare, I grimaced. I was so sure he knew about my connection to Mae. But now I felt I made a grave mistake. "I'll forget you ever mentioned it. Don't fret, I haven't forgotten about our understanding. Was there any other purpose to your coming here?"

I blinked and stood straight.

"As a matter of fact, there was. Now that we've got Kalbrook out of the way, there is a matter regarding Reikag Vykin that I wanted to discuss," I replied.

"Ah, Reikag Vykin. Yes, he seems to be late for his shift today; I was wondering about him. You haven't seen him at all, have you?" the Diramal asked.

"As a matter of fact, I have. As of today, I've taken the Reikag under my command," I said.

The Diramal's eyes opened wide as he leaned forward over his desk. His stare broke through layers; it felt like he was looking at more than just my face.

"I didn't hear that," he said. For the first time in a long time, I heard the Diramal's voice meld. I understood the words, but it sounded like he spoke a different language. I stiffened as I caved in to the unspoken command behind them.

"As I said, I've taken Vykin under my command," I responded.

The Diramal took a deep breath and nodded his head.

"That's what I thought."

The Diramal growled and cursed as he stood, flipping his desk over. I was astonished at his strength, as the desk had been built into the floor. As the contents of the Diramal's desk flew off, I stepped back defensively and dropped my arms to my side, ready for the Diramal to attack me. He stood still, his shoulders rising and falling as he stared at the mess he made. Finally, he turned around and looked out into the deep darkness outside the base.

"I wouldn't presume anything about you, Diramal, that I don't already know. But I'd say you seem greatly displeased by the idea of Vykin no longer being under your wing."

"Yes, you're very observant, Amat," the Diramal said. His vexed tone suggested a level of vulnerability in his mood.

"Would it console you to know that I don't intend on taking him into the field?" I asked.

The Diramal turned and faced me.

"Why is that?" he asked.

"That will remain my business. But I think a better question is why are you acting like you have no say in this?" I asked.

The Diramal growled.

"That will remain my business. The most I can tell you is what I've said before. Certain circumstances would have it so."

I took a step forward as I tried to comprehend what he meant by that.

"Who is Blick to you?" I asked.

The Diramal turned his back to me, once again.

"You're dismissed, Jinn-hid," he finally said.

"So, the Reikag is—"

"Is yours. That'll be all, Criptous," the Diramal broke in.

I slowly took steps backward before turning away from the Diramal and exiting his office.

XX
Neuro-chip Free
(Amat)

I made my way to the cafeteria as quickly as I could. He sat at a table near the entrance with his head down and his hand covering his face. As I got closer, I saw that the Reikag was sweating so profusely that it seeped through his uniform and there was color to his cheeks. But none of that was very surprising. I greeted the Reikag as I took a seat across from him.

"Despite it being a dumb question, I'll just go out and ask it. How are you holding up?" I asked.

The Reikag gave me a sidelong look; his eyes were tired. Blick slowly opened his mouth to speak, but struggled. He swallowed and closed his eyes.

"I-oi . . . I-oi'm doing alwight," Blick said.

I tightened my mouth and nodded my head, trying to keep from laughing. *I can't laugh; I probably sounded just as stupid, if not more, when I had my injection.*

"*He* . . . how did m-meeting go . . . with Die-mal?" asked Blick.

I blinked and nodded. Blick sounded so simple-minded, it was almost sad. I wondered if he would even notice me laughing at him. Still, I held back.

"Better than anticipated. You're a free man, Blick," I said.

Blick grew a big dopey grin on his face.

"Fwee?" asked Blick.

"Yes," I replied.

Blick gave a strange laugh and looked away.

"I-I don't know what say."

"I imagine you don't and that's probably for the best, for the time being. Why don't we walk this off back to my quarters, 'ey, Blick?" I asked.

Blick slapped the table, inhaled deeply, and smiled.

"Great sounds, I wike walks!" Blick exclaimed.

I nodded my head and smiled awkwardly at others who'd noticed us. I took Blick's arms from across the table and helped him up. He almost fell back, but I was there to pull him up straight.

"Whoa there, Blick. Take it easy," I said, as I slid to Blick's side of the table and put his arm around my neck.

"Yeah, walks really nice. Good for get out," he said.

We received a few disturbed looks from people entering the cafeteria on our way out. But fortunately, Blick stayed quiet most of the way to my quarters. To most, he would have just seemed drunk, given his stumbling stride.

***

By the time we reached my quarters, Blick was speaking straight again, and he only seemed a bit weary. I helped him to a seat on the couch, and Blick gave a sigh of relief as he lay back. A sigh escaped me as well as I took a seat. I was tired from holding Blick up and compensating for his lack of strength. I tilted my head back and rested my eyes.

"Feeling better?" I asked.

"Very," Blick replied. "Don't remember a whole lot."

"There wasn't much worth remembering. Except, do you remember what I said about where you stand with the Diramal?" I asked.

"Enough to know that it was big news." Blick turned his head toward me. "I've been officially reassigned."

"That is correct," I replied.

"Thank you, really," Blick responded.

"You're an asset to me, Blick. You've proven that much in giving me those sources. You did all that with a neuro-chip in your head, knowing the risks your actions would entail. Thus, there should be no reason for any further misunderstandings between us. If there are, it won't end well for you." I lifted my head and looked at the Reikag. "Do we understand one another?" Blick nodded his head. "You've earned my trust, but my friendship, that will take more to regain."

"Understood, sir," said Blick.

"Good," I said, resting my head back and closing my eyes.

"When should we return to the hangar?" Blick asked.

"The hangar?" I raised an eyebrow.

"Yeah, for the mission," Blick said.

"Is that where you think I'll be taking you?" I looked back at Blick, and he seemed confused. "No, no, Blick. What I have in mind for you is something of far greater importance and responsibility."

"Well, what is it?"

"I'll show you when you're ready to move again. The sooner the better," I replied.

"Alright, mind if I rest for maybe ten minutes?"

"Ten minutes seems reasonable enough," I replied.

I proceeded to send Lara a written message via my fizer.

I counted, in my head, the seconds that went by till I reached ten minutes' worth and led Blick through the halls of Y'Gůtsa, to a particular residence.

"What are we doing here?" Blick asked.

"You'll see," I replied.

I knocked on the door.

"Who is it?" Lara asked.

"It's Amat."

The door slid open, revealing Lara's welcoming expression. She frowned at the sight of Blick.

"Amat, is there a reason you brought *him* here?" Lara asked.

"I try to have a purpose behind every action I take," I replied, leading Blick inside the quarters.

Lara locked a furious gaze onto Blick as he passed.

"The others home?" I asked.

"Mom's resting and Lia's in her room. What are you—"

"Go and get them, please. There's something I need to discuss with you all." I turned toward Lara when she didn't move. "Quickly."

"Right away, sir," Lara replied.

Blick cleared his throat, sensing the awkward tension.

"It's nice, this place, better than my quarters, I'd say," Blick said, trying to change the subject.

"Even for the former Ward of the Diramal?" I asked.

"You'd be surprised what little that title gets you," Blick said.

I took a seat and waited for Lara to come out with Lia and our mother.

"Amat, what are we doing here?" Blick asked.

I looked up from my seat and saw my mom walk in, holding Lia's hand, yawning. Lara walked right behind them. My mother's gaze stuck on Blick like glue as soon as she saw him and not in a good way.

"Amat, what is this young man doing here?" she asked, scanning Blick up and down.

I raised my finger.

"A question that seems to be on everyone's mind at present and one that I intend to answer. But first, take a seat, all of you. This will all go smoother if you're settled down," I replied. Lara sat next to me, Blick and my mother sat in chairs across from one another, and Lia at our mother's side. "Perfect. Now, Mom, both you and Lara seem a bit upset that Blick is here. I assume that's because you remember the things I told those reporters over three years ago regarding the last mission on Anua."

My mother's gaze still stayed on Blick as she raised an eyebrow and nodded her head, frowning. Blick leaned back in his seat, uncomfortable.

"A mother never forgets, Amat, so you'd be correct. What entitled you to do all those things to my son, not to mention the things you did to my nephews?!" my mother exclaimed.

"Mom, please, I don't have time—"

"No, I want to know, before I hear any more from you. What is your problem? My son harbored you, putting himself and the rest of us at great risk. If I was aware of the history between the two of you, I would *never* have allowed it. And to make matters worse, right when you gained my son's trust, you stabbed him in the back. So, give me one good reason why I shouldn't grab you by the neck and throw you out of here myself," she growled.

"Mom—"

"I'm not talking to you, Amat!" my mother barked, giving me a stern stare. She shifted her attention back onto Blick. "Tell me why I should hear my son out on whatever it is he has to say about you."

I sighed heavily.

You're gonna hear it, regardless of what Blick has to say to all that.

Blick leaned forward, looking down at his feet as he collected his thoughts.

"Mrs. Criptous . . ." Blick started, raising his head to my mother. "It's true what you say about me. I've done terrible things to Amat and other members of your family. All I can say to that is, I regret them with the deepest sincerity you could know. In my defense, our rising conflicts were mainly due to Amat's actions. But in his defense, I could have done better. I could have held back from indulging in his aggression toward me. Especially after he stopped going out of his way to excessively compete with me in our training at Lazithia. Part of that was due to jealousy."

I raised an eyebrow, looked over at Blick, and him at me.

"Even though it might have been hard for you to see at the time, I noticed that your father cared very much for you, Amat. He was harsh, at times, yes, but he had your best interests at heart. At that point, I'd spent years under the Diramal's care, and he never showed me an ounce of worry or affection like the way your father did for you. And I hated you for being so blind to the fact."

He shifted his attention back to my mother.

"As for the incident on the moon, I can honestly say those actions were not my own. My code three neuro-chip had been activated and someone forced me to attack your son, Mrs. Criptous. I swear that to be the truth, by the light of Anua, and I should be doomed to walk in her shadow for the rest of eternity if it is not. I'd imagine it was an executive order of the Diramal's, in the hopes that Amat would hand me back over to him and lose his trust in me."

My mother sighed and nodded her head.

"You asked me why you should hear what your son has to say about me. I would answer with this: your son, Mrs. Criptous, is a great young man. He puts the lives of those he loves before his own. He's grown to consider his actions before he carries them out. I've only been reacquainted with him a few days now and I can see that much in him. Whatever he has to say to you, I'm sure he has your best interests in mind . . . like his father did him," said Blick.

My mother stared at Blick in silence for a long moment, her gaze seemingly piercing through him. Deciding if she could be satisfied with Blick's words.

"Well, Amat, what do you have to say then?"

I lifted my head and looked over to my mom.

"Thank you, Mom," I said. "Well spoken, Blick. The reason I've brought him here today is due to where I stand with the Diramal.

According to the Diramal, we have an understanding and in recent days he's been far too generous to me. But his words are worthless to me. That is why I felt it necessary to appoint Blick as the security of this family."

"What?!" my mother, Lara, and Blick all exclaimed.

"Blick, you will be responsible day and night to remain in the presence of this family, ensuring the Diramal doesn't attempt to harm or pry into their lives while I'm away." I shifted my attention to Blick. "From time to time, I'd like it if you also checked on my Uncle Gordon and Aunt Sally."

"Amat, I-I can't be trusted with this. The safety of your family is a burden I could never live to bear, should I fail," Blick said.

"Then don't fail. If you do, you'll have more than your burden to worry about," I replied.

"Amat, this is outrageous!" my mother exclaimed.

"I agree, Amat. If security is what you want, why not just keep me here to watch over everyone?" Lara butted in.

"Is your trust so easily regained?" my mother blurted. "Are you so sure this one won't put us in as much danger as you hope he will in safety?"

"All of you, be quiet!" I barked. "On the subject of my trust, *Mom,* it is not so easily gained to begin with. If it were, this family would have likely seen worse done to it three years ago. Blick came to me, pleading to let me take him back into my good graces. So, I gave him the task of acquiring certain information that could be crucial in taking the Diramal down. Lara, you know this." My mother sighed as she threw her arms up. "He gave me this information at the drop of a hat and when I wasn't satisfied, he went out to bring me more. I think it's safe to say where Blick's loyalties lie and the amount of risk his being here entails. And, Lara, your place is under my command; I need your skills on the battlefield."

"I won't have him around Lia; what if his code three neuro-chip is activated again?" my mother asked.

"Do you think I would have put him in this position without having taken care of that? Do you think I'd be sitting here if I hadn't figured out a way to permanently remove my own neuro-chip and not be able to do it to someone else?" My mother crossed her arms and looked away. "On the subject of Lia, shall we see what she and Lara think?" I looked at both my sisters. "Lia? Lara? How do you feel about this?" I asked.

Lara shook her head.

"I have to say, Amat, there's part of me that stands firmly with Mom on this." Lara looked over to Blick and then back at me. "Another part of me trusts your better judgment, not just as my commander, but also my older brother. And you gave Blick your serum?" Lara asked.

"I did," I replied.

Lara nodded.

"Then I shall also have to admit, I sensed the honesty in Blick's voice when he gave you his justification to hear Amat out, Mom." Lara and our mother looked at one another. "And if he really feels that way, without his neuro-chip, perhaps he can be trusted."

"Lara." My mother's voice was stern.

"But I would still advocate for myself to take up this position you are assigning to Blick," said Lara.

I turned my attention to Lia and asked her the same question.

"I don't know, Amat, I don't want to make Mommy upset," Lia replied.

"It's okay, Mom's not gonna get upset. Just tell us how you feel about Blick," I said.

Lia looked at Blick and bit her lip. My mother tightened her grip around my little sister. Lia looked over to me.

"Can I see him closer?" asked Lia.

I looked at my mother, who shook her head at me. I shifted my attention back to Lia.

"Sure." I smiled.

As I stood, my mother tugged Lia closer. Lia reached her hands up to me and I looked into my mother's eyes.

"She'll be alright," I said.

My mother removed her arm and as I took Lia away, my mother held her breath. I gently pried Lia from my mother's arms and guided her across the room, kneeling at her side as she stood to examine Blick.

"Your eyes are very interesting. On the bottom half of your irises, they are yellow, yet at the top, they are a vibrant red-orange," Lia said.

Blick blinked several times as he thought of a response.

"Thank you," Blick said with an awkward smile. "I've never really known the reason behind it, but they've been that way since I was born. Perhaps a strange mutation of my parents' genetics occurred when I was in my mother's womb."

"Did one of them have the red eyes of a Cho'Zai and the other yellow eyes?" Lia asked.

"I can't remember what both my parents' eyes looked like. I barely even remember my mother's face." Blick's eyes revealed a sincere longing at the mention of his mother.

"Do you mean you lost her?" Lia asked.

"I . . . I've lost them both, yes," Blick replied.

Lia stood, walked up to Blick, and gave him a hug. Blick kept his arms to his side, and his attention switched from me to my mom. I gave him a nod and Blick lightly patted Lia on her back. Lia sniffed.

"I'm sorry for you. I lost my daddy, but I don't know what I'd do if I lost my mom," Lia said, wiping a tear from her cheek.

Lia ran up to our mother, arms open.

"Mommy." My mother took my younger sister into her arms as she wept. "I think we should let him stay." Lia looked back over to Blick. "He needs us just as much as we may need him."

Blick looked deep into Lia's eyes with a curious expression. He swallowed and looked down at his feet. If I didn't know any better, I'd say he was on the verge of tears.

I took my seat back beside Lara.

"I don't want to presume anything has been decided, but it's looking like Lia and Lara are on board with the idea of Blick staying here for the time being. So has anything about *your* opinion on it changed?" I asked my mother.

My mother sighed.

"Fine, but know this, Vykin, Amat and his father aren't the only ones in this family who would do anything to protect it. Anything," she said.

"I understand, Mrs. Criptous. I swear to you, I won't put this family through any more trouble than it's already endured. And I will do my best to protect it against any threat."

"We'll see. I suppose this . . . arrangement is effective immediately?" my mother asked me.

"Affirmative," I replied.

"Well . . ." My mother stood from her seat and let go of Lia. "Make yourself at home then, Vykin."

My mother walked away and took Lia with her.

Lara and I stood and said our goodbyes to everyone, including Blick. After which we headed straight for the hangar, expecting the troops to be ready by the time we got there.

XXI
Cracks In My Wall
(Amat)

I saw Olson had beaten my return to the hangar. He had his arms crossed and was shaking his head, observing Log arguing with some of the men and women. I frowned and walked up to him.

"Olson," I called.

Olson turned his head toward me and then shifted his attention back onto Log.

"Amat," Olson said and leaned past me. "Lara."

"Olson." Lara smiled.

"Is there a problem or is Log's confrontation limited to those individuals?" I asked.

Olson smacked his lips.

"Unfortunately, the former, the troops seem to be lacking initiative and at this rate, the launch is likely to be delayed."

I raised an eyebrow.

"How late exactly?" I asked.

"About an hour and a half. Log and I have been trying to get them to pick up the pace, but as you can see, they're taking their time loading the Fades," said Olson.

My ears flinched and perked up.

"An hour and a half," I said calmly.

"Yes, sir, that'd be my guess," replied Olson.

"*Mm*, an hour and a half," I repeated.

I walked forward and took in some of the activities they were doing. A lot of the men were sitting on cargo, drinking. Some of the women looked to be talking with the men, laughing, like this was some social gathering. Less than half of the people in general looked to be doing something productive.

"AN HOUR AND A HALF!" I barked.

The shout echoed through the hangar, stopping everyone in their tracks. All eyes were on me. All the smiles faded from their faces. It was like they were seeing me for the first time.

"The last squadron under my command lasted nearly three years, with minimal casualties." I continued to speak loudly enough for my voice to carry. "Granted, those men and women were all Alphas, among the best of the best, next to the Cho'Zai. They fought under me, in the worst areas of this country, and won against impossible odds time and time again. Do you know how they did it? Discipline. Something I can't even sense within any one of you. Instead . . ."

I marched through the crowds up to one of the men sitting on a box of cargo with food and drink in hand. I raised my leg and kicked the box forward; the man fell back and spilled everything all over himself.

"I see those among you eating, drinking, sitting on precious cargo, and laughing it up amongst yourselves."

I looked down at the man who fell to the ground.

"You hungry?!" I bellowed.

"Y-yes, sir!" the man stuttered.

"Then you should have thought of that before you reported for duty this morning." I pulled the man off the ground. "The time for pleasantries has passed. Due to your procrastination, we are an hour and a half behind schedule. That is unacceptable! If you expect to survive the missions I'll be leading you into, you are all going to have to tidy up your priorities and sharpen your senses or you are going to die within your first few minutes of combat! Under me, you'll not be doing simple recon missions or clearing areas that have already been run through. You are on the front lines now, and you will be facing the horrors of this war to their maximum."

I turned around to Log and Olson.

"On another note." I marched up to Log. When I came up to him, I grabbed his wrist and raised his arm. "Alphas Olson and Lara Criptous, get over here!" Olson and Lara made their way promptly to my side. I took Olson's arm and raised it as well. "These three, Olson, Log, and Lara Criptous, are your superiors, just as much as I am. If they tell you to do something"—I turned to the men and women that had been arguing with Log—"there should be no argument. Alphas Olson, Log, and Lara

Criptous are to be taken just as seriously as me. Remember their names and faces well, or you'll be dealing with *me*."

I lowered Olson's and Log's arms.

"Our mission, in case you all forgot, is to save as many Skivs and Warvs as possible. And every minute you waste here, could mean another innocent Skiv is killed. You're on their time now; their blood is on *your* hands. Now get to it! I will not accept the launch commencing five minutes past our target time. That leaves you all one hour to finish prepping these Fades!"

The men and women immediately got back to work and stepped to their duties. The hangar filled with all kinds of clutter and voices. I turned back to my siblings.

"May Anua save the trooper that disappoints you directly," Lara said to me.

"I doubt they will after that speech. Why don't you go around and get them familiar with you before we launch."

"Yes, sir," Lara said, leaving the group.

I turned to my cousins.

"I've heard there's been some difficulties between you two. Have you made up with one another?" I asked.

Olson and Log looked at one another. Olson gave Log a half smile and reached out his hand. Log looked down at it and then back up at his brother. Log shook Olson's hand.

"I'm sorry about the other day," Log said.

"It's alright, I'm just worried about you. I understand you're getting older, but you're still my little brother. It's my job to look after you, both of you," Olson replied, glancing at me.

Log nodded and considered his reply.

"You don't have to worry about me. Either of you," said Log.

I wasn't so sure about that, but then and there was not the place to discuss it. Unless one of them brought up an issue, I wasn't going to make any enquiries.

I placed my hands on their shoulders and they leaned in, with us staring deeply into each other's eyes.

"Our family is its own squadron, a pack. If any one of us falters, as do we all. We must always look out for one another, no matter what we're individually capable of," I said.

Olson slapped his hand on top of mine.

"Yes, sir," he said proudly.

Log gave a solemn nod.

I sensed something that lured my attention toward the entrance of the launch bay. It was Mae, looking in my direction. I looked back at my cousins as I pulled away from them.

"*Mm*, if no one has anything else to add, we can leave it at that for now. When we return, we're going to talk, all of us. Agreed?" I asked. Olson nodded his head. "Log?"

"Sure," Log replied, avoiding my eyes.

"Good. See to it that the Fades are ready within the hour."

"Yes, sir," Olson and Log replied.

I made my way to Mae.

"Io-Pac Kalbrook," I began.

"Jinn-hid," Mae replied.

"How much of that did you hear?" I asked.

"Enough," Mae replied, nodding her head.

"I suppose you think I was too hard on them. Knowing you and your tendency to a kind heart."

Mae kept her gaze on me while I turned to look at the men and women at work.

"You say that as if it were unwise to hold a kind heart," Mae replied.

"In a world like ours, it is futile."

I looked back over into Mae's eyes and waited for her reply. When she didn't, I eased my gaze back onto the soldiers at work.

"No," said Mae.

"No, what?" I asked.

"I didn't think you were too harsh. There were many stragglers, and they'd cost you time and potential lives outside these walls. You said what needed to be said, in a tone that needed to be harsh," said Mae.

"But?" I asked.

"But . . . you've changed." I looked over to Mae. "Yet there's much about you that remains the same."

Mae started marching away. Before she got too far, I called out, "Perhaps I never allowed you to know me so well. Perhaps there is much about me that remains the same, but not in the way you think."

Mae turned around and faced me.

"Such as?" she asked.

"Who you are to me," I replied.

I held my hands behind my back, turned, and walked away. *I'll let her sit with that for now,* I thought with a smirk.

XXII
Promotions
(Amat)

An hour had gone by, and I spent it wandering around the base; fetching a few things that would help with some of the challenges I foresaw. When I returned, I found the hangar clear of the clutter that our cargo and supplies made up.

"Amat!" a voice from behind me shouted.

I turned around and saw Log approaching me.

"Log, you're looking better than last I saw you," I replied.

"And feeling so, sir," Log said.

I nodded.

"What do you need?" I asked.

"The Fades are ready, sir. All that's left is to load the troops and head out," he said.

"Good, there may be hope for them yet. Are Olson, Lara, and Io-Pac Kalbrook here as well?" I asked.

"Yes, sir, by the entrance," Log replied.

"Then let us head that way."

A brief silence fell between myself and Log as we walked beside one another until I was ready to break it.

"Log, I'm going to tell you this now while we're alone, to avoid any confrontation it may stir with the others." I pulled something from my coat—an insignia. "This is the mark of an Io-Pac," I said, offering it to Log.

Log stopped, bewildered.

"Amat, you're not thinking of—"

"I am," I said, cutting Log short.

"I-I can't accept it," said Log.

"You will have to. To maximize this mission's efficiency, I am going to divide our forces into fourths. You, Olson, Mae, and I will have our own command of each quarter. I saw how the troops ignored you when you tried enforcing their productivity. They shrugged you off as a kid who didn't know any better. And while this will help, you will also need to find your inner leader, Log, promptly. Or they will not follow your commands and you will lose more than you can afford to out there," I said.

"I can't carry the weight of that responsibility," Log said.

I leaned in close to him and placed the insignia in Log's hand.

"You can and you will." I stood straight. "Place that in your pocket for now, and put it on after we launch, Io-Pac Log Criptous."

***

Log led me to the others; included among them was Zothra. It wasn't to my liking, nor my surprise. Nevertheless, I briefly went over the coordinated areas of my choosing, telling each member where they would land and where they would look for Skivs and Warvs. Mae and Lara would take several of the troops under their command to the city of Zoiqua, a place that once held the largest marine mining and fishing operations in the country. The city itself was mostly submerged beneath sea level, shielded within Laquar domes, south of the state Trinadone's shores.

Olson would take his troops to the north, to a city called Skergel. I received word from Sarak that there was a high concentration of Skivs and Warvs on a reconnaissance run she performed a couple weeks back.

Log would go to the east, to a city called Atheika, a place that was once green and lively. Back in the day, its people had a reputation for protests and rallies against the use of neuro-chips. Having experienced the extreme of their restraining potential, maybe my time would have been better spent over there with the protesters, rather than at Gallethol. Not to my surprise, Sarak said most of the city was covered with Warvs who'd overthrown at least one of the military bases in the area. I was counting on this to be a challenging mission for Log to command, in the hopes that it would pull him from his boyish tendencies and force him to take charge.

Zothra and I would be going to Ion, a highly industrial city once, filled with Skivs and Warvs alike. Ion had the headquarters of Levi-rails, a company responsible for installing magnetic rails beneath the roads and manufacturing vehicles and trains that hovered along them.

"Right, everyone knows where they're going?" I asked.

"Yes, sir," Olson, Log, Mae, and Zothra replied.

The Tyrant of Unity

"Good, dismissed, except for you, Olson. You stay a minute. Zothra, go and get Fades one through thirty-two loaded with troops. Those are the ones we're taking. Mae and Lara, you have thirty-three through sixty-four. Olson, you'll have sixty-five through ninety-six. Log, the rest gives you an extra two Fades' worth of troops under you, compared to the rest of us," I said, directing Olson away from the others.

"Yes, sir," they all replied.

I remained quiet until I was sure we were out of earshot, then looked back over my shoulder to make sure Zothra wasn't hovering over us.

"What's wrong?" Olson asked.

"Everything, haven't you noticed?" I asked.

I smiled and Olson scoffed.

"No, I pulled you aside"—I reached into my pocket and pulled out another Io-Pac insignia—"because I wanted to give you this."

Olson looked down at the insignia and back at me in awe.

"What's this for?" he asked.

"To acknowledge your services to me," I said, pinning it onto Olson's jacket. "A few years ago, we were total strangers to one another, Olson. As sad as it may be, time disintegrated our bond as family. At least that's how I see it. Despite all my arrogance, all my pride, and my rage, you still reached out after all that. Since then, you've helped to revive me from what might as well have been a waking grave, neither dead nor alive."

I stepped back. Olson took a moment and stepped forward.

"Time never made a difference for me, Amat; we're family, always have been. No promotion, gift, tragedy, or mistake will ever strengthen or weaken that bond," said Olson.

"Then use it for the reason I'm really giving it to you, to better command respect from these soft grunts. If they won't respect your authority at the rank of Alpha, they *will*, at Io-Pac. Or at least, they won't want to see how I'd react if they don't."

Olson nodded.

"Don't get too used to that method, Amat, or you'll become just like the man you seek to destroy," Olson said.

"I'll never," I replied.

Olson nodded as he took a deep breath.

"If you ever start to, I'll be there to brighten your path," said Olson.

Olson saluted me and I, him.
"Thank you, sir," Olson said.
"As you were, Io-Pac Olson Criptous," I responded.

XXIII
Recollection
(Quavek)

In my quarters, I always roamed freely outside my human skinsuit, as I found it too cramped. My quarters were always locked in the event anyone attempted to enter unannounced—not that I had many visitors to begin with.

I rummaged through my belongings and found a case with four very small yet highly sophisticated cameras. I linked each one to my computer so I could receive their feeds. For a mission as simple as observing two individuals from afar, I could have just accessed Gordon and Sally Criptous's neuro-chip feeds. But if there was some detail I desired to analyze closer in their quarters, these cameras would grant me a free range of sight.

I received a message through my fizer from the Diramal. He informed me that Gordon was asleep, and Sally had left their quarters. Making it safe for me to enter without being noticed. I took the case of cameras and walked up to the vent in my room, removed the cover, and slid the case inside. My body was designed to be manipulated; even my shelled head could extend and squeeze in on itself, changing its size. For this occasion, I did just that. I also had a total of four arms, two on either side. The ones at my rib cage tucked in and melded into my body. A pair of edged bones that sprouted from my back shriveled and sank into my flesh. I flipped, hooked my feet into the vent above, and hoisted myself into the vent. My legs pushed against the walls of the vent, nudging me forward as my arms guided the case. When I had to turn corners, I sprouted my other arms from my chest to help me reposition myself. Though these vents were also tight and cramped, I felt it less restrictive than the skinsuit.

When I reached the Criptous quarters, I waited patiently and listened. When I heard no movement, I slowly removed the shield to their vent and pried myself out with my legs, landing softly on the ground. I looked around to ensure no eyes were upon me and opened my case, extracting one of the cameras. Crouching low, with my back arched; crawling across the floor, stretching my legs into wide steps, hardly making a sound. I hid the first camera on a shelf at waist level, for a human that is, and hid it well. I side-stepped into the living room and placed a second camera on the table that held up their glass screen television. Scaling up along the walls of the quarters, I hid a third on the rim of their light overhead.

At this rate, I had eyes and ears in almost every corner of the quarters except the bedroom, and I needed to be careful not to wake Gordon. I slid the door open. Gordon Criptous rested on his bed; his stomach rose and dropped with every snore. I crept in, more mindful than ever not to make a single sound. Staying low, I examined the room and determined the best place for it—on the edge of the railing, beneath the bed. I carefully opened my case, and the sound of the locks flipping triggered a snort from Gordon, but he remained asleep. I took the fourth camera and positioned it. Gordon yawned and turned toward me, smacking his mouth. As he turned, I could see his eyes cracked open slightly. I altered time, slid the case under the bed, jumped onto the ceiling, and blended with its texture and color.

Gordon was awake, and his attention was *slowly* drawn to the bottom of his bed. *If he finds that camera, I'll kill him,* I thought to myself. But he didn't. Instead, he managed to roll out of bed, quite literally. By the sound of it, he hurt himself mildly. His attention was naturally drawn elsewhere, outside the room. *He'll surely notice the vent on the floor; I'll need to move fast before he starts to get too suspicious. If he's even got the sense to.* I dropped to the ground lightly and squeezed under the bed to reclaim my case. I looked around the room, strategizing my next move, and found another vent on the wall. Removing the shield and quickly sliding the case inside, I covered it once again as I entered. I looped around to my initial entry point, scaled across the ceiling and waited until I saw Gordon in a position where I could return the shield to its proper place.

"How did this fall down?" I heard him mumble. "Torúga, Didron?! Did one of you break the vent?"

No one answered, fortunately—that meant he was still alone. Gordon growled as he picked up the shield and placed it on the kitchen counter.

"I'll have one of them *fix it* later."

I pushed myself forward to get a better look into the quarters. Gordon marched about the living room, sorting random things into place. I slowly moved across the ceiling, continuously blending my skin with its texture. It helped too that Gordon kept his head down. When I was over the shield, Gordon was crouched over something in the living room, but he had been moving about so swiftly from one thing to the next, I felt I had to be quick as well, so I hung from the ceiling by my feet and grabbed the shield. I pulled myself up and scurried back to the vent, putting the shield back in its place. Gordon made a noise that indicated he'd been startled.

"What?! Wait . . . Torúga, Didron, whichever one of you fixed the vent, I thank you for it!"

I sighed with relief and made my way back to my quarters.

***

When I made it back, I promptly activated all the feeds from the cameras I'd installed and brought them up on my computer. Conveniently, it seemed as though Sally had just returned from wherever she'd been.

"Torúga? You're just returning?" Gordon said.

"Yes, I was out getting us lunch," replied Sally.

"So, was it Didron who was here earlier and fixed the vent?" asked Gordon.

"The vent? What do you mean?" asked Sally.

"The vent, up there; one of you must have removed it or maybe it fell off earlier. But one of you put it back up. You must have," said Gordon.

"Oh, Gordon, I'm sure there was nothing wrong with the vent in the first place," said Sally.

"But I saw it! It was here, right here on the floor—"

"Okay! Just . . . enough. I'm not in the mood for that right now. Let's just sit and eat."

Gordon growled as he sat at the table.

Sally set the table and sat with Gordon. Gordon was about to open his mouth and say something, likely about the food based on the way he grimaced at it.

"No, before you say anything, just eat what you can, and I'll throw the rest out."

Gordon grumbled and started eating his rations.

"You know, Olson, when he was here the other day—"

"Olson was here?" exclaimed Gordon with a mouthful of food.

"He was!" Sally smiled. "He . . . told me that he and Log had been going through a lot."

"Log! Why the boy's practically nine years old, what could he possibly be overwhelmed with?" Gordon chuckled.

"Right." Sally sighed. "Well, in any case, he said he's worried about Log. He said they'd been interrogated by the Diramal's Cho'Zai… apparently, over the past year, Amat has somehow freed himself from his code nine neuro-chip. Some of us recently learned about this."

Gordon dropped his utensils and stopped chewing. He spaced out, staring blankly at the wall.

"Amat . . ." Gordon whispered. He turned to look Sally in the eye. "You mentioned Amat, Sally?"

Sally perked her ears and tilted her head at Gordon.

"I did."

Gordon stared down at his tray, his gaze moving back and forth as if he were contemplating something. I could barely hear him mumbling words to himself over the feed.

"Gordon?" Sally placed her hand over her husband's.

Gordon looked at Sally and stood, wiping his snout clean.

"I have to go get something," Gordon said.

Gordon walked into their bedroom and Sally followed him in. I looked over at the camera I placed under their bed. Gordon went to a corner of the room and knelt. He lifted a flap in the floor, a hidden compartment I must have overlooked while I was in there. Gordon pried up some documents, and I zoomed in, trying to take a closer look, but he moved before I could get a clear view. Gordon walked back into the kitchen and laid the documents on the counter. He started to look through all of them, passively, as if he was recounting the contents.

"Gordon what—what is all this?" Sally asked.

I started to scan every page he laid out and tried to unravel their content.

"Good, it's all still here."

He started to collect all the pages and put them back in their folders.

"No, no!" I exclaimed as several scans were suddenly canceled after having lost their visual on the pages. Gordon walked up to Sally and held her arms. Fortunately, he didn't close the document and one of the pages had script left visible, so I started a new scan.

"Sally, you said Amat is no longer under the influence of his neuro-chip?"

"Apparently so, according to Olson. He told me the other day that somehow Amat had discovered a way to free himself of it some time ago and the Diramal learned of this just recently."

"He'll be in a lot of trouble then; they all will if our boys have been helping him," said Gordon.

Gordon marched back to the folder, grabbed it, and returned to Sally. But before I lost the exposed document, I received confirmation of a match—in our classified records. I opened the file and reviewed it.

"I don't have a lot of time, nor do any of the boys."

"Gordon, what are you—"

"Sally, listen, I need you to get these to Amat, or pass them on to Olson or Log to give to him. But he *needs* to see these. Bod informed me of their existence and told me to retrieve them during my days at I.I.D. They could be the world's only chance at bringing down the Diramal. Our family's only chance at redemption," said Gordon.

It was then that I finished reviewing the gist of the documents and decided their potentially damaging value.

"Oh, indeed they are, Gordon Criptous... But not if you or your wife are unable to pass them on to Amat . . ." I said.

I stood, squeezed into my human skinsuit, and marched to the Diramal with twitchy movements to inform him of my findings.

XXIV
Broken Promise
(The Diramal)

I placed my hand over the shell once again and my consciousness passed into a far-off, dark dimension. The ground was wet, and I could hardly see anything. I waited patiently for Drakkar to show himself. There was a subtle wind in the distance, but I couldn't feel it blow on my face.

"*Mm*, Diramal…" I heard a voice say, sounding far off from where I was.

I turned around and there his figure was, zooming up to me as if out of thin air. He caught me off guard, but I made sure to keep my composure.

"You're back so soon," Drakkar said.

"Yes, to update you on our arrangements with Amat," I replied.

"With the exception of the Varx, you gave him command over all forces of the base."

"Yes," I replied.

"*Mm*, good. I sense there were several things that occurred during this that upset you. Something that involved . . . Blick," said Drakkar.

"Amat made him part of our arrangement. Given the need for subtlety, I decided it would be best not to raise tensions with him over it. Nevertheless, I was still displeased by the change."

Drakkar chuckled as he hovered around me.

"Don't trouble yourself with it too much, Diramal. The boy merely put Blick in charge of protecting his family while he's away. Seems he doesn't trust you enough to keep your word on not harming his family—and with good reason. For you will have to break that promise if you desire to remain in power over the humans," he continued.

"What do you mean?" I asked.

"The Qi'val, Quavek, will explain. Until our next meeting, Diramal," said Drakkar.

I was abruptly pulled back into my body, gasping for breath. I stumbled back and rubbed my hand over my chest. Quavek . . . that must mean she discovered something about Gordon and Sally Criptous. I should hurry back to my office and debrief her.

***

I made my way back and shortly after I arrived, so did Quavek.

"Diramal, sir, I bring grave news concerning Gordon and Sally Criptous," Quavek said as she limped through the doors.

She saluted me and I, her.

"So I've been informed. What have you found, Quavek?" I asked.

"Sir, I don't presume to know exactly how he got his hands on it . . ." Quavek walked up to me with a data crystal in her hand and placed it before my computer's projector light. A looped recording was displayed along with certain documents being referenced. "But Gordon Criptous has access to transcripts documenting the classified encounters between yourself and the Zeltons from twenty Galizian years ago. He intends to pass these on to Amat upon his return."

I sighed.

"Gordon must have gotten his hands on these when he worked at I.I.D. Though he never knew its contents, Bod knew that I had gone missing for several hours in the early days of our encounters with the Zeltons and that a transcript had been sent back to Galiza shortly after my return. Curse me for ever having documented it in the first place," I said.

I rested my face in my hands and moved my fingers through the hair of my skinsuit. A tense silence filled the room.

"What shall I do about this, sir?" Quavek asked.

I raised my head and squinted my eyes.

"Nothing."

"Nothing, sir?"

"I know what must be done and Amat will surely dig into it after he hears about it upon his return. I won't have one of my best tied to it, to deal with the consequences thereafter." Turning my head, I examined one of the Cho'Zai that guarded the room. "You there." The Cho'Zai turned his attention to me. "Front and center."

The Cho'Zai moved beside Quavek and stood tall.

"What is your name?" I asked.

"Kroth, sir," he said.

"Mm, sounds Arkillian," I replied.

"I am, sir," Kroth replied.

"Well, to make it sound more human, let us change that to Roth and you'll have the surname Amberson," I said.

"Yes, sir," said Kroth.

"Roth, you are going to carry out a mission that, in a few days' time, may cost you your life. Measures will be taken to ensure your identity and location about the base are withheld from Amat Luciph Criptous, his cousins, and any other close associates of his with clearance. But it is likely they will find you and kill you once they hear of the mission's details."

"I accept, sir. What's the mission?" asked Roth.

"You're going to kill Gordon and Sally Criptous. You're going to make it look as though it was Gordon's doing and you're going to retrieve a series of transcripts within Gordon's possession," I commanded.

"Understood, sir. I take it this mission is to be carried out immediately?" asked Roth.

"It is. You'll be in contact with Quavek. If you have any questions regarding the location of the quarters or where Gordon keeps the transcripts hidden, she will inform you," I said.

"Yes, sir, I'll be on my way then," Kroth said, as he saluted me and I, him.

"You're dismissed, Quavek, you've done well," I said.

Quavek bowed and limped out of my office. *Dead or alive, this won't end well for me. But at least this way I can buy myself a little extra time before Amat finds out about Kroth and proves what I sent him out to do.*

XXV
Ion City
(Amat)

Sitting in silence, I stared blankly across the way, frowning at the troops seated opposite of me, with Zothra at my side. The Cho'Zai maintained an antagonizing smirk on his face, occasionally glancing at me. I never so much as looked in his direction.

"You know, it's a long way to Ion, sir," Zothra finally said.

"*Mm*," I replied, nodding.

"A conversation might help to kill the time, maybe break the ice between us," said Zothra.

"There's no better method for killing time than a deep train of thought, which you are disturbing," I said.

Zothra chuckled.

"May I ask, then, what has you so preoccupied, sir?"

"What has you so damn curious?" I asked, finally turning to face Zothra.

Zothra looked deep into my eyes, bearing that same subtle curvature in his lips.

"What can I do to gain your trust, Jinn-hid?" Zothra asked.

"Severing your allegiance to the Diramal would be a start, but even then, I wouldn't know if that'd be enough. Not that I would even want you to in the first place," I said.

"Well, I don't see why you wouldn't. A Cho'Zai like myself, breaking my bonds to the Diramal and tethering myself to your better judgment. That'd be a whole world of information at your disposal," Zothra said.

Zothra leaned forward, pressing his elbows onto his knees. I scoffed.

"What reason would you possibly have to betray him?" I asked.

Zothra looked back at me.

"What reason did you have?" Zothra asked.

"As if you would be the only member of our kin that doesn't already know," I said.

"I don't, I only know of your rivalry between one another. On the day of the first mission launch to Anua, three years ago, I was away on an assignment in Zeta. 'Course, you'd know that to be a fact if you read my file," said Zothra.

"So, you weren't on the secondary science team, like the news said you would be," I recollected.

"As it stated, it was the secondary team; you were the primaries. The purpose you and your troops served was to decide whether or not the first ship was safe enough for a science team to enter. When you confirmed that it was not, I was reassigned," Zothra replied.

I nodded. In my head, I didn't know to count that as a truth or lie.

"What do you know about it then? Because surely, you must know something after having been assigned as my babysitter," I said.

"I know the Diramal wants you for something." Zothra leaned in close and whispered, "He knew there was someone like you out there. Someone with the power to manifest a quantum field around himself… and capable of much more perhaps." Zothra leaned back in his seat. "He won't tell anyone how he came to know this or what he truly intends to use you for. Perhaps it was as simple as turning you into a weapon to be used. But he knows… exactly what you are."

I took a deep breath and held a stern expression as I leaned in close to Zothra.

"What I am is nothing short of human. Which the Diramal couldn't be further from," I whispered.

I stood and started to walk away.

"And that is my reason, Criptous," Zothra blurted from his seat. "That is my motivation in seeking your trust."

I scoffed. *It'll be impossible to gain. It would require so much that even I wouldn't know where to begin. But perhaps time will tell.*

***

I'd gone up to the front of the ship to talk with Sarak. It started out as a friendly conversation; she always appreciated the company up there. She told me about how she spent her time off over the past few days. Spent a lot of it cleaning the Fade, apparently. She also sent messages back home to her family. She couldn't be sure if they were alive or dead, having received nothing back from them. But she had checked records from the base in which they resided. It was still operational, and their names remained on the list of civilian occupants.

"That must be hard, not receiving word back. With the amount of trouble I've caused my family, I find it hard enough to leave them behind at Y'Gůtsa in the hands of someone I share a complicated history with," I said.

"There must be something about this acquaintance of yours that allowed you to find trust in him. Something Anua opened your heart to. Otherwise, would you really have left him with such a delicate task?" asked Sarak.

I tilted my head. I suppose, maybe, there was some part of me that sensed Blick was not my enemy at heart.

"I'm not sure I would have. So perhaps she did. On a less troublesome subject, I've been having to play 'good soldier' around the Cho'Zai Zothra."

"Zothra?" asked Sarak.

"He's one of the Diramal's best. He's spent all day, thus far, trying to get on my good side. May Anua scorch me if I ever let that happen," I said.

"I see. This must be concerning you, too."

"Not as much as my family. If need be, I can handle myself and take Zothra on. But there is something he said just before I joined you, something that I've wondered about. Which the Diramal may have the answer to," I said.

"What's that?" asked Sarak.

"I . . . I can't—"

The Fade's radar sounded as it detected in-coming enemies and quickly bounced at the sound of loud thuds on the plating.

"What just hit us?!" I asked.

"Aerial enemies, sir, we're under attack. Activating automated defenses," replied Sarak.

"How many do you detect?" I asked.

Sarak brought up a holo-scanner. The Fade was displayed at the center of a blue sphere, where in and out of it popped several red circles. Sarak squinted.

"Maybe half a dozen, I'm not sure," she replied.

"How far are we from Ion?" I asked.

"If I can maintain our course, five minutes, sir."

"Get us as close as you can and tell the other Fades to have their troops suited and armed up."

"Yes, sir," Sarak replied.

I rushed down to the troops and barked orders.

"Alright, that's our cue. We're coming up over the target area! Suit up, gear up, arm yourselves."

I swiftly dressed in a QS-25, grabbed a belt, and buckled it around my waist, and attached four knives. I went to the racks to grab a pistol and my E.S.P. 101, one of the last of its kind since all manufacturing of its ammunition had ceased. Luckily, I'd managed to reverse-engineer the formula for myself. I'm not able to make very much of it at a time, as the process is very extensive, and the materials are not easy to come by. But I have my resources.

The process for making the ammunition uses a thin square cut of seed quartz crystal, hung in a hot body of water at three hundred fifty degrees Celsius. The water is then mixed with potassium hydroxide and a magnet is placed underneath the container holding the water. Drop a few tiny pieces of natural quartz crystal at the bottom of the container and place some electric wires in the water, amplifying over twelve-hundred volts of electricity. The mixture of electricity and potassium hydroxide causes the water to spin. Over the course of about six days, the thin-cut seed becomes thicker from the specs of natural quartz lacing themselves around the seed. This then develops dimensions about the seed, and electric charges are laced onto layers of the crystal, serving the gun with ammunition.

I was about to reach for the E.S.P. 101 when someone placed their hand over it before me. I looked over my shoulder and saw it was Zothra.

"Thought these were out of stock due to lack of ammunition," Zothra said, examining the weapon.

"I make my own," I said, yanking the gun from Zothra's grasp.

I loaded the E.S.P. 101 with a crystal. I had about seven on me, and each crystal carried about two hundred rounds; more than the standard form of ammunition would have granted me.

The Fade rocked again, and I nearly lost my balance.

"Alright, form up, form up! Switch on comms," I demanded.

With my team in position, I shut off the lights inside the Fade and opened the hatch. The alien crafts made high-pitched zipping sounds that could just barely be heard over the harsh wind blowing and the guns firing. One of the alien craft was hit badly and nearly collided with the lowered hatch. We all flinched and stepped back in case there was a direct impact. As the alien craft stalled and fell, I shouted orders at my troops over comms to rush out of the Fade. I waited until all of them had left and only Zothra remained. He walked up to me, unfazed by all the chaos that surrounded the Fade, his eyes fixed on me.

"After you, Jinn-hid," he said.

I frowned at Zothra as I primed my helmet to envelop my head and jumped out. I wasn't going to argue with him, not then and there, prolonging Sarak's risk of having to remain over the area. The sounds of the conflict slowly faded out as I dropped further and further down toward Ion. Zothra hovered beside me for a time, despite having a heavier build than myself. The Cho'Zai glanced over and saluted me before diving down toward the city. Soon after, I activated the gliders, formed by nanomaterial preserved in the suit, as had the others, and landed gracefully on the surface.

I rolled onto the street, pulled my E.S.P. 101 from a holster on my back, and took in my surroundings. I let down my guard when all was clear and activated my fizer. It displayed a holographic list that told me who was still alive and who was dead. I opened a channel to those who remained.

"Jinn-hid Criptous calling to all troops. I'm glad to see most of us made it down safely." I brought up an overall map of the city and saw where all my troops were located. "I see everyone is scattered at present. Let us all meet in Kaito Plaza, at the city's center. Use the map on your fizers to find it and be on your guard. Though the city may seem quiet, the invaders surely know of our presence, and they'll be sending their numbers our way. Criptous out."

I turned around and paused when I saw someone casually sitting on a pile of rubble. He tilted his head and waved his hand.

"Stirring speech, sir," he said.

I could tell from his voice it was Zothra. He stood and walked up to me.

"It was Kaito Plaza you said, right?" asked Zothra. When I didn't respond, he continued, "Right, shall we, then?"

Zothra gestured to the road ahead. I altered time and finally made my way to the Plaza. Didn't stay far ahead of Zothra for long, though, as, before I knew it, he was there pacing beside me and all I could do was let it happen.

***

With everyone gathered in the plaza, I started to strategize my next move.

"Alright, listen up, all of you," I shouted, the alien dub from the cryptic at my throat was faintly audible outside the confines of my helm. "You all know why you're here, to search for Skivs and Warvs and bring them back to Y'Gůtsa. At least for a time till they can be relocated to another base with more room for them. In order to efficiently execute this mission, we must *thoroughly* search the city; we'll call it four days till we meet back here with whoever we manage to find. 'Course, this task would be a lot quicker if we divide our numbers . . ." I trailed off in that moment; it only then occurred to me that I had never looked over any of the profiles among the troops. Not that I had the time for it anyway. I'd become accustomed to my former squadron of Alphas, having known every man and woman in that pack, so selecting subcommanders was not something I often needed to consider. "I need volunteers to lead three teams. Before I begin asking each of you your qualifications and ranks, would anyone like to step up?"

I could see the fearful expressions they held through the constructs of each of their helms. Some looked down at their feet, while others shared awkward glances. I wondered if they were scared of volunteering because they lacked the courage to take up the responsibility of a leader. Or perhaps some of them did possess virtues of a leader, but in this opportune moment they were downplaying their own capabilities.

"Well, if it'll do you some good, there's at least one man here with a pair between his legs. I'll step up to the task," a man said, walking up past the formation, lightly brushing those in his way aside.

I nodded as I examined this trooper.

"Anua's courage shines through you, soldier," I said, saluting the man. "What is your name and rank?" I asked.

"Shím MgKonnol. Here my rank would be considered a Duka, but back home, that would be a Húsba," said Shím.

I lifted an eyebrow.

"And where is home?"

"Irenole, in the Dronomen Islands," said Shím.

I don't think 'Húsba' is a rank that exists anywhere in the world, but he shows promise, and he seems optimistic. Perhaps such qualities will suffice for those under his command.

"*Mm*, very well, Duka MgKonnol, hold up your fizer," I said.

I walked up to Shím as he raised his arm to me. All the fizers have a small red light on their side that is associated with their vital sign location on the holo-map. I activated his map, zoomed in on everyone's signals, highlighted a quarter of them, put in an overriding code, and made them blue.

"There we are. Those of you with blue lights on your fizer will be under the command of Duka MgKonnol here, and you will cover the east side of the city. Regardless of your rank, even if it is technically higher than Shím's, he is your commander for this operation. You follow *his* command without question. Is that understood?"

"Yes, sir," all the troops with blue lights said.

"Good. Duka MgKonnol, lead your troops well."

"I will, sir," replied Shím.

As Shím and his troops marched out to the east, two women came toward me. I noted that the small lights on their fizers were still red.

"Will the both of you be taking command of the other two groups I mean to send out?" I asked.

"We would like to volunteer ourselves, sir, yes," the one on the right said.

"Interesting how two of you would come up together. Do you know each other?" I asked.

"Yessir, we do," the one on the left said.

"Hm, that's convenient, I admire the courage shared between you both for the task at hand. What are your names and ranks?" I asked.

"I'm Kyla Torlen, this is Iana Dovan. We both hold the rank of Duka as well, sir," the one on the left said.

"Very good. Show me your fizers now."

I gave Kyla and all those under her command a purple light on their Fizer and Iana a dark orange.

"Duka Torlen, I want you and your troops to cover the south side of the city. Duka Dovan, you will cover the west side of the city," I commanded.

"Yes, sir," they both said.

"The same rules apply here with Dukas Torlen and Dovan. Follow their command, even if your rank supersedes their own."

"Yes, sir," the troops responded.

Really though, across all the soldiers the Diramal had given to me, the rank of a Duka would have likely been the highest rank among them.

"The rest of you will follow me to the north side of the city," I said.

"Yes, sir," the remaining troops replied.

Zothra stepped beside me.

"Interesting strategy; looking forward to how it turns out," said Zothra, showing the red light on his fizer.

Shut. Up.

***

I led my troops through northern Ion, running up and down the maze-like streets. We had searched thoroughly for many hours, but made very little progress finding Skivs or Warvs, out in the street or in the ruined buildings. Yet there was something strange also in the lack of corpses we found, both among the militia and the invaders. *If most of the people in this city aren't dead and they're not here, where are they?* As the day ended and I saw that many of the men and women under my command needed to rest, I opened a channel to Shím, Iana, and Kyla to see if they'd had better luck.

"Dukas Kyla, Iana, and Shím, this is the Jinn-hid. Come in," I said. They all acknowledged. "We have found no sign of live Skivs or Warvs. Have any of your groups?"

"Negative, in fact, we've hardly found any remains of our kin," said Kyla.

"Unfortunately, that would be the same for us too, sir," said Iana.

"Well, I'm glad to be the bearer of better news, as we've found about seventy-two Skivs over here, sir. But I must say, we've noted the strange circumstance of there being hardly any corpses out here as well. Other than the common fellow soldier and invader. Makes me wonder, could they have found refuge beneath the city?" asked Shím.

"That's an idea. Perhaps we should redirect our search to the mines of Ion. Iana, Kyla, keep searching as you make your way to the edges of the city. Contact me if you manage to find any Skivs or Warvs before leading your troops below the city."

"Yes, sir," Kyla and Iana replied.

"Shím, I want you to hold your position. I'm going to call in a Fade for you to get those seventy-two Skivs out. If there are any Warvs among them, assign some members of your troops to board the Fade with them, so things don't get out of hand," I said.

"Roger that, sir," Shím said.

I cut the signal and opened a new channel to Sarak, hoping she was still alive to receive it.

"Jinn-hid," she said, before long.

"Sarak, it's good to know you're alright. How's the condition of your Fade?" I asked.

"Her plating is badly worn, sir; wasn't too long ago that I brought her back to base. She'll need some work before going out again," Sarak said.

"How are the others?" I asked.

"Most of them endured at least some damage, but Fades seven and twelve are in the best shape right now, sir."

"Tell the pilot of Fade seven I need a rendezvous, east side of Ion city; there's a Duka commanding a fraction of the troops there by the name of Shím MgKonnol. Sending you his coordinates now. Pass them on to the pilot and tell them that Duka MgKonnol has seventy-two Skivs he needs picked up and rendezvoused back to base," I commanded.

"I will, sir," replied Sarak.

"Good, Criptous out," I said, closing the channel.

I opened a channel back out to Shím.

"Shím, I have a Fade en route to your location. Once you've exchanged the Skivs, search the rest of eastern Ion and meet the rest of us down below," I said.

"Ryne. Understood, sir," Shím replied.

"Criptous out—"

"RIGHT, YOU LITTLE LILLIGS, LISTEN UP—"

I cut Shím's transmission short.

Zothra stayed well at my side as we proceeded. The competitive nature of the Cho'Zai's persistent pacing with me, reminded me of my introduction to Blick. It almost seemed that Zothra was attempting to put both my patience and awareness to the test. In my frustration, I desired only to remain ahead of the Cho'Zai but to a fault. For there were several instances, where I had pushed the limits of my quantum field to such an extreme that there were many an instance where one of my troops triggered a surge signal to halt my race with the Cho'Zai and momentarily regroup.

We came to a huge mound of buildings that had collapsed over one another. The rubble was so high and wide we couldn't see to the other side. Running up and down the street; only to find there were many more tall buildings that had been torn down. *A blockade maybe?* I looked up at the other tall buildings that surrounded us—I didn't see anything, but I suspected. *Maybe we were running into an ambush. Those roofs would make good long-range positions.* Activating the map on my fizer, I determined how much more ground we had to cover. *Seven more blocks north, eight blocks to either side of that. That's a lot of ground we wouldn't be covering.* I heard a set of footsteps walk beside me.

"Is there a problem, Jinn-hid?" Zothra asked.

"There's a hill of debris in our way, and we have no way of telling what's on the other side. Given that it stretches down several miles of road implies an ambush may be set on the other side," I replied.

"Might I make a suggestion, sir?" asked Zothra.

"Not under my command, you won't," I replied, walking back toward my troops. "Those of you with moonsights, come forward," I said. Dozens of troops did as commanded. "I need all of you to take positions at the tops of these buildings, pronto. Give me eyes over this hunk of debris. Anything, *anything* that seems concerning in the slightest, inform me."

"Yes, sir," the men and women bearing moonsights said.

As they took positions, I opened a channel to all their comm signals. "Does anyone see anything out of the ordinary?" I asked.

One by one, they all replied with the same answer: "Negative."

But I still wasn't convinced. *That doesn't mean there's nothing there.*

"Everyone, hold your positions. I'm going over. Moonsights, watch my back."

"Yes, sir."

"Allow me to accompany you, Jinn-hid," Zothra said, stepping forward. "If it is what you suspect, a place set for an ambush, it would serve you to have an extra pair of eyes."

"I have more than a dozen positioned around the clock," I replied.

"All the same . . ." Zothra persisted.

"Fine," I replied, begrudgingly.

Together, Zothra and I carefully climbed over the wall of rubble, peeking our heads over the top. We stood atop the rubble, vulnerable to any and all potential threats lurking nearby.

"I don't see anything," said Zothra.

I ground my jaw and nodded with a sigh of relief.

"Nor do I." I opened the channel to my moonsights. "Moonsights, we've confirmed the area ahead is clear. You may return with the others." There was no reply. In an echoing whisper that gradually got louder in my head, I heard the beckoning warning: *"Amat, look behind you!"* I turned around to see an invader in place of where one of my men should have been. It fired a huge orange magmic orb toward the rubble.

"Criptous, get to the other side!" Zothra shouted as he yanked back on my shoulder.

We fell toward the ground; time naturally began to alter around me as I observed the orb hurtle into the rubble. The impact blew a hole in the blockade and in a *bursting* shock wave, the Cho'Zai and I were sent, tumbling back across the road. Before rolling too far back, I got myself on my feet and skidded across the road. Steadying myself, I observed that many of my troops had been severely injured, if not killed by the blast, as they lay still on the ground, hardly moving. The rest were in a frenzy, shooting in random directions, howling and barking profanities. I looked back over to Zothra. He nodded at me and took off running.

It was obvious which side had the upper hand. Watching briefly, as the invaders moved swiftly, striking down those who were overwhelmed by the enemy's element of surprise. Still, there were those who managed to put up a good fight and guarded themselves well. Observing the chaos, I caught sight of an alien who approached me. Its movements seemed so smooth and slow; I was entranced by how deep of an altered time state I had entered. In a daze, I sluggishly pulled my E.S.P. 101 from my back, overthinking in my swayed aim. I tried to steady myself as my heart beat pulsated in my ears. The alien did not falter in its dash toward me, as my finger twitched over the trigger. I wasn't prepared when instinct finally took over and the unsteady grip of my gun sprayed my aim across the alien. I almost lost my handle on the gun when I heard the *booming* launch of another large orange orb dashing down toward my troops. The shot had been unleashed from a nearby rooftop. I shook my head as I gathered myself and fired at the stationary invader, but I was too far away to get a good shot on it. Looking to the walls of a nearby building, I took a deep breath and scaled my way up, running so fast that the bottoms of my boots maintained traction against the wall. Once on the roof, I leaped as quickly as I could to the next one over. The invader was aware of my presence at this point and how fast I was moving.

"Amat, pull away!" my father's voice said.

The next moment, the alien across the way fired another orb ahead of my path, shattering the roof. I altered my route as my father advised and avoided getting hit by the blast. Extending my hand out to the falling pieces of debris, twisting my arm to position them back in place. Making it so I could hop from platform to platform until I reached the ledge and jumped the gap to the third building. The alien that stood on its edge swiftly aimed its cataclysmic weapon at me and, in turn, I aimed my palm at the creature, 'versing its movements. I held the alien there, just before colliding into it, slamming the back of my E.S.P. 101 into the creature's face. We tumbled along the roof, both of us struggling to straddle the other. The alien placed all four of its hands on my E.S.P. 101, pressing the top edge of it against my neck. I swiped my suit's claws at the creature's chest. Wrenching the gun from the creature's fading grasp and in a swift maneuver I fired at one of the alien's two hearts.

Recovering to my feet, I passed my eyes over each of the nearby rooftops to ensure there wasn't a second invader armed with a similar weapon. Distracted, two left claws yanked at my leg and pulled me down the edge of the building. Tumbling down in my fall, I whipped my aim down sight and shot the alien before it could do much else. Quickly shuffling options in my mind, as the ground dashed up to meet me, I noticed that the building had windows on its side and whirled into one of them.

Growling, I pushed myself off the floor and rushed back to the window, firing down at the invaders while trying to avoid my own kin. Another tug, this time on my shoulder. Spinning me around, the invader launched its two right fists into my gut and ribs, followed by a head butt. I swung my gun into its ribs and then my arm across its face. Holstering my gun, I charged into the alien while it wrapped its arms around me, desperately trying to pierce its claws through my armor. The seeps of my armor clenched, crushing its fingers and claws as I continued to run. I hoped to hit the alien's back against a pillar, but with the creature's wide, prickly body obstructing my vision, I charged us down into a gaping hole. We fell four stories down; the alien's body fractured and shriveled on impact.

I pried myself from the alien's corpse and rushed to the nearest window facing the conflict. A fall from my current level was one I could survive, so I dove through the window and rolled onto the ground. Stopping on a knee, shooting invaders surrounding me, saving a few of my kinsmen in the process. An alien punched me so hard in the face my grip on my gun loosened and it dropped. I pulled out my pistol, but before I could aim it, the invader caught my arm and held it off to the side. I was careful not to fire, as I could have hit one of my own. With my free hand, I swiftly grabbed one of my knives as the alien scraped its two right claws, sparking across my armor. Gasping as the seeps momentarily tightened across my chest, I swiped my knife at the alien's waist. The alien fell to a knee and let go of my arm. Three quick shots to the gut brought the alien down.

More invaders came in from around the corner of a building, but not close enough to anyone to harm them yet. I sheathed my blade, yanked a grenade off my belt, and rolled it in their path. The explosion obliterated two invaders caught at its center, burning, and twisting the rest into the air from the shock wave.

I stood and pain wracked my body. Immediately, a towering invader punched me in the back as it came around to face me. Keeling over, I tried to bring up the aim of my pistol as quickly as I could, but the alien disarmed me. Ramming into the alien, hard enough to push it away, I unsheathed two knives from my belt. Despite its colossal figure the alien was very agile at avoiding my every swing and jab. The alien was finally brought to a knee, when a low, spinning swing of my body finally landed in one of the creature's outer legs. With my enemy momentarily pinned, I jumped into the air, flexing my feet and kicked one across the face of the alien. It pried the knife from its leg as it stood, and I rushed in for another attack. The creature stopped me, restricting both my arms, pulled me down, and launched both of its left knees into my chest. The blow knocked the wind out of me, sending me shooting backward as my blades fell from my grasp.

A drowsiness engulfed me once again, while my head plotted a way to end this in a hurry. I retracted my helm—with my natural quantum field still active—to catch some fresh air and cough out a gush of blood. I growled a curse.

"Amat, look up the road," I heard my father say.

I raised my head and saw a pistol resting on the ground. *I hope that's loaded. If it's mine, it should be.* Taking a deep breath, I sprung off the ground and raced for the gun. I moved as if the alien was at my heels, unsure if it truly was. Stumbling down to grab the pistol, I turned around and saw the large alien pouncing at me. After shooting it twice, the full weight of the invader fell onto me.

"DAW!" I exclaimed, snapping out of my altered time state.

A short silence, and the air filled with cheers from my troops. I scrunched my face as I pushed the large alien off me and stood, enveloping my helm around my head. The troops went on cheering and despite trying to catch my breath, I howled with every bit of air I had in my lungs: "SSTOOOOOOOP!"

They all fell silent and looked at me, slouched over my knees, panting. I pulled myself out of my quantum field before proceeding. "Fools, what are you thinking? Do you want to bring another wave of the invaders down on our heads?" I stood tall, calmed my breath, and stepped before them. "Look around yourselves, take in what we just lost. This was but a skirmish against a small band of invaders and we lost far more than they did. This is *no* time to celebrate."

I couldn't see their faces, but I knew that I had crushed many spirits.

"Account for the dead; use what you can off them. If they were a friend, pray to the Mother for their safe passage into the Luminous Paradise. Take shelter in the nearby ruins for tonight; it'll be the last place our enemies will suspect if they come looking for us," I said.

The troops remained silent and saluted me as I walked past them. After recovering my E.S.P. 101, I headed toward a nearby ruined building—stopping along the way to kneel beside a fallen soldier, placing a hand over her chest, praying that all who died that day would be granted peace in the Luminous Paradise for their sacrifice. Finding refuge, I reached out to Shím, Kyla, and Iana to let them know we would be taking shelter for the night, and I advised them to do the same. Settling down on an old, rusted cot; my body sank to the ground. My back was slightly discomforted, but I didn't care enough to reposition myself. Only a few short seconds passed before I drifted off to sleep.

XXVI
Warv
(Log)

My eyes were fixated on the ground, my hands gripped together tightly, my palms sweating as my legs bounced, and my mind craved another shot of Diazep. I felt cold and on the edge of making a scene, battling raging thoughts, voices piling on top of each other. But I wouldn't reach into my bag and do the injection here for everyone to see. Still, that didn't help me cope with my *need* for that next hit and soon. Finally, I stood, walked up into the cockpit, and asked the pilot when we should expect to reach Atheika.

"At this rate, maybe about ten more minutes, sir," the pilot replied.

"Good, that's good," I said, patting the pilot on the shoulder.

"Are you alright, sir?" he asked.

I looked over at him, confused. Then I noticed his expression was slightly concerned, perhaps about my appearance.

"I'm fine, thank you. Just get us to Atheika," I said.

The pilot cleared his throat.

"Yes, sir," he said.

I walked back over to my seat and lowered my head, holding it in my hands. My legs were back to bouncing once again. *Ten minutes, you can do this.* I sniffed and rubbed my face. Before long, my eyes started to feel dry, and I found myself blinking a lot. Losing track of time—that whole ten minutes felt a lot longer. Perhaps it was, or perhaps it just seemed that way, as that same horrifying face popped back into my mind again and again. It was so clear I thought I was seeing it right in front of me. A discomforting sensation filled my ear, as if something was reaching and squirming inside it. I wanted to put my hand up to it, scratch the inside and dig out the wriggling, phantom parasite, but I wouldn't allow myself to cause a scene. Reluctantly, I tightly clenched my hands together. I tried closing my eyes and attempted to meditate, thinking it would help, but in my every attempt, that same face popped into my mind. *What are you?!*

Finally, the pilot announced that we were about to fly over Atheika. I sprung up and barked commands at my troops, marching to my bag. Snatching my bag from the wall, I proceeded to step into my Quantum Suit and geared up. Ready to go before anyone else, I continued to shout commands at my troops until they'd fallen in line. If I had to wait much longer to take that hit, I wasn't sure what would happen. My fangs grazed over my lips again and again as the hatch *slowly* opened. Just as the hatch became level, I turned back to my troops and barked for them to exit the Fade. The sound of a quivering screech carried across the air as an invader craft whipped past the hatch and fired two shots, launching many escaping soldiers into the overhead of the Fade and sending others into a tumbling descent. The rest of us jumped back, cursing and crawling across the floor. It was then I realized I hadn't shut off the lights within the Fade. I did so, growling, and continued to urge the others to jump out, past the now flaming and brittle hatch. When the only other occupants of the Fade were those who could barely move from the blast, I made my own descent. Holding tightly onto my bag; I couldn't afford to lose it in the fall. I nose-dived toward the surface, passing several of my kin until finally I deployed my glider wings and hovered to the roof of a tall building. I retracted my helmet. I turned on a dim light on my Fizer to illuminate my raw sight. *Ripping* open the bag, inside I found my pinch gun, and five doses of Diazep that had dissolved in some water. I eagerly loaded up the gun, careful to spill as little as possible, and injected it into my neck. There was a sharp pain that came with it, only to be relieved a few brief moments later, by the flush of dopamine that filled my mind, shutting out the voices and shattered memories within it. I no longer saw that malicious face, nor did I feel the discomfort in my ear.

Finding my feet, I sighed with relief, slugishly took the bag over my shoulder, and enveloped my helmet over my head. A harsh impact knocked me to the ground from the side; my bag slipped free from my shoulder and tumbled toward the edge of the roof. I activated my suit's quantum field with the intent of catching the bag before it fell. Stopping to look back at the approaching invader, I launched my elbow into its face. It stumbled back on its four feet. I briefly looked back at the bag, slowly continuing to tumble away. I pulled my Gyrat from over my shoulder, but the invader was already within arm's reach of me before I could take aim. Adapting my strategy, I swung the gun at the alien's ribs and raised it at the alien's lengthy, flailing arms until it knocked the weapon away. Frustrated, I could feel my mind palpitating with blood, my veins filling with adrenaline. I flicked out my claws and rushed into the alien, knocking it to the ground. It raised its two left arms to my helmet and neck. Without hesitation, one by one I grabbed each arm and bent them back ninety degrees.

I'm not going to let you stop me! I shouted in my mind, as the alien's cries echoed in the quantum field.

I scraped my claws across the alien's face several times; still it had fight in it, reaching up with its right arms. I pulled so hard on one of them that it completely tore off from its rib cage.

Not letting you stop me! I yelled in my mind once again.

I pounded my fist into the invader's chest, cracking the roof as I howled rabidly into the invader's blank face.

Twitching my head back, I saw the bag drifting off the edge of the roof. I had never been more willing to jump off the edge of a building as I slid out toward the edge. One hand extended back as I reached out for the bag with another. Only after I'd gotten hold of the strap had I dug my claws into the roof above me. Slipping further before finally my claws planted themselves well within the edge of the cement roof.

"Ha, thought you'd get away," I said to the bag.

I grunted as I pulled myself back on top of the roof with the bag in hand. I rolled on my back, caught my breath, then sent out a surge signal and opened a channel to my troops.

"Attention, everyone, this is Io-Pac Log Criptous. It's safe to assume everyone has touched down on the surface at this point. Some of you may already be in a quarrel with the invaders; I know I was. I'm sending a pin to all your fizers. Make your way there and we will decide our next move. Over and out."

I pushed myself to my feet more vigorously than I had to. It felt like I could race across Galiza without pause or launch myself with such force as to jump over a building.

I made my way to the rendezvous point like a madman, keeping to the rooftops and likely raising suspicion from anyone or anything nearby. I jumped gaps between buildings, smashed into windows, and charged

The Tyrant of Unity

through whatever obstacles rested in my path, even weak walls in some instances.

There were a few who'd made it before me. Slowly, the numbers grew as more and more men and women found their way to the rendezvous point. I paced and moved around as I waited, unable to keep still, which stirred some suspicious gazes from those under my command.

"Judging by our numbers here, seems we lost a few additional friendlies post-descent into the city. This means the enemy is not only aware of our presence, but *alert*. From this point forward, each and every one of us should be on our guard. Now, for the plan I've decided on. The layout of this city is shaped like a circle, so what I propose is we divide into two groups. Half of you with the green lights on your fizers will start at the city's center, the rest of us with the yellow lights will start on the outskirts of the city. We'll move in pairs, and once we start finding one another, reach out over comms. We'll meet back here with whatever Skivs and Warvs we can bring back with us. Understood?" I asked.

The troops mumbled a reply. Some of them, I'm sure, didn't say anything.

"I didn't hear that," I said.

"Yes, sir." They spoke a little more loudly, but I still wasn't satisfied.

I curled my fingers into fists.

"What is this? Are you all tired? Do you not respect me because I'm younger than most of you? Does that mean I should expect most, if not all, of you to die out here and the rest of our kin with you? Because you don't have the grit, you don't have the ferocity it takes to be out here? Somebody give me an answer!" I shouted.

"No, sir," the troops said with more chorus.

"Should I call in the Fades, ask them to take us back? Should I explain to the Jinn-hid that we had to retreat because I sensed the pack under my command lacked diligence and allow him to deal with you?" I asked.

"No, sir!" the troops shouted.

"Are you gonna listen?" I yelled.

"Yes, sir!"

"Are you going to fight to your last breath?"

"Yes, sir!"

"Who is your commander?" I shouted.

"You are, sir!"

"You're all right about that. I expect nothing less than your best out here. When everyone's in position, wait for my command and I will say when we can start to close in on the city. Now, find a partner and move out. You," I said, pointing to a woman, "what's your name?"

"Krollgrum Kita Yatů, sir," she replied.

"Krollgrum Yatů, you're with me," I said.

"Yes, sir," Kita responded.

I turned my back and took off to the outskirts of Atheika with Kita at my side. On the edge of the city rested scattered shrew trees, tall thin-trunked trees with white leaves that glittered in the darkness. Only all the leaves had long since fallen from their branches.

I brought up the map of Atheika on my fizer and monitored everyone's location until I saw that one group had gathered at the city's center and the other along its borders. I opened a channel to the troops.

"Attention, this is Io-Pac Log Criptous, we're all in position, disperse on my mark. Mark," I said.

I closed the channel, deactivated the hologram on the fizer, and looked over to Kita.

"Let's move," I said.

I entered a quantum field via my QS-25 and sprinted directly into Atheika. Kita and I ran through the first building in our path only to find it mostly in ruin, with scattered bodies of fallen invaders and fellow kinsmen. The next couple of buildings were the same, so I signaled for us to pull out and catch our breath. We were both panting hard, our chests falling and rising. I rested my hands on my knees while Kita put her hands behind her head and stood straight.

"You should raise your head, sir, easier to let your lungs breathe," Kita said.

I slowly straightened my back. We nodded at one another.

"How's your suit doing on invader blood?" I asked.

"Still half-full," Kita replied.

"About the same for me. Next building we enter, we'll stock up on some samples. Come on, let's walk for a bit."

***

"What's in the bag, sir?" Kita asked as we exited the building.

I looked over at Kita, then down at my bag holding my Diazep.

"Supplies for the mission," I replied.

"Ah, I see. It seemed curious; not a common accessory I've seen officers bring onto the battlefield," said Kita.

"*Mm.* How long have you been in this war?" I asked, trying to change the subject.

"Two years, sir," replied Kita.

"You must have been promoted to Krollgrum recently then," I said.

"No, sir, I've held that rank for the past year. I was awarded it for pulling surviving members of my squadron out of a burning Fade. It had been shot down, just a few miles from base. Defenses had been scrambled and the Fade was in such bad shape there was no way they'd be able to send anyone in time to put out all the flames."

"How many did you save?" I asked.

"Fifteen. There were others, but I couldn't get to them in time," said Kita.

"That's still a lot of lives. Even if you'd only saved one, that person might have had a family to go home to or lived to fight another day, week, or month in this war." I stopped to face Kita. "Your promotion was well deserved; they are not always so."

"Was your recent promotion to 'Io-Pac' well deserved, sir?" Kita asked.

I paused before answering.

"In a way, yes. Was I ready to receive it? I—"

An incoming assault of enemy fire grazed the shoulder of my armor but fortunately, did not wound me.

"Take cover!" I shouted as I altered time.

I ran and hid behind a pile of rubble. Peeking my head just slightly over, I tried to determine where the fire was coming from, but just as quickly ducked my head back down as the heat was too heavy to risk exposing myself. Strategizing my next move, my thoughts were interrupted when I noticed that the ammunition was of orange and purple colors—ammo commonly emitted from Gyrats and Magplazes. Our kin's weaponry. *Could these be Warvs attacking us?*

Kita sent out a surge signal. I pulled out of my quantum field and opened a channel to Kita.

"Io-Pac . . . hold . . . I think . . . fighting—"

"Come again, Krollgrum Yatů," I said, cutting Kita short.

"I said I think we're fighting Warvs. The ammunition they're firing looks to be from Gyrats and Magplazes. We should disarm them, give them a chance to hear us out," said Kita.

"Roger that; I'll draw their fire. Once I have it, get up the adjacent building, jump over to their position, and disarm them," I said.

"Yes, sir," said Kita.

I altered time and fired at the Warvs as I moved swiftly from my position, up the street. It was hard to tell, but I estimated that there might have been four holding positions in an opening of a ruined building. Suddenly, incoming fire sprayed across my path from above. My feet stomped against the ground as I quickly halted and changed my path, scaling up a building that held no hostiles. Hiding in one of the lower levels, I crawled across the floor to a small opening where I could observe Kita moving into position. But the Warvs pinned the Krollgrum with suppressive fire. I stood and raced over to the next building where the second group had taken refuge.

Closing in on their position, a Warv noticed me. She shifted her aim to me, but I dove onto her and thwarted her aim before she could fire. We slid across the floor as the other three turned their heads toward us. I took aim and fired at one of their weapons, disarming the Warv and immediately raced up to the other two as they unleashed their fire. Pushing my quantum field to carry me more swiftly, I dodged past their shots. Stripping the Warvs of their weapons I backed up and lifted my arms passively to signal that I would show no further aggression. The Warvs stood their ground, until one of them rushed me. I threw the guns out of the opening as the Warv pounced on me and launched her fist at my helm. Catching her arm before the blow could land, we wrestled until I managed to straddle her and twisted her arm to the verge of breaking. With one hand holding the She-Warv's arm in place, I raised my other.

I regulated time, retracted the Warv's helm as well as my own, and tried to speak to them.

"Stay back! I don't want to hurt any of you, but if one of you comes any closer, I *will* break this one's arm," I warned.

The Warvs looked at one another and then back at me as they raised their hands in submission. They retracted their helms, revealing their faces so that we could speak. How worn, were their suits; one of them even looked to have quite a few scrapes and holes in it. At this time, I didn't hear any more fire coming from down the street, so I assumed Kita was successful in taking care of the others.

"What do you want, *Militia?*" one of the Warvs asked.

"My name is Log Criptous, my cousin is the Jinn-hid, Amat Luciph Criptous. He's launched a fleet of men and women to rescue as many of our kin that we can, whom we've neglected out in the waste for the entirety of this war. If you come with me and the one under my command across the way there, I can promise you all shelter, food, and safety," I said.

The Warvs all looked at each other in silence, then back at me.

"How do we know we can trust you?" asked the same Warv.

"I could have easily killed you, all of you. Instead, I chose to disarm each of you, and I've made more than one attempt during this exchange to express my intentions," I said.

"How do we know this isn't some trick you're feeding us? How do we know this isn't some ploy for you to turn us into one of the Shadow Scar?" asked the Warv.

A wave came over my head at the mention of the word "Shadow Scar," followed by a chill that tensed my spine.

"What—what was that word you said?" I asked.

"Shadow Scar, they're an outside threat from the invaders. We've heard stories that they're the result of some secret experiment program. Genetic modifications that certain militia among yourselves created. We've been fortunate enough not to have any encounters with them. I'm sure that if we did, we wouldn't be standing where we are now. Few who face them survive," said the Warv.

Slowly, I started to hallucinate as my eyes barely adjusted to the darkness. The faces of the Warvs seemed less and less human and were covered in tentacles. A familiar pain grew in my ear, becoming more irritating with the increasing transparency of the delusion. I shut my eyes and tried to calm my breathing as my heart started to pound out of my chest. I opened them and looked back at the Warvs. The illusion had fled.

"I—I'm familiar with the term. My cousin saved a Skiv, a few days back, a little girl with her family. He asked me to speak to her and it came up in conversation," I said.

"That reassures us of *nothing*," barked the Warv.

"She told me about the Shadow Scar. She said they killed her father while she hid in a pile of rubble. One found its way back to her, one with tentacles on its face. Its very presence inflicted a depth of fear she'd never experienced; made her ears ring," I said.

The Warvs shared glances.

"We've heard stories of an identical Shadow Scar," said the first Warv who I'd knocked down. She stood and walked up to me. "They all have their peculiarities, but word of that one has spread vastly throughout the Waste. You said this cousin of yours, Amat Luciph Criptous, he offers us hospitality?"

"He does, on the essence of Anua, I swear it," I said.

The She-Warv stiffened.

"We will allow you and those under your command to roam this city uncontested by our forces and allow you to take the Skivs into your custody. Should they choose to accompany you. But we will *not* go with you," said the She-Warv.

I was confused; I was so sure she and the other Warvs would have embraced the opportunity.

"I don't understand," I said.

"We have it under good authority that someone in the militia is behind the making of the Shadow Scar. To our eyes, this third-party threat is far more villainous than all the invaders put together. So long as whoever commands them remains in power, we will continue to take our chances here in the Waste," said the She-Warv.

"You have it under good authority? What intel do you have?" I asked.

"Skivs and Warvs alike who have remained out here from day one," she said.

I took a moment to reflect on everything the she-Warv had said.

"I regret that you won't be coming with us, after we came all this way, but may I ask one thing of you?"

"That would depend on the request," she replied as she raised an eyebrow.

"Will you and yours help me and my troops locate what Skivs remain in this city? Help us offer them a chance at receiving salvation?" I asked.

The She-Warv sighed and shook her head.

"No, we will not assist you in this task, either. As heart-wrenching as it is to know the Skivs will likely die out here without your aid, we will not partake in the act of lending as many as we can into your care so that they can be added to the ranks of the Shadow Scar either. But as I said, we will not interfere further with your mission. Seeing as how your intentions are pure," said the She-Warv.

I nodded my head, reluctantly, as I finally let the other She-Warv go, releasing her arm. I walked up to the She-Warv I had been talking to and slowly reached out my hand. She looked down at it skeptically and back up at me as she joined her own grip with mine.

"Here's to first contact between Warv and militia," I said with a smirk.

The She-Warv scoffed.

"Here's to being human," said the She-Warv.

That caught me off guard, though I tried my best not to show that it did. I opened a channel to Kita, told her we were going to move on, and parted ways from the Warvs. For now...

***

Kita and I said nothing more to one another for the remainder of the day, and as it faded, I felt the shivers creep in and the sweat seep. Kita stayed well by my side both in altered time and out of it. Without making it obvious, I had tried on several occasions to slip away from her, but she always took that as a silent command for course correction and trailed after me. It wasn't until I started to feel lost in my own navigation and stumbled in my steps that I finally had us set up camp for the night.

Hopefully, Kita can occupy herself with that while I take another hit of Diazep. Unless . . . she knows and that's why she hasn't let me out of her sight!

"Are you alright, sir?" asked Kita.

Dodge that question!

"Are any of us?" I replied.

"No, I just mean, you've led us on a path that's nearly crossed over the other pairs east and west of us, twice over in the past four hours. We've hardly gained any ground north in all that time. And I can't help but notice you seem distracted."

"Who isn't?" I said, vexed. "When you've got a father who can't recognize you or any other member of your family. When your family is being pressured by the most powerful bodies in the militia. When you've been asked to suddenly take command of a force who doesn't have the slightest bit of respect for you, and you're haunted by the memory of . . ." Kita retracted her helm and a dim light on her shoulders illuminated her face. Her eyes were sad. "That should be a sufficient answer. Get a camp ready. I'm going to secure the area." I stopped myself and raised my finger to Kita. "And don't you judge me for any of that. Because *you* asked." I marched, altered time, and found a place I could use the contents of my bag in peace . . .

XXVII
A City Submerged
(Mae)

It was strange seeing Amat again, after so long. I never suspected I would after parting ways over three years ago. Starting out, it was hard to forget about him. Though we were separated at opposite ends of the world, I kept well informed on his involvement against the first wave of invaders. It was, after all, a little hard not to be.

When they launched their full invasion, I'd been called back to fight on the Eastern Utopion front by my older sister. She pulled many strings to see that through. I'd forgotten all about Amat by then, and my feelings for him. In the rare instances I recalled him, I'd think of myself as childish, dreaming out a fantasy. But now that I find myself by his side once again, I . . . well . . . I'm reminded of why I liked him in the first place and how I fantasized about where our relationship could go. But several years have passed. The thing is, now he finally made his first remark toward me, when he told me certain things hadn't changed about him—in the way he felt toward me. Which has me wondering if I was the only one who felt that way to begin with. *But damn it, Mae, that could mean anything.* I just hope he doesn't find out that it was me who arranged for the transfer under his command.

"So, you and my brother go way back?" asked Lara, Amat's younger sister, sitting right beside me.

I flicked my head toward her, bringing my attention back to the present.

"We do."

Lara nodded and smiled.

"What, has he . . . said much about me?" I asked, holding back the eagerness in my tone.

"No," Lara said bluntly. The remark made me raise my brows. "He doesn't tend to talk about particular people. That is, except for the Diramal and my father."

I suppose that brings . . . some relief.

"I'm sorry, I'm not trying to upset you. Just trying to break the ice if we're going to be working together," said Lara.

"I see. *Uh*, you're an Alpha, right?" I asked.

"Yes, sir," replied Lara.

Yeah, they don't make 'em like they used to. This one talks too much.

"I joined with the intention of finding a way to free my brother of his code nine neuro-chip," Lara said. I pricked up my ears. "After the Diramal broke his body and revived it through a mark-one regenerator."

"Oh, I didn't know all that. I mean, I knew that he'd been promoted to the rank of Jinn-hid at the start of the war, but I never . . . Goddess." There was that feeling again. I looked away at my feet as my expression tensed.

"You don't have to hide your concern around me; I could tell by the way you interact with him," Lara said.

I scoffed.

"You know, for an Alpha, you have an interesting way of expressing yourself," I said.

Lara raised an eyebrow.

"You know, for an Alpha turned Io-Pac, you have an interesting way of hiding your most sensitive feelings," replied Lara.

I chuckled.

"Fair enough. Do you treat all the girls who have an interest in Amat this way?" I asked.

"As far as I know, he's only mentioned one . . ." Lara let that sink in for a moment. "'Course he never specified who."

I gazed at Lara awkwardly.

Perhaps Lara's not as immature as I initially thought.

"Well, I can attest there's been more than that. Though, he's never seemed to notice," I said.

"I wouldn't be so sure—"

"Is there a point to why we're talking about your brother like this?" I cut Lara short.

"Of course there is. Put blatantly, my brother has been through a lot, more than you're likely aware. He's put a lot on the line to protect me and other members of my family and I noted how your mood shifted when he entered our conversation in the hangar. And regardless of what your intentions are, I'm trying to make sure you don't add to the weight he's already carrying," Lara said.

I heard the pilot call my name and rank and to meet her in the cockpit. I said nothing more, just stood and headed that way.

"You called for me," I said to the pilot.

"Yes, Io-Pac Kalbrook, we are nearing Zoiqua. Shall I proceed to take us over the target area?" the pilot asked.

"That's good, but no, take us out, away from the coast. We'll have a better chance at gaining an element of surprise if the enemy has defenses installed in the area," I replied.

"Yes, Io-Pac Kalbrook," said the pilot.

I stepped out of the cockpit and barked orders at the men and women to suit up and gear up.

"Those of you who can pilot a Dailagon, with me," I said.

Among the many faces I saw fall in behind me, I caught a glimpse of Lara. As I walked down to the lower level of the Fade, where two columns of Dailagons were docked, I opened a channel to the pilot.

"Pilot, reach out to the other Fades, tell them to relay this message to the men and women under my command. Any one of them that knows how to fly a Dailagon is to partake in piloting one of their own with me. The Fades will bring the rest down. Dock in the landing zones and release them into the city," I said.

"Yes, Io-Pac Kalbrook," replied the pilot.

"Only on my mark will you and the other Fades submerge to the city," I commanded.

"Understood, Io-Pac Kalbrook."

I reached the lower levels and strapped myself into the cockpit of a Dailagon.

"Pilot, open the Dailagon hatches," I said.

A few moments later, the hatches slowly unlatched. I opened a channel to everyone under my command.

"Those of you currently in Dailagons, if your hatches are opened, deploy and plunge toward Zoiqua," I said.

I activated my Dailagon and dislodged it from the Fade. I dove into the sea; it was dark, perhaps as dark as you would expect it to be at the deepest depths of the ocean. On the interior of the Dailagon's canopy, my surroundings were illuminated by a molecular display. Yet in this perception, the extent to which I could perceive things at a distance was limited. So, I transitioned the display to Lidar vision and was able to distinguish my surroundings much more clearly.

I looked to either side of me and saw several other Dailagons following my lead.

"We're gonna do some reconnaissance out here, pilot. Stand by for further orders, until we know the area is secured," I said over comms.

"Understood, Io-Pac Kalbrook."

The other Dailagons and I moved slowly in formation with one another, scanning the area with our eyes. From what I could tell, the terrain was rigid and rocky. It wasn't very clear to see, but there was a sense that a lot of life had managed to remain preserved down there. And that was confirmed once we'd gotten a little further. Slowly, a large Glawchomic gracefully squirmed its way past our formation. If I had to guess, it was likely a hundred-plus feet across. It had three glowing purple eyes, one at the center of its head. The top line of its teeth were spaced out evenly and rested over its wide bottom lip. Tentacles that gradually got smaller at the front of its body, dragging all along the bottom of its stomach. Seven escas sprouted along the grand fish's spine. Its tail fin was thin and featherlike. At either side of its body were short transparent fins that held patterns much like a Xintaflub; an insect on Galiza that resembled a butterfly. I held my position to admire the beauty of the fish as it slowly swam past us. *Beautiful. It's reassuring to know that we humans aren't the only ones surviving this war.*

Once the Glawchomic passed us by, we pushed just a little further beyond and found the city of Zoiqua radiantly resting in a wide trench. The city itself was shielded from the water with a Laquar barrier. The same material S.E.F.'s space suits are made of. *Well, I think if a Glawchomic can swim comfortably in the area, there's no reason to suspect there's much, if any, threat outside the city barriers.* I opened a channel to my pilot and gave her the "okay" to dock the rest of the men and women into the city.

I led the small fleet of Dailagons at my side to come around and escort the Fades into the city. But once the first one submerged into the ocean, slowly along the rocky surface, dozens of paired orbs lit up. They lifted from the surface and took on the shapes of invader fighters. I silently cursed as I realized an assault was about to be launched.

"Invader forces detected! Disperse and retaliate, protect the Fades, see to it that they reach the city," I shouted over comms.

The other Dailagons dispersed, and in the same instance, the invader forces did the same, only much more quickly. Within the first moments, four of my Dailagons had already been taken out. I yelled a curse as the same thing nearly happened to me. I pushed my Dailagon to its maximum speed, which made me perceive things slower than they were actually moving, but nothing like a QS-25, and even at this rate the alien crafts were far swifter. But this wasn't my first time fighting the invaders from a cockpit. Previous experiences taught me the key to surviving this form of conflict was observation and thinking ahead of the enemy.

To get my bearings, I maneuvered my way through the conflicts, avoiding the enemy head-on. After clearing my tail and getting a feel for my surroundings, I looked constantly from my canopy to my scanners and pinpointed an incoming enemy fighter. Spiraling down from above, if I continued my course straight ahead, I'd put myself directly in its line of sight. I pulled back on my joystick and drifted in a crescent motion as I aimed the Dailagon's nose up at the alien craft and blew it out of the water. The maneuver slowed my speed, mildly, before I accelerated the Dailagon to its max speed once again.

I looked to my left and saw that someone under my command was taking heavy fire from an invader craft tight on their trail. Before both crafts passed me by, I positioned myself on an opposite line of sight from my ally. We hurtled toward each other and at the last moment, I twirled over them as they passed me by, aimed my guns down at the rear of the alien craft, and fired. Debris scraped against the plating of my Dailagon, but the damage was not severe. I went on to assist a handful of others and dealt with a few additional enemies that had taken me head-on.

"What's the status on the Fades?" I shouted over comms.

"This is Alpha Lara Criptous, Io-Pac Kalbrook. I can confirm seven Fades have docked at this rate. The eighth is en route," Lara said.

A Dailagon came over my position and was obliterated the moment it was overhead of me. I growled as my Dailagon was knocked off balance and quickly adjusted to maintain top speed and mobility.

"I'm not going to lie to myself and say we can keep this up for as long as we please. The Fades need to pick up the pace and the ranks need to be quicker about emptying them. That or the rest will have to pull out and return to base," I said.

An alien craft aligned itself behind me. My scanners warned me of its presence before it fired and I pulled back on my speed, rotating off to the side as the alien craft passed me by. In the blink of an eye, I twirled back around, found a shot, and took it.

"By my count, we're already down twenty Dailagons of eighty-four and this quarrel hasn't gone on ten minutes," I said.

I looked over to my left and witnessed a Dailagon in a dive, chased by an invader craft over the city. The invader managed to land some shots that nipped the Dailagon just slightly, preventing it from recovering the dive. The Dailagon proceeded to fall into an amplifier that manifested the Laquar barrier. Fortunately, there was a webbed array of structures in the shape of octagons and the Laquar quickly filled the gap. An idea dawned on me.

"Pilot of Fade thirty-seven, this is Io-Pac Kalbrook, are you receiving me?" I asked over comms.

"Roger that, Io-Pac Kalbrook, I read you loud and clear," said the pilot.

"Are you and the other Fades en route back to base?"

"We are, sir," said the pilot.

"Delay that route. Come back, take positions beside the trench, do not submerge yourselves. Inform the other Fades to do the same. Let me know when you are in position," I said.

"Yes, sir."

"The rest of you still with me in Dailagons, last as long as you can through this. I have a plan. When the Fades are in place, be ready to form up on my position," I said.

"Yes, Io-Pac Kalbrook," replied various voices over comms.

"Those of you who have already reached the city, find cover in the buildings and remain there. Do not roam or draw attention to yourselves; this is for your own safety and the success of the mission. Alpha Criptous, ensure the docked Fade makes it out okay," I said.

"Roger that, Io-Pac Kalbrook, the eighth Fade is ascending now," replied Lara.

On and on that battle waged and there didn't seem an ounce of give in the invader's persistence. Thus, I continued to lose Dailagons and their pilots with them. Before long, however, I'd heard back from the pilot of Fade thirty-seven.

"Io-Pac Kalbrook," she said. "We are in position. Hovering a hundred twenty-five yards West of the city."

"Thank Anua. Alpha Criptous, delay the next Fade," I said.

"Yes, Io-Pac Kalbrook," replied Lara.

"All of you rally to my position and head toward the Fades. On my mark, Fade thirty-seven, you and the others are going to fire down toward the water," I said.

"Understood, Io-Pac Kalbrook. Standing by for your mark," said the pilot.

When I saw that what remained of the Dailagons were at either side of me, I led them out and away from the city, with the invader forces behind us firing still. Two more Dailagons had been taken out, and by my count, less than half remained.

"Hold formation, squirm as you need to, but do not break formation," I ordered.

I had a lock on the positions of the Fades. They held a circular formation with a wide center. *That'll do.*

"Fades, we are coming up on your positions. Dailagons, be ready to emerge at ninety degrees in three, two, now!"

Three more Dailagons had been taken out in the break before we emerged out of the water. I waited just a moment longer till we cleared the sight of the Fade guns and as the invader forces chased after us, I finally blurted, "Mark!"

All thirty Fades unleashed their fire and mowed down each of the remaining invader forces as they rose or even passed through the line of sight. The battle had been won, but at a great cost.

I gave a sigh of relief when the Fades let off and it was clear the invaders had been dealt with.

"Alpha Criptous, how many more Fades need to dock?" I asked.

"Twenty-four, Io-Pac Kalbrook," replied Lara.

"See that they do. Fade pilots, you may continue your route back to base. Everyone who participated in this battle, fallen and alive, fought admirably. If it were so simply done, I'd commemorate you all," I said.

"Even if it were so simply done, I don't think I'd be able to accept whatever you had to offer, without having your leadership and strategy acknowledged first, sir," said Lara.

XXVIII
Marks Of Sanctuary
(Amat)

A dark void had once again entrapped me in the confines of my unconscious visions. A layer of water covered the ground, soiling my shoes. The darkness: so mesmerizing I could hardly tell if my eyes were open or closed. An infant's cries sounded in the near distance. They did not promptly disturb me, as I was unsure of the cause for the infant's distress. I slowly turned around, looking in every direction, to find no distinct outlines or figures in the distance. Suddenly, the cries burst in a thunderous chant that seemed to emanate itself throughout the void. The cries grew louder, and their frequencies strained my ears and churned my insides. The pain brought me to my knees, and I slouched forward. My body felt as though it was dematerializing and yet reforming at a molecular level simultaneously. Pressing my palms to my ears did not dull the wail of the cries. Despite my suffering, a gracious aura surrounded me and filled me with a sense of weightlessness. Like the sensation one feels when they are graciously weighed down into a body of water; the moment their muscles give and their eyes are entranced by the glistening of sunrays, dancing and stretching down from the water surface. That was the sensation the aura provided to me, a sense of complete tranquility.

Relaxing my eyelids, they opened to the sight of a radiant being. Streaks of light stretched and faded from his body. It was hard to tell on account of how brightly he shined, but certain aspects of his body seemed to morph and shift constantly. My eyes adjusted to his radiancy, and I noted that this being was kneeling beside someone—a woman. I tried to stand and approach this being, but something about the aura that surrounded me kept me in a fetal position.

I opened my mouth to speak and call out to the being, but my mind had run a blank on the concept of communication altogether. The being stood; the motion sent chills down my spine. My strength faded as I extended an arm to the being; I didn't know why, but I was overwhelmed with a sense of longing for his presence. The being slowly turned his head back toward me, but before I could make out any details in his face, a chant of my name reached my ears and lured my attention elsewhere. Once I turned my head back I was suddenly faced with my father and standing on my own two feet.

I looked down at my body, felt around it with my hands. I turned back the other way; no one was there.

"Amat," my father called, once again. I slowly turned back to face him. "Are you alright?"

"I . . . I don't know. I mean, I feel fine. I'm just not sure of what I experienced a moment ago," I replied.

"You saw something?"

"Someone, yes."

"What did they look like?"

"Beautiful," I said. I paused as I reflected on the event. "I felt a deep connection to him; not knowing how or why. I heard a child crying before he presented himself to me, and he was kneeling beside a woman. She looked familiar, but I can't say for certain who she was."

My father sighed as his gaze drifted from me.

"Ah, it sounds as though you witnessed something of great importance, Amat."

"You sound as though you know more about it than I do," I said.

My father shifted his attention back to me.

"Even if I did, I would not be allowed to reveal any more than you yourself understand about it."

"Because you're just a memory in my head?"

"Because it is for you to discover these things, Amat. The most important things that we receive are the things that most challenge us, put us in uncomfortable circumstances. Do you know why that is?"

I shook my head. My father walked up to me, got on his knee, and grabbed onto my arms, looking up at me.

"Because it is in those circumstances that we have our greatest growths and gain our most precious knowledge. Do you understand?"

"Yes, sir," I replied.

"Good. Now, before I leave, understand this. I am more than a constant memory that resides within your mind. There is a plan, Amat, that exists within and beyond the physical universe. Part of me has decided to stay behind and guide you up there and in here," my father said, pointing to my head and heart.

"I understand," I said, nodding.

My father smiled.

"I trust that you do. It is time we part now. Wake up, my son." My father gently traced his fingers over my eyelids, closing them. "Wake up."

I stared up at the cracked ceiling as I lay there in the cot, contemplating who that being was. *My father told me I would have to find out for myself. Perhaps, if I can learn how to control these dreams of mine, I can discover the being's identity.*

"Jinn-hid," a man said.

I looked over in his direction and recognized him as Zothra.

"It's been several hours since we made camp. Night has surely passed by this time. The troops are getting ready to leave."

I grunted as I sat up and stood.

"Has everyone stocked up their QS-25s on invader blood?" I asked.

"Yes, sir," replied Zothra.

I nodded.

"What about our casualties and wounded?" I asked.

"Eighty-seven were killed in the scrimmage, sir. Six were wounded, but they've been tended to."

"Are the wounded well enough to travel?" I asked.

"I inspected each myself, sir. Four of them seem well enough to continue with the mission. However, one of them is bleeding internally in both her legs. Our medics have done everything they can to mend her, but she is surely on her way out if she does not receive extensive care soon. The other is a man; he was close to one of the blasts that hit us. It forced him back against a wall and he hit his head. He's non-responsive and there are questions surrounding his condition."

"Very well. Take ten of our troops, give them orders to stay behind and guard our wounded. I'll arrange for a Fade to take them back to base. Once that's taken care of, report back to me and we'll move out," I said.

"Yes, sir," replied Zothra.

Once Zothra left my sight, I opened a channel.

"Shím, Kyla, Iana, this is the Jinn-hid. I need an update on your mission statuses. Have any of you located any additional Warvs or Skivs?" I asked.

"This is Kyla, sir. We've still had no luck in finding Skiv or Warv. We were attacked, early this morning. Twenty-three troops were lost and four have been wounded, all of whom will need to be taken back to base."

"I've wounded to care for as well, Kyla. I'll be calling in a Fade later to send them back to base. Give me your coordinates and leave some of your troops behind to guard your wounded. I'll have the Fade pick them up as well," I said.

"Yes, sir," said Kyla.

"This is Iana, sir. We had a run-in with a large force of Warvs. Contact was attempted but unfortunately, our efforts to reach out proved useless. We had no choice but to retaliate. Thirty-eight were lost in the battle. Two were wounded, but they are well enough to travel. We have, however, cleared our region of the city's surface and are ready to take our search beneath it."

I sighed, dreading the thought of how many Warvs died in that fight, on top of the thirty-eight that were lost under Iana. I should have asked if Iana had taken a count of the fallen Warvs. They were human, after all. But a greater part of me didn't want to know the answer to that question.

"It's alright, Duka Dovan, the Warvs left you and your troops with no other choice. If you are ready to start your search beneath the city, you may proceed," I said.

"Thank you, sir," said Iana.

"This is Shím, sir. Unfortunately, aside from the seventy-two Skivs we found yesterday, we've had no luck finding any more. Oddly, the invader forces have relentlessly thrown themselves at my troops since finding the Skivs. The last attack was just under ten minutes ago."

"Have you taken heavy casualties?" I asked.

"We haven't had time to account for the dead, sir, but I can say that we've lost several."

"As soldiers, it is expected that we should die on the field of battle; it is what we are bred for. If they cannot be accounted for, merely pass them on to the nourishing arms of Anua so that they may be received into the Luminous Paradise. What matters is that you get those Skivs safely back

The Tyrant of Unity

to base. Have you cleared your run of the eastern end of the city, Duka MgKonnol?" I asked.

"Almost, sir. I've sent troops up ahead while many of us march beside the Skivs to protect them."

"Very good, Duka MgKonnol. Send me a lock on your location, I'll arrange for the Fade to meet with you as well and pick up the Skivs. After the extraction, you may proceed to wander beneath the city," I said.

"Yes, sir," said Shím.

"Criptous out."

Moments after I finished calling in a Fade to reach the various locations I'd discussed with my subcommanders, Zothra returned to me.

"I've arranged for ten men and women to stay behind with our two severely wounded, sir. Shall we move out?" Zothra said.

"Yes, we shall," I said.

Before the end of two hours in normal time, my troops and I had managed to search the rest of the city's northern region, to no avail. We hadn't encountered Skiv, Warv, Invader, and certainly not these Shadow Scar I'd heard so much about.

I ordered my troops to make their way below the city's surface. With Ion once having been a highly industrial city, the ground below it had been hollowed via tunneling systems. Their appearance resembled something like what you'd call a crystal cave. The underground submersion interfered with our particle sensor grid, and we had to rely on lights attached to our weapons and helms to clear a path. All along the walls and overhead were the same material, a form of crystal called Azorkanite.

I led my troops into the mines as others continued to make their way down and follow the rest. I kept my aim up and opened a channel.

"Be on your guard, everyone. If there're enemies down here, the terrain down here will provide them with ample cover to remain hidden from our eyes," I said.

Zothra stayed close to my side, though he seemed less on edge about the place.

"Sir, do you really think that Skivs or Warvs could have found refuge down here?" Zothra asked.

"I think it's very possible," I replied.

"Even if they are, or were, there's no doubt that these mines run for miles. Ion City, when it was still lively, dug through its own depths for centuries before this war broke out," said Zothra.

"Just as you doubt there could be some surviving members of our kin down here, *Cho'Zai*, I doubt that they would have ventured so far from the surface. If there is anyone down here, dead or alive, I trust we won't have to travel far to find them."

Zothra scoffed.

"Should we find anyone down here and bring them back to base, if there's one thing they should be grateful for, it is your optimism, Jinn-hid," said Zothra.

"Or perhaps, more simply, my sense of observation. Do you see all this Azorkanite that surrounds us, Cho'Zai Zothra?" I asked.

"Is that what it's called?" Zothra asked, seemingly impressed but sarcastic too.

"You may notice that it's transparent—the crystal. You may also notice that on its outer layer, it holds a light blue-green coloration and if you look closely enough, you'll see that beyond that thin layer, the color of the crystals is a darker blue. That is its natural color, but it's lighter on the outside because that's what happens when the crystal has prolonged exposure to dense oxygen and wind flow. One final thing to note is that the air is not so thin down here, which means these tunnels lead to a way out and an abundance of wind is finding its way throughout this system."

"Fascinating, and how did you learn all this?"

I gave Zothra an annoyed, sidelong look.

"Call it a hobby of interest." I took a moment before saying anything else. "I came across the knowledge in my research to discover alternative ammunition for this E.S.P. 101. Along that path, I discovered that certain crystals could hold an electric charge. For me, it was only a question of which one would serve as the best magazine."

"I see."

I gave a light laugh.

"You know, for someone who up until the other day seemed so eager to know me, you seem unamused by what I've just shared about myself," I said.

"No offense intended, sir, but if this is your way of opening up to people, I dare say it could be improved upon."

"I'd like to think the same could be said for how you acknowledge your superiors in certain respects. If that's truly how you see me."

"Duly noted, sir," said Zothra.

Zothra and I continued to walk in silence for a moment and I couldn't help but notice there was a part of me that was starting to trust him. Granted, it was very small and I wasn't entirely open to the idea, but he had saved my life the day before and there was reason to acknowledge that much about him.

"Perhaps if you started sharing a bit about yourself with me, I'd consider being a little more open with you," I said.

"And what would you seek to know about me, sir?" asked Zothra.

"Start with something simple, like telling me where you're from," I said.

Zothra turned his head over to me. A smile grew on Zothra's face, and he chuckled.

"The answer to that question is not so simply answered, sir. Not even by myself."

I wasn't quite sure what Zothra meant by that, but at least he sounded honest about it. *Perhaps the Cho'Zai had a complicated upbringing, and he doesn't like to talk about his past.*

"What can you tell me then? Reveal something about your character to me."

"Something about my character," replied Zothra ominously. "Over ten years ago, when we were at war with Afeikita, I was assigned a classified mission. I'd been sent with another Cho'Zai, Xaitúkeiba was her name."

"Curious name," I butted in.

"Yes, it is. I called her Kib for short. Together, we'd been sent to negotiate with this arms dealer, Quabe Zúnyút. Of course, he had a reputation for playing on both sides of the war; guys in his line of work always do. Intel told us that he was going to give members in the Kintabú alliance a whole arsenal of not just guns, but artillery, high-grade tech, and Anua knows what else from Druteika. At the time, they were among the leading militaries of the world. So, long story short, we had to track Quabe down, arrange a meeting, and convince him to sell his arsenal to the Utopian militia. We had just over a month before Quabe would receive the shipment and his initial exchange would be carried out. In that time, Kib and I got familiar with one another."

That made me turn my head.

"Ha, that alone impresses me. Didn't know you Cho'Zai could have feelings for others," I said.

Zothra looked right back at me, sternly. I wasn't intimidated, but it was certainly the first time I'd seen this expression on his face. It revealed to me that he was sharing a sensitive incident from his past and didn't discuss it with many people. Finally, he looked away and continued.

"As I was saying, Kib and I got close. Three weeks go by, we make contact with Quabe and arrange a meeting. Days later, we convince him to hand over the arsenal. We meet in a secluded location, and Quabe arrives with what we believe to be the Druteikan weapons cargo. At this rate, Kib and I are backed up by a few of our people from home. As we make our approach, hired guns of Quabe's flood out the trucks, shots are fired, our backup drops faster than we can retaliate and Kib gets hit, bad. I pick up Kib and get us out of there, but I take a shot to the leg. The deal's a bust, and I have Kintabú on my tail who chase us into the next day. Overnight, I contact . . . the Diramal and explain what happened. In addition to his frustration, he orders me to kill Kib, telling me she's dead weight. That the priority was for me to make it back to Utopion to debrief and reformulate our strategy to obtain the weapons. I didn't say it directly to him, but I refused to carry out the Diramal's execution order. I continued to run through the jungle for another day with Kib in my arms. But by that second night, Kib's wound got infected, she was deathly sick, and going into shock. It was only after I knew she wasn't going to make it, after I saw how much she was hurting . . ."

We stopped and faced one another.

"That I gave her to Anua. I made the choice out of mercy, not self-interest or because the Diramal told me to. So with all that said, does that tell you something about my character that satisfies you, sir?" asked Zothra.

I nodded.

Zothra frowned as he caught sight of something past me.

The Tyrant of Unity

"What's that?" he asked.

I turned around and saw a part of some inscribed insignia imprinted on the wall, down an alternative path. We could barely see the markings with just the lights on our helms, but it was clear that something was there.

"I'm not sure. Let's go find out," I replied.

I led Zothra and the rest of my troops down a winding path that looped back up to the insignia. It was blue in color, on a wet, tan rock. I soon realized that it was composed of invader blood. The insignia almost seemed to resemble the invaders themselves in the sense that it was a large raindrop-shaped body with eight arms extending in various directions. I stared up at it as I tried to contemplate its purpose, its meaning.

"You ever seen anything like that, sir?" asked Zothra.

"No, but it was no doubt drawn with invader blood. Perhaps they were down here, and the insignia is a tribute to something. Maybe their dead?" I asked.

"It could also be a warning sign displayed by the Warvs," suggested Zothra.

"Sir . . ." a woman in my ranks called out. I turned my head to acknowledge her; she was standing before an extension of the path. "There's another," she continued.

I came to her side and there was at least one more insignia of the same design further down the path. I placed my hand on the woman's shoulder.

"Well done," I said to her.

I looked back at the rest of my troops.

"We continue this way," I commanded.

As we pressed deeper into the mines, one blue blood insignia led to another. There must have been at least a dozen we followed before we heard what sounded like moaning. I halted my troops and signaled for them to be on their guard. A tight segment in the path made it so I had to squeeze my way forward. As I neared the clearing, someone exclaimed: "Ouch!" It caught me off guard, but I wasn't so quick to violence, recognizing the voice as human. I looked down swiftly and the lights on my helm revealed a lonely male Skiv. His clothes were dusty and worn and he raised his hand to my lights.

"Who—who are you?" the Skiv asked.

I slowly stepped forward from the tight space, raising my hands peacefully as the Skiv backed away. I retracted my helm and my eyes immediately adjusted with their enhanced vision.

"It's okay," I said. "My name is Amat Luciph Criptous, I'm here to help you and any others that might be with you."

The Skiv broke into hysteria as tears trailed down his cheeks.

"You're not real. You can't be. The Goddess is dead. We destroyed her and for that, she unleashed this chaos upon us all. You're not real, I already lurk in the shadow of Anua."

The Skiv trembled as he went on to mutter words to himself. I was going to try to communicate with him further when I caught sight of something that moved just barely out of sight, past the man. I stood and slowly walked deeper into the clearing to find hundreds of additional Skivs huddled together. Frightened, shocked, likely just as broken as the previous Skiv I came across. It broke my heart to see my kin so shattered. *How did they all get down here? Were they led by those insignias? If so, who then led them to the insignias?*

Suddenly, I felt a chill flow past my face. At first, I thought it might have been just the natural temperature of the mines, but then I felt it again, just a subtle breeze blowing through my hair. *Wind,* I thought to myself.

I looked back and saw that Zothra and the others were starting to come through from the small gap. I allowed my helm to envelop my head once again and joined everyone else.

"Hold on, hold on. That's enough of you to come through for now. There are people here and they're all in shock. I don't want to overwhelm and risk them getting hurt," I said, once a handful of troops had joined me.

"What should the rest of us do in the meantime, sir?" the man at the edge of the slim pathway asked.

"Just hold your positions. See to it that whoever brought our people down here don't give us any surprises if they come back," I said.

"Yes, sir."

I turned my attention back to Zothra.

"If these people are so overwhelmed, how do you expect to get each one through that narrow space without them losing their minds?" asked Zothra

"We won't have to take them back out the way we came," I said.

"What do you mean?"

"I just had my helm off, briefly, stepped a few paces toward the cluster of Skivs and felt wind on my face. That means there's an opening nearby, a large one, most likely. Capable of seeing us all comfortably out of here," I said.

"What about enemies? Say there is an opening somewhere nearby. How do we know it's not guarded?"

"I intend to find out. We'll send a few troops out to investigate the path or paths ahead, if there's more than one. We'll find out for ourselves where the opening is and if it's safe to lead our kin through it," I said.

Zothra nodded.

"Very well then, sir, I will see it done," said Zothra.

Zothra eased his way past the Skivs to the other end of the clearing.

"Sir, there are three tunneling paths at the end of the clearing. Only one seems to have a breeze emanating from it. I still feel it would be wise to allow only me to go on ahead and scout for potential threats," said Zothra, over comms.

"Agreed. I'll start bringing some more of the troops through as we attempt to get the Skivs more comfortable around us," I said.

"I didn't approach them, sir, but I did observe several Skivs acknowledge my presence and they seemed unfazed by me. Perhaps you need not be so cautious as you and the others start to interact with them," said Zothra.

"I'll take that into consideration. Good luck, Cho'Zai Zothra. Criptous out," I said.

I started out with just that initial handful of my troops to wander around and interact as calmly as we could with the Skivs. I also gave my troops orders to retract their helms so that the Skivs could see who they were talking to and feel more comfortable. We didn't dedicate too much time to any one specific Skiv at a time. We prompted them with a series of questions concerning their safety: if they remembered how they got down there in the first place, if they knew where they were. Unfortunately, many of the Skivs were in a daze. Not paranoid, like the first one I encountered, but seemingly half awake. As if they'd been sedated, their awareness repressed. The children were the most aware, but then they, too, were more like the first Skiv I encountered—paranoid and scared. I suppose it was a high expectation to assume some might have been sound of mind, buried for who knows how long within, not just darkness, but Galiza itself.

After a close examination of one of the dazed Skivs – whose hair had been shaven clean off his scalp – I noted strange markings along the top of his head. Tiny swollen indentations in a perfect row that ringed about his scalp. Curious, I moved to examine another dazed Skiv and gently felt around their scalp, shifting their hair aside to find identical markings.

"Jinn-hid, sir, I've reached the end of the tunnel. There was a sentinel of invaders waiting for me. I dealt with them on my own. Though, I'm not sure if they had any patrols set to come this way, but now would be a good time to start moving the Skivs out of there," said Zothra over comms.

"Very good, Cho'Zai Zothra. Do a quick scout of the immediate area, see to it there are no nearby patrols or additional sentinels, and we'll rendezvous with you shortly," I said.

"Yessir."

I closed the channel and arranged for the rest of my troops to ease their way into the clearing, in small groups at a time. Leading the Skivs out through the central tunnel with care, complemented by their half-asleep states of mind. I'd been assigning my troops to escort the Skivs out of the mines, families at a time, at their own pace.

As we neared half of the Skivs to be moved, I overheard a heated conversation coming from the other end of the clearing.

"Hey, come on, stop that," I heard a voice shout.

I turned to face the noise. At first, I thought maybe it was a Skiv who was barking replies to one of my troops, but then I heard the same voice shout insults that couldn't have been mistakenly directed at one of my soldiers.

"Come on, you waste muck!" I heard the same voice blurt.

I raced towards the yelling, ready to set this insubordinate trooper of mine straight. The two finally came into view as I witnessed my trooper reach down and yank the Skiv off the ground.

"On your feet," the trooper growled.

The Skiv immediately broke into hysteria, screaming and flailing his body all about. I rushed up to my trooper and instantly separated him from the Skiv, pushing him to the ground.

"May Anua rip your tongue from your throat, soldier, restrain yourself!" I barked, towering over him.

The Skiv went on wailing until all fell silent to the sound of screeching invaders beckoning from deep within the mines. Everyone stopped what they were doing and I'm sure their breaths trembled. The trooper pushed himself off the ground in a rush. I raised my hand to him and put my finger to my snout. The screeches sounded again, and I pinpointed they were coming from the left-side tunnel at the end of the clearing. I signaled for the trooper to remain still as I slowly made my way toward that left-side tunnel. *Goddess, please, if you can hear me, spare us from a conflict with the invaders.*

Steps away from the tunnel, the screeches continued to echo through the mines, and my heart pounded as I prepared myself to look down its long, dark path. Rocks were *launched* against my back and shoulders as an invader burst from the ceiling above. Four arms swiftly latched themselves around my upper body before I had time to gasp. I fell to the ground; the wind knocked out of me. I altered time, naturally, until my helm reformed itself around my head and a good thing too, for the invader latched on to the left side of my reforming helm, leaving half of my face unguarded. I felt blood trickle down from my scalp. I twisted back, launched my elbow into one of the invader's pincers, and rolled out of its grasp. The rest of my helm was allowed to fully envelop my head. I gave a heavy sigh, after finally relieving myself of the tight pressure that occurred with my natural time alteration. Our eyes locked, the invader's and mine, as we pushed off the ground and raced toward one another. I pulled out one of my knives, launching toward the creature, stabbing it in the chest. The invader squirmed still once we hit the ground and I jerked the knife deeper into its flesh, cracking its sparse bones. As its body gave out, I looked up at the ceiling above and along the walls, witnessing several other invaders emerging from the stone and crystal. I growled a curse and stood to fight.

One by one, my troops were cut down by the overwhelming forces of the invaders. Yet within all that chaos, I couldn't help but observe none of the remaining Skivs had been attacked or targeted by the invaders. Despite my troops being heavily outnumbered, the Skivs were curled up helplessly on the ground, with not so much as a scratch to be seen on their bodies. It was almost like… the invaders were protecting the Skivs . . . from us, the militia.

The ground began to tremble, as a result of the invaders sprouting from the walls, and the clearing started to cave in on itself. I noticed this while fighting neck and neck with an invader, after a large chunk of stone collapsed beside us, inches away. Both the invader and I were distracted by it. I quickly ended our conflict before looking up at the wall and noticed the cracks etching their way along the crystal and stone. *No.* It wasn't long before more and more chunks of rock and Azorkanite stacked on the floor. With the conflict waging on, I noted something even more peculiar. The invaders were tending to the Skivs, moving them down that left tunnel. *Where are they taking my kin?* I raced toward the left tunnel to see where the invaders were taking them. Dodging around falling debris, I made short work of those who stood in my way, but before I could reach the tunnel, a firm hand tugged at my shoulder. I was spun around and led back toward the middle tunnel by one of my own troops. This wasn't willingly; in fact, I tried all the while to pull from this trooper's grasp on me and run back toward the left tunnel as the space in the clearing was starting to get dangerously tight. In a swift and mighty movement, the trooper hooked his arms underneath my armpits, pressing our bodies closely together and *leaped* back into the middle tunnel, clearing the impact of a large piece of Azorkanite. blockading the clearing altogether.

I snapped out of my altered time state. Outraged, I *howled*, "No!" as I rushed up to the crystal and bashed the sides of my fists against it. I went back into my altered time state to hit the crystal harder and break through it—relentlessly bashing against the Azorkanite until it looked on the verge of shattering, and, even then, it would not break apart. I was pulled away once again to face the trooper. Struggling against his firm grasp on my shoulders as he shook me, I couldn't overpower his strength. I snapped out of my altered time state once again and the trooper with me.

"Criptous, sir, stop!" the trooper shouted. After having registered his voice, I saw that he was Zothra. "You got as many Skivs out of there as you could. The rest are gone."

I gazed down, panting, dousing my rage before turning back to the crystal and falling to my knees. A tear fell from my left eye as I softly placed my hand on the crystal. I lowered my head to say a prayer for those I couldn't save.

"Sir, the others are waiting with the Skivs. We need to send for a Fade, or the invaders will surely attack us again," said Zothra.

I sighed and stood begrudgingly.

"Then let's move out," I whispered, marching my way down the tunnel.

XXIX
9247-Nacilag
(Olson)

We've been out for two days in the city of Skergel. There's been no sign of Skivs or invader forces, but there are plenty of Warv forces to be found. The city's filled with them; we can't even set up camp without fighting for some ground to settle in. It feels strange fighting against my own race. Funny, I can just as easily remember a time, not too long ago, when such a concept felt as normal as eating intermittently throughout the day. I wonder if Amat has a similar perspective; he seems like he would. Otherwise, would he provide the Warvs the same opportunity as the Skivs in receiving sanctuary?

Attempts to make contact with the Warvs and inform them of our intentions have obviously not gone over successfully. Perhaps if they were more spread out and in smaller groups, we could apprehend them more easily and create a dialogue. At this rate, I've decided my time in Skergel would be better spent locating Skivs. And the apparent lack of an invader presence within the city concerns me less. My guess is, the Warvs have proven a worthy opponent for them, and they're simply biding their time. Perhaps until resources grow scarcer here.

The persistence of the Warvs has cost me a considerable number of troops under my command. I can sense those that remain grow uneasy. Some might even be plotting a mutiny.

Thus, to put everyone's concern at ease, I considered that by using the underground passages, we would be assured a safer path around the city. Granted, this would rob us of much exploration throughout city surface and the chance to save many lives in need. But we'd likely be avoiding future attacks more than we'd be missing out on unaccounted Skivs.

The city of Skergel is sacred to our kin, across all cultures, much of the city's architecture pays tribute to the Goddess herself, in various interpretations. But what gives Skergel its *true* greater value is what lies beneath it.

The depths of Skergel were used as tombs. The history of the tombs, while there is controversy among our people as to how far back it occurred, we all share knowledge of a calamity that happened at least a few thousand years ago. In a time prior to the existence of Anua's presence. The ruins spread across Galiza, put there by our ancestors, stood tall and lively. The ancestors were immensely intelligent in mind, heart, and soul. But, as a species, they'd reached a state of mourning, hardship, and scarcity. Many have speculated as to why that is, but none can be certain.

They lost their way, certain members of our ancestors, who sought to divide our race. These members, a select few, were held in such praise and resources, while the rest were discarded, left to starve, and fend for themselves in what remained of the wilderness. Cities and technologies had consumed most of the natural world. It was only a matter of time before those discarded, rose and waged a war that could not be sustained. The integrity of this ancient society started to collapse on a vast scale. But before we could wipe ourselves out, the Goddess made herself known.

It is said that she was once a beautiful body in space, teaming with life and all things our world lacked. But she made the choice to hurl herself across space and time, enveloping herself in a flame that found its way to Galiza. The blaze was so great that it scorched our world, turning the cities of our ancestors to rubble, changing the air we breathed, resetting… everything. There were some scattered across the planet, who were able to detect the imminent disaster and took refuge beneath the surface.

It is also said that as Anua sacrificed the life of her body to purify our own, her flame went on to surround the planet for four *long* days before finally dousing. Leaving the Goddess with nothing but powder and ash on her surface. But, as the story goes, she went on to restore this world to its former beauty over the course of four additional days. Giving what remained of our ancestors a chance at a new way of life.

The remnants of our ancestors gathered the remains of those who fell victim to the scorch and brought them here, to the city of Skergel. Buried them deep underground, forming walls and paths out of their blackened bones. That much was revealed to be true once I got down there to see it for myself. The ground itself was covered in dust and stone, but all along the walls and roof were burnt bones of various shapes and sizes.

I had led my troops to the nearest entry point to the city's underground—pinned on my fizer. Fortunately, no Warvs intercepted our route. The passageways were long and tight; you could barely walk side by side with someone comfortably without scraping shoulders or the wall. I took the lead, navigating my troops through the tombs. Already a long way in, we were fortunate not to be met with any sign of threat or foe. Still, I could sense my troops' faith depleting, feel their eyes pressing on me. *A mutiny may still dawn on me. At any moment they could, all of them, overwhelm me, knock me out, and leave me for dead. Anua, forbid it.*

We were nearing our exit point when I noticed the ground begin to crack and dust started to fall below our feet. I raised my fist and blurted, "Halt!" My troops paused in their tracks and immediately became uneasy as they bore and primed their weapons. "Steady yourselves, the path ahead may be unstable. Our exit is just ahead, but I will go on alone and make sure one can pass safely," I said. Not even those closest to my back replied.

I took my time, edging forward, shifting my weight back so that if the ground in front of me broke, I would fall to the ground behind me. I moved tranquilly and listened intently. At the sign of any further dust fall, I would retreat to my troops. Well into the unstable ground, I came across a wide crack to the right of the path. It looked bottomless as I leaned over just slightly to view its contents. Holding still a moment, I caught wind of dust trailing down another crack beside me. After taking a deep breath, I raised my front foot to walk back . . . *crack!* The ground beneath me ruptured. Hardly having time to gasp before I fell far enough to see the lights on the guns and helms of my troops fade slightly. I turned around to face the darkness and deployed my suit's glide wings. Falling deeper, a large metallic body came into view. From above, it resembled a beak or an egg shape. Starting wide from the bottom end and curving down as it grew narrower at the other.

"Io-Pac Olson, sir, are you alright?" a woman's voice asked over comms.

"I . . . yes, I'm not harmed. I'm hovering down to some kind of buried object," I replied.

My unsteady landing on the object caused me to slide down its smooth, curved body but I managed to stop my fall before drifting from its edge. The woman's voice returned, distorted by white noise. All I heard was ". . . get you out . . ." but by that time I was too intrigued to see what this object had to offer. To assure my troops, however, I managed a simple reply.

"Roger that, trooper, I'll be standing by till then," I said.

I got on all fours and climbed my way up and around the object, trying to make some sense of what it could be. There were no windows, no attached weapons. But then I caught sight of something that looked like large, faded script. Inspecting the markings further, I made it out to be the number nine. Gazing ahead, I could faintly make out additional markings and recognized the nearest one to be the number two. The next was a four and after that, a seven. The numbers stopped at a dash and on the other side were the letters N, A, C, I, L, A, G. I read it all from left to right. *Galican-7, 4, 2, 9.*

"Goddess!" I gasped. "I think I've discovered some kind of ancient stellar ship."

XXX
Shadows In the Blacklight
(Mae)

The city of Zoiqua was illuminated by a dark hue of neon light. It was the first and only city that gained its power solely through Galiza's core, a few centuries past. Up until recent years, it served as a large mining grid.

The dark hue of blacklight illuminated the ocean air within the city's Laquar dome. The architecture was unlike any other on Galiza. Tall, twisted coral-like spires with blue and orange bulging windows formed from a gel-like substance. At the center of Zoiqua was a bright yellow light that reached the top of the Laquar barrier.

It was the third day in our search for Skivs and Warvs. There hadn't been many Warvs accounted for, live ones anyway. Much of the alien presence there appeared vacated. The city was practically filled with fresh corpses. The only conclusion I could draw was that the Warvs and invaders had an all-out war of their own recently. Or possibly . . . *No, it can't be that.*

The second day had passed, and we'd found no indication of a single threat within the city. Thus, I dispersed my troops, allowing each to roam freely rather than as a collective unit. Amat's sister, Lara, requested the honor of continuing the search with me personally. At first, I questioned the suggestion, but then I sensed she wasn't trying to be difficult on the way to the city. *She's just looking out for Amat's best interests.* She reminded me of my older sister in that respect. It was the concept of company that finally made my decision. *At least I'll be distracted from my superstitions about the fresh corpses lying about.* As a soldier, bloodied bodies didn't bother me; it was the curiosity of what could have given rise to such rapid bloodshed. After all, those invader fighters we fought during our arrival couldn't have been stationed outside the city for nothing. It's possible that they were trying to keep us out, but I speculated they might have been trying to keep something in.

The Tyrant of Unity

Varying reports from my troops informed me there had been plenty of Skivs found throughout the city by the end of the third day. A full count had yet to be taken, but at the rate we were retrieving them, we might end up doubling the numbers we arrived with, minus our casualties.

"You know, you never answered my question from earlier, Io-Pac Kalbrook," said Lara, breaking a persistent silence between us since we divided up.

I looked over to Lara.

"What question?" I asked.

"The one regarding your intentions with my brother," Lara replied.

"My intentions . . . I haven't quite figured them out. I haven't even thought about Amat much since we parted ways three years ago," I replied.

"Yeah, I don't buy that. Like I said, Amat doesn't tend to talk about particular people in-depth. Ninety-five percent of his conversations consist of battle strategy and family matters. The rest are threats and sympathy. So, unless the Diramal monitored his interactions with you throughout your time at Gallethol, I find it extremely coincidental that he asked for you by name to serve under Amat. Unless . . . you had submitted a request for transfer . . ." said Lara.

I stopped and looked at Lara.

"You've got a lot of character, Lara; makes you stand out as an Alpha. It's a luxury Amat, myself, and those of us in the program prior to the war seldom had by the end of our five-plus years of training. Those of us that did were the only ones that really understood one another."

"And now that you've lost your sister, you think Amat is the only one left who can," Lara said. I turned away and proceeded forward. "If that's all there is to it for you, I'd ask you to respectfully keep your distance from him." I stopped as Lara came to my side. "Amat's not much for emotional support. But if there's anything else and he senses that, don't betray his trust. That's all I have to say about it."

Lara continued ahead.

"At the very least, I consider your brother a very dear friend . . ." I said, walking at Lara's side. "The last thing I would do is hurt him."

Lara turned to me and nodded.

"That's reassuring—"

A loud shriek and croak echoed across the air, followed by some gunfire, stopped us dead in our tracks. The shriek couldn't have been mistaken for anything but an invader; but the croak . . . I'd never heard anything like it before. Lara and I quickly whipped our heads in the direction of the noises and aimed our weapons. The shrieks and croaks continued to persist for a moment longer.

"One of those things is undoubtedly an invader, but I couldn't tell you what's making that *croak*. Should we investigate, Io-Pac Kalbrook?" asked Lara.

I may have an idea; I think it could be . . . I gulped. *Oh, please, Goddess, don't let it be that.* I took a deep breath.

"Yes," I replied reluctantly.

We ran through the dimly lit streets, following the sounds of the rummage until we found ourselves very close to them. The cries stopped. Lara and I acknowledged one another with a nod and proceeded with our guard up. We made our way around a row of small, conch-shell-shaped buildings. Beyond them rested a wide opening with scattered piles of rubble across the basalt ground. As well as numerous fresh invader corpses, the aliens' limbs were shriveled and stiff. Many brutal and fatal wounds embroidered their bodies. Limbs that looked to be forcefully torn off. Deep, elongated cuts across their bodies, with their intestines trailing out, like someone had opened them up for an autopsy. Missing eyes, heads, and gaping holes along their bodies that were too big to be mistaken for any standard bullet wound.

Lara growled a disgusted remark.

"Anua's shadow!" Lara gasped. "What would have gone so far as to inflict such . . . gruesome . . ." She couldn't finish the sentence. "I've never seen such vast brutality displayed before."

"I have, but only once," I replied.

"When—"

"Shh!" I replied, raising my hand to Lara.

I could hear . . . something moving in the near distance. Something slimy and squishing grotesquely. I slowly made my way toward the sounds and signaled for Lara to follow my lead. As these noises grew nearer, they were accompanied with the sounds of crunching and tearing, like something was . . . feasting. My breath shivered as the particle sensors on my hud slowly revealed the origin of the sounds. Easing my guard down at the horror of its appearance and the sight of its mouth sucking and drooling over the exposed brain of a fallen invader.

A creature with a pointed nose and scaly—no, smooth skin—black in color, sat there. Its big, empty eyes bulged from their sockets, with a thin pattern of gold around the edges. Four long, pointed fingers with webbing between them made up its hands. It had a well-defined physique. Four legs were squatted in a seemingly natural position. Knees rested high above its head. Thin appendages sprouted and rattled from its back as it roared a croak. Its bottom jaw split open, outward, and stretched out its elastic tongue at me.

The tongue pierced through my gun, obliterating it to pieces; the tip latched onto my shoulder and yanked me toward the creature. I screamed as I fell to the ground and quickly activated the quantum field of my suit as the creature's tongue continued to pull me closer toward itself. In a frenzy, I unsheathed my knife and stabbed the creature's tongue again and again, but still it remained on my shoulder. Lara drew a splice and severed its tongue. The creature squirmed what was left of its tongue back into its mouth. In just as quick a motion, it leaned forward and leaped through the shell wall as I unholstered my pistol and fired in its direction.

Cursing as I ran out of bullets, I pulled myself out of the quantum field and Lara helped me to my feet.

"Are you alright?" she asked.

"I'll be fine."

Suddenly, the air filled with overlapping cries. Aside from the croak, there was one that stood out to me; I'd heard it before, years ago. It was a haunting, loud, rapid gurgle. A shiver crept up and down my spine as my eyes widened and goosebumps covered my arms.

"We need to get out of here," I growled.

I couldn't waste any time minding Lara's reply; the memory of that gurgle was too horrifying to risk sticking around a moment longer. I knew that if what the call belonged to found us, we wouldn't stand a chance. Retreating the way we came, I kept looking over my shoulder to make sure Lara stayed at my side. She'd been jogging backward, covering our rear. I rushed over to Lara and grabbed her by the shoulder.

"We cannot fight what's coming our way with just the two of us. Now come on, run and enter a quantum field!" I yelled as I shoved Lara forward.

Lara and I raced through the neon-lit streets as the various muffled cries followed close behind us. I looked to either side of us and perceived, just barely, shadow figures dashing atop roofs and through rugged buildings. I kicked up my stride, grabbing Lara by the arm as I passed her. *Come on, keep up with me, Alpha, I will not lose another person to these things.*

I ran so fast that the signs of quantum fade were surely creeping up on us both. But the adrenaline in my veins made me oblivious to them. My eyes were locked on the path ahead. Searching for a place we could take cover and hide from our pursuers, I turned a sharp corner and yanked Lara by the shoulder to ensure she remained at my side.

We took refuge in a small shop, safe from the shadows lurking in the dark. Deactivating our quantum suits as we hid behind the front desk.

Both Lara and I retracted our helms and stood tall. For me, it was barely enough to have my head exposed; the tight hug of the QS-25 against my body intensified the pressure in my chest.

"Sir, what . . . what were . . . we running from?" asked Lara.

Out in the distance, we could hear gunfire topped by various cries and screeches like the ones that chased us. Tears fell from my eyes, from a combination of the stress on my body and the thought that maybe we'd made those things someone else's problem. I stiffened my back and placed my hands on my head.

"Only the Goddess . . . may know."

"But . . . you seemed so . . . knowledgeable about what they might be capable of. Have you—"

My eyes widened and I raised my hand to the sound of the gurgle, crying very close by.

"Wait," I whispered, half out of breath.

I allowed my helm to envelop my head and very carefully, walked toward the outside of the shop, scanning the area with the particle sensors. I kept my hand raised at Lara, telling her to stay still. Suddenly the gurgle sounded again, loud enough to echo across the air, sounding as if it could have been just above us. Standing like a statue, I dared not break my pose as that shiver returned to my spine.

"Sir," I heard Lara whisper in a shiver. "You are unarmed."

It was then I remembered the creature we faced earlier destroyed my gun and I had no more ammunition for my pistol. I growled as I plucked my knife from its sheath. The slightest sound from the scrape of steel leaving leather seemed to bring the gurgling creature *crashing* down onto the street just outside the abandoned shop. It let out its haunting call as I rushed back to Lara. My chest tensed as I tried to keep from panting through my nose and glanced back at the creature. I didn't get a very good look at it, except for a quick glance at its back before it *spun around*.

The creature propelled itself through one of the red glowing ion windows. Lara and I flinched but neither one of us screamed. The creature let out a slower, quieter gurgle before starting to walk about the shop. Every step was a heavy smack against the floor, as if it were . . . barefoot possibly? An additional set of synced steps sounded that might have served as hind legs and had more of a peg sound to them, *clicking* across the ground. The creature took in the atmosphere, sniffing deep, as it moved around the room.

"*Mm*, catch your scent once and I'll never forget it . . . human," the creature said.

Its voice was deep, and it was hard to discern if it was a male or a female. Lara looked over to me as she raised her gun to her chest. I gingerly placed my hand on her arm and shook my head. *Bash! Thrash!* The creature was suddenly pushing things over, making a mess of the shop. Pounding the ground like a wild animal till it cracked and trembled slightly. My grip tightened on my knife; if fate would have us fight this thing, I would be ready.

Suddenly it slapped its front feet—which resembled fat-fingered hands—onto the ledge of the counter and growled a sigh. It did not look down at us, but I could tell, as it took one final deep breath in through its nose, it knew we were there. Lara gazed up, ready for whatever came next with her gun in hand. I couldn't bring myself to gaze up, for fear of meeting its own. Sweat trickled down my face and neck as I gulped.

"*Mm*, too easy," the creature said.

It pushed off the ledge and scurried out of the shop. My breath trembled as I slowly raised my head to gaze over the counter. Shortly after, I gathered the courage to stand and head out of the shop.

"Sir—"

I raised my hand once again to Lara.

"Wait. Here."

I was mindful of every step, pressing lightly against the broken glass and over the fallen shelves in the shop so as not to trip over them. A deep breath before stepping out of the shop, armed still with only my knife. I took my time observing the area. While not immediately visible, I felt it was still nearby. I quickly spun around and gazed up at a tall building beside the shop and caught sight of a blur falling toward me.

I altered time and crouched down, just avoiding its arms as they moved to wrap around me. Trapped between its front legs, I sliced at its lower abdomen. The creature gurgled a roar as it stood on its four hind legs. I rolled from out beneath it, just as it landed its forelegs back against the ground. In the blink of an eye, it reached behind its back and planted its weapon's glowing head into the ground. The light from the weapon dimly illuminated its face, enough to see its jagged teeth. The top of its head had three broad, flat corners. Its lack of lips seemed to give it a natural grinning expression. Broad, edged bones seeped out from its skin at the elbows, shoulders, and from the back of the head, down the upper back. Serving almost as built-in body armor.

A series of shots disrupted our stare as Lara rushed to my aid. A few of them penetrated the thing's side, but hardly seemed to faze it. The creature proceeded to plant its pegged limbs into the ground with such force that it outlined a crack in the road. I charged the thing while it was distracted. The creature jumped and twirled, prying a boulder of basalt rock from the ground. I halted, in awe of this display. As the thing rotated, it jabbed its glowing weapon at my chest, but I shifted out of the way. Before landing, the creature let go of the boulder with its legs and propelled it at Lara, who dove out of the way.

Landing in a wide stance as the creature reeled its weapon back, Lara sent out a static shock. I looked her way as she'd tossed her splice toward me. Rotating in the air, I reached for the hilt as it landed in my grasp, flicked it to manifest the weapon's blade, and held it horizontal to the creature's second blow. The creature's weapon was like that of a dual pitchfork, with thick arched blades, and the splice's blade moved right through the crevice, halting the weapon where the blades interlinked. They rested inches away from my chest as the creature's superior strength began sliding me backward.

We were at a stalemate, and my arms trembled to keep the blades at bay. The creature arched its back and leaned its face centimeters away from mine, revealing its gory smile. It chortled at me. I flexed my muscles and tightened my grip around the blade as I lifted and twisted the creature's weapon off to the left, dodging right. Sliding the splice out from between the creature's weapon, I swung it around for another blow at the creature's foreleg. The creature bellowed something that I couldn't comprehend, in a language I had never heard. The words chanted across the air, coming in waves, delaying and overlapping.

Lara mounted herself on the creature's back and tried to strangle it, awkwardly, as she avoided the large boney spikes along its spine. With my limited view, I watched as the spikes shifted from left to right and smacked Lara so hard she fell to the side. I rushed forth and thrust the splice toward the creature's waist, but it pounced back. It crept low, standing its ground, its bloody grin just out of sight. The creature mouthed some words and dashed off. Just before it was out of sight, I heard the words it uttered loop in my ears.

"Your sister put up a better fight than this," the creature had said.

XXXI
Unforgettable Faces
(Log)

Second day into the mission, and the morning was awkward. Not for me; I could sense how Kita . . . wasn't intimidated by me, but she seemed reticent. After I'd spelled out each of my circumstances to her. Other than following protocol when we encountered trouble with invaders, she didn't say much to me. Just before we set up camp and the Diazep started wearing off, I decided to break the tension.

"You've been mostly quiet today," I said flatly.

Kita was taken aback, as if she'd been lost in thought, and I'd just pulled her out of it.

"Sorry, sir?" she asked.

"Until this morning, you were quite the conversation starter. Something on your mind?" I asked.

"Oh, uh, yes, you could say that, sir," Kita replied.

"Well? Despite our success today, it won't do for both of us to be preoccupied with our thoughts. So, let's hear it," I said.

"Is that an order, sir?"

"Only, if it must be. I meant it as a genuine interest," I said.

Kita rolled her shoulders.

"Well, in all honesty, sir, I . . . I've been thinking about what you said last night. In that moment, I only meant to express a genuine interest, out of concern for the mission's success. And knowing what I do now, about you, I do not wish to upset you again. As Io-Pac, your focus is as vital to the mission's success as my cooperation is with your command."

I nodded. "I commend you on being so concerned with the mission's success, despite the fact our directive is surely very different from what you're used to when it comes to tracking and finding Skivs," I said, gesturing to the seven we'd found who were walking ahead of us. "Tell me why." Kita considered a moment. She knew the answer, but her body language suggested she was hesitant to be entirely honest with me. "Is it personal?"

Kita shifted her attention to me.

"It may be," she replied. I lowered my chin to her. "My family is somewhere out here, sir."

I tilted my head.

"I thought all relatives of military personnel had priority in receiving shelter within the secure bases," I noted.

"Biological family," Kita corrected. "My biological father gave me up when I was a newborn. He entrusted me into the hands of a family he knew well. From what they told me, he recognized bellicose mannerisms in my mother that could have gotten me killed. Unable to provide for me on his own, my biological father brought me to the purest souls I have ever known on this Galiza. So, when the war came, I was given sanctuary by default, but my family was not. And while I know chances are slim, I am determined to find them with the opportunity your cousin has granted me here."

"That is very honorable," I remarked, as the effects of the Diazep started to wear off. "I appreciate your faith in me, Krollgrum Yatů. But I must level with you, I am not mentally fit to take on the position I have been tasked with. And in the coming days, if the state of my health worsens, I may need someone to take my command. For the sake of the mission. Can I count on you for that?" I asked.

Kita looked over to me, and I could feel her gaze through her helm. She gasped at the implication of my selflessness.

"You can, sir," she said.

"Good," I replied.

***

On the third day, the Diazep didn't invigorate me as much as it had the day before. It was barely enough to recenter my focus . . . for a time. Halfway into the day, Kita and I had to fall back in a skirmish against the invaders. We came across more Skivs, a family, a boy and his parents—at least I assumed they were related. I couldn't really give them too much of my attention once we made contact. It was subtle initially, and I thought I might have just been drowsy the first few times I witnessed squirming appendages extend from their faces. Watched as features of their faces caved into gaping holes.

"Io-Pac? Sir—"

"What?" I cleared my throat, cutting Kita short. "Sorry, my mind drifted off just then."

"The lead commander of his own operation lost his focus?" the father blurted.

I shifted my attention to his face, and through my particle scanners, I could see that his face wasn't a face at all. Coated in squirming tentacles stretching out of gaping holes. I retracted my helmet and saw him with my own eyes—the illusion was gone.

"I didn't get much rest last night. And this is the Jinn-hid's operation; I am only the commanding officer of the troops occupying the city," I said.

The father glanced past me to the seven Skivs at our backs, and shrugged.

"I suppose this war gets to us all then, even you militia," replied the father. "Your Krollgrum was telling us you can get us somewhere safe, take us away from here. Is that true?"

"It's why we're here," I said.

The man looked over to his child and wife; she nodded to him.

"Lead the way then," the man replied.

***

Fourth day into this mission—the Warvs have kept their word in avoiding my troops. Across the board, I'd received reports the invaders were pushing their numbers on my troops ruthlessly, as they found more and more Skivs. Almost seemed to me like a pattern had been developing. First few days we found next to no Skivs, maybe a few Warvs, then all of a sudden, the invaders got on the defensive as we started collecting Skivs. *Curious . . .*

I didn't know what it was, but something about that face in my head had been so persistent that the Diazep ceased in obstructing it from my conscious. Not that it would've made much of a difference that day, since I'd used the last of it the day prior. I'd likely developed a tolerance. Couldn't have been worse timing.

We were meant to remain out in the waste for another day, but I knew I wouldn't last. I barely managed to keep it together as it was. So, I called everyone back to the rendezvous point early. I'd grown anxious and the ever persistent delusions corrupted my mind with an *overwhelming* paranoia. *If I can't lead this mission to its success, I will at least get everyone back to base as safely as possible with the last speck of sanity available to me.* Kita had noticed and she'd taken the liberty of talking with the Skivs we were escorting as conversations came up. She never said anything, but I could tell she was watching over me silently.

"Krollgrum Yatů," I said, as she walked at my side. "I . . . I can't explain why, but my mind has been plagued with . . . horrors and sensations that I can't very well explain. I'm on the brink of losing myself to it, which is why I'm sending us home early."

"Yes, sir—"

"I'm not finished," I said, cutting Kita off. We paused and faced one another. "The time has come for me to hand you command of the mission. I'll inform the others over comms of this. In the event I act out, you are to restrain me no matter the circumstance. You will remain at my side until we return to base, and you are not to let me out of your sight until then. Understood?"

Kita straightened her back and presented the front and back of her hand.

"Yes, sir," she said.

"Thank you."

At the rendezvous point, Skivs roamed harmoniously among their militia liberators. It wasn't vivid at first, but something about the Skivs' naked faces dizzied my conscience. Something in the vague illusion about their faces made my heart skip beats. I nearly collapsed in terror when the tentacle features finally came into focus. I placed my hand on Kita's shoulder for support and she just as quickly held me up.

"Sir, what is it?" Kita asked.

I could barely think of what to say as I licked my snout and breathed heavily.

"Just . . . t-take me somewhere isolated," I said.

"Yes, sir."

She pulled me to my feet and led me toward the crowd. I couldn't help but stumble alongside her, sluggishly.

"Wait, no, no, no," I said, clutching Kita before we got too deep into the crowd. Kita stopped and looked over at me. "Don't take me through there. Go around the crowd, take me into one of the buildings."

"Yes, sir," she replied as we changed our path.

Some noticed my odd behavior, though I doubt they knew who I was behind my armor.

As we wandered inside a nearby building, the manifestation of my fear intensified. I didn't know what I felt so afraid of until a little further when I fell to my knees and grunted loudly.

"Io-Pac Criptous?" exclaimed Kita.

It was then that all the imagery I'd witnessed in that . . . was it an interrogation? It seemed that way in my head, but I couldn't be certain. I remembered not only the face, but everything it had shown me, through just the incitement of fear itself. I clasped my head with my hands. My claws would have drawn blood from my scalp if it weren't for the protection of my helm. I howled tirelessly until my lungs felt sore; no doubt there were many among the troops and Skivs who could hear me. Kita squatted beside me, squeezing my shoulders, shaking me, shouting words I couldn't make sense of. My mind was a war zone of terrors. Finally, I fell limp and the last thing I remember feeling was my body twitching frantically as I passed out.

I woke up lying flat on the ground with a trooper sitting beside me, who I took for Kita. She shifted as she noticed my head turn.

"Io-Pac Criptous?" Kita asked.

"*Mhm*, Krollgrum Yatů," I said; my throat hurt to speak. "Is all well?"

"Uh, yes sir, all is well. You managed to rile the troops and Skivs with your screams. But I gave them assurances before things got out of hand and they stood down."

"Good, have the Fades been called in for evacuation?" I asked.

"Yes, sir, they should be arriving in a few hours."

I sighed with relief.

"Well done, Krollgrum Yatů."

Fatigue quickly weighed over my eyes and even in the comfort of my suit I felt cold, shivering like nothing could warm me.

"You should continue to rest, sir. If you're not awake at the time of the Fades' arrival, I'll see you to them myself."

I gave a subtle nod in reply as I closed my eyes and almost immediately fell back to sleep.

Utter darkness surrounded me. A sound, like a deep exhale of breath, filled my ears, growing louder and louder. I whipped my eyes open to the sound of gunfire. I was so confused; to me it felt like no time had passed at all, as if Kita and I had only just stopped talking. Loud booms echoed across the air and shook the building, making dust fall from overhead.

I sprang up, rushed to a nearby opening in the walls, and observed the battle waging below. At first, I couldn't tell if they were Warvs or Invaders; my QS-25 wasn't activated. I entered a quantum field, ready to join the rumble, but just as I was about to jump out into the street, I caught sight of a large orange ball with a tail shooting toward me. The shot landed just a few feet beside me as I leaped back. The force of impact tossed me across the room and against a wall. *Howling* as pain shot through my back. A ringing filled my ear, and my heart raced with anxiety as I pushed myself off the ground, having to use every bit of strength I had in me to do so. Stumbling forward, I pulled my Gyrat from my back and rushed out. Rolling onto the ground, I fired quick bursts here and there at passing enemies; invaders. Not far from my position, the troops had formed a line around the Skivs, while a select few roamed around the street and inside buildings. Distracted as I was, one of the aliens managed to rush up to me, swiping both of its left-hand claws at my torso. I shifted back, but it still managed to scrape my armor. Unfazed, I pounded the back of my gun against the invader's chin and in just as quick a motion, I pulled the trigger of my Gyrat as I raised my aim up across the creature's body.

(Kita)

I'd witnessed Io-Pac Log Criptous jump down from the building and join the fight. It was no surprise to me; I would have awoken him myself if I hadn't been taking count of our casualties and the Skivs we'd found. The invaders' attack had come from nowhere. Despite the distance that separated us, I still intended to keep my promise and stay by him through the thick of this battle.

Dealing with those who intercepted my path to him, I viewed Io-Pac Criptous take out a handful of invaders with his Gyrat. One faced the Io-Pac in hand-to-hand combat, distracting him from a second invader plummeting overhead. I quickly ran across the walls of a nearby building. As the Io-Pac killed his initial opponent, the falling invader descended just a few feet above the Io-Pac's head. Launching myself from the edge of the building, I collided with the invader before it could land on the Io-Pac, nudging my elbow into its side. Skidding across the ground, the invader and I rushed to our feet in a stumble as I drew and flicked the hilt of my splice, forming its long, rectangular blade. I jumped into the air acrobatically and landed on the invader's shoulders, swiftly moving the edge of my splice across its throat.

I rushed toward the Io-Pac, pulling him to his feet as I ran by, leading him toward the line that protected the Skivs. The Io-Pac yanked away at me, pulling so hard that we collapsed into a pile of rubble. As the Io-Pac grabbed me by the shoulders and shook me, he shouted words that reverberated.

I raised my hands to him and revealed my face. All went black, but the shaking had stopped. I gestured over to my fizer and yelled as loud as I could: "Open a channel, sir."

The Io-Pac looked over to his fizer as I allowed my helm to envelop my head. Then he returned his gaze to me.

"Can you hear me now?" the Io-Pac shouted.

"Loud and clear, sir," I replied.

"I don't want to be taken behind the lines of our troops. If I'm placed too close to the Skivs, I'm afraid something bad will happen. I can't be near them right now."

I didn't quite understand why, but I respected his decision, nonetheless.

"Understood, sir," I said.

"How long till the Fades reach us?"

"They should be arriving any minute, sir."

The Io-Pac looked over the rubble, at the troops that guarded the Skivs, and then among the chaos that surrounded us. I was concerned he might have been overwhelmed by it all; perhaps he was plotting in that moment. Like a snapping twig in a silent forest disturbs unsuspecting prey, he whipped his attention back to me.

"We need to spread out our numbers. Keep the line around the Skivs, but push the troops out. The invaders have sentinels positioned somewhere in these buildings bearing heavy—"

Boom-boom-boom-boom! A set of sizeable explosions hit our line of troops in four separate locations. One of the blasts emitted a shock wave that knocked us down.

(Log)

I slowly pushed myself off the ground. The sound of my heartbeat pulsated in my ears. An inescapable pain buried deep within my right eardrum, so burdensome I clasped my armored ear. The pain persisted and an irritated growl escaped my snout. Mirage waves blurred my vision as I crawled over the rubble, taking in my surroundings, processing them as if it were the first time I had witnessed such horrors—their full embodiment: doppelgangers of the creature with the tentacle face. They were unmoving, facing my direction, no more than twenty paces out. I raised my aim.

"Sir, what—" Kita's voice became distorted as I altered time.

The aquatic-featured monsters remained unfazed as I held them down the sight of my Gyrat and fired, killing two while the many others began to disperse. I noted a third, revealed behind the fallen two. It had the same appearance as the others, only this one was much smaller in size. I was uncertain of myself, but then I realized . . . *Goddess, is that a child?! Am I mistaking the Skivs for—*

Smack! Something hit me hard on the side of my head, enough to knock me on my back and out of my quantum field. Looking up, I saw Kita standing over me. She raised the back of her gun and hit me once again on my forehead. I passed out on impact . . . all was dark, all was silent.

XXXII
Sphike
(Amat)

Final day of the mission—there hadn't been much need to stick around any longer as we had found no additional Skivs. Fortunately, Dukas MgKonnol, Dovan, and Torlen were more successful in collecting our kin from beneath the surface of Ion City. Following the skirmish in the mines, I called in several Fades to take the Skivs we found back to base. Two days ago, we went back down in an attempt to reach that same clearing, but it was caved in at the entrance as well. It still troubles me how the invaders managed to snatch back more than half of the Skivs from me. *But this is a war after all; not every life can be saved. As soldiers, we're burdened with such an impossible task, protecting everyone from the terror of our enemies—the innocents especially. And while often failing to do so, we only manage to protect the perpetrators—those that instigate war and loss altogether.*

The appointed officers and I had all regrouped with our troops for a scheduled recovery from the Fades by midnight. Kyla had requested and managed to recover some additional Skivs earlier in the day. *Might make one or two of the Fades a little crowded, but I won't deny them passage back to base.*

While we waited, I kept myself isolated from most everyone else, looking over the large group of my kin. A firm nudge against my shoulder abruptly pulled me out of my gloom. Acknowledging the soldier, I couldn't say who he was until he spoke.

"How do you do, sir?"

"MgKonnol. What brings you over my way?" I replied, as he took a seat beside me.

"Oh, I just spotted you from afar . . ." Shím said, pointing towards the crowd of people. "Couldn't help but notice you seemed down. Figured you could use some company."

"Truth be told, I'm all alone 'cause I wanted some time to myself."

"Oh, I know, sir," replied Shím, as we looked at one another.

I couldn't see his face, as it was covered by his helm, but I could sense the grin past the armor, through the tone of his voice. When Shím didn't leave, I simply nodded and looked away from him. Shím remained quiet, not seeming the least bit impatient, content with the silence we shared.

"The way you interact with me, at least just now, you seem so familiar to me," I said.

"Familiar, sir?" asked Shím.

"Comfortable, like we have a history," I said.

"Ah, I see. Well, I wouldn't say I know you so well myself, sir. But you know, when I was much younger, little older than a small karn, I vividly remember meeting your father," said Shím.

"My father?" I asked, shifting in my seat.

"Yes, sir, I couldn't have been more than ten years old. My family moved us over, illegally, to Utopion. A few years passed and the I.I.D. caught up with us, prepared to send us back to the Dronomen Isles. As it happens, your uncle ended up serving as our representative in court to remain as citizens, since we'd been here five years already and well planted in the nation by that point. Your uncle fought a good case but the only way to remain in the country was to pay a large sum of money per member in the family, to the sector. Your father attended the final day of the trial and presented the seat of justice with a unit drive. Granting us our citizenship. We spent hours thanking the man for what he had gotten us out of."

I let that soak in my mind for a moment. I could see the whole thing play out as Shím had described it, scene for scene.

"Yep, that sounds like Dad. I know he did that kind of thing for people regularly. It's nice to meet someone he had an impact on, aside from myself and my family."

"Ryne, it's an even greater honor to be serving with his son. Can imagine no better way paying off my debt to him."

"You shouldn't think of it like that; he wouldn't have. Is your family still with you?"

"Yes, sir, always," said Shím.

The way Shím said it made it sound as though they'd passed or maybe been separated, and he didn't know if they were still alive, but were rather with him in spirit.

"Shím, my father worked hard to accomplish the things he did in life. He did a lot for himself, but also did the best he could to pass down his blessings onto others. Like you and your family. I'd hate to see any of it go to waste," I said, looking over at him. "If at any point you'd rather invest yourself in something else, just say the word and I'll discharge you, honorably."

"You mean, of duty, sir?"

I nodded.

"It's a very generous offer, but with the state of the world, what else could I possibly do with my life? Sit around inside a military base, eating that glop they feed us, waiting for this all to blow over? No, I'd rather die on my feet, sir," said Shím.

"Very well. All the same, if there's anything you'd ask of me, don't hesitate," I said.

"Thank you, sir."

I could hear the Fades starting to hover down over us. I stood.

"Let's go home," I said.

Shortly after we boarded the Fades, a female Krollgrum approached me and gave me the count of Skivs we collected from Ion. It was just over fourteen hundred.

I sat beside my troops, with a cluster of Skivs filling the empty space between the line of seats to either side of the Fade's interior. I kept to myself, tried to find peace in the quiet of my mind, forget about those that I couldn't save in that mine. Silence my edgy questions as to what those strange signs meant and what the invaders were doing with our people. Finally, I stood and walked to the cockpit, where I met with Sarak.

"Almeida, if they're still en route to base, can you open a channel to Io-Pac Log, Olson, and Mae Kalbrook's positions?"

"I shall check on Io-Pac Kalbrook and Io-Pac Olson Criptous' statuses, sir, but I saw that Io-Pac Log Criptous returned a day early with his troops," said Sarak.

"He arrived yesterday?" I asked.

"Yes, sir."

"Did you find out why?"

Sarak hesitated as she glanced away from me.

"I think it would be best if you find out on your own, sir. I fear it is not my place to speak on such things."

I sighed a growl. *Log . . . what did you do?*

"Just open a channel to Olson and Mae, then," I said.

"Yes, sir."

I turned around to a screen behind Sarak's seat. After some time, I overheard Sarak talking to someone over comms.

"I have Io-Pac Olson Criptous and Io-Pac Mae Kalbrook on comms for you, sir."

"Put 'em through," I replied.

Moments later, both their faces lit up on either side of the small screen I stood before. I couldn't help but notice that they both looked distraught in their own way. Olson's expression held a certain level of agitation and fervor, whereas Mae seemed more shaken and disconnected. I tilted my head at both of them.

"Olson, Kalbrook, report," I said.

Olson opened his mouth, only to choke on his words, and Mae could only stiffen her back as she bit her lip.

"Not all at once. Olson, shoot," I ordered.

"Ah . . . well . . . I would say the mission in Skergel wasn't as successful as we would have hoped. The city was filled with Warvs at every turn; we were forced into taking submerged routes to get around the city."

"Any invader contacts?" I asked.

"Minimal, if any. The same could be said for the Skivs. But Amat, we found something . . . beyond extraordinary beneath the passages of Skergel," said Olson.

I crossed my arms and shifted my weight.

"I'm listening," I said.

"Just before we were about to surface from the passages, I stumbled upon some frail ground and fell down a wide pit. At the bottom, I discovered something artificial—a ship," said Olson.

"A ship?" Mae and I spoke at the same time.

"A large one, yes. I'd say on par with the invader crafts that darken our skies. Some script along its plating seemed to resemble a name: 'Galican-7, 4, 2, 9.'"

"Did you . . . investigate its interior?" I asked.

"I'm afraid we couldn't. There was no obvious opening, and we didn't have any way of penetrating the plating. Except charges, but I didn't want to risk bringing that cave down on our heads in the process."

I nodded.

"When we return, I'll ask Blick to see what he can find on the name. Galican, was it?"

"Yes, sir."

I nodded.

"In the meantime, I'll work on arranging a mission dedicated to investigating what's inside the ship. Do you think you could find it again when the time comes?" I asked.

"Yes, sir."

"I'll hold you to that then. You're dismissed, Olson."

"Yessir."

Olson left the screen and Mae filled it. Silence fell between us; she still seemed distracted by something.

"Io-Pac Kalbrook?" I asked.

"Yes, sir?" Mae stiffened.

"Would you please report your findings," I said in a calm and tender tone.

"Oh, yes. Um, sorry, sir, I'm just a little distracted by something I encountered on the mission."

"Maybe start with that, then."

Mae seemed taken aback. Not offended, just caught off guard.

"You'd think I was crazy," she said.

"My cousin just told me he found a potential starship beneath the surface of one of the most sacred cities in all Galiza. In the past week and a half, I've heard and considered much that until recently seemed out of the ordinary. I doubt there's anything you could tell me that would make me question your sanity, Mae. I trust you."

The regard put a smile on her face, briefly.

"Thank you, Amat. I don't feel comfortable sharing the details over an open channel. But perhaps when we return to base?"

"Sure," I replied.

"Thank you. Oh, before I forget the count for our recovered Skivs, it's—"

Mae's signal was lost at the sudden rocking of the Fade. I stumbled back but pressed my hands to the ceiling and caught myself.

"Contact! Detecting seventeen, *twenty,* alien aircraft. Initiating defenses," blurted Sarak.

The Fade rocked again. I could hear the cries and screams of the Skivs in the background.

"Where are we hit?" I asked.

Sarak inspected the Fade's damage.

"Lower levels, sir, we've lost our Dailagons, all but two."

I looked out of the cockpit, briefly altering time, naturally, and observed the alien aircraft targeting the lower levels of the other Fades.

I faced Sarak and leaned in by her side.

"How far are we from Y'Gůtsa?" I asked.

"Too far to survive this heat if it persists, sir," replied Sarak.

I took a deep breath and nodded.

"Just keep her flying straight then."

"Yes, sir."

I exited the cockpit and forced my way past the crowd of Skivs till I found Zothra and ordered him to follow me. We rushed to the sublevel of the Fade; gushing wind blew past us from the opening in the plating as we carefully made our way to the two remaining Dailagons docked in the Fade. After entering the cockpits of each, we opened a channel to one another.

"All systems go, dislodging from the Fade," I said.

"Dislodging," said Zothra.

I dropped down into the air but noticed that Zothra failed to fall with me. He cursed and growled as I got the impression something was wrong with his lodge. But by then, I was too preoccupied to concern myself with Zothra's dilemma.

I altered time. Though my natural ability for it seemed to make the Dailagon slightly more durable and agile, the alien craft were still far superior in both. I twirled the diamond-shaped craft as I recovered and responded to the attacking alien presence. A pair zipped by one of the Fades and fired shots at the plating. I quickly fell in behind them and pushed the Dailagon to its limit. I lined up a shot and fired on one of them; the rounds left some damage but did not destroy the craft as both peeled away from each other.

I cursed as they moved out of sight and maneuvered vigorously to keep the damaged craft intact; it lost me entirely before I could align a second shot. My scanners rang and warned me of an incoming threat from above. I eased off the speed and swiftly maneuvered the Dailagon into a forward rotation. It happened so fast, but my perception of it all seemed so slow. When the nose of the Dailagon was facing down towards the ground, I pushed forward on the throttle and once again corkscrewed in a plunge as the alien craft from above shot at me. I pulled up and found myself looping beneath Sarak's Fade, recognizing the same opening and briefly noticed Zothra outside his Dailagon. Doing what, I couldn't say. My eyes widened as the scanners informed me of another lock from the pursuing craft and we were right in line with Zothra's position.

If I let it shoot down this line of sight, it might kill Zothra.

As if it were second nature, I swiftly eased off the speed just slightly, pulled back on the joystick until the nose rotated clear of the Fade, and punched the throttle forward, *powering* ahead. A shock wave from the blast briefly stiffened the joystick.

(Zothra)

I triggered the ejection of my Dailagon from the Fade, but only fell a few feet before the craft jerked to a stop and growled as the straps over my chest pressed tightly. I could see Amat successfully leaving the Fade as my cockpit lit up with yellow flashing lights and rang with sirens.

"Warning, lodge jammed," an automated voice repeated time and time again.

I altered time, opened the canopy, and pushed myself out of the cockpit, careful not to fall forward out of the Dailagon's opening. The harsh winds blowing past seemed to force themselves down my lungs as I looked around for the jam. Behind me, I could hear a sort of metal creaking. I turned around to observe two arms diagonally positioned from each other, refusing to retract from the Dailagon's rear. I altered time and made my way up to the arms at the tail of the Dailagon, positioned myself beneath it, and pressed my legs against it. The arms creaked and raked against the Dailagon's plating as my whole body tensed. Intuition told me to look down at the opening. I saw a Dailagon being pursued by a Zelton Sphike, perfectly in line with me.

If that thing fires, I'm dead.

I reverted my attention back to the arm and pushed up with all my might. The Dailagon made a peculiar maneuver as the Sphike fired. The arms popped out of place and I grabbed onto the falling Dailagon before it could slide under me. Through my interaction with it, the craft and I dropped just slightly faster as we moved closer and closer to the incoming fire. The craft slid out of the opening as the Sphike's shots landed on the Fade. I was alive, but I wouldn't be for long if I didn't get back in the cockpit. The Dailagon was tumbling out of the sky as dead weight. Still moving in altered time, I pulled myself ahead of the falling Dailagon. Letting go of the craft, it fell slower than myself, allowing me to re-enter the cockpit. Now we were moving fast again. I couldn't trouble myself with the canopy or straps, as I had to get the craft's systems up and running. The ground rushed toward me and the city buildings fell past as I finally got the systems active. The engine hummed loudly, and the joystick shook from the opposing force of gravity. A wind picked up from below. *I must have nearly hit rock bottom.* Pulling at the joystick, I slowly rotated the nose of the craft up and charged the throttle forward. Its launch delayed, the Dailagon finally sped forward, back to the skies to join Amat in the fight.

(Amat)

As I propelled forward, I flipped the Dailagon once again to face the alien aircraft. Twirling as we raced toward each other and fired rapidly at one another. Fire from the alien craft grazed my Dailagon once, then twice. My shots flew right past the alien craft until only the smallest gap divided us, and finally I blew it out of the sky, piercing through its blazing wreckage.

The sight of a second Dailagon overhead caught my eye as it chased an alien craft. Drifting around the alien craft in a half circle with the Dailagon's nose aimed up, the Dailagon fired till the enemy craft was no longer aerial.

I guess Zothra made it out after all.

I refocused my attention. An alien craft rose from beneath me and faced me head-on. My perception of everything seemed so slow once again. I eased my speed and tried to maneuver out of its line of sight, but the ends of the craft's guns were already lighting up with green flashes. I ejected from my Dailagon, shooting out of the cockpit as the canopy *whooshed* back. Slowly, the alien craft's green rays hit and obliterated my Dailagon as the thrust beneath my seat tired. Options raced through my mind.

Okay, I can either stay in the seat, deploy my chute, and risk getting gunned down by a passing alien craft. Or I can jump onto that alien craft and take my chances trying to get into it.

Intuition lured my head to the left and I saw another alien craft swooping toward my way.

I'll take the ladder!

Unbuckling my straps, I sprung out of my seat, diving down toward the alien craft that took out my Dailagon. It slowly turned back as I unsheathed my knife. I swung my arm down as the alien craft began speeding onward; the tip piercing and scraping across the plating before the blade finally nestled me to a stop. The speed alone was enough to strain and tug at my arm as the craft danced about the sky. My eyes squinted in the strong wind to keep from tearing up. With my free hand, I reached and gripped the edge of the severed plating so tightly that my fingers bled. Prying and stabbing the knife down into the plating to pull myself forward, I used swift movements to keep from falling off the craft. Edging my grip further up the crevice and stabbing my knife into the plating once again, I hoisted myself closer to the canopy. Reaching the head of the craft, I observed there were, in fact, two crescent-shaped canopies at either side of the craft's front. The pilots persisted in their *riotous* maneuvers, as if the occupants inside knew I was barely holding onto the plating of their craft. Sheathing my knife, I fired into the right-side canopy until it shattered open. In a swinging entry, I crushed the pilot's chest with my feet. The alien in the next seat over to the left quickly whipped out a pistol-like weapon, but I kicked it out of the alien's grasp before it could fire and then launched the toe of my boot into the creature's face. The alien swiftly refocused and *latched* its claws around my leg, pulling me close. Quickly aiming my pistol, I shot twice at it, until its grip loosened and ceased.

Squirming to the left-side cockpit, I pushed the dead alien out of the chair, seating myself in its place. Analyzing the layout of the panel, the only thing that seemed vaguely familiar were two levers with cylindrical grips, parallel to one another. I gripped them and pushed one forward as I pulled the other back, turning the craft to the right. The maneuver was *sharp.*

These controls are sensitive.

I was almost about to open a channel to Zothra and rejoin the fight when I realized: *this side of the cockpit has no firing trigger.* I took a guess at the purpose behind having two cockpits as I turned my head to the right-side cockpit.

Their crafts must be designed for a pilot to fly while the other selects the targets. Curious, but for how fast they move, I suppose it makes sense. I'm gonna need to get a little creative in this.

I regulated time and opened a channel to Zothra.

"Cho'Zai Zothra, come in, this is the Jinn-hid."

"Roger, Jinn-hid, I read you. I saw you deploy from your Dailagon; do you need us to rendezvous back to you?"

"Negative, I've commandeered one of the alien crafts. I managed to latch on shortly after ejecting from my Dailagon. Not that it would be easy to notice, but I'm in the one with a broken canopy on the right side and I can only pilot the craft. The gun triggers are separated from the flight controls in the adjacent cockpit."

Suddenly, a burst of fire from one of the Fades was directed my way and nearly hit me. I growled a curse as I recovered.

"Sir, are you alright?" asked Zothra.

"I'll get back to you, Cho'Zai," I replied.

I quickly opened a channel to Sarak.

"Sarak, come in, this is the Jinn-hid," I said.

"I read you, Jinn-hid," said Sarak.

"I'm sending you a lock on my location. I'm currently inside an alien craft and one of the Fades nearly took me out with it. I need you to tag me as a friendly across all the Fade sensors; do it now."

"Oh?! Uh, yes, sir. Right away."

"Jinn-hid, come in," said Zothra, as I converted the channel back to him.

"I read you, Cho'Zai, what's the count on the alien forces we're facing?"

"Not including the craft you're flying, twelve, from what my scanners tell me, sir."

How do I cut down that number slightly?

"Cho'Zai, I'm sending you a lock on my location. I need you to fly beside me. Even if it's only for a few moments. I want to try something."

"Yes, sir, making my way over to you now."

Zothra fell into a paired formation with me, but nothing happened as a result.

"What should we do now, sir?" Zothra asked as I also contemplated that question.

"Intercept an enemy craft. Do whatever you have to, I'll stay at your side," I said.

"Yes, sir."

Zothra took the lead and I remained at his side. The Cho'Zai fell in behind an alien craft that was supermaneuverable. Yet the Cho'Zai demonstrated no audible hesitation or struggle, over the comms. He gave the impression he was absolutely focused, hugging the craft's trail as if it were his own. We looped beneath and over a Fade, arching high over the battle. It was then that Zothra found his shot. The alien craft dove back down and toward the battle; Zothra took his time before he fired. Only when other passing craft were in sight to see their ally's total obliteration did Zothra fire. Still in formation, Zothra and I recovered.

"Jinn-hid, I'm detecting several alien craft heading after us, sir," said Zothra.

"Good. Break off and retaliate. I can handle myself from here," I replied.

I didn't know how many enemy craft fell in behind me, but judging from the number of green rays that passed me by, I imagined it was the majority that remained. Applying every aerial technique I knew to the controls of the alien craft to weave around every shot, I quickly became an expert out of necessity.

As I gained my bearings and formulated a plan, I stuck to the skies, before eventually luring the chase down toward the city surface below. Keeping to the buildings, hugging their rooftops and corners. The longer I let it go on, the better their aim adapted to my maneuverability. One shot knocked me off course and forced me into a dive toward the street. As I pulled back on the levers, trying to recover in a struggle, I saw my path ahead would culminate in a narrow alleyway.

Perfect.

I positioned my craft sideways and jolted forward through the alley. I couldn't see what followed behind me, but I could hear the rumble of crashing and bursting crafts as the fires lit up the walls beside me. The force of the explosion rocked my craft sideways, forcing it to scrape against the walls as I curved my path back up to the sky. I saw that the firing had stopped from all the Fades and heard no further sounds of conflict. The battle had been won.

XXXIII
Orphaned
(Amat)

As I piloted the alien craft back to Y'Gůtsa under guard of the Fades, my mind endlessly nagged me with presumptions of the news I would soon discover about Log. I wondered if Olson would get there before me and how he would react to it. My only hope was to be disappointed by the fretful assumptions that had addled my brain, because at least then, the reality of the situation wouldn't be as bad as I envisioned it to be in my mind.

When in range, Sarak opened a channel to Y'Gůtsa, informing the base of my status. Everyone observed in awe as a craft of the notorious off-world enemy was gracefully settled within the confines of a human facility. A team of M.I.S.T. personnel was accompanied by a small group of armed Cho'Zai who promptly surrounded the craft. I scoffed at the sight of them.

Do the red eyes really think invaders would be so senseless as to infiltrate a base full of their enemies in this manner?

A gleeful expression from one of the researchers turned my head as I passed her after exiting the craft.

"Ah, what a marvel," she said.

I made to continue on my way, with an awkward expression on my face.

"Jinn-hid," she said.

I stopped.

"Yes?" I asked, quizzically.

"I'm Doctor Rika Rogen," she said, showing me the front and back of her hand. I did her the same courtesy. "Daughter of Xandall Rogen. I believe you two met three years ago, in the second mission to investigate the arrival of the first alien vessel."

"It was more of an extermination. As brief as our time was together, I remember your father well. And I'm aware of his passing. I was sad to hear of it; your father was a man I would have liked to have known better."

Rika gave a grim smile and nodded as if I'd reminded her of the pain Xandall's death brought her.

"I'm sorry, I didn't mean to upset you—"

"No, no it's alright. Taking up after him, sometimes I'm reminded of the things he taught me in military engineering. Almost feels like he's still around me, guiding me through the process."

That made me tilt my head—it almost brought back to mind the dreams I have of my father.

"Curious," I replied. I looked past Rika and saw my family wandering through the hangar. "Well, I should be going. I can see you have other duties to attend to. It was nice to have met you, Rika," I said.

"Likewise, Amat, or Jinn-hid. My apologies, sir."

"It's a rank, Rika, and you're not a soldier. Don't fret over it," I said, walking away.

Approaching my family in the open allowed many a Skiv and soldier alike to recognize and acknowledge me with a salute. I replied in kind as I walked past. Among their faces, I noted Olson's the quickest. He tried to hide it, but I could see through his eyes the torment and concern that rested within them. Much of my family shared the mournful look on their faces. The muscles in my face slackened helplessly as I sensed what was about to unfold.

"What's wrong with Log?"

Olson shook his head.

"Log is an entirely different matter," Olson said.

"What does that mean? What's happened?" I asked.

Olson broke down into tears while Mom came to his side and hugged his shoulder.

"Amat, your Aunt Sally and Uncle Gordon... Olson and Log's parents are dead."

My heart sank as my eyes filled with tears and my legs stumbled back. Sniffling, I looked at Olson, walked to him, and hugged him fiercely.

"I'm sorry," I said, as Olson cried into my shoulder. "I'm sorry."

Olson continued to cry vigorously before his weeping turned into rage.

"I want to kill him, Amat, I want him dead," Olson growled.

I looked Olson in the eyes. There was something there I had never seen in him before. A hate that had been molded much deeper than any ordinary outburst.

"Who?" I asked

"Olson, calm yourself. As much as you may wish it to be true, we can't be sure that it was him. This isn't like your Uncle Bod, where Amat or anyone of us can say for certain who was at fault," my mother said.

"What are you talking about?" I asked.

"A Cho'Zai killed my parents, Amat," said Olson.

A hand slapped itself on my shoulder.

"Sir," a voice said beside me. I turned my attention to Zothra. "I just wanted to say that it was an honor fighting beside you out there."

Olson gave the Cho'Zai a scornful look.

I nodded my head.

"Same to you. Forgive me, Cho'Zai Zothra, but I have personal matters to attend to now. So, if you would please, excuse yourself," I replied.

"Of course, sir. Until our next mission," said Zothra.

Once Zothra was out of earshot, we continued our conversation.

"What was that about?" asked Olson, still holding a furious look on his face.

"It's a long story, I'll tell you later. For now, I need to know which Cho'Zai was involved with Aunt Sally and Uncle Gordon's death?" I asked.

"Roth Amberson is the one who's *killed* them. Blick briefed me on the details; there'd been complaints from the neighbors, and Amberson was sent to inspect the activity. He gets there, finds Mom brutally beaten to death. Dad gets in a frenzy and attacks Amberson, which prompts the Cho'Zai to shoot him in self-defense. And if that wasn't *spiteful enough*, Amberson was decorated for his actions by the Diramal."

I looked at Mom.

"You think that sounds plausible?" I asked.

"I think we shouldn't act rashly, which would include *killing* anyone, especially a Cho'Zai." My mother glanced at Olson, to which he grimaced. "When the Diramal manipulated your father, you wanted to kill him every bit as much as Olson wants to kill this Cho'Zai, but you didn't—"

"Because I couldn't, and I still can't. But, Mom, if I had nothing more to lose and the consequences were anything but extreme, I would march into his office and shoot him dead, *today*," I said. Several eyes turned their gaze on me, but I didn't care. I turned my attention back to Olson. "I'm as eager to move on this as you are, Olson, and we are going to get to the bottom of it. But first, I need to know what has happened to Log."

Olson nodded.

"I'll take you to him," Olson said.

As we started to exit the hangar, I heard Lara and Mae call out my name.

"Lara . . ." I looked over to Olson. "She should know too," I said.

Olson nodded as I made my way over to the girls. My focus was mainly on my sister, though I vaguely noticed Mae's troubled expression. I could hardly concern myself with that right now.

"Amat, is everything alright?" Mae asked once I'd reached her and my sister.

I looked at Mae, and she flinched at my stern stare. I wasn't upset with her, but in that moment, I struggled to contain my rage. Holding back my temper, I shook my head at Mae as I looked at my sister.

"Lara, something's come up. You need to come with me and the others now," I said.

Lara could sense the tension and became worried.

"Why, what's wrong?" Lara asked.

"Now is not the best time or place to discuss it," I said, glancing at Mae.

Mae tilted her head.

"Amat, I don't mean to impose here, but you know you can trust me, right?" Mae slowly reached to grab my hand.

I frowned, then shifted my attention down at Mae's hand and into her eyes.

"Let go of my hand, Mae." Mae slowly looked down as she retracted her grasp. "Lara, go and catch up with the others." I waited for Lara to walk out of earshot. "I don't know what happened in your mind when I made the comment the other day about who you are to me. But right now, I have priorities that supersede *you*. And whatever, *that* was"—I gestured to Mae's hand—"I don't have time for it."

I slowly turned away from Mae and marched off. She rushed to my side.

"No, wait, Amat. I'm sorry, I didn't mean to upset you. I just meant that we're friends. I can see something is off, and I just want to help." I stopped and turned to Mae impatiently. "We are friends, aren't we?"

I sighed.

"There are very few who I consider friends and then there's family. Between the two, the latter comes first, and you aren't in that circle. So don't try helping me, Mae . . ." I leaned in close and whispered, "You can't."

I marched passed Mae, back towards my family, as her eyes started to well up.

"I'm sorry," Mae cried.

"You are *forgiven*." I growled the last word, vexed.

Both my mother and Lara seemed to note that I left Mae upset.

"What was that all about?" my mother asked.

"Nothing. Take me to Log, Olson," I said, marching ahead of the group.

Olson led us all through the infirmary to a room that held Log in isolation and under heavy surveillance. Two guards stood outside and another pair in his room, armed, which made me all the more anxious. There was also a third, a woman who sat at his side, wearing a concerned expression. Log's eyelids were shut and ringed by blue-purple circles, indicative of exhaustion. Whether he had drifted or was sedated, I couldn't say. His skin had a pallor to it; a combination of wet and dried sweat that looked like paste covering his face and neck.

"Who are you?" I asked the woman.

The woman stood promptly at my appearance.

"Jinn-hid . . ." She presented the front and back of her hand to me, while I did her the same courtesy. "I am Kita Yatů, sir. Rank, Krollgrum. Io-Pac Log Criptous paired me with him during the mission. At the end of the fourth day, he gave me command."

I turned my head slightly as I looked at Kita quizzically.

"Why would he give a Krollgrum command of the mission?" Kita opened her mouth to speak, but I stopped her. "Disregard the question. Answer me this instead. I imagine there's a reason for the heavy security presence here, perhaps linked to my cousin's condition?" Kita glanced away and nodded. "So, tell me, how many know the reason he's here like this?"

"I-I'm not sure, sir. I would say those involved with his court-martial, the Diramal, and maybe a handful of others," said Kita.

Court. Martial?! My eyes went wide, and my mouth tightened

"Then that makes the details of his incident a private matter still. You two . . ." I said, gesturing to the two guards at either side of Log's bed. "Out."

"But, sir, we've been charged with keeping Io-Pac Log Criptous detained. In the last few times he's woken up, he's—"

"Io-Pac Olson, Alpha Lara Criptous, and I are also military. We are quite capable of restraining him should Io-Pac Log Criptous prove difficult. I won't say it again," I said, while opening the door for them to leave.

The guards hesitated a moment before marching out. I slammed the door shut behind them and locked it. I walked to the opposite end of Log's bed. Blick seemed a bit surprised that I hadn't asked him to leave.

"Io-Pac?" Lara asked, looking at me.

"That's not important right now, Lara. As for you . . ." I said pointing at Kita. "The only reason you're still here"—I pulled up and chair and sat across from Kita—"is because I assume you have some light you can shed on *why* my cousin is under heavy surveillance, in the infirmary sweating like ice left out in the sun, scheduled for court-martial."

Kita stumbled on her words for a moment before gathering herself. She seemed intimidated by my stare and avoided my eyes, as if she'd gotten the impression I might lash out if she looked at them for too long.

"Well, sir, I don't know all the details, but I've speculated."

"Make sure you tell it all, because once it's said, you're gone too," I replied.

"Amat," my mother blurted sternly.

I shifted my gaze to her. Her stare was the only one that could have cooled my temper in that moment and once it had, I cleared my throat and gestured back to Kita.

"Report, Krollgrum Yatů." I spoke slowly but sternly.

"Yes, sir. I suppose I may have noticed some peculiarities in Io-Pac Log Criptous's behavior as early as the first day. But what was really going on became more apparent by the third day, the day before we returned to base."

"Peculiarities?" I asked.

"Abnormalities, sir. He seemed very distant, spaced out, not in a focused manner. Sometimes we'd start a conversation and right in the middle of it, he'd be walking half asleep, staring at his boots, or dead ahead. In the few times that I saw him without his helm on, he did seem like he was sweating a lot. By the fourth day, it was clear, even in the confinement of his suit, I could see his body shivering. It showed in his attitude as well. He was paranoid; sick. When I asked him how he was feeling on the first day, he confided that many personal matters were on his mind."

I nodded my head as I considered what Kita had said.

"I see, continue."

"Well, sir, as for your question regarding Io-Pac Log Criptous being scheduled for court-martial, it's because during our final conflict with the invaders, Log gunned down a handful of Skivs. Two of them were parents to a child who is now an orphan."

I couldn't believe my ears. My eyes widened and my nostrils flared. I didn't pay any mind to my family's reaction but heard my mom gasp and Lara recite a prayer in a whisper. I pushed myself off my seat, cursing under my breath. Pacing in a circle as I calmed my rage. I stood behind the chair and gripped the rim of the backrest so hard the metal dented. After sighing heavily, I sat back in my seat.

"This might seem a strange question, if the answer is 'no.' But I need to know. Was there, at any point in the mission, a time where you saw my cousin use any sort of devices on himself that would suggest a form of self-injection?" I asked.

"No, sir, I did not. But there were several occasions throughout the course of the mission where the Io-Pac excused himself from me for an extensive period. I assumed he was relieving himself, but he carried a bag with him. And after one of these occasions, he returned with the bag no longer strapped across his shoulder."

Olson sighed as he rubbed his forehead. Blick seemed confused, as did Lia. Lara and Mom wept. I leaned forward and dug my fingers through my hair, scraping my claws across my scalp.

"Shit!" I exclaimed as I sprung up and kicked my chair back. Pacing back and forth with my hands at my waist, I chuckled, amused by how surreal this day was becoming. Forwarding my attention over to Olson, I said: "He's been using again." Gazing down at Log's disgusting, sweat-drenched face, I continued: "You got hooked again, and when I specifically asked you the other day if you had, you said you didn't. Goddess! That's—that's gonna be a wonder to defend in court, which you better damn well hope they don't know about."

Finally, my attention drifted to my family, and I calmed down somewhat after seeing Lia's reactions to my outburst. I sighed, trying to work out how to best proceed, but knew I didn't want my little sister to observe any further.

"Blick, take my mother and Lia out of the room for a moment," I said.

"What? No, we're not going anywhere," my mother said. "Get your hands off me," she growled at Blick.

She marched up to me, grabbed me by the chin, and made our eyes meet.

"What are you about to do?"

I breathed heavily in silence before answering.

"I'm going to wake him up." I spoke just loudly enough for only my mother to hear. "I don't want you or Lia to see what will happen once I do," I said.

"In his current state of mind, Amat? I've never heard you suggest anything so *unwise*."

"He needs to know about his parents, Mom. He needs to know what he's gotten himself into and we need to understand why. The only way we're going to be able to do that is by Waking, Him, Up."

My mother gave a heavy sigh as she let go of my chin and walked toward my little sister, leading her out. Blick followed them outside, glancing back at me with a face full of sorrow before closing the door. I turned back toward Kita, and the next instant, the door opened once again. It was my mother who emerged through it. She leaned back against the wall with her arms crossed.

"Mom, I told you to wait outside with Lia," I said.

"Blick is with her."

"So now suddenly you've grown to trust him?" I asked.

"When Log wakes up, Amat, if you manage to calm him enough to tell him the horrible truths you intend to reveal, he may very well need a motherly presence at his side. He's still only a child, after all."

"He's fifteen," I said.

"That's young enough to need comforting after losing a parent. You should know, you were his age when your father was killed."

I sighed. "Very well," I replied.

I walked over to some cupboards in the room filled with various medications and liquids, pulled out a syringe, and loaded it with adrenaline.

"Olson, come around the other side. Lara, Yatů, get his legs," I said.

Olson stood on Log's left as we pulled back his shirt and revealed his chest.

"Hold his shoulders," I said, pressing my free hand down on his right.

I raised the syringe over my head and pounded it into Log's heart. Log *gasped* as he opened his eyes. He took one glance at Olson and wrenched forward, barking, flailing, resisting.

"Log, Log, Log! Calm down, it's us. Amat, Olson, and Lara," I said.

"Log, calm down. It's alright, we're not going to hurt you." Olson spoke at the same time as me.

Out of the corner of my eye, I saw my mom approaching to intervene. I whipped my head in her direction and raised my hand to her.

"Not yet," I said.

"I can help," she replied.

"It's not safe," I barked.

Suddenly Log's growls were soothed. He still breathed heavily, and his shoulder blades rose off the bedding. I slowly turned my head over to him and saw a hand grasping Log's left. It was Kita's.

"Just when I thought you'd exhausted your use to us," I said. I looked over to Log; he was looking up at the ceiling with crazed eyes. "Log, can you hear me?"

"Log, are you alright?" asked Olson.

Kita leaned in, trying to align herself with Log's sight.

"Log?" Kita spoke.

Log's panting paused. In fact, his entire body ceased to move. Finally, he passed his gaze over us.

I glanced over at Kita with a raised eyebrow.

"It's clear he seems to be more attentive to you, so I'll need you to ask him for the information we require." Kita nodded her head at me. "Ask him what he remembers from the last day of the mission."

"Yes, sir. Log?" Log slowly shifted his eyes over to Kita. "Log, what can you remember from the last day of the mission? What was going through your mind?"

Log blinked repetitively as his chest rose and fell intensely.

"F-faces. The same one . . . everywhere, everywhere," replied Log.

"Whose face, Log?" asked Kita.

"Zz . . . Zz . . ." Log couldn't sound out the name.

I looked over to Kita, but she was just as confused as me. I looked over to Olson who held a puzzled expression on his face, observing Log struggle.

"Any idea what he could be trying to say?" I asked.

"No . . . wait. Considering his behavior began changing after our interrogations with the Diramal's Cho'Zai, he could be trying to name 'Xaizar.' He was the one who took Log in for questioning," said Olson.

I turned to Kita and raised my eyebrows at her to proceed.

"Log? Is it 'Xaizar'? Is that what you're trying to say?"

"Xaizar. M-man with n-no face. *No face,*" said Log.

We all tilted our heads. I sighed as I glanced back over to Olson.

"You said it was in the interrogation that Log met with Xaizar personally?" I asked.

"Yes."

"Ask him about the interrogation; ask him what he saw," I told Kita.

"Log, what did you see when you were alone with Cho'Zai Xaizar?"

"F-face. Took. Off. Face. Tentacles squirming out. Ringing in my ear. Afraid. I'm so afraid." Log's eyes swelled with tears and his voice trembled.

I started to piece some of what Log was saying together. I couldn't very well make sense of his 'no face' statement. But it was clear that my younger cousin saw something in that interrogation that stuck with him; made him paranoid to the point that he killed several innocent Skivs. Now that I understood that much, it was time Log understood what he'd gotten himself into.

"I've heard enough; we get the idea. It's time we tell him what's happened. Krollgrum Yatů," I said.

"Yes, sir," Kita replied. "Log, there's something you need to hear, so listen closely, okay?" Log, still breathing intensely, managed a nod of his head. "On the final day of the mission, during that last fight we had against the invaders, do you remember it?"

Log gasped as he squeezed his eyes shut and tensed momentarily.

"R-r-remember. Yes."

"Just before the Fades arrived, there was a blast that hit the two of us . . . do you remember what happened after that?"

Log took a deep breath.

"Yes. I saw him, his face everywhere."

"Xaizar's face?" asked Kita.

"Yes. Ch . . . Ch . . . child. A child stopped me. Too small to be Xaizar." Log started to cry. "I killed . . . innocents."

Kita gave a sympathetic sigh.

"You did. Log . . . you're going to face a court-martial. Do you understand what that means?" Kita asked.

Log stared blankly, his eyes filled with hopelessness and his jaw dropped.

"I do," said Log.

A moment of silence passed over the room.

"Good. Now, tell him one final thing . . ." As I explained what I would have Kita relay to Log about the death of his parents, my mother walked up to my side and took Log's free hand. Before I noticed it, Log's attention shifted to me.

The Tyrant of Unity

"Amat?" Log said. I paused my speech and acknowledged my younger cousin. "Olson? Aunt Judi? What's going on?"

"Log..." Kita opened her mouth as if to stop me from telling Log about his parents, the look on her face saying it would be too much for him to take. I gave her a silent command through my stare, and she leaned back in her seat as I continued, "I'm... there's no easy way to say this. Seems that way for every subject of today's discussions."

"Say what?" asked Log.

I held a tight grasp around the railing of the bed. It was still all so hard to say aloud.

"Your parents are dead, Log. They were killed while we were away on the mission." I spoke calmly to soften the blow.

His jaw twitched and tensed as his anxiety fled his eyes, replaced with a deep, *deep* dread. They were like tiny lone stars glittering in a thick and despairing darkness. His body seemed to deflate. Log leaned over into his older brother as Olson cradled his head and shed some tears himself.

"Oh... no... no, Goddess!" Log wept.

Log continued to cry and wail for a time. I couldn't help but think how I'd never seen my younger cousin so... broken. Not just in his mourning, but that, combined with his state of mind, made him seem so fragile. All I could hope to do was be there to help rejuvenate his strength. Finally, Log settled.

"How? How did it happen?" Log asked, looking back at me.

I looked over to Olson before answering.

"We don't know the truth for certain. But we know that a Cho'Zai by the name of Roth Amberson was involved. He was made to look like a hero in a situation where your father allegedly lashed out in a severe outburst and killed your mother. Amberson acted in self-defense by shooting your father dead," I said.

Log's face turned pink as he tensed his body.

"That sounds like a filthy load of—"

"Ow!" Kita blurted as she pulled her hand away from Log's crushing grasp. I don't think he was entirely aware that she was holding it.

Log shifted his attention to Kita, as if noticing her for the first time.

"Krollgrum Yatů. *Uh*... forgive me, I didn't mean to harm you."

Kita collected herself and calmly replied, "It's alright, Io-Pac." She looked over at me and I gestured for her to leave. "Well, I should be going. This is family business, after all."

My mother gently touched Kita's arm as she walked past and whispered some words of gratitude to her. Once Kita left the room, I couldn't help but notice that Log appeared embarrassed. But regardless of what he felt about Kita, we had more important things to discuss.

"As I was saying, we know Amberson was involved. Olson and I can agree that the next move should be to find out the truth about what really happened. Which starts with finding the Cho'Zai."

Log nodded. "How soon can I leave with you?" he asked.

"Amat," my mother broke in, "he's in no condition to join you in whatever mission you're going to carry out."

"I never said he was coming along," I replied.

"Excuse me," said Log.

I turned my attention back to Log.

"Were it any other circumstance, Log, I wouldn't deny you this," I said. "But you are scheduled for court-martial; you're psychologically unstable and I can't afford the risk of you jeopardizing this investigation Olson, Lara, and I will be undertaking."

Olson looked as though he wanted to argue in Log's defense, but after a moment's reflection, he too could see that Log was a liability.

"You can't do that to me. You can't tell me that my parents are dead, reveal that they might have been murdered, and say you'll investigate their deaths, only to leave me out of it," said Log.

"I told you what you needed to know, and asked you questions that we needed answers to. We're done now. Olson said it himself, earlier, you are an entirely different matter from your parents, Log. If you want to see justice for them, you will have to stay out of it. In the meantime, I need you to get yourself on the mend in all ways that need mending. Do I make myself clear?" I asked.

Log growled before answering.

"Yes, sir," he replied begrudgingly.

I turned to my mother.

"Will you stay with him?" I asked.

"I will."

"I'll have Blick and Lia join you. Olson, Lara, let's go," I said.

I walked out of the room, allowing the guards to return to their positions, and ordered Blick to continue looking after my family.

"I'll guard them with my life, you have my word," replied Blick.

I hesitated before replying.

"I trust that you will."

It was hard to admit, but I meant it. And I saw the effect it left on Blick.

"If I'd known what would have happened to Olson and Log's parents, I would have checked—"

I raised my hand to Blick.

"No. That was not your fault, so don't apologize for it," I said.

"I could have done more, still," Blick persisted.

"Did you check in on them as often as you could, in the time leading up to their deaths?" I asked.

"In the time that you charged me with watching over your family, I was only allowed time for one inspection of your aunt and uncle. Just before they died, I suspect."

"Then you did all that was asked of you. That is enough," I replied.

"Thank you, sir." Blick kept his head hung low, ashamed. Perhaps burdened with feeling some amount of responsibility for the incident, as if he could have stopped it.

I nodded my head.

"Go on, resume your duties." I gestured at the door to Log's room.

Before leaving the med bay entirely, Olson, Lara, and I made a stop at the regenerators, and I extracted some more nanites.

XXXIV
Anua's Hidden Child
(Amat)

Olson and Lara accompanied me to my office to form a sample of my serum.

"What should we do while that prepares itself?" Lara asked after I'd finished writing the code to reprogram the nanites on my computer.

"Let's go to my quarters," I replied.

When we reached my quarters, I walked promptly up to my AI computer and asked it a question.

"Computer, do a search for Cho'Zai Roth Amberson. I want to know his current location."

"Searching for Roth Amberson . . . failure to locate Cho'Zai Roth Amberson on the premises of base Y'Gůtsa," replied the computer.

"Does Cho'Zai Roth Amberson reside in a different base?" I asked.

"Searching . . . access denied. Failure to locate Cho'Zai Roth Amberson."

I crossed my arms and shifted my weight.

"Excuse me. Overwrite, by request of Jinn-hid Amat Luciph Criptous," I said.

"Access denied. Failure to locate Cho'Zai Roth Amberson."

"Let me try," said Olson, as he stepped before the AI screen. "Computer, this is Io-Pac Olson Criptous requesting access to the location of Cho'Zai Roth Amberson."

"Searching . . . access denied. Failure to locate Cho'Zai Roth Amberson."

Olson looked back at me.

"Did you update my status in the system?" asked Olson.

"I did, but there's no reason why it shouldn't recognize my authority and grant my request," I said. "Not that there was any question of it beforehand, but it's certainly safe to say that the Diramal was involved with the event. And he made damn sure we wouldn't be able to gain easy access to the trail once we found out."

"Let me try," Lara said, stepping forward.

The same result.

"What other options does that leave us with then? Should we just start wandering the base in hopes of bumping into the man?" asked Lara.

I sighed as I thought of an alternative but risky plan.

"I have one other idea," I said, as I eased Lara out of the way of the AI screen. "Computer, give me the location of Io-Pac Mae Kalbrook's quarters," I said.

***

I hesitated before knocking on Mae's door. Not because I was worried about a likely outburst, but because I dreaded the thought that we wouldn't find Amberson in good enough time if she refused to cooperate. Finally, I took a deep breath and knocked on her door; moments later, her voice sounded on the speaker just beside it.

"Who is it?" Mae asked.

"Mae . . . it's Amat," I replied.

"Amat? What do you want?" She sounded surprised at first, but her tone quickly shifted to irritation.

"I need your help with something."

"My help? You expect me to give you that after what you said to me earlier in the launch bay?!" blurted Mae.

"I know it's improper of me to ask something of you right now, but I wouldn't have come unless I could solve this any other way," I said.

"Since when has that been a problem for you?"

"What?" I replied.

"Being on your own, shutting people out?" I cursed, lightly banging my head against the door, growling as Mae went on. "That's one thing, but acting like you're opening up and then completely shooting me down is beyond insulting. You made it clear you don't need me and I'm sure it will stay that way even after I help you."

I banged the side of my fist against her door.

"Damn it, Mae, my aunt and uncle have just been *murdered* by a Cho'Zai while we were away on the mission. My clearance has been deemed inadequate for finding the bastard. My younger cousin is in a state of paranoia, withdrawal, and is due for court-martial. I *need* your help!" I barked.

I breathed heavily and pressed my hands against the walls on either side of the door. Silence . . . then the door opened. I raised my head and there she was, holding a skeptical expression on her face. She looked me up and down, passing her glance over Lara and Olson before inviting us in. As I walked past her, I gave a sigh of relief and nodded respectfully. Mae nodded back.

"Alright, let's get it over with. What do you need from me?" she asked after the door closed behind us.

"I just need you to look up his name, Roth Amberson, and find his quarters for me," I replied.

"That's it? Then you're gone?"

"Then I'm gone," I said.

Mae marched promptly to her AI console.

"Computer, give me the location of Cho'Zai Roth Amberson's quarters, by request of Io-Pac Mae Kalbrook."

"Searching . . . there are no profiled Cho'Zai in Base Y'Gůtsa with that name." I clenched my fist in a fiery rage that was about to burst until I heard what the computer said next. "But there is a Cho'Zai Kroth, located in quarters 'KL,' one-eight-seven. Is this the Cho'Zai you meant?"

Mae looked back over to me.

"It very well could be," said Mae.

"Kroth, that's a peculiar name," said Olson.

"The peculiarity of his name is a matter for another day. What's important is that we have what we need," I said.

"Maybe, assuming he did kill your mother and father"—Mae gestured to Olson—"your aunt and uncle. He might have been issued a different name to further conceal his identity and whereabouts."

"It's a likely scenario," Olson said.

I stood up straight and faced my family.

"Olson, Lara, would you give me and Mae a moment in private? I'll join you both outside shortly," I asked.

Lara and Olson shared a glance, then looked at me. I raised my eyebrows at them.

"Sure," Lara replied. "We'll be waiting outside."

Lara gave me a knowing smile as she turned her head and left with Olson. When we were alone, I faced Mae. She avoided my gaze.

"Thank you for this." I spoke tenderly.

"Yeah sure, no problem," Mae replied in an insincere tone.

"Not to use it as an excuse, but the last time we spoke, I was overwhelmed with a lot of bad news I'd just received. I just want you to know the way I reacted was not your fault." Mae did not respond and continued to ignore my eyes. "Hey," I whispered, lightly lifting her chin with my finger.

Our eyes locked, staring deep into the contents of our souls. An unspoken truth was shared between us and the next moment, our snouts met. The intimacy took my mind into the clouds, casting from it all that was wrong in the world. I looked into her eyes once again. Mae glowed with an aura I hadn't seen since perhaps the first day we met, if that. Her face lit up, her whiskers seemed to complete her, her hair glistened smoothly, and her eyes sparkled with passion. Mae took a stumbling step forward as I walked away from her.

"*Uh* . . . can we talk later?" Mae blurted, before the door to her quarters opened for me.

I paused and twisted toward her. "We may. If not today, soon," I said.

With that, I left to rejoin Olson and Lara. Lara had a prying look on her face.

"I imagine that went better than expected for you," she said.

"What are you talking about?" I asked.

"The secluded moment you requested with Mae." Lara giggled.

"That's my business."

Lara opened her mouth to say something else but cleared her throat and held her tongue instead. I turned to Olson and observed his amused smirk.

"What's got you in a good mood all of the sudden?" I asked.

Olson shook his head.

"Nothing, I'm just happy for you," Olson replied.

"I should say, we both are," Lara butted in.

"Why?" I asked.

"You're opening up, Amat. That's a good thing," Olson said.

We walked back to my office to collect the serum, sure that by the time we reached it, it would be ready.

XXXV
Breaking The Unbreaking
(Amat)

With the serum on hand, we gathered all we required at the base armory and walked to Cho'Zai Kroth's quarters. There was a pad beside the door, and it asked for thumbprint identification to access the quarters. I pressed my thumb on it, stating my name and rank as it scanned. The pad processed my identification and denied me access. I growled deeply. Popping the strap away, whipping my arm around, I fired my pistol and destroyed the pad. I looked over to Olson and Lara. Olson bore a confused expression on his face, whereas Lara's held a semi-impressed one.

"I'm getting a little tired of this crap," I said.

Olson and I pressed our hands against the door and forcefully slid it open. Olson and Lara swiftly armed themselves and took in the state of the very spacious quarters before entering. I scoffed.

Strange, I didn't think anyone could make their quarters messier than Log made his the other day.

We cautiously dispersed into different sections of the quarters and I wandered to a corner of the room on my own, inspecting all the clutter on the ground. Then moved to a room that, to my surprise, was filled with a variety of different torture weapons.

"Well, even if we don't have the right guy here, we've certainly caught a creep," Lara said from where she was.

I rummaged through all the devices, finding a 'muter,' a device that strains your vocal cords to the point that you cannot speak or scream. There was a wired suit that looked designed to envelop the human body and perhaps shock them in some way. There was even a surgical laser used for both fine cuts and seals in an operation. Before I could recognize anything more, I heard the hammer of a pistol pull back behind me. I froze, unfazed but attentive.

"Turn around slowly," said the man behind the gun.

I did as he instructed and slowly raised my hands to give him extra reassurance. The man seemed confused by the syringe and the color of its contents in my hand.

"What's that?" asked the Cho'Zai. I could tell he was by the color of his eyes.

Since I saw that he hadn't captured Olson or Lara, I played dumb. I assumed they were hiding somewhere in one of the other rooms within the quarters.

"Nothing, just one of your little toys I found on the ground here. Kroth, is it?" I asked as I spotted Lara and Olson carefully making their way behind the Cho'Zai.

"Never seen a serum like that in my life. Plus, drugging my targets isn't exactly how I carry out my duties."

"I don't imagine it is, based on the description I heard of how you left my aunt and uncle a few days back. Which is my business in being here in the first place," I said.

"Huh, how unfortunate this turned out to be for you then. As I suspect you were the one who planned to surprise *me*," replied the Cho'Zai.

"Well, I certainly expected one of us to surprise the other," I said.

Olson got right behind Kroth and pistol-whipped the back of his head, which only seemed to infuriate the Cho'Zai, as he fired a shot without aim. The bullet ricocheted off Lara's armor as the seeps momentarily clenched shut over the edge of her rib, knocking the breath out of her. The Cho'Zai turned toward Olson as my cousin threw another punch at him. He caught Olson's arm and bashed their heads together. Olson fell to the ground as I altered time and sprinted into Kroth, pounding his back against the corner of the doorway. The Cho'Zai looped his arms beneath my chest, just before I was about to reach up with the syringe and tossed me across the room.

Lara recovered, altered time, whipped out her splice, and swung it this way and that at the Cho'Zai. Kroth evaded every blow. I hugged the syringe and protected it as I rolled atop the kitchen counter and hit my back against some cupboards. In their struggle, Kroth managed to grab Lara's blade hand, low, in a downswing, and aimed his gun in her face. Lara swiftly dropped the blade into her other hand and cut the barrel in half, tearing the rest of it out of the Cho'Zai's grasp. The Cho'Zai's hand had been wounded, distracting him. Lara reeled back and pierced the angled top of her splice through the Cho'Zai's shoulder into the wall, pinning him there. I blurted Lara's name just before I threw the syringe at her; my sister's reaction was delayed but timely enough that she caught it sailing towards her and stabbed it into Kroth's neck.

Kroth growled as he slapped Lara to the ground and pried the splice from his shoulder, drowsy. I rushed to my feet as he stumbled toward Lara and made like he was about to strike her with the splice. I crashed into him once again, standing tall this time. Kroth had become so weary that the splice had fallen out of his hand. We pressed against one another. Kroth dug his claws through the seeps of my armor, digging just slightly into my shoulder. With one hand, I grasped and crushed his throat while the other pressed the rest of the serum into his neck. Slowly, his strength faded, even though he was determined to fight with all his vigor before finally passing out. I let him fall to the ground as I pried the needle, then regulated time and checked the Cho'Zai's pulse.

"Is he alive?" Lara asked.

"He is," I replied.

"No, I mean Olson."

I glanced back and we went to Olson's side, whereafter I scanned his body with my helm's hud.

"He'll be alright; we should let him rest for a while though," I said.

"Anua blesses us. Let's restrain Kroth."

"No, I'll handle that. Shots were fired, so check in with the residents of the nearby quarters. Ease their concern, we don't want anyone contacting security," I said.

"What if he wakes up?" Lara asked, gesturing to Kroth.

"Won't happen; I made an adaption to the serum's programming. Part of what those nanites are stimulating in Kroth's brain is his vasovagal reflex. A reaction triggered by low blood pressure that causes the individual to feel faint and pass out. Should keep him under for at least an hour; now go."

"Yes, sir," Lara said.

Lara walked out of Kroth's quarters and shut the door behind her, leaving the room momentarily to check in with the nearby residents.

I cleared the living room of most of the clutter and placed a chair at its center. Trailing back into the room with all the devices, I located some plasma restraints. Dragging Kroth's body into the chair, I locked his wrists behind his back and his calves against the legs. Calibrating the ratio of the Cho'Zai's ankles and wrists, in addition the chair legs to ensure that the restraints would instill a burning sensation at even the slightest flinch made by the Cho'Zai. As I finished, Olson groaned, slowly pushing himself off the ground. My cousin retracted his helm, placed his fingers on a bruise, and winced at the touch.

"Are you alright?" I asked.

Olson peered up at me.

"I'll be fine," Olson said.

Olson walked up beside me and pulled the hammer to his pistol as he aimed it at Kroth's head.

"No!" I barked, as I forced Olson's aim up.

Olson gave me a startled and almost insulted expression.

"I thought we were here to kill him."

"All has been settled with the nearby residents." Lara slowed her sentence as she reentered and noted the gun in Olson's hand. "Why the gun, Olson?"

"It's what the bastard deserves, isn't it?" Olson exclaimed.

"Not yet. First, we question him," I said. Olson still seemed confused. Lara nodded.

"Amat's right. Don't you see, Olson, the opportunity we have here? You pull that trigger now and we kill him without cause in the eyes of the public. We get him to confess, our actions here are justified and more," said Lara.

"If we can get him to admit the Diramal hired him to kill your parents, we can take the Diramal down for conspiring to commit an assassination on civilian residents of the base," I butted in.

"You're thinking we take down two for one, then?" asked Olson. Lara and I nodded. "And what if we can't break him?"

"Then you can finish him off and I'll handle the repercussions," I said.

Olson sighed as he put away his pistol, begrudgingly. He looked over at Kroth.

"Can we wake him up?" Olson asked.

"We shouldn't. Brute force inflicted on him might keep him knocked out longer than the nanites' programming. But he'll come out of it, shortly. In the meantime, we wait, *patiently*," I told Olson.

Olson made his way to find a seat on some furniture, impatiently kicking some clutter out of the way. Lara remained by the door. I grabbed a chair and sat in front of the Cho'Zai, keeping an eye on him. I wanted my face to be the first thing that greeted his waking. I wanted him to fear my intent, to know that his time in this life would soon come to an end.

Within forty-five minutes, Kroth finally coughed and cracked his eyes open, raising his head to me. Olson stood promptly from his seat. Lara came to his side and placed her hand on his shoulder to calm his eagerness. They shared a nod as Olson shrugged Lara's grasp off.

"About time," said Olson.

The Cho'Zai, still overwhelmed and disoriented, struggled to open his eyes wide and as he collected himself, he could only seem to keep them squinted. Wincing as the he pulled far enough from his restraints to momentarily *sizzle* his flesh. I looked down at my fizer and activated a mechanism on it. Then I slowly stood and reached my hand around the back of Kroth's head, grasping and jerking at his fur.

"Look at me," I growled, as the Cho'Zai panted. "You know who I am?"

The Cho'Zai laughed hysterically, despite his suffering.

"I knew you from the moment I set eyes on you. I knew there'd be no mistaking you when I saw my door had been forcefully opened. You're that fatherless Criptous bastard," replied Kroth.

I tilted my head. I wasn't insulted, merely curious about what prompted the insult. Yet there was something mischievous in the Cho'Zai's eyes, as if he knew something about me that I did not.

"You'd dare say such things to the Jinn-hid—"

I raised my hand to Lara, cutting her short. Looking back at the Cho'Zai, I yanked back on his head as I released my grasp.

"You've got some guts, spitting insults from where you sit, in the presence of those you tore something precious from," I said.

The Cho'Zai sighed, casually rolling his neck.

"If you're referring to that couple I had a run-in with a few days past now, you should know as well as anyone that the husband lashed out and killed his wife; would have done the same to me if I didn't do what I did." The Cho'Zai held a sinister grin as he lowered his face, glancing up at me.

Without hesitation, Olson launched his fist across the Cho'Zai's jaw. Olson grabbed the Cho'Zai by the collar and motioned to hit him again, but Lara pulled him back. I said nothing in reply. Olson had every right to unleash a fraction of his fury at a time until Kroth served his purpose.

"Ooh." The Cho'Zai spat dark blood onto his floor. He slowly moved his eyes to Lara. "Forgot you were here. It's alright little *weija*"—my eyes widened, as did Lara's—"let the pup have at me."

The Cho'Zai laughed again, and I swung my claws across the Cho'Zai's face. Hard enough to leave a few bleeding lashes.

"You'll learn to watch your mouth when you address my sister in the progression of this interrogation," I said.

The Cho'Zai sighed, as he returned his confident gaze to me.

"Your sister, yes, I heard about her." Kroth leaned forward as much as his restraints would let him, focusing his attention on Olson. "You look to be about the same age as the Jinn-hid here, which must make you the older brother. Last I heard, the younger one was being held in captivity at the med bay till he recovers from his own psychological breakdown. Must run in the family."

Olson clenched his hand tightly around the Cho'Zai's neck, his sharp claws pressed tightly against Kroth's skin. All I had to do was say the word and my cousin would have ripped the Cho'Zai's throat out.

"Olson," I said, calmly.

Olson turned his head toward me, and I shook my head. He reluctantly let go. I leaned forward and whispered: "I wouldn't tempt him if I were you. I'm sure he doesn't intend to make your death quick. And since you've already gotten his blood boiling, I wouldn't try stirring hers as well," and gestured to Lara.

The Cho'Zai laughed hysterically again, coughing as he momentarily choked on his own black blood. I was reminded of that peculiarity from the two Cho'Zai who attacked me in the bathroom at the S.E.F. base three years ago and of the Diramal as well when I noted the similar discoloration of his blood. Before I could pay it too much mind, Kroth spoke.

"You think pain and torture frighten me?" The Cho'Zai chuckled. "You think your petty cousin and your stuck-up sister intimidate me? You think you can break me with words?"

"No. Words are just for play. I don't know what breaks you, Cho'Zai. But I will find out," I said.

"Ooh, you really know how to make an interrogation *invigorating*, don't you Jinn-hid?" said the Cho'Zai.

I paused before replying, studying the Cho'Zai's character. I could already tell, from what I'd seen, this interrogation would be a battle of wits.

"Your tone suggests you're confident that you'll find a way out of this. That maybe the Diramal will catch what we're doing here via your neuro-chip's feed and send more of your kind, here, to save the day. But remember that serum Lara here injected you with"—I leaned in close and flicked the edge of my claw against the region Lara had penetrated the Cho'Zai's neck—"right *there*. The serum is of my own making. Liquified nanites programmed to knock you out and dissolve your chip."

The Cho'Zai and I stared at one another in silence.

"Huh, fascinating," Kroth said, unimpressed.

I scoffed.

"You hide your fear well," I said.

"I have no fear to hide. But you, Jinn-hid, oh yes, you have fear you hide exceedingly well. You convert it into rage, which you suppress patiently until you find yourself on the field of battle, killing everything that isn't human," Kroth replied with a fiery look in his eyes.

I pulled away from him and glanced over to Olson. I never liked using torture as a means of getting what I needed, but with Cho'Zai in particular, it seemed the only way to get anything out of them.

"Olson, Lara, why don't you go back to the other room, see if you can find something in there that'll loosen Kroth's cooperation with us," I said.

"Yes, sir," Olson and Lara said in unison.

Still, there was no shift in Kroth's mood, no doubt in his confidence.

"I saw a muter back there, when I went around earlier. Make sure to grab that along with anything else you find," I told Lara. "Wouldn't want to cause a disruption."

Before long, they returned with a variety of different things. I did not intend to use any myself. The suffering Kroth was sure to receive was not mine to give. Lara pressed the muter to Kroth's larynx, where it stuck. The Cho'Zai let out a painful sigh as the muter pulled at the skin surrounding it. Kroth bared his fangs as if he meant to growl; if he did, the muter did not allow it. Olson then grabbed the wired suit and tossed it over the Cho'Zai. A cord extended from it, attached to a remote. Olson pressed one of the buttons, unsure of what it would do and, like shifting magnets, the suit adjusted itself around Kroth's body tightly. The Cho'Zai let out another wheeze of discomfort. The wiring of the suit hugged extremely tightly to Kroth's skin, crushing and weighing down on his body. Its texture looked rough and sharp, so I wasn't surprised at the Cho'Zai's initial discomfort. Olson looked down at the remote and pressed another button. The suit sounded like electricity was running through it, and small streaks of blue current curved and stretched themselves away from the suit as Kroth spasmed in silence. I turned to Olson after a moment.

"Right, you've figured out how it works, now shut it off," I said. Olson's gaze was glued to the Cho'Zai as he jerked and tensed his body.

"Olson!" Lara's shout quickly got his attention and he shut off the suit.

"Do a better job of controlling yourself," I said.

Olson cleared his throat.

"Yes, sir," my cousin replied.

I turned back to the Cho'Zai as he panted heavily. Once he settled, I reached my fingers through the wide gaps in the wiring and removed the muter from Kroth's throat.

"*Hooowwooo*, nothing like a bit of electricity coursing through your nervous system to wake you up in the morning! You should try it yourself, Jinn-hid, might set your mind straight on this whole misperception you have of me," the Cho'Zai said.

"I think I'll pass. Compared to the first two years of the war, I would argue my mind has never been sounder. Getting back on track, let's talk about you and who hired you to do what you did to my aunt and uncle."

The Cho'Zai *tskd* and shook his head.

"Jinn-hid, Jinn-hid, Jinn-hid, we've been over this three times now. Yes, I shot and killed your uncle in *self-defense*. I did nothing to violate your aunt. However . . ." The Cho'Zai slowly stared at Olson. "Were she alive and not with your father, Io-Pac, there may have been a few things I would have liked to try with her." The Cho'Zai grinned sinisterly as he chuckled.

Olson breathed heavily as he looked over at me. I tucked the muter back onto Kroth's throat. Once it latched itself onto his skin and I had backed away, Olson activated the suit once again. The suit hugged tightly at Kroth's flesh once again, without remorse, popping bones and joints as the Cho'Zai shriveled into his seat. Finally, I raised my hand when I'd seen enough. Olson relieved the suit and I removed the muter. Dark shades had manifested on the Cho'Zai's skin to either side of the suit's wires.

I walked around the room while the Cho'Zai caught his breath. On the ground, I found a silencer casually resting in a corner. I walked back up to Olson.

"Take this," I whispered. "If he plays games again, fire, but don't kill him."

"Yessir," Olson said as he took the silencer into his grasp and applied it to his pistol.

Olson kneeled and pressed the barrel of the silencer to the Cho'Zai's knee.

"Ho, as if a shot to the kneecap couldn't be solved with a little trip to the infirmary and time in a regenerator." Olson's finger pressed against the trigger, but I rested my hand on his shoulder before he could fire.

"Who said you'd even have the chance to see the infirmary once we're done with you, Cho'Zai?" I asked.

"I just did," he said.

I turned my back and slowly paced away from the Cho'Zai.

"You know, I'm surprised by you," I said, as I turned back around. "What kind of man can endure so much pain without a crack in his spirit and inflict so much cruelty on others without the slightest bit of remorse?"

"Who ever said I was a 'man,' Jinn-hid?"

"I would not go so far as to call you inhuman; you Cho'Zai were bred for the services you carry out. And I've found there is at least one among you who can find it in himself to make up his own mind on orders he deems unethical," I said.

"Perhaps you don't know him as well as you think, Jinn-hid."

I would have continued this conversation were the circumstances different, but I would not allow the Cho'Zai to lead me astray.

"You have methods and characteristics about yourself, Cho'Zai, which are no doubt beyond barbaric and savage," I said, as I slowly paced back toward him. "But if I were to outright call you a monster or a heartless, cold-blooded brute"—I stopped and stared Kroth down—"it would only empower you further. You *are* just a man, certainly nothing more, but you have great potential to become something far less, if you are not already. You are nothing, no one. You are blessed in the eyes of our kin but in the Mother's, you are a stain on her beloved planet."

The Cho'Zai looked up at me and chuckled.

"Oh, Jinn-hid, if only you knew what I truly was," Kroth replied.

"Enlighten me and I'll spare your knee," I said.

The Cho'Zai let his head fall back, as he smiled up at me.

"Go ahead, do it," he said.

I looked over to the other devices Olson and Lara had laid out, and picked one that looked peculiar. It was a metallic, cylindrical container capped off on one end. A green light streaked down one side of it with a small label below. *Vi-warmigols*, it read. I'd heard of their use during the war with Afeikita—they were a live biological weapon. Their use was made illegal after the effects were deemed extreme and almost impossible to contain. They operated as a sort of parasite, and they'd be released into enemy encampments; often where the wounded and infirm were kept. They enter through any kind of opening they can squirm into on the human anatomy. Within hours of entry, they make their victims delusional and force them to tell the truth when interrogated. But on a larger scale, they also gave rise to a disease, sprouted from the corpses of their victims, which nearly wiped out half the population of Afeikita.

If I use this, we will have to burn Kroth's body as soon as we're done with him. Otherwise, it could lead to a catastrophe for everyone else on the base. No doubt Olson laid this one out as an option.

I didn't like the risks that were involved with this plan, but it seemed the only option in breaking the Cho'Zai. I stood, found some gloves, and placed them on my hands. Walking back to Kroth, I placed the muter over his throat and nodded for Olson to shoot his knee. The Cho'Zai took tense breaths as he looked up at his ceiling and squirmed tightly against his restraints; smoke rising from their burning constraint.

"Step back," I told Olson, as I unraveled the cap to the container. "I'm doing this myself."

I set the cap aside and carefully reached my fingers inside. The Vi-warmigols were sliming and slipping around my grasp as I pulled two out.

"Amat," Lara blurted, once she caught sight of the parasites.

I turned back to meet her fearful gaze.

"Don't worry, we'll take care of it when we're done with him," I said.

I turned back to place *one* of the parasites into Kroth's gushing wound and carefully placed the other back in the container. Lara turned her gaze away in disgust. The Cho'Zai tilted his head and clenched his fists as the Vi-warmigol escaped my sight. I twisted the cap back onto the container.

The Vi-warmigols were each about a quarter inch wide, four to five across. They were purple; their bellies were flat and lighter in color than their rounded backs. They had dozens of small limbs branching out along either side of their bodies, with wide, gaping mouths that encompassed their faces.

I reached to Kroth's throat and removed the muter.

"Ah, a Vi-warmigol, clever, clever, Amat Luciph Criptous. You've won, congratulations. In a matter of hours, perhaps even minutes, I'll be so disoriented that I won't know how to dodge your questions any longer."

"You don't sound the least bit worried," Lara interjected.

"I've no reason to be. At this rate, death is assured and sooner than I would have anticipated. No use doubting the inevitable."

"If we can both agree that the Vi-warmigol will certainly make you compliant with time, tell us what we want to know now. No more games and we'll end this more promptly before you face the worst of it," Lara tried to bargain.

"No!" Olson blurted. I stood and turned to face my cousin. "Lara, the limits of his suffering are not yours to determine."

"Olson, the longer you let this persist, the more he will twist your heart and damage your character," Lara said.

"It's not your parents he killed! Amat, he hasn't suffered nearly enough for what he did to my mother and father. Neither of you saw the bodies, I did. Mom . . . you could hardly recognize her." Olson turned to Kroth as he flailed his gun at him. "I couldn't recognize my own mother!"

Standing tall, I reached my hand out for the gun. Olson hesitated, shifting in his stance and attention from Kroth to me.

"You plan on using that thing again anytime soon, you could end his suffering more abruptly than you'd like. I will give it back when it's time," I said. Olson reluctantly handed me the gun and I stepped closer to him. "We've done more than we should to him. And Lara's right, if you don't allow yourself to let go of what you're feeling as we're going through this, no matter how much pain you inflict on him, it'll never be enough. You'll find yourself becoming worse than he is." I placed my hand behind Olson's neck. "If we become worse than our enemies, we become worse versions of those we despise. We cannot allow ourselves to forget who we are. Someone I looked up to in the earliest years of my life taught me that. Is he still in there somewhere?"

Olson calmed his breath and nodded. I turned back to the Cho'Zai.

"What is your answer, Kroth?" I asked.

Kroth nodded with a sigh.

"I will admit to it. I will admit what you cannot, Jinn-hid. I read the report on the first mission you took to the moon. It stated your father acted . . . cowardly. Mentally unfit to command his squadron and started a three-year war with an alien race, which we currently still find ourselves fighting. All this pain and suffering humanity has endured, Criptous, is your father's doing. You said it yourself, I believe. He. Fired. First. Carrying out such an act could only make one a traitor to his kin, no matter how much good he tried to spread among them beforehand. Your father is surely condemned to walk in the shadow of Anua for all eternity. Never to see the Luminous Paradise."

I stood there, on the edge of being unhinged, as Kroth and I locked eyes. The Cho'Zai grinned at me, hoping, knowing that I would react to his words. They didn't have the same effect on me that the Diramal's sometimes did, forcing me into conformity with his demands. It was merely the fact that this Cho'Zai was desecrating the truth behind my father's loss of sanity and judgement. His innocence of the whole situation on Anua.

But was he, is he truly innocent if he—like the Cho'Zai said—fired first? a foul voice in my head questioned.

My father had the most genuine heart than any other man I've ever known, I argued back.

If he had a genuine heart, he allowed it to be corrupted by his mind, said the voice.

No, the Diramal saw to that. There's no denying what he did to my father in that conference room, I replied.

Then perhaps your father's heart was not as strong as you believe. Perhaps he was weak and susceptible to manipulation. But in that scenario, the Diramal still did not kill your father. If anything, he warned your father of the dangers that would await him and you on that ship, which he was right in saying.

No! I shouted inside my thoughts.

Yes . . . your father is the reason for all that your kin suffer.

No!

"You see it now, don't you, Criptous—"

I altered time and kicked Kroth in the chest. The chair burst apart and the Cho'Zai tensed so hard, part of his wrists were severed from his hands as he shot across the room onto the ground.

"Amat?!" Lara's yell came in a delayed echo.

I ignored Lara. I couldn't control myself and I didn't feel myself. Something or someone had possessed my actions, but I couldn't call myself back enough to put a stop to it. My mind was on autopilot.

I charged up to the Cho'Zai and pounced onto him, whipping my fists relentlessly across his face, growling, howling. Every hit felt like a shock wave pounding off Kroth's face. Finally, I pulled myself out of my altered time state, unholstered my gun, cocked it back, and pressed the barrel tightly against the Cho'Zai's forehead. His face was bloodied and hardly recognizable.

"Amat!" both Olson and Lara cried.

"Stay!" I roared, louder, pointing my finger back at them.

The Cho'Zai sighed as he leaned his head back against the ground. A gory smile grew on his face, and he broke into hysteria once again.

"So, it *is* still within you, all that rage, manifested from all that fear that I mentioned earlier. You fear the truth that you now see; you deny it by lashing out at me and now here we are, at the result of this little game of ours where *I* stand the victor. Now, finally, I'll give you what you want, Criptous. I confess, four days ago, the Diramal gave me the mission of killing Sally and Gordon Criptous. The story about Gordon killing his wife was a cover-up to make the scenario seem plausible. On the contrary, old Gordon Criptous seemed as right as rain when I saw him in his final moments. Shame you and yours couldn't see him that way for yourselves once more."

I raised my hand and slammed the bottom of my gun onto Kroth's head.

"Anua's light, Amat, that's enough. We got what we came—"

"Not yet!" I barked back at Lara. "Why did the Diramal give the order?!"

"Oh no, can't reveal that much to you."

"You'll tell me," I said, pulling the hammer back on the pistol.

"You'll shoot me, more likely," replied Kroth.

"Tell me, or I'll let the Vi-warmigol fester inside you while you still breathe," I said.

"It already does. I probably wouldn't have shared that much with you if it didn't."

"Perhaps you should ask him a more specific question, Amat. He won't know how to avoid it," said Olson.

I nodded.

"Try all you want, Criptous, but bear in mind you haven't broken me on any level yet."

I pressed the barrel more harshly against Kroth's skull.

"Did the Diramal know something about my aunt and uncle before giving you the orders to kill them?" I asked.

Kroth shook his head and remained silent for a moment.

"He might have," replied Kroth, seemingly struggling to hold the words back.

"Were you there when he received this news?" I pressed.

"*Mph . . . mm . . .* yes."

"What did *you* hear?" I asked.

Kroth growled.

"F-f-files, transcripts, recovered from I.I.D. Your uncle . . . was going to pass them down to you."

"What was in the transcripts?" I asked.

"I don't know." Kroth shook his head.

"What were the contents?!" I barked.

Kroth shut his eyes tight as he winced, trying to hold back the answer.

"Something about an encounter . . . between the Diramal and the Z— invaders. During a deep space S.E.F. mission, nearly twenty years ago."

I took a moment to process that.

"The Diramal had a meeting with the invaders?"

"Yes."

"You were about to say something else, before you said the word 'invaders.' You were about to say another name, what was it?"

Kroth mumbled and shook his head from side to side, fighting the urge to cooperate.

"Say it!" I barked.

"Z-Z-Zeltons. The invaders are called Zeltons. But that's . . . that's all I know. All I know."

"No, I'll bet you have the answer to at least one more question—what is the name of the file?" I asked.

Kroth grimaced.

"F-file one, one, seven, nine . . . 'Důlabega quadrant incident.'"

"That's good enough for me," I said, standing up. I pressed a button that deactivated the running mechanism on my fizer. "Olson."

My cousin came to the other side of the Cho'Zai as we lifted him to his feet by the arms. We both grunted at how heavy Kroth was.

"Lead the way, Lara," I said.

"Where are we taking him?" asked Lara.

"To the Diramal," I replied.

XXXVI
Exile
(Amat)

Our way to the Diramal's office was slow on account of Kroth's incapacitated leg. More than halfway there, the Vi-warmigol seemed to be taking a more drastic effect on Kroth's psyche and stamina. By the time we reached the office, the Cho'Zai was speaking gibberish, trembling and shouting at unseen horrors, and the sight of him would put the fear of Anua into any unsuspecting passer-by. Black veins bulged throughout his body, and dirty blood seeped into the whites of his eyes. He was wet to the touch, drenched in his own sweat.

Upon arrival, there were two other Cho'Zai standing guard at the doors of the Diramal's office, who expressed obvious concern at the sight of the four of us. I subtly commanded the others to stay back as I stepped before the Cho'Zai, untroubled by their demeanor.

"Jinn-hid, what do you mean to do with that Cho'Zai?" one of the Cho'Zai asked, a male.

"I've brought him to see the Diramal," I said.

"I don't think so, Criptous. Judging by the condition of that Cho'Zai in your custody, one can only assume the worst. And if the current state of him was your doing, you'd be wise to hand him over to us and turn the other way with your companions," the other Cho'Zai said, a female.

"I wasn't asking," I replied.

The Cho'Zai and I shared menacing stares. She turned her head, armed with a wogue—a spear-like weapon—and knocked its metal in a specific sequence on the door to the Diramal's office. Four more Cho'Zai came marching out. I caught a glimpse of the Diramal between the column of his bodyguards. He stiffened as he caught sight of Kroth. I clenched my fist and bared my fangs as the doors closed.

Taking a few steps back, I hovered my hand over my pistol, and noted the positions of the lights overhead. I took one glance at Olson and Lara.

"Stay close," I said.

Olson and Lara nodded as they enveloped their helms over their heads. I altered time, unholstered my pistol, spun around, and shot out all the lights. My eyes promptly lit the hallway back up for me, as I turned to face the Cho'Zai and fired at one of them, but she somehow managed to dodge the bullets. With my free hand, I pulled out a knife as I ran to meet them. One of the Cho'Zai, armed with a wogue, lunged it at my shoulder. I twisted out of the way of its path, while another came to my side and punched my face into the edge of the blade, which cut around my cheekbone. I took a few steps back as Lara and Olson had met with their own adversaries. The Cho'Zai with the wogue proceeded to swing it at my waist but I arched back and avoided the blow. After pulling myself back up, the second Cho'Zai jumped in the air and extended his leg out toward me, knocking me flat on the ground. Standing over me, the Cho'Zai made to strike a lethal blow, but I stabbed him in the leg.

Looking through the gap between his legs, I saw the Cho'Zai bearing the wogue stepping closer, spinning her weapon round and round. With the knife still in the towering Cho'Zai's leg, I twisted the blade and tore its edge out through the Cho'Zai's calf. The Cho'Zai stumbled back, close and fast enough to the wogue that it cut into him. I rolled away and found my feet. The male Cho'Zai looked up at me as I raised my pistol and fired twice. The female Cho'Zai hit her dead companion aside with the shaft of her wogue as she approached me.

I raised my forearm to her first swing, and as nano-steel scraped against nano-steel, I thrust my knife toward her gut, but she twirled her wogue around and batted my blade away. When I spun around, she reeled back, thrusting her weapon forward. I swiped it away with my knife and pistol-whipped the Cho'Zai. She fell to the ground as I fired my last bullet and killed her.

Turning my head to Lara, I caught the eye of a short-snouted male Cho'Zai who promptly raced toward me and I, him. At the last minute, he ducked and lifted me off the ground, ramming me into the wall, denting it. Looking around, I noted that Olson had already taken down one of the Cho'Zai he faced. Whereas Lara was struggling to fight the scruffy-haired Cho'Zai she was left with, taking a blow to the head so hard she fell to a knee.

I raised my knee into *short snout's* gut and stabbed him in the shoulder blade. The Cho'Zai sprung up so fast that I lost my grip on my blade. We met at eye level and the Cho'Zai clenched his fingers around my neck, pinning me to the wall once again. I growled, witnessing how relentlessly the scruffy Cho'Zai fought against my sister, moving to strike a lethal blow at her.

I pushed back against *short snout*, escaping from his grip only moments before being pinned back against the wall. Lara had rolled out of the way, still using every technique she knew to her advantage. In just as swift a movement, I punched *short snout* in the face and lifted my knees to my chest, launching them forward. The Cho'Zai stumbled back as I fell to the ground. I spent only a brief second to catch my breath, as *short snout* stood ready to face me head-on. We circled one another, charged, and just before we would have collided, I skipped to the side, running against the wall, falling behind *short snout*. I reached over and wrenched my knife from his back and threw it into *scruffy hair's* hamstring, giving Lara the upper hand.

With my back to *short snout*, he collided with me, and we crashed to the ground. The Cho'Zai sat on my back and placed one hand underneath my chin, while the other wrapped around my eyes. Through the cracks of his fingers, I could see a loaded pistol beside a fallen Cho'Zai. I reached for it; the edge of the handle met with my fingertips. Just out of reach. I flicked out the claws of my suit and edged the gun closer to me. The Cho'Zai lifted my head, arching my back as I pulled at his grasp, to no avail. As he yanked me closer to him, I managed to slide the pistol closer to me as well. The Cho'Zai lowered his snout and gnashed his teeth beside my head, as I finally grasped the gun, aimed it back against the Cho'Zai's side, and fired, one, two, three, four times until his grip on my head loosened. I stood, ready to assist Lara, but she was in the process of delivering her final blows to *scruffy hair*. I looked to Olson, who had done the same, and regulated time.

We all took some time to catch our breaths. Olson pressed his weight against his knees as he made his way over to Kroth. Lara leaned against the wall.

"Everyone alright?" I asked.

Olson and Lara nodded.

"Do we still have Kroth?" Lara asked.

Olson kneeled beside the Cho'Zai and felt his pulse.

"Just barely," Olson replied.

"Then let's not waste any more time," I replied.

I took Kroth's arm, and together, Olson and I dragged him through the dark. The Cho'Zai wheezed with every breath. Lara kicked open the doors to the Diramal's office. He eased his way back into his seat as we shoved Kroth before him.

(Log)

A thousand whispers filled my ears; each was somehow equally as clear as the other as I rested in my bed, eyes sealed shut. Simultaneous physical, emotional, and psychological pain coursed through my body and spirit. In a way, I endured a fourth source of pain, one that I could not particularly describe or single out, yet it was there, and it was the worst to endure. It instigated an entirely new type of madness within me, perhaps because it was alien to me. Perhaps it was merely my being overwhelmed with all that had happened? *No*, I thought. *No, this is something entirely different.*

I wondered if the guards noticed my discomfort; I wondered if they were even there. A subconscious attempt to open my eyes. But I didn't even have the strength to do that. The sweat that covered my body like a spread had dried and continued to manifest as it operated more like a paste. At the slightest movements that I could manage, I felt the sheets beneath me tear slightly from my skin. I could feel the heat steaming off my flesh from my fever. It encased me in a cocoon of warmth. I didn't feel like I was in the med bay; I wasn't sure where I was. I didn't feel human. I felt like this slime, this thing, too broken and shattered to be anything.

The whispers cursed and spoke down to me. They convinced me the death of my parents was my fault, that I was a murderer, a psychopath. That I'd let down my brother and my cousin, my whole family. That I was too weak to mend the damage I'd done. That I wasn't needed. I could never be loved again, if I ever was. I always got in everyone's way, including my own. *I can never stand up for myself, let alone anyone else. I deserve to die . . . death, death, DEATH!*

I saw something in the dark stretches of my mind. A skinny, naked, pale body far in the distance, suspended in a pink bubble, curled into a ball. Next, a thick, sticky, brown, shape-shifting substance that appeared from nowhere. Emanating sounds of smacking and squishing as it shifted in shape. I couldn't behold the entirety of its appearance, as I only had a few moments to observe it before returning to the sickly individual. He was closer to me this time, or perhaps I to him. The echo of his faint weeping drifted across the air. My vision once again engulfed by the shifting, ominous brown mass. The sight of it ailed me with a deep sickness in my heart . . . no, my soul. Snapping back to the pale, hairless being, who continued his cry, hovering closer to me. A faint waterfall sounded in the distance. There was no sign of water anywhere, just me, this person, and the shadow that engulfed us. Yet the sound of the running water indicated to me the imminent arrival of something. Confronted with the brown mass again, this time accompanied by many dimmed screams and cries; its movement seemed to mold all the shouts together. I could feel every single one of their pains and agonies added to my own burdens. The naked being reappeared—now he was right in front of me. The sound of the falling water was louder, and the man's cries seemed to echo throughout the void. My shoulders were heavy; invisible weights dragged them down. I was met with the brown mass; the screams were gruesome and filled with a wrath that felt directed at me. I had never sensed so much hatred. If there was ever a place worse than the shadow of Anua, this was it. It was a trap, a trap of my own suffering; a place where I could never hope to see the light of day or the next life, ever. I would remain here, stuck forever. It was truly a fate worse than death to be condemned here, and much of its terrors were indescribable. Once again, I was met with the shivering, pale man. I rested on the ground as he hovered above me. We were face to face and I recognized his as my own. He wept so powerfully that as his tears fell on my face, each one felt like the pour of a heavy waterfall, crashing against rocks with such force that would make the *world* tremble.

Overwhelmed, I couldn't help but open my mouth and, with every bit of strength I had in me, let out a spastic cry. My eyes cracked open; it hurt to move, but I had to. I had to let out all this pain in whatever capacity I could. I didn't care how ridiculous or disturbing it seemed, I had to fight against the guards' restraints to release my internal torment.

"I'm sorry, I'm sorry, I'M SORRY!" I cried out. "I love you; I love youuuu! Can't I say it to them one last time? Can't I hold them, see them? MOM! DAD!" I howled at the top of my lungs.

My ears pulsed and rang at the frequency my voice had reached. I didn't feel the needle, but I could sense the liquid sedative seeping into my body as I went limp and allowed myself to drift back into my mind.

"How many times does that make tonight?" one of the guards asked.

"I don't know, at least eight would be my guess," the other replied.

The next moment, I was asleep.

(Amat)

The Diramal maintained a calm composure as a tense silence filled the room. My eyes and the Diramal's were locked as I scowled at him. Slowly, the Diramal shifted his attention to the limp Cho'Zai on the ground and back to me.

"Is there a reason you've brought a diseased Cho'Zai before me and assaulted six others, Jinn-hid?" asked the Diramal.

"This one doesn't look familiar to you?" I asked.

The Diramal shook his head.

"The only Cho'Zai I'm truly familiar with are the four that I hold in my closest counsel," replied the Diramal.

"Perhaps a closer look will freshen your memory," I said, walking up to Kroth's head.

I grasped the Cho'Zai by his fur, dragged him up to the Diramal's desk, and set his chin against the edge. Kroth whined as I harshly landed his chin against the table. The Diramal stared plainly at the Cho'Zai.

"No?" I asked.

The Diramal slowly shifted his eyes up at me.

"If that isn't enough, then this will most certainly do it justice," I said, as I walked beside the Diramal in his seat.

"What are you doing?"

Without replying, I activated the base's intercom. The Diramal reached his hand over to stop me, but Olson and Lara had dashed to his side and held down his arms. The Diramal growled at their restraint. I proceeded to press a few buttons on my fizer and held it up to the intercom. It played back a recording of Kroth's confession to having been issued orders for my aunt and uncle's assassination. The Diramal's hand clenched into a fist as I paused the recording.

"All residents of Y'Gûtsa, that was a testimony by Cho'Zai Kroth, otherwise known as Roth Amberson, who was reported to have stopped a 'disturbance' in the quarters of Sally and Gordon Criptous. But as you just heard for yourselves, he was under orders to assassinate them, by our beloved Diramal. Perhaps our great leader would like to share his reasoning behind his decision to cruelly cut short the lives of these innocents and then set into motion a devious coverup," I said.

The Diramal did not hold a menacing expression on his face, yet I sensed he wanted to get away quickly. I slowly reached for my knife while we locked eyes. In a swift movement, the Diramal pried his arms free from Olson and Lara's grasps, standing tall and throwing them back against the wall. I altered time and raised my blade over my shoulder. The Diramal grabbed my wrist with one hand and with the other, he wrapped his fingers around my throat, lifting me into a wall. I bared my fangs and tried pulling away from the Diramal's grasp at my throat, but he was too strong. Oddly, his grip was not suffocating.

A flood of whispers drew my eyes to his; overlapping in my head until I finally heard them with clarity: *Don't think you've won, Criptous. Our war is far from over.*

The voices were nauseating, and even though I heard the Diramal speak those words, clearly as any normal conversation, there was another voice whispering in the background, in another language…

In the blink of an eye, a shot was fired and the Diramal fled the room. I regulated time, and a bullet penetrated the wall behind me, close to my head as a growled yell was cut short. Lara had stopped just before me. I raised my head and saw her, frozen in a pose, the edge of her splice resting inches away from my scalp. Her eyes filled with dread at the thought of what would have happened if she followed through with her swing. Steadily, I lowered her arm and stood, putting my sister at ease.

"He's gone," Olson said, his gun still in his grasp. Both Lara and I looked to him. "The Diramal."

The Tyrant of Unity

"Regrettably, yes," I said, gracefully moving my sister aside as I walked to the center of the room.

I walked over and sat in the Diramal's chair. With the intercom still active, I continued to speak.

"Residents of base Y'Gůtsa, if you couldn't hear the recent commotion clearly, the Diramal lashed out at me and fled his office. As Jinn-hid, I deem his acts of conspiracy worthy of expulsion from office and residency of the base. Unfortunately, seeing as how he's fled the scene, measures will have to be taken to track and capture this traitorous tyrant. Any sighting of him should be reported to a nearby militia representative, apart from the Cho'Zai. Given their involvement in carrying out and concealing treacherous actions by our *former* Diramal, they, too, will be on watch lists and should be deemed unsafe. Efforts will be taken to ensure their discipline and compliance with my authority. Thus . . . at this time, I will take on the duties and responsibilities of the Diramal. I will lead us all to victory over these invaders that have obstructed our world and our great Mother. Criptous, out," I said, cutting the intercom.

I looked over to Olson, who was staring at Kroth, still barely alive, his body swelling. I sighed as I walked beside my cousin and placed my arm on his shoulder. Olson raised his pistol and shot Kroth in the head. We stood in silence, staring at the body.

"Dispose of his corpse and feed it to the furnaces before it rots a disease throughout the base. When you're done report back here, we have much to do," I said.

"I will . . . Diramal Criptous," said Olson.

XXXVII
Shine
(The Diramal)

I'd never heard Y'Gŭtsa so silent; hearing my steps echo through the halls as I strolled past the humans, frozen in time by how deeply I had altered it. Funny, to them, I'm imperceivable as I move through the very fabric of time itself. *I wonder, do I, in this moment, cease to exist? Am I neither here, nor there?*

I have fallen, but not surprisingly. On the contrary, it was to be expected. I knew the repercussions of killing Gordon and Sally Criptous. I did not, however, anticipate how swiftly Amat would discover the truth and how quickly the tides would turn against me. Despite my influence over the humans being stripped, I still have the upper hand. It'll only be a matter of time before Criptous plays into my hands once again.

I found myself strolling into the med bay and I seemed to recall hearing that Log Criptous had found his way in there upon his return to the base. I casually made my way behind the main desk and inspected the rooming list for Log's name.

He resides in room 418.

I tossed the list aside and headed that way. When I reached the door, I found the remainder of Amat's family standing outside of it, with Blick in their company. Two guards stood before the door and two more at Log's bedside, were revealed as I stepped into the room.

Xaizar must have done a real number on you for there to be this much security around you, I thought, as I leaned in close to Log's face.

I reached my hand toward Log, and lightly tapped his cheek with my fingers, stroking my claws lightly down his face. I folded all my fingers back except my index finger, digging it slightly deeper against Log's cheekbone and whipping it across his face. A thin, bleeding cut streaked just below his eye. I pulled back and left the room.

This is a warning to you, Amat, if only you can see it as such. Your whole family is in front of me, and I could snap each of their delicate necks with the push of a finger at each of their chins.

I paused at the sight of Blick once more, reached my hand out toward him, hesitantly, and finally stroked my fingers over his hair, gently.

'Who is he to you? Blick?' I heard Amat's voice echo in my head.

I pulled back my hand and clenched my fist as I made my retreat to speak with Drakkar. I needed to inform him of what had happened and ask what he would have me do next.

When I reached an elevator at the center of the base, I pressed my hand on the door, and extended my quantum field around the elevator itself so that it could move in the same space and time as me. It was the only one that went down to the restricted area in which Drakkar and the items were located. Inside, there was a flat insignia below all the other buttons. I reached into my coat pocket and pulled out an emblem and pressed it to the insignia. A shadow crept over the insignia as the elevator doors closed and I was carried down through the depths of the base.

The doors opened to a different pair of Cho'Zai than the ones who had greeted me before. A man and a woman at either side of the door could not perceive me within the dimension I walked. I entered the doors across the hall and sighed before placing my hand over the large scale. After closing my eyes, my hand trembled as I was taken, consciously, into Drakkar's domain.

For a moment, I was truly nowhere, between my body and the world I crossed into. It's cold there, dark, entrapped in utter silence. Your mind splits in two there. The presence of the heart cannot embrace the divide into this realm; it is shunned, and the soul is devoured.

A vision of Drakkar's domain burst before my eyes—an endless void, drenched in ankle-high water. I hesitated before stepping aimlessly across the void. Walking further, I noticed the black stretch before me seemed to move; disfigured shapes shifting and molding into one another. I'd never witnessed this before. A few more steps and a grand figure sprouted from all the misshapen entities, twisting and sprouting up over me. It smashed a boulder of a fist before me and then another somewhere far off in the distance. A large head turned outside in from its neck until I was met with a face that had an ever-changing pattern of characteristics to it.

"Diramal," Drakkar bellowed.

"Drakkar," I replied. "I've never witnessed you in such a form."

"I take on many shapes and names, the likes of which even the Hanu combined are unaware. I sense you are . . . *troubled* with the news you bear."

I hesitated before answering, unsure of how Drakkar would respond.

"Amat Luciph Criptous has taken my place of power over the humans. He will soon discover much once he starts prying into our concealed data banks."

"Most of which the boy will not be able to make sense of. You see this as a threat, Diramal? Perhaps you are not as cunning as you seem. I sense you selected the one called Zothra to be our eyes and ears surrounding the boy; how does their trust fare?" Drakkar's voice was meshed with at least half a dozen others, as disfigured entities and peculiarities sprouted and faded from the shadow's form.

"Zothra told me that he feels Amat may not fully trust him, but they have created a sort of mutual respect for one another," I replied.

"That will do for now. So long as he can inform us of what the boy is capable of and his activities, that will suffice, until Amat serves his purpose . . . to us," said Drakkar.

"Yes, Drakkar," I said, lowering my head.

"Fear not, Diramal, the boy will continue in his pursuit to rally his people under his wing and inevitably grow our army, before the Zeltons fulfill their purposes in the *waste* of Galiza. His cousin, Olson, discovered one of the many human vessels that we buried when we dominated their final hidden settlement here. And once we have bound them to our cause, we will do the same to the last three races."

"Yes, Drakkar."

"Do not allow the boy to intimidate you, Diramal; the ones that came before did not. For now, keep to the shadows."

Suddenly, I was cast out of the realm and returned to my body. Gasping for breath as my eyelids whipped open. The racing thump of my heart forced me to hunch over. A gleaming light lured my eyes to the side, followed by the sound of a *strong* beat. I looked over to the sphere that held the shifting gaseous colors, then stepped away and clenched my fist in alarm as the orb illuminated brighter than it was a moment ago. It meant only one thing. Somehow, even on the edge of their greatest doom, the humans were gathering strength.

XXXVIII
Artificial Organism
(Amat)

Zothra stood before me as I sat there in the Diramal's seat. Having not fully embraced the title of Diramal, I was disgusted with it, knowing the shame and scorn it held. Taking the rank and power of my most devious enemy was not something I foresaw when removing him from office.

"Diramal?" Zothra pried, after I'd stared blankly at my new desk for a time.

I glanced up at the Cho'Zai, scooted up, and cleared my throat.

"Cho'Zai Zothra, over the course of the past few days, you've proven to be a valuable . . . soldier. On numerous occasions, you've saved my life, or at the very least, spared me from a great deal of physical pain. But I still can't bring myself to trust you fully; you are, after all, a Cho'Zai."

"Whose loyalty lies solely to the Diramal, sir," replied Zothra.

I scoffed.

"Ah yes, but which one? That is the question that rattles my mind, still," I said.

"To the one in power, sir," Zothra replied.

"Perhaps, but words can only give so much assurance." I stood and walked up to Zothra. "In order for me to fully trust you, to allow you into my circle of inner allies, you will need to prove yourself, for one of your rank."

"And how might I do that, sir?" asked Zothra.

I stiffened and took a deep breath.

"Find the former Diramal and bring him to justice," I said.

There was no break in Zothra's expression, but he did take a moment before replying.

"I'll do my best, Diramal Criptous," Zothra said.

"I'll accept nothing less. Dismissed," I said.

Zothra and I saluted one another and the Cho'Zai left the office.

I sense it would be wise to assume his priority will be to keep the Diramal in hiding. Until he brings me results, I will continue to exercise my suspicion.

Olson opened a channel to me when he started heading back. I had asked Mae and Lara to watch over my family in Blick's place while I held an audience with him and Olson. Before long, they were both present with me, standing side by side.

"Diramal Criptous," Blick said.

"Diramal," said Olson.

"'Sir' will do just fine," I said. "Now, we have much to discuss, the three of us. Blick, you have access to the former Diramal's classified files, yes?"

"Yes, sir," he replied.

"Are you familiar with either of the following: The Důlabega Quadrant Incident and or Galican-7, 4, 2, 9?" I asked.

Blick gave a confused frown as he reflected.

"No, sir."

"I need you to find out for me why these things are relevant. They may be vital to the future of this war. From what Olson told me, he discovered a rather large starship beneath the city of Skergel, bearing the inscription 'Galican-7, 4, 2, 9' on its plating. I want to know, if possible, how it got there, where it came from, and above all else, I need to know if there is more than one."

"Yes, sir," said Blick.

"The Důlabega Quadrant Incident is a report of an apparent dialogue between the former Diramal and the beings we have been at war with over the last three years. We uncovered the file name in our interrogation of the recently deceased Cho'Zai Kroth. He also mentioned it was numbered 1-1-7-9, if that'll assist in its discovery," I said.

"It should, sir," replied Blick.

"Olson, I want you to take a small squadron back to Skergel, properly equipped to investigate the ship. Any M.I.S.T. personnel we have on hand, take them with you, inspect the troops before take-off, and ensure there are no Cho'Zai that accompany you. Once you've breached the shell and secured the interior, report your findings to me," I said.

"Yessir," said Olson.

"You are both dismissed."

Olson and Blick saluted me before leaving the office.

As soon as they left, I accessed the Diramal's computer and prepared a message for all the other active bases across the world, announcing that a new Diramal had assumed power. I relayed orders to each of them, stating that the recovery and salvation of Skivs and Warvs would be our top priority in the coming months while a route off planet was to be arranged. Failure to carry out these orders would not have repercussions; however, should anyone try to stop these plans from proceeding, they would be met with a full retaliation from the Utopian armies.

I'd typed up a pardon and exited the office to see Log in the med bay. Upon arrival, I witnessed Mae sharing a seemingly pleasant conversation with my mother. Lia had fallen asleep beside my mother, as it was already late in the evening. Walking past her, Mae and I shared a glance. I gave a half smile as I nodded in reply.

"Amat?" my mother began. I stopped and turned toward her. "Will you not stop to say hello after all that's happened, share a little with us?"

"When I am done talking with Log, possibly. I have much to see to with the new status I have acquired."

"You can't spare a few minutes for your family?"

"What I must do concerns the safety and well-being of my family, and time is of the essence. Now more than ever. I assume Lara is inside with Log?" I asked.

My mother frowned and nodded. I turned back and entered Log's room, frowning at the sight of the bandage on his left cheek.

"What's that about?" I asked the guards, pointing at Log's bandage.

"We're not sure, sir," said Lara.

"One moment he was just resting in his bed, the next a long scratch manifested on his cheekbone. The cut is not a deep one, however, should patch up in a few days," one of the guards said.

I sighed uncomfortably at the possibility that it might have been the Diramal's doing, to send as a warning. If the guards were Cho'Zai, I might have assumed them, but I doubted a pair of Dukas would risk their hides to violate the cousin of the Diramal, or even if I were still just the Jinn-hid.

"Leave us," I told the Dukas.

"Sir," said one of the Dukas as they exited the room.

I walked up to Log. He still looked awful, but the bags under his eyes had faded slightly.

"Has he gotten any better?" I asked.

"I'm not sure. When he's awake, he still doesn't seem himself," said Lara.

I placed my hand on Log's shoulder, shaking him slightly until his eyes cracked open. He turned his head over to me and tried to lift his hand to his bandage, but his restraints held it down.

"Amat? What's happened? Did you find Amberson?" asked Log.

"'Amberson' turned out to be an alias to keep us from finding him. But we found him, justice was served, and we used what he had to say about your parents against the Diramal. Both Amberson and the Diramal are gone now," I replied.

"Dead?" Log asked.

I shook my head.

"Olson dealt with Kroth, but the Diramal got away. All that matters, presently, is that he no longer holds dominion over our people," Lara added.

I shifted my jaw and sighed. *We would all be better served if he was dead or imprisoned at the very least. The Diramal still has power through the Cho'Zai.*

"Who serves in his place, then?" asked Log.

"You're looking at him," I said.

Log let out a heavy sigh as he nodded.

"How does it feel?" asked Log.

"Uncomfortable, but this is not why I came. We have more important matters to discuss." I lifted my pardon letter to Log and tossed it on his chest. Log glanced at it, confused. "When you are called to attend the court-martial, present that pardon to them, gifted to you by Diramal Criptous."

Log seemed caught off guard as he looked at me, then back to the letter, and sighed with relief.

"Amat . . . I-I don't know what to say—"

"I'm not finished. There's a catch to this that you must agree to fulfill," I interjected, cutting Log short.

"What is it?"

"First and most importantly, you need to get healthy. Until then, you will be deemed unfit for combat and excluded from future missions until I'm satisfied with your temperament. You'll be assigned a counselor and mandatory meetings with this individual."

Lara nodded her head approvingly.

"Yes, sir."

"Lastly, you orphaned a child, a little boy, on your last mission. You will apologize, personally, for your actions, regardless of their context. You will take it upon yourself to see this boy is looked after, whether that be in the form of you taking him into your care"—Lara's eyes widened—"or finding him a home under the care of others, you will carry out one or the other before you return to the field," I said.

Log gulped.

"Amat," broke in Lara, "don't you think that's a little extreme?"

"It may be, but it's a necessary responsibility, dear cousin," I said, shifting my attention back to Log. "That is why I have provided you with a choice; either option carries a heavy burden. Whichever one you choose, this is not a test to reignite my faith in you, but for you, in yourself."

"It seems a big task to take on myself, but one I am certainly responsible for. I will do as you ask, Amat, as best I can," said Log.

"I've seen your best, Log, do better," I said.

"Yes, sir," Log said, lowering his head.

"Now rest, we will talk more later," I said, as I walked out of the room.

"Forgetting something, aren't you?" my mother called as I walked past.

I stopped and walked back.

"And what might that be?" I asked.

My mother raised an eyebrow, and I reluctantly gave my mother a kiss on the forehead, in front of Mae.

"Thank you." My mother's tone was passive.

"Welcome," I replied, as I started to walk away.

"Ahem," my mother blurted.

"*Yes?*" I asked, pausing once again.

"I've been catching up with your friend Mae, here, and she expressed to me that you agreed to talk with her in private about something. She also told me of a coarse conversation you shared earlier. I believe you owe her a specific time and date to discuss a few things, as you said you would."

I turned around to face Mae and wrapped my arms behind my back. Mae looked a little uncomfortable with the situation, yet said nothing.

"Mae, I do recall you mentioning that you had something important you would like to discuss with me, over comms on the Fade. How about we discuss it at fourteen hundred hours?" I asked.

Mae slowly nodded her head, and her eyes brightened.

"That sounds good, Amat, I'd like that," she replied.

"I look forward to it," I said. "Am I dismissed now, Mother?"

"*Mhmm,*" my mother replied. I could sense the smile on her face as I turned around and carried on my way.

I walked to the hangar to inspect the progress on the alien craft I had recovered. It was mostly empty, the hangar, which was no surprise to me. A handful of engineers worked on every other Fade down the line. I didn't see any sign of Olson; I suspect that meant he must have already flown out.

Finally, I found myself standing before the alien craft. Funny, for the first time, I seemed to fully embrace its appearance, observing its resemblance to the invaders themselves. At either side of the front, there were two forward arching arms; the two at the very front were shorter than the ones that paralleled them. At the rear, there were another two arms on either side, arching back. At the top of the craft, there was a spine-like feature stretching all the way down the middle. And of course, two circle-shaped cockpits with a broken canopy on one side that resembled eyes.

Very curious.

At first, it looked as though no one was currently working on the craft, but then I peered a little closer and saw someone inside, through the broken canopy. She seemed so focused on what she was doing I didn't want to disturb her, but the moment after I'd set my eyes on her, she turned her attention to me.

"Oh, Jinn-hid!" I recognized her voice from earlier, but I couldn't quite recall her name.

It's actually . . . well, not that I care enough to correct her.

Drained of the desire to start a conversation with anyone, I started to walk up the column once again.

"Wait!" The young woman banged her head against something. "Ow!" She called me by rank again as she stumbled her way out of the ship, but I didn't stop. She ran up to meet me. I stopped, but not for her. I faced the next ship over, covered in drapes and for good reason. Sometimes I'd visit her in the weeks that came after our crash.

"Do you know what's underneath those cloths?" I asked.

"Yes, of course I do, sir. It's the Peroma."

"That she is," I whispered, pressing my hand against the plating through the drapes. "Lost the left wing, a year and eight days ago. Haven't been able to fly her since."

"You mean you haven't found someone willing to patch her up."

I glanced over at the young woman. Seeing her face, I was certain she was the same girl I'd met earlier, Rogen's daughter, but I couldn't for the life of me recall her first name.

"That too. I'm sorry, I know we met earlier, but remind me of your name."

"Rika Rogen, sir."

She seemed slightly sensitive to the request.

"Rika, right. How goes the inspection on the alien craft?"

"Oh, quite well, sir. We, well, *I've* been learning more and more about the tech behind the craft. How the altered time field that it amplifies differentiates from how the aliens themselves manifest the field."

I faced Rika and crossed my arms.

"Yeah? Enlighten me," I said.

"Well, as you know, sir, and if you don't, I'll say it anyway. The aliens manifest the field through their biology. It's a natural process they conduct in their blood; atoms dividing create a quantum break in space and time around their physiology. But *that*, the ship, it's a non-biological body, it's a mechanism. Thus, the field needs to be conducted and amplified—"

"Through a core engine, I imagine," I broke in.

Rika gave an exhilarated smile.

"Ah, one might think. But to your surprise, you'll find it is something far more sophisticated."

I tilted my head with intrigue.

"Can you show me?" I asked.

Rika nodded.

"Right this way, sir." Rika gestured to the alien craft and then scurried back over into it, enthusiastic as ever.

I walked in behind her. She continued her explanation from the pilot's seat.

"Good, you're here. Now, make sure you can see. I've discovered that this button here seems to be the trigger to put the ship in a quantum field and when we activate it, I noticed something emanating from above, so I removed the plating overhead . . ." Rika pointed above her as I looked up at an empty interior. "And watch what happens."

Rika, with her finger still raised, pressed the button on the panel and the next moment, a teal-colored liquid light filled the opening, followed by the sound of a deep pulse. I stared up, starstruck at the scene.

"Do you see what's at the *heart* of their technology, Jinn-hid Criptous?" asked Rika.

I nodded.

"Yes, I think so. The ship is . . . organic," I replied.

"Well, it's not entirely organic, seeing as how it's not alive. But one might say that it's artificially organic. Thus, imprinting the same, if not a similar process of their own biology into their crafts."

"How soon could you adopt this technology to our craft, say—"

"The Peroma for starters? Could have her repaired and equipped with this tech in a week, sir."

I nodded my head. Wasn't quite where I was going with the conversation, but I liked where it led.

"I'll hold you to that, Rogen. In one week, I'll expect her to be in tip-top shape," I said.

Rika smiled, pleasantly.

"Yes, sir, you can count on me."

XXXIX
First Date
(Amat)

I retreated to my quarters to rest my head, consciously casting into the deepest depths of my mind. It returned me to the void, where five beings hovered above the ankle-high water, four of them radiant, one of them so entrapped in shadow I could hardly perceive it amid the void. But they were there, nonetheless. Each of them staring at me, but between them all, I felt the shadow's gaze pressing on me the hardest.

    I sensed none of them were male or female, but they were, each of them, distinct from one another in presence and hidden appearance. There was one I felt most drawn to. Its light seemed somewhat dimmer than the others, but that was not what pulled me to it. It was a connection, one that seemed to stretch back from a time too far to measure. Coming closer, its light became ever more radiant, to the point that it seemed to be hiding its features. I squinted my eyes at the nauseating light that engulfed it. Before coming face to face with the being, it raised its hand to me. I looked down at its palm, pressing on my chest. I raised my arm slowly to remove its hand. Oddly, the being imitated my motion. I paused before extending our arms to one another. As our fingertips neared, I could sense… knowledge teeming in the back of my mind. Ancient knowledge, long forgotten, concerning…

    I might have discovered exactly what, if I hadn't allowed myself to be distracted by the dark figure down the line. Ominous whispers of words I could not compute filled my ears as the dark figure lured me to it. Unlike the radiant being, as I got closer to the shadow, the more I saw of its features. I was allowed only a split second to process the features of its face before the being vanished into thin air—it was my own.

    Confused, I turned around to find the other four beings lying limp on the ground, deprived of their light completely. Their bodies were decayed and shriveled. I squatted down beside them. It was hard to make out, but there was one that seemed to resemble the remains of my own kin and another of the invaders. The remaining two were more of a mystery. One was insect-like, the other, perhaps wormlike.

I heard a pair of boots stomping themselves in and out of the water that covered the surface. Turning around, I recognized my father and stood to face him.

"Father," I said.

"Amat, it is good to see you once again," he replied as he met me at my side.

"It is good to see you as well."

"Do you recognize any of the beings that lie before you?"

I turned my head to look down at the carcasses once more.

"Two of them, but just barely. But I'm not sure what my interaction with them meant."

"If you were to look deep enough inside yourself, you may find that untrue."

"What is that supposed to mean?"

My father sighed before replying.

"All I can tell you, Amat, is that each of these beings are connected to your past, present, and future. Whether you saw it as such or not, what you witnessed was a testimony to a very possible future. A future that will be of your making. In it, you will face an ancient foe, greater in power and strength, and viler than the Diramal himself. In being unable to comprehend this future, you are blind to it, and if you remain this way, you will be at this foe's mercy."

I shook my head.

"You're not making any sense," I replied.

My father looked down at the bodies in silence, took a few steps away from me, and stood in place of the dark figure.

"When you first witnessed these beings, they were illuminated"—I nodded my head—"yet there was a fifth that stood here, embodied in shadow. You walked up to it and before long, you saw a face. Dare I ask whose it was?"

I hesitated before answering. There was no doubt that I saw my own face imprinted on the dark figure's head, even if it was only a moment's glance. I couldn't say why, but it chilled me to the bone to express it aloud.

"I can't be sure."

"Yes, you can," my father said, turning swiftly back toward me. "Do not fear what signs are presented to you in this place, Amat. If you refuse to acknowledge them, your worst fears about what they could mean will surely come to be."

My father and I stood in silence before he raised a questioning eyebrow and I nodded.

"I saw myself," I replied.

"I see. How did it feel?"

"Strange, I didn't understand it. But I sense that it *is* a warning. But of what? That I'm a threat to myself?"

My father lowered his chin, his stare intense upon me.

"To others?" I asked.

"Is that what your heart tells you?"

There was a subtle sense of confirmation in my gut after my father posed this question.

"I fear it may be. But if that is the case and I am a threat to my own future, what must I do to make sure the worst does not unfold?" I asked.

"Perhaps you would be wise to expand on that question and not think of it in regard to your own future, but as you said earlier, others as well. A great leader is not made for his own sake, Amat, but for the sake of others. You must reach those whom you are meant to guide to the last twinkle of light that shines at the heart of shadow. Do you understand?"

I nodded.

"I will try to. I will pay closer attention when next we meet and out there in the world," I replied.

"Good. It is time we parted, Amat. You must wake up. Wake up."

I opened my eyes to the darkness of my room, sweating slightly. I rubbed my face and walked out of bed to my AI module.

"Computer, what time is it?"

"Current time is 1:17 p.m.," replied the AI.

Almost time to call Mae. I would've hoped I had more time to check in with Olson and Blick, but I did make a promise to Mae.

I stepped away to freshen up and did some chores around my quarters to tidy up. With some time to spare, I called Mae a little early. Something told me that wouldn't be a problem. Her face filled the screen and by her expression, she seemed excited to see me, despite her obvious efforts to hide her emotions.

"Amat, hey, you're a little early."

"Is that a problem?" I asked.

"Oh no, I just wasn't expecting you to call till a little later," said Mae.

"Yeah, well, I ran out of small things to keep myself occupied. I stayed up late last night, then overslept."

"I see. I stayed with your family through the night, mostly talking with your mother. We came back to their quarters early this morning and I slept in the guest bedroom," said Mae.

"I thank you for that, keeping an eye on them. I wouldn't have tasked you with it, if it weren't for . . . well, a lot of things," I said.

"Like your aunt and uncle?"

"Yes," I answered.

"I don't think I expressed my sympathies to you about it earlier. And I'm sorry I was challenging," said Mae.

I nodded.

"It's alright, Mae. I was already upset with something prior to you approaching me; it had nothing to do with you and I shouldn't have been so impatient with you," I replied.

"So... there's no hard feelings?"

I snorted.

"Do you think I would have kissed you if there were?" I asked, smugly.

Mae blushed.

"*Pfft*, you kissed me? Clearly, you've let it go to your head already. I let it happen," Mae said.

"Really?" I asked, unimpressed.

"Were it any other circumstance, I would have had you pinned to the ground the moment your eyes closed," she said.

"You seem confident I wouldn't have seen that coming," I replied.

"You wouldn't know. It's been years since we sparred."

"As I recall, at the graduation party, it was *me* Pac Yondůgůl acknowledged for being the best in our squadron," I said.

"As I recall, it was you who said *I* was as equally skilled an Alpha as you."

"You'd be wrong. You fail to recall I said you were the 'next best' and *perhaps* equally best Alpha in the squadron," I said sarcastically.

Mae rolled her eyes as she smiled.

"Wow, as if that's so much different from what I was saying," Mae replied.

"I'd like to think I just have a memory that serves me well."

"So I see," said Mae.

We shared a smile.

"So, if you're still open to talking about it, what was troubling you from Zoiqua?" I asked.

Mae sighed.

"Well, although I never said it outright, I did lose my sister a little less than a year ago. But . . . I didn't lose her to an invader or a Warv. We'd been separated from our squadron in an ambush; it wasn't clear who the enemy was. My sister found me pinned down in the rubble, passed out. The way she barked at me as I finally woke, it almost seemed as if she'd been trying for hours to shout me back from the dead." Mae gave a nervous chuckle. It was clear she didn't like talking about this subject. "She helped to carry me out of there, but we didn't make it very far before . . . that *thing* found us."

"What do you mean?" I tilted my head, intrigued.

"A creature, but it wasn't alien, Amat. Unless, maybe it was, but it wasn't an invader. I didn't get a good look at it, but I could hear it and it was unlike anything I'd ever heard before. I was too weak to fight, so my sister, she. . ." Mae's jaw was tight as she sniffed. "She put me somewhere safe and out of sight while she fought it. She didn't survive." Mae broke down in tears as I looked at her sympathetically. "I know . . . I know she had some final words that she cried out, but I couldn't hear them over the call of this *monster*. I'm sure she was asking me to help her, but I couldn't gather the strength needed to save her." Mae took a moment to collect herself. "I brought this up because I encountered this creature once again in Zoiqua and this time I saw it, heard it speak, and Amat, it remembered me."

I sighed as I considered all that Mae had shared.

"I'm sorry, Mae, I can only imagine the trauma you must have endured in both those scenarios. Losing your sister and being met once again with the thing that killed her."

"Do you not feel a similar way with the invaders after what they did to your father?" Mae asked.

"The only fear I felt in that scenario was losing my father. After his passing, I had every intention of avenging his death and thus there was no room for fear of my enemy."

"You weren't scared at all, over the course of those few days?"

"Only of losing more of my family than I already had. Though we weren't all the closest at the time, since I'd been away for so long, losing my father reminded me of just how valuable my family is, who they are to me, how they contribute to my life."

Mae's gaze trailed off from me, filled with gloom.

"My sister was the last bit of family I had tied to this world."

"That's not true," I said, as Mae looked at me once more. "You aren't a Criptous, but it's obvious that there are . . . several among us who've taken a liking to you, Mae. There's at least one who's happy to have you in his life and, in essence, I'd say you do have family here, if you'll have us."

A warm smile grew on her face.

"I would need some time to accept this, but the invitation is well appreciated, Amat."

"Of course. You know, you're not the first I've heard tell a story like that. The Skivs refer to the creature you spoke of as a Shadow Scar. Their origins remain a mystery, but there does seem to be more than one."

"That much was revealed to me as well. There was another that Lara and I encountered shortly before we met with the one I just mentioned. We found it feasting on the corpse of an invader."

"I guess that answers the question regarding their relationship with the invaders."

"I know you said you don't know anything about their 'origins,' as you put it, but do you have any sort of hypothesis or suspicions around these Shadow Scars?"

Taking a moment before answering, I reflected on one of my dreams I'd had over a week before. Seeing the columns of humans in capsules, being mutated, experimented on, turned into… what could only be described as monsters.

While it was a dream, much suggests it might have been a premonition of some kind.

"No, I don't. But sometimes it doesn't matter *why* something is, especially something dangerous. Sometimes it just needs to be put to rest so that others can be placed out of harm's way. If I could put a stop to these Shadow Scar or the Invaders tomorrow without ever knowing their purpose or origin, I would be satisfied knowing they would never return."

"So that things could go back to the way they were?"

"So that our kin could be at peace," I replied, nodding. "A global peace. After a crisis like the one we face, I'd trust we'd all be closer than we've ever been. If that day comes, and this war ends and our people can rejoice in dominion over our home once again, would you care to go out together?" Mae's skin somehow grew paler and the depths of her irises glinted with excitement. "Unless, of course, you wouldn't find that appropriate—"

"No-no, I'd gladly go out with you, Amat, when this is all over, the war and such. Despite there being not much to do—"

"There will be everything to do, everything to see, basking in the long-forgotten sunlight for one," I said.

Mae smiled.

"Ever since the invaders darkened our skies, I've thought of nothing but our sun and starlight. The darkness that covers our world is crueler than that of the natural night," said Mae.

"I'd have to admit, I've felt a similar way about Anua. Though I know it would likely be heartbreaking to behold her now, I've missed her gentle light—" I said.

"Amat?" asked Mae, her voice sounding distorted. The display was engulfed with white static. "Amat, you're breaking up."

"Mae?" I asked, as her display was replaced with another figure.

Slowly, a familiar face came into view.

"Congratulations on the promotion . . . Diramal Criptous," said the former Diramal.

I took a moment before replying.

"It's funny, I would acknowledge you, but the only way I've ever known how is by your rank, which you no longer have."

"This is true; shame I still can't reveal my true name to you."

"Scared I'll laugh?"

"You'd become overwhelmed with the knowledge it would grant you."

I tilted my head.

"Interesting of you to hold back something like that. Seeing as how you seize every opportunity you have to overwhelm and wound me," I said.

"Oh, make no mistake, Amat, I have no intention of holding back my fight with you in the slightest. Have you visited your cousin Log recently?" I didn't say anything. "You might have noticed a scar across his left cheekbone—if they didn't already patch it up by the time you got there. Ever stop to wonder how he might have received it?"

"After seeing how you could move like the invaders . . . like me, without a QS-25, I suspected as much from you when I saw the bandages. That aside, I'm more curious as to how you and members of the Cho'Zai are able to alter time without a suit."

"Should you live long enough to see humanity off this planet and escape this war, I've no doubt you'll have all your questions answered. But this is not why I interrupted your quality time with Miss Kalbrook."

"Then why have you?" I asked.

"To show you something. Something that may answer questions or leave you with more. Observe."

The Diramal reached behind his neck, unlacing something. I frowned. I heard a sort of 'zipping' sound as the Diramal pulled his hand up over his head. His skin loosened as though it opened from behind. His face started to deform. Before I could see what else was about to unravel, the base rumbled and the signal was lost. Blue lights illuminated the base and loud sirens sounded. We were under attack.

XL
Hide And Strike
(Amat)

I dashed to the hangar, where soldiers and engineers alike rushed this way and that, prepping and launching Dailagons. The sound of war echoed from the opening at the end of the runway. I found Blick barking orders up and down the column. I called out to him, and we approached one another.

"How bad is it?" I asked.

"Sensors picked up over fifty invader craft hitting Y'Gůtsa."

Fifty?! I blurted in my mind.

"Are they targeting any particular area about the base?" I asked.

The base trembled beneath our feet, nearly knocking both of us off balance.

"As far as I know, 'Z' level seems to be where they're targeting."

"That's impossible. 'Z' level is submerged below ground level."

"We detected multiple unidentified signatures, large in scale, drilling through the surface. We have a team tracking and moving on their position. You should also know that we moved the majority of the Skivs down there, sir."

"Amat!" a woman's voice shouted behind me.

"Diramal Criptous!" a man yelled.

I turned around and saw both Mae and Zothra rushing toward me.

"Io-Pac Kalbrook, what are you doing here?" I asked.

Mae seemed taken aback by my addressing her by rank.

"The base is under attack, sir, I thought it necessary to—"

"No," I said, pulling Mae aside by her arm, away from Zothra.

"Ow, what is wrong with you?!" Mae asked as she wrenched away from me.

"Your duties lie with my family. I gave you the order to protect them. Have you forgotten what I told you not a few minutes ago about how important they are to me?" I asked.

Mae paused before replying.

"No, sir. You were very clear on that."

"Not clear enough. If I was, you wouldn't be standing here. Where are they?" I asked.

"In their quarters, safe."

"They may not be for much longer. There is a second assault en route to the base. The invaders are somehow drilling into the lower levels. If they flood the base, that'll leave many vulnerable, including my family," I said.

Mae nodded.

"I understand. I'll see myself back to them."

"Dismissed, Io-Pac Kalbrook," I said, as I turned briskly back to Blick and Zothra.

When I regrouped with them, I got straight to the point.

"Blick, you seem to be handling things well here in the hangar; can I count on you to lead the defense against the aerial assault?" I asked.

Blick stiffened.

"Yes, sir."

"Step to it then," I said. I turned to Zothra. "You're with me, Cho'Zai."

The way I saw it, if it could be helped, I'd have no intention of any Cho'Zai going rogue under my command. Of course, I couldn't keep all of them constantly under my watch, but if I could keep any under my surveillance, I would and did.

After having made a stop at the base armory, Zothra and I headed straight for 'Z' level, where we met with the defensive front. The hall was completely crowded with civilians and soldiers alike. All the non-militia were eager to gain access to the elevator and ascend into the base before the invaders landed their assault. As I pushed past all the desperate and frightened faces, there were moments where I saw those who were clearly Skivs being shoved aside and cursed at by longer-standing occupants of the base. A frenzy broke out among the crowd and certain members of the civilian and Skiv groups fought like wild beasts, slobber flying, growls, howling, claws scraping, fangs gnawing, blood dripping. I tried shouting over them all and breaking up rumbles where they stirred. Still, the conflict waged. Seeing no other alternative, I unholstered my pistol, aimed it up at the ceiling, and fired two shots. The metal roof rang as the fighting and the screaming dissipated.

"That is enough!" I barked. "We are all human here, Skiv, civilian, Warv or otherwise. I do not care. The ferocity I just witnessed here disgusts me. If there is any man or woman among you non-militia who desires a fight, say the word and I will gladly make a place for you on this front." I waited. No one spoke. "If that isn't to your liking, you will *all* ascend from this level, in an orderly fashion, and there will be *no* further conflicts. Those who have just been injured in the skirmish have priority in leaving this level and will be brought promptly to the med bay."

From then on, the room remained silent and those that were non-military left the level, in groups at a time. While we waited, I sought out the officer who had taken charge of the command and along the way, I ran into Shím. He approached me slowly with a grin on his face.

"Diramal Criptous. Thought that might have been you I heard shouting earlier."

"Duka MgKonnol, we're here looking for the officer leading this front," I said.

"We, sir?" asked Shím.

"Cho'Zai Zothra and I," I replied, half gesturing to the Cho'Zai.

"Ah, I see. In that case, let me lead you to Pac-Qua Quim."

Shím led us through the crowd to a woman seated with her back slouched, looking down at something, maybe some plans, surrounded by a group of Krollgrums. Shím whispered something in the woman's ear. She placed her hands on her knees and stood, slowly. The first thing I noticed about her was the woman's muscular frame. Her features were strong and broad. She had at least a forehead on me and at first glance, I would say her size was on par with Blick, if not maybe slightly leaner. She gave me a stern but respectful look as she walked up to me, with Shím at her side.

"Diramal Criptous, allow me to introduce you to Pac-Qua Quim," said Shím.

The Pac-Qua, with the same expression on her face, reached her hand out to me. I frowned as I grasped her hand and thought: *Mmm, tight grip.*

She shook me so vigorously I jerked forward. I cleared my throat as I rubbed my shoulder.

"Real peachy, isn't she?" remarked Shím.

"You two are close?" I asked.

"Well, our paths have crossed more than once, that's for sure."

"Does it talk much?" blurted Zothra.

Quim very slowly moved her gaze to the Cho'Zai, as I too turned my head back at him. Zothra stared right back at the Pac-Qua, unfazed by her unblinking stare.

"*She* does, in fact," said Quim. "Introductions waste words. We Dövar don't divulge in small talk. If I speak, I do so sparingly."

I turned back toward Quim.

"A Dövar? You are someone who's been killed and revived by a regenerator?" I asked.

Quim nodded.

"Shím tells me you've taken command over this front; I've come to offer my aid and leadership in conjunction with yours. Would you care to share your defensive strategy with me?" I asked.

"There's not much to say," Pac-Qua Quim said, as she turned around to face the wall behind her. She gripped a device at her side and held it in front of her. "The scans show that whatever the invaders are gonna hit us with will come through this wall here. We're standing in a hallway, so the only strategy is to stand our ground and await their arrival."

I crossed my arms, contemplating an alternative strategy. I glanced up and down the hall, noting the doors, each hiding someone's quarters. *Hiding...*

"You're wrong," I said.

Pac-Qua Quim raised an eyebrow as she faced me.

"How many militia do we have down here with us?" I asked. "A few hundred, give or take?"

"Probably, sir."

"What if we disperse those numbers?" I asked.

"Disperse, sir?"

"Hear me out on this. Assuming we can evacuate the rest of the Skivs and civilians from this level in time, what I suggest we do is divide our numbers into groups of three or four, taking positions in each of the quarters on this level. That way, when they arrive, it won't be a bloodbath; we'll have the element of surprise as they fill the level," I said.

Pac-Qua Quim crossed her arms and nodded.

"And what if some straggle, find a way to access the elevator, and flood the base that way?"

"We will assign a handful of troops to each entry point that this elevator reaches. They will be given orders to shoot anything that comes out of it until they hear word back from us," I said.

"Ha, not that I have any say in the matter given my rank, but if I did, I would wage my earnings on it. That's a solid plan," said Shím.

"As would I," said Zothra.

I glanced back at the Cho'Zai as he nodded at me and then shifted my attention back to Pac-Qua Quim.

"Is that what you're suggesting we do, Diramal Criptous?" asked Quim.

"It is," I said.

"Then I will see it done, sir."

I nodded respectfully at the Pac-Qua. Once the last of the Skivs and civilians had left 'Z' level, there wasn't much time left for preparation from Quim's updated scans. We had to move fast, establishing a channel over comms, designating soldiers to rooms that they had to access forcefully, and assigning handfuls of militia to take positions at the exit point of every opening. As the last of the troops took up positions in the quarters around 'Z' level, a rumble sounded at the other end of the wall. Quim still stood before it. She looked down at her tracking device.

"The enemy is about to breach!" she yelled, stepping back from the wall.

I took up residence in an abandoned room alongside Shím and Zothra as we heard the sound of loud machinery drilling into the base.

"This is Diramal Criptous, activate your QS-25s. Stand by for contact," I said.

The sound of the drilling shifted into a deep rumble before finally coming to a halt. I let everything else fade into a blur as I honed my focus on the open doorway, my Gyrat aimed down sight. No screeches echoed in the halls, no screams, no chaos, nothing but the sound of a deep *woob* that filled my ears. Still, I kept my guard up.

A pair of invaders came into view, creeping past the doorway. *Why do they move so slowly? Unless...* I looked to my side and saw that Shím had raised his aim to the enemy, but I eased his gun down and shook my head at him. Zothra hadn't raised his aim at all and seemed to notice the same thing I had. The invaders were not in an altered time state. I deactivated my quantum suit, sent out a surge, waited a moment, and spoke over comms.

"This is the Diramal. The aliens' guard is down, I repeat, the aliens' guard is down." I paused a moment, observing how the invaders' movements were far more fluid. "They are not in an altered time state. Unless absolutely necessary, do *not* fire once they pass you. Stand by. At the sound of any conflict, initiate the attack. For now, just activate the blend mode on your suits," I said.

Shím, Zothra, and I proceeded to activate our blend modes. The QS-25s could mirror the main feature of the Fade suit. The only thing was the QS-25 could not create enough power to generate a quantum field and blend in with its surroundings in unison.

"Does anyone have eyes on the elevator?" I whispered as many more aliens wandered passed. By this point, several invaders had investigated our room, as I'm sure they did others, but were unable to perceive us.

"This is Krollgrum Valhi, sir. I have eyes on the elevator."

"Have any of the invaders entered it, or attempted to?" I asked.

"Negative," said Valhi.

"Good. If they do, just let them. Remember, we have people at every entry point. Continue to stand by for just a little longer. On my mark, we alter time and strike," I said.

I waited until the gaps between groups got longer and I sensed most, if not all of them, had entered the hall.

"Three . . . Two . . . One . . . Mark," I said.

I deactivated the blend mode on my suit and entered an altered time state, rushing out to the hall with Shím and Zothra at my side. We stood with our backs together, as others hurried out of their own quarters, catching the invaders off guard, and gunning them down. By the time the invaders altered time themselves, to retaliate, their numbers had been so severely cut down that there was no question who the victors were.

XLI
Buried Fortune
(Olson)

The M.I.S.T. personnel and those under my command found our way back to the passageway that led to the hidden starship, Galican-7429. The hole in the path seemed bigger than I remember it being. If it was, that meant more of the surrounding ground could have been prone to crumble as well.

Once we secured the area and confirmed the ground was strong, I commanded several of my troops to set up a zip line down to the ship, connected to the roof overhead. As the officer of the operation, I went down first, this time landing softly on the plating. A handful of my troops followed down right after me. Despite my confidence that we would encounter no threats down there, I kept my guard up as I walked to the head of the ship. Upon inspection of the main deck, I shined the light on my Magplaz through the dusty glass that clouded its contents.

It was hard to discern the contents of the deck aside from a central seat, some panels at the front of the deck, and certain interfaces along the wall that appeared to be active still.

Finally, the M.I.S.T. personnel and most of my troops had made it down, while the rest remained topside to guard the zip line. The researchers brought many devices with them, one being a sort of laser drill that was used to create a hole in the plating. It was cylindrical in shape and probably didn't exceed any more than two feet high, with a wide diameter. Before activating the drill, a pair of the M.I.S.T. personnel wandered around the hull, with a smaller device in hand, aimed down at the ship as they walked across it. I suspect they were looking for a location where the plating was at its least dense. After detecting a suitable region, the drill was situated over it. When activated, the drill locked itself down, and a yellow light illuminated from beneath, as the lasers carved out a hole in the plating, followed by a deep *clunk* sound.

The drill was retracted from the ship and moved out of the way. To everyone's surprise, the plating was replaced with an orange shield. We all looked at one another quizzically. I crouched down and inspected the shield, reaching my gun toward it. The weapon seemed to pass straight through the shield as if it wasn't there. I pulled it back, more quickly than I pushed it in, and the head of the gun was severed. I stood up as we all stepped back and stared at my disabled Magplaz in shock.

"That could be a bit of a problem," I replied.

I tried the trigger and the gun oozed out its molten munition. I swiftly tossed it aside before the munition could pour over my suit and looked back at the shield.

"Should we attempt to find another way into the ship, sir?" one of the men at my side asked.

I tilted my head as I noted something: *The shielding only severed my gun after I moved it more quickly.*

"Hold on, let me try one more thing," I said.

I crouched down beside the shield once again and hesitantly reached my hand toward it.

"Sir?" the same soldier spoke, as he took a step beside me.

"Wait," I replied, as I raised my hand to him.

I eased my hand across the shielding. Taking a deep breath, I *slowly* pried my hand back out . . . intact. Sighing with relief, I stared at my hand and wiggled my fingers.

"That's as I thought. It seems so long as we move slowly through the shield and we are extremely careful not to make any sudden movements on our descent, it should be safe to enter here," I said.

One of the scientists gulped.

"Do we have any more rope?" I asked as I stood.

"Uh, yes, sir, we should," one of the scientists replied.

"Whip it out then; we'll use it to ease our way down. The plating is too smooth to tether the rope to it. I'll need you four to hold the rope and stay behind while the rest of us go down," I said, gesturing to the four soldiers on either side of me.

"Yes, sir," they replied.

One at a time, everyone lowered themselves into the ship, past the sensitive shielding without incident, while the four appointed soldiers countered our weight on the rope. As the first one to enter the ship, the instant my feet touched the floor, the hallway lit up in a gentle twilight, as if my presence awakened the ship in some way. Armed with a pistol, I inspected my surroundings. As anticipated, I encountered no threat.

The halls were blue in color, dimly lit with purple lighting along the floor and pillars of dark blue lights stretching down to either side of the walls. The setting almost gave the impression that the ship might have been in a low-power mode.

With everyone on the ship, I ordered the troops to accompany the scientists wherever their curiosities led them. Wandering solo, I set off in a direction I hoped would lead me to the main deck. It remained elusive, but I found myself in what could have been used as the mess hall. I began second-guessing myself when noting the lack of tables and chairs, with much of the wide, red room being quite empty—dimly lit with the same purple and blue lights. It wasn't until my curiosity lured me to a series of evenly spaced interfaces along the walls that I formed an idea of the room's purpose. The display on the screen immediately acknowledged my presence. I saw no method of scan, yet I felt something shiver down from my shoulders, through my spine, and within my gut as the interface made a noise. It then presented a peculiar outline that resembled a hand, but not my own. Despite this, I stepped out of my QS-25 and pressed my hand to the outline as it illuminated. A surge of energy burst throughout my body, causing me to keel over and shout. The sensation was hard to describe. It wasn't like a shock, and it certainly wasn't soothing. It still wouldn't do it justice, but the best way I could think to describe it was friction. Like the feeling you get between your hands after rubbing them together vigorously for a time and then holding them close, but in a far greater magnitude.

Catching my breath after having pulled my hand away, I couldn't help but notice I felt profoundly invigorated in my psyche and spirit. I wasn't sure I'd ever felt so ecstatic, even as a child. Despite this, I didn't want to repeat the experience.

Before leaving, I glanced at the interface one last time and then down at my hand, to find something very strange indeed. I'd witnessed the nerve pattern in the palm of my hand illuminate in a neon yellow light as it faded. My breath caught and my eyes couldn't keep from blinking as I turned my hand over. I grabbed it, pressing thumb to palm. Everything felt fine. In fact, everything felt great. My skin felt so smooth, like a child's cheek. I didn't know what to make of it.

I could drive myself crazy trying to work out what happened here.

I stepped back into my suit, exited the mess hall, and continued wandering about the vessel in the same direction until I found the main deck.

The lights were brighter in this room. At the very end, there were two pairs of seats, positioned at an angle from each other, with diamond-shaped transparent screens set before them. A little closer to me was a sort of dark gray podium. Before it rested two tall pillars. I took a few steps forward and a series of long pins extended from the ground, forming a chair. The ends were rounded and smooth. I exited my suit once again, reached my hand over them, and felt a sort of kinetic energy emanating from each one. Not that I was planning on sitting in the chair to begin with, since the design of the seat looked uncomfortable as is. But at least now I could see more clearly how the commanding seat was set to operate. The seat was lined up with the two pillars that may very well have operated as controls, closely set before the podium. *Which might have its own interface when activated.*

I walked over to one of the seats up front and tapped the glass screen where a star-like insignia was displayed on it. The star faded and in its place, a sort of digital layout presented itself to me, but it was hard to say of what exactly. My head ached trying to make sense of it. There was writing beneath the outlines, but in a language I was not familiar with. Though some of the markings bore some resemblance to letters in my kin's alphabet. *I wonder if I press any of these buttons it'll lead me to a record or log within the ship's mainframe.*

Slowly, I pressed my finger against one of the smaller outlines on the screen. Immediately after, came a deep rumble that sounded like it was coming from somewhere outside the ship. I looked up and around, frightened that I'd made a mistake. Outside the window, I could barely see a glowing teal light on the right side of the ship. I rushed to that side of the deck to get a better look at what was going on, but before I could get more than two steps in, a loud burst filled the cave and a stream of light shot ahead of the vessel. I cursed as the loud boom rang the cave like a bell and the ground shook below my feet. A few seconds passed, and the quaking finally came to a stop, which I was grateful for.

Over comms, it was a riot; my troops thinking the eruption was a potential assault. In a blaring exchange of dialogue, I reached out to them, settling each one before they did something rash. I gave a sigh of relief once it was over with.

Well, I think it's safe to assume the rest of you control different aspects of the ship, I thought to myself, glancing at the other three screens.

I turned to face the central seat and exhaled heavily, nodding my head.

Assuming you are the command seat, if there's any sort of computer in this room that would have access to the ship's database, without a doubt, it would be yours.

I walked back to the command seat, pausing before I settled into it. I took a deep breath and rested myself on it. The pins were weighed down slightly. I gasped on contact and strained my entire body as energy surged throughout it, emanating from each point of the pins. My body trembled as I forgot how to breathe from the sheer amount of shock I was in. My breaths came out in quick gasps; seconds apart from each other.

A set of pins pressed themselves up to the back of my neck and scalp. All became black. I was still conscious; I could still feel my body and my discomfort, but my sight was blinded. Seconds later, it was as if my eyes adjusted to the dark and I could make out abstract shapes that changed every time I blinked. Among the shifting sceneries, one bore a small orange light, high above me. It didn't take me long to recognize it as the hole we entered to reach the ship. I blinked again and saw four figures guarding a rope. It was then I realized . . .

Goddess, I'm connected to the ship!

Promptly after the realization, I received a message. It didn't come in the form of words, but rather a sensation of confirmation.

Wait, is the ship . . . I paused, getting the sense that the ship didn't like being referred to as "the ship," or maybe it was that it didn't like being referred to in the third person. *Are you, can you understand me?*

I got another sense of confirmation and I swallowed deeply.

C-Can you show me how you got here?

I felt that the ship could not show me every detail; that the imagery would be disorienting and hard to make sense of.

I think I understand. Show me what you can.

The ship agreed and my vision of the dark exterior surrounding the ship vanished—suddenly replaced with the view of a great battle, from the ship's perspective and . . . a third presence. A man, perhaps the former commander of this vessel.

Though I could sense the urgency and intensity of the situation, my vision was clouded with some sort of static blur. I could hear the commander's voice shouting orders as he took the ship head-on with the enemy. The opposing forces were too dark in color to perceive, blending with the black of space behind them.

I observed as the battle waged on, trying to keep track of everything that was occurring until realizing the occupants of the ship and their allies were losing the conflict. Yet there was a resolute spirit about these people who fought ever stronger in the face of death and defeat. The defenders rallied and fought with a might that drove their attackers back from whence they came. But not for long. The defenders had settled and had a few minutes to recuperate before the attackers returned in greater forces. They brought something with them this time around, but it was hard to see. It started out as a round blazing glint, slightly larger than the stars in the background. As the enemy forces stormed in closer, it grew brighter. I could hear the commander's worried voice, distorted over comms. ". . . ons . . . tles . . . this . . . Stordar Glīzen . . ." The large flaming ball grew closer to the point that it became blinding. ". . . Galican . . . overwhelmed . . . ix . . . attack—" All went dark, the vision had cut short, and I was back in the cave.

How long ago did this happen? I asked the ship once I caught my breath.

The ship replied with the sensation that the event occurred a very long time ago. I then asked the ship a series of questions, all at once: *What was the origin of conflict in that battle? What race of beings commanded you? Who is Stordar Glīzen?* I felt weightless as my consciousness found its way back into my body. My mind was dizzied as I felt myself twirling and falling toward the ground. As my chest met with an abrupt impact, I was completely reunited with my body. Gasping and coughing for breath as I struggled to push myself off the floor, an uncomfortable pressure stirred in my chest.

"Io-Pac Olson Criptous, sir, are you alright?" one of my troops asked.

I glanced at her boots as I collected myself and stood. I didn't know why, but I noted that she wasn't armored in her suit. The insignia on her jacket shoulder left exposed.

"Duka, is there a particular reason you removed me from that seat?" I asked.

The Duka stiffened.

"Sir, you were struggling for breath, your body spasmed, and I thought maybe you were in distress."

I sighed as I rolled my neck and shoulders.

"I didn't realize it had reached that extreme. I was interfacing with the ship. It showed me . . . something," I said.

The Duka nodded.

"I see. I was just passing by with a group of the M.I.S.T. personnel when I saw your body flailing from down the hall. Should I remain here for any others and warn them not to interact with this seat, sir?" asked the Duka.

"Yes. Don't touch anything else inside here, especially that interface there," I said, pointing at the diamond screen that controlled the ship's weapons.

"Understood, sir."

I walked into my suit as it enveloped me, and I turned to the Duka one final time.

"As you were, Duka," I said.

The Duka and I saluted one another.

My body ached as I resumed wandering around the ship. I continued to observe things I didn't understand. Given what I had already exposed myself to, I had no intention of finding it out for myself.

"Io-Pac Criptous!" a voice shouted ahead of me.

I raised my head and paused briefly to find one of the M.I.S.T. personnel rushing toward me.

"Io-Pac Criptous, sir, we found the core of the ship." The scientist spoke with such passion and his eyes filled with wonder.

I couldn't quite find it in myself to share his excitement, as I'd be more surprised to discover the ship had no core at all.

"Ah, well done," I said, noting the scientist's name, "Doctor Xīrith." I patted him on the shoulder as I passed him by.

"I should think you'll want to see it for yourself, sir. It is truly a marvel to behold." I stopped and turned back to Xīrith "Unlike anything we have."

I raised an eyebrow. *Might as well.*

"Which way?" I asked.

"I'll show you, sir." Doctor Xīrith's face lit up.

Xīrith led me through the halls of the ship, marching with delight.

"Have there been any incidents with any members of your team?" I asked.

"Oh, we've certainly had our fair share of surprises in our investigation, sir. But we've suffered no casualties that I know of, if that's what you're referring to."

"Good," I said.

"Ah, here we are," he said, as we walked through a doorway.

On the other side was a dark room, spherical in shape. A long bridge rested ahead, leading up to a tall structure at the center of the room.

"This way, sir."

We walked across the bridge and the door closed behind us—the room was utterly dark. Slowly, the structure at the end of the bridge cracked open, releasing pressure. Light shined through the crack, stretching across the room. The streaking lights were so strong they looked like glowing blue blocks. The structure opened more and revealed a live, burning star, four times bigger than myself. Arching arms were directed down at it, perhaps to maintain its size and conceal its heat, as I couldn't feel it, even at close range. There was, however, a gentle breeze that emanated from the star.

"A star core. You were right, Doctor Xīrith, this truly is a marvel to behold. Have you conducted any examinations yet?" I asked.

"We've learned all we can for now, with the tools we have on hand. But I sense there is much more to be discovered that will require better equipment, sir."

"I'll have it arranged when I report back to the Diramal," I said.

"Very good, sir."

"When you and your team have finished up here, report to me over comms, and we'll return to base," I said.

"Yes, sir," said Xīrith.

XLII
Warter
(Log)

I stood no more than seven feet away from a table of four officers, two Pac-Quas, and two Ho-Jinns, one man and woman of each rank. I held Amat's letter of exemption in my hand, nervously tracing my index finger around the envelope's crisp edges. I'd freshened up and dressed in uniform, yet I found myself distracted by the task that awaited me after the court-martial.

How will I even approach the boy whose parents I killed?

"Io-Pac Log Criptous," the female Ho-Jinn said. I looked up at her, caught off guard. "Will you approach the court closer, please."

Coming to the edges of the table at which the officers sat, I extended the letter to them. The male Ho-Jinn halted me.

"That is close enough, Io-Pac," he said.

I cleared my throat and raised the letter.

"I, uh, have a letter of exemption here from Diramal Criptous," I said.

The officers looked at one another, confused. Finally, the female Ho-Jinn reached her hand out to me.

"Let me see it," she said.

I placed the letter in her palm as she grasped it. Without delay, she reviewed the contents of the exemption. She read it so quickly, I questioned whether she processed any of the information.

"So, it is. Given that these are orders from the Diramal, we have no choice but to dismiss you from this court and drop all charges of reckless leadership, hysteria, and cold-blooded murder."

The female Ho-Jinn gave me a hard stare of disgust. I sensed she had much more on her mind she wanted to say, but for the sake of professionalism, she held her tongue.

I could only give an awkward nod and walk out of the room.

"Send in the next!" the female Ho-Jinn blurted, irritated.

The Tyrant of Unity

Walking through the halls of Y'Gůtsa as I tracked down the location of where all the Skivs were being held, I heard whispers of the attack on the base from the previous day. They'd likely been dispersed about the base for a time until accommodations could be made.

I received and opened a message on my fizer. It was from Kaia. The message said: Heard you came back from another tour. Need a restock on some more of the good stuff? Or maybe another night at your place?

My breath trembled as I fought the temptation to reply and ask for more Diazep. The withdrawal still held its grip on me. Just thinking about how nice another hit would feel reminded me of how weak and queasy my body felt without it. Hesitant to reply, I was spared of the choice when I heard someone call for me.

"Io-Pac Log Criptous?" a woman's voice said.

I looked up and saw that it was Kita.

"Krollgrum Yatů, ah, this is an interesting coincidence," I replied.

"Interesting, indeed, it's good to see you out of the med bay, sir," said Kita.

"It feels good being on my two feet again. Where were you headed?" I asked.

"Just to my quarters, coming from the mess hall. What about yourself?"

I took a moment before answering.

"To find the kid," I replied.

"The kid?" asked Kita.

"You know the one," I replied.

"Oh, that one. I hope you haven't been too hard on yourself over that."

I tilted my head.

"I don't see why I shouldn't be. I orphaned a child, put several innocent lives at risk. Not to mention the lives of those under my command, leading them while under the influence," I said.

"True, all true. But while you are guilty of these things, I can't believe that you did them in your right mind. I've always been able to sense when someone's out of character, sir. I live with the moral that no one in this world is born evil. I look at someone like you, in a situation like yours, and I see someone who is suffering severely. I do not approve of the things you've done, sir, but I don't see what good it would do to hold them against you. Knowing that the source of your faults is not your own."

It felt like a stream had poured itself out of my heart. No one had ever told me anything like that before, ever. Reflecting on how often I'd been shot down by others, including Amat and Olson. People constantly underestimated me, took advantage of me, pushed aside my perspective and I let it happen, all of it. I'd always blamed myself for it, thinking I was the problem. But not in that moment.

I wasn't crying, but a single tear found its way out of my eyelid. I wiped it away and sniffed.

"Thank you, Krollgrum Yatů. No one's ever told me anything like that before," I said.

"Just expressing my honesty with you, sir," Krollgrum Yatů replied.

I sighed as I collected myself.

"If I may; I'd like to request something of you, Krollgrum," I asked.

"Yes, sir?"

"My cousin, the new Diramal, pardoned me from my charges related to the incident on my last mission. On the condition that I talk to the kid and either find him a new home or take him myself."

"I see." Kita seemed confused as to where I was going with this.

"It frightens me to my core, but I'm going to do it either way. I wouldn't mind for someone to be there at my side when it happens, though," I said.

Kita and I held a silence, staring at each other.

"Oh, you mean me."

"Well, there aren't too many other familiar faces around." Kita seemed taken aback. "Sorry, I didn't mean it to come off that way. I'm not forcing this on you, but it would help if you came."

Kita gazed blankly at me. I gave her a half smile, as if to say I understood that she didn't want to go. I walked past her in silence.

"Wait, sir…" I paused as Kita walked up to my side. "You didn't hear my answer."

"Ah, forgive me, I mistook your silence for it. What is your decision then?"

"I'll do it. I'll accompany you to see the child."

"Thank you," I replied.

Together, Kita and I made our way through the halls of Y'Gŭtsa, making our way down to the lower levels where the Skivs were still being kept. Though no longer on level 'Z,' on account of the large gaping holes from the invaders' breach. On level 'Y' the Skivs crowded the halls. I paused, reflecting on a thought.

"What is it?" asked Kita.

"It's just occurred to me; I don't know the kid's face, let alone his name," I said.

I continued to explore the level, until I was met with a handful of Dukas going around, taking names, and assigning quarters for the Skivs. Each of the Dukas looked overworked and concentrated so intensely on their tasks it seemed the slightest distraction could cause them to lash out. Without hesitation, I approached the one closest to me, taking note of her name pinned to her coat before asking, "Excuse me, Duka Hŭvas, I am Io-Pac Log Criptous, I'm here to inquire about a Skiv, a young boy, orphaned, no older than ten years and no taller than waist height."

Only after I'd mentioned my name and rank, did the Duka raise her head to me, gazing at me with wide, unblinking sore eyes. She looked me up and down before replying.

"We've reviewed a lot fitting that profile."

The Duka looked back to her glass pad and went on poking away.

"I imagine so. In that case, could you tell me where you send these children?" I asked. The Duka sighed irritably as she rolled her eyes at me, which I chose to ignore. "Surely, you don't just set them up with quarters of their own and expect them to look after themselves."

"No, we don't. When we find kids who don't have parents, we send them to the Pens on 'P' level. Until we can figure out a reasonable living situation for them, that is where they will stay, under heavy supervision. Now please, if you'll excuse me, sir," said the Duka.

"Of course, thank you, Duka Hŭvas," I said.

"I take it you don't recall the features on the boy's face," said Kita, as we started to walk away.

"When we get there, I can help point him out to you." Said Kita.

I glanced over at her.

"You say that as if you'd recognize him."

"I would."

Kita went on to explain how, after she'd led the evacuation from our last mission, she found and comforted the child whose parents I'd killed in my hysteria.

"Did you explain to him that the commanding officer of the mission was . . . is responsible for his being an orphan?" I asked.

"No," replied Kita. "So far as he knew, I was the commanding officer of the mission. I never thought you'd be in the position to do this, but I figured if anyone was to explain that to him, it would have to be you and only you."

I nodded and lowered my head.

"You feel shame for it."

"Of course I do," I replied.

Kita shook her head.

"You shouldn't." I squinted, confused by her words. "You carried out an unforgiveable act, yes, and you should carry that with you as a reminder not to make the same mistakes again. But as I understand it, you wouldn't have made such mistakes if it weren't for a certain interaction you had with Cho'Zai Xaizar. For that, you shouldn't feel shame for your internal torment, but rather acknowledge the courage you've found to take responsibility for your actions and offering this child what you can to support him. That is what we're doing here, isn't it?"

"Your logic bewilders me. Do you talk this way with all your commanding officers?" I asked.

Kita looked over to me with a certain faint gleam in her eye.

"No," she replied.

Once we reached the Pens, there was a collage of kids there, running around, screaming, and laughing. I'm sure it had been too long for them since last they were able to do such things. There were some, however, that kept to themselves and looked gloomy still. Perhaps they had seen too much horror to reinvigorate the spirit of their youth. I hope I wasn't the horror that stole the boy's young spirit.

"That's him, there," said Kita, pointing at a lonely child sitting with his head down.

Studying his features until they were crisply defined in my mind, my breath caught; there was no mistaking him for Xaizar. Not that I still had his face glued to my mind, but I was overwhelmed with the reality that I nearly took a child's life along with the others, all because of that haunting image I was scarred with.

"You didn't catch his name by chance, did you?" I asked Kita.

"Warter," replied Kita.

"Warter. Thank you, Kita, I'll go on alone from here."

Kita nodded.

"I'll be here when you've finished speaking with one another," she said.

I gave a half-smile and made my way over to the child. My mind raced with a thousand different outcomes of how it would turn out; most of them unpleasant and the ones that weren't felt like lies to myself. I held my breath as I took my final steps toward the boy and introduced myself. I waited and eventually he looked up at me. He held a frown on his face, a frown I had been all too familiar with of late. His eyes did not shed tears, but they did look to be covered with a light liquid layer of dread that distorted his irises.

I knew I had to break the silence, and with it, my voice cracked.

"Hey, kid. Warter is it?" I asked, awkwardly.

Warter blinked.

"How do you know me?" asked the child.

I sighed as I contemplated how I should answer that.

"Mind if I sit with you?" I asked.

"Could I really tell you 'No'? You're an Io-Pac."

It was a peculiar question. Technically he couldn't, as in our culture I could order the surrounding guards to grab Warter, tie him down, and explain everything to him that way. But I didn't perceive it like that. In my mind, Warter had the higher authority. If he wished me shunned from his company, I wouldn't force my apology or my assistance on him. Even if that meant going back and facing the court-martial.

"You're an observant one," I replied as I lowered myself beside Warter.

"Vigilance is something you become accustomed to when you've spent nearly three years in a war zone, among other things."

"Sounds like discipline may be among them as well."

"My father wouldn't have it any other way after he lost my little sister. He blamed himself so deeply that he wouldn't have anyone making a mistake like that again."

"And your mother?" I asked.

Warter gave a light laugh.

"My father was strong, but my mother was the leader of our family. She kept us all together, scouted for resources and shelter; she did much on her own."

"But... wouldn't your father have had an easier time fending off any enemies she might have come across when she did things on her own?"

"Precisely the reason why she wanted him staying with us."

"Your parents sound like they sacrificed much for you."

Warter nodded.

"Right to their last breaths," he said.

I paused before replying.

"I'm sorry." The words felt like ash in my mouth, as if even the gesture of an apology couldn't begin to repair the damage I'd done.

Warter snorted.

"Forgive me. I hear an apology, but I can't believe you truly know just how much pain I'm in since militia's families get a free ticket to salvation within these submerged, armored bases."

I tilted my head, partially offended by the child's words. Yet I maintained my composure.

"I would think that among the various lessons you learned in the Waste, one of them would be that sometimes, even in concealed walls, there are still many dangers," I said.

Warter turned his head to me.

"It's true; my family was given sanctuary in this base. Yet it was just over a week ago that my parents were killed by a Cho'Zai, under orders of the former Diramal. Not to mention the countless lives of comrades I've lost who fought by my side to bring you here. As a soldier and certainly as a commander... of sorts, I know loss all too well."

Warter gave a stubborn frown and shrugged, looking away. A long moment of silence passed between us. If I queried what Warter was thinking, something suggested to me that he'd give a reply along the lines of: "I can't tell you what you can or cannot do, but I don't have to tell you everything about me. Unless maybe you'd order it out of me." Strange, in a way I was intimidated by Warter. He looked so young, but like Lúvi, there was a certain maturity about Warter that suggested he was psychologically older than his physical age. War will do that to a person. I should know, having to fight in this one when I was hardly twelve.

I knew what I did next was a risk in how it would play out. But I saw no other way and even if I did, perhaps this was the best of my choices after all. I cleared my throat.

"I'm gonna tell you a story, Warter. How you take it is entirely up to you and once I'm done, you'll decide how this conversation proceeds." Warter turned his gaze back onto me with intrigue. "So, listen closely. Not too long ago, there was a young Alpha, who was related to a very powerful, caring, and focused commander—a Jinn-hid whose position had been compromised in what he hoped to achieve with his command. Thus, the Diramal, at the time, commanded two of his Cho'Zai to pull aside two of the Jinn-hid's closest allies, his cousins, for interrogation. During which one of the cousins endured a highly . . . disturbing . . . encounter with one of the Cho'Zai, which drove him to some very poor choices. This Alpha was confronted with a lot of pain and fear that he didn't know how to control, so he acquired medicine that relieved him of this suffering, but only for hours at a time and he became reliant on it. Later, his cousin, the Jinn-hid, tasked the young Alpha with a mission he was not ready for and executed it . . . poorly. He made a grave mistake, one he wishes—every day since—he could take back. The combination of the interrogation and the medicine unhinged the Alpha and, in the swelling of his insanity, he took innocent lives. He deprived a boy of his parents, the one whom he sits beside right now . . ."

Finally, the tears rolled down Warter's cheeks. He frowned so hard the skin on his forehead turned pink. The young boy looked me up and down, and his bared fangs appeared, ready to rip out my throat. No doubt, the thought crossed his mind.

"I can't bring back your parents, Warter, and were it under any other circumstance, we would have likely never met. It was never my wish to rob you of them. And all I can do is offer you a choice. I can find you a place you'll be well looked after, surrounded by good people who are willing to take you into their home. Or I can take you under my wing and look after you. Either way, I will do my best to make up for what I took from you, knowing it will never be enough."

Warter breathed heavily as his eyes lowered to the side of my waist.

"I'd sooner take that gun from its holster and shoot you dead where you sit than accept anything from you," said Warter.

"Perhaps your wish will be granted then. My cousin Amat Luciph Criptous is the new Diramal. The only reason I'm sitting here and not standing before a court-martial is because he made it so. He told me to present you with this choice and if I couldn't carry it out, I'd face the consequences of my actions. I can tell you now, Warter, I've lived a harsh life and I've always dealt with it improperly. So, if I can't make this right, I might as well allow you the opportunity to receive your justice."

I unholstered my pistol and slid it over to Warter. The boy did not touch it immediately; he didn't even raise his hand to it. No one else in the room saw it happen. Warter glanced up from the gun and at me.

"My father was a Mond before the war, and throughout my life, he trained me in his ways, in the practices of Anua. Though I meant what I said about killing you, I acknowledge your willingness to admit your fault. You've robbed me of everything I've ever known, and I see you suffer from it. Killing you would be a *mercy* and I don't think my father would have wanted me to. I think he would have told me to take you up on your offer and make things right. But if you fail, Io-Pac, I will take that pistol and be done with you," Warter said, sliding the pistol back to me.

XLIII
The Důlabega Quadrant Incident
(Amat)

I walked to the breach and inspected the alien mechanisms that had drilled into the base. They were red in color, perhaps three feet taller than me. Not very wide, rectangular in shape, and oh yes, the large drill at the front of each vehicle. I walked up beside one and stepped onto its track wheel. Atop the vehicle, I observed the same marking that I found in the passageways below Ion.

Strange, I thought. *If the marking is of the invaders' making, was there a correlation between its placement in the mines and the large group of Skivs that had found their way down there? Also, why did the invaders enter the base without altering time? The Skivs were placed down here; could the invaders have had some way of knowing that? If they did, that would suggest there is something that they find desirable in those we've discarded to the waste.*

"Diramal Criptous," I heard a woman say.

I turned my head to find Pac-Qua Quim, stepped down from the alien vehicle, and approached her.

She reached out her hand to me. I looked down at it before uniting our hands and shaking them.

"I see promise in you, sir. I look forward to the chance of serving under your command again," she said.

"It was an honor fighting at your side, Pac-Qua Quim, and I see promise within your character as well," I replied.

Pac-Qua Quim and I nodded at one another as she turned and walked away. Her expression had not changed, and she maintained the same blank stare.

"Diramal Criptous," Blick said to me over comms.

"Criptous here," I replied.

"Sir, I've found some information on the subjects we discussed the other night," said Blick.

"Roger that, Reikag Vykin. Meet me in my office and we'll talk about what you've discovered," I said.

"Which office, sir? Old or new?" Blick asked.

I was thrown off by the question, then I remembered I did technically have two offices. My office as a Jinn-hid and now the Diramal's.

"The old one. Criptous out," I said, having a more positive reflection on my office as a Jinn-hid than the Diramal's.

I'll need to select a new Jinn-hid soon, though.

I reached the office shortly before Blick and waited patiently for his arrival. Blick walked through my door with his arms full of documents and slammed them down on my desk. My head ached at the thought of scanning through every scrap of paper. I sighed, shifting in my seat, and gesturing to the documents.

"What's the summary of all of that content?" I asked.

"Locations, records, and analytics to more than a thousand starships buried across the globe."

My eyes widened as I slowly leaned in closely and scanned one of the documents, observing blueprints and various forms of records about a vessel named *The Kalizar-5809*.

"Over a thousand, you say?" I asked.

"Yes, sir."

I leaned back in my chair and nodded.

"I want more teams launched amongst our allies, like the one Olson is leading to investigate the Galican vessel. Take these documents, find out which bases are closest to each individual ship, and relay orders to investigate. I want to know if and how many of these ships are operational. They may serve as our salvation from this war and to the habitable planet that revolves around Anobose," I said.

"Very good, sir. I'll start on it right away," Blick said, as he leaned over to collect all the documents off my desk. "Oh, and before I forget"—Blick reached behind his back and handed me a data crystal—"I couldn't find the physical transcript, but I did find this. It's a recording of the dialogue shared between the former Diramal and the invaders." I looked at Blick and the data crystal with intrigue. "I'm not sure you'll be able to make much sense of it, but I hope it helps you nonetheless."

"You listened to it then?" I asked.

Blick nodded.

"Will there be anything else, sir?" asked Blick.

"No, you've done well here, Blick. Report back to me when you've finished coordinating with our allies."

"Yes, sir."

When I was alone, I accessed my computer, connected the data crystal, and opened the file to the Důlabega Quadrant Incident. The first few seconds were silent. Then, there was the sound of a door opening in the background, followed by footsteps and subtle screeches, identical to those of the invaders.

"Ah, you must be Fargon's ambassador," a voice said, sounding very much like the Diramal.

There was a reply from an alien, presumably who must have spoken in their native tongue, as I could not make out what they said.

"That I am. Shall we sit?" the Diramal asked in a pleasant tone.

The sound of chairs moving filled the background, followed by a distorted reply from the alien.

"Yes, I believe there's been a terrible misunderstanding about the whole incident that occurred in the Tronmine System. Those ships were not our own; they'd likely been hijacked by Vix forces."

Vix?

Before I let my thoughts trail too far, I refocused on the recording. The alien on the other end of the conversation screeched and choked a reply.

"No doubt there were still members of our kin on board those ships. The Vix have grown fiercer in the climax of this war. They are restless in their assaults on our people, still. Despite your fronts to defend the restoration of our army and strength, their forces find ways of attacking our refuges," said the Diramal.

The alien gave a long reply, hissing and chirping.

"We've grown concerned with our lack of communication between the other settlements; you're not alone on that. As I said earlier, the Vix are ruthless in their determination to wipe us out. I can tell you, however, that the settlement on Galiza fares well and we are restoring our numbers every day."

The alien spoke more slowly, collectively, and suddenly it sounded like several guns had been cocked and loaded.

The Diramal gave a sigh, followed by a sinister chuckle.

"You Zeltons have always been the wisest of the bunch. Your kin just have a natural intuition about yourselves. But the one who is deeply wise often has a sincere flaw in their wit, when strategy and cunning come into play."

There was a moment of silence . . . and then a burst of screeches and shrieks piled on top of one another. I paused the recording but saw that it went on for a while longer. I scrolled the marker up the timeline, played it, and the chaos continued. Stopping it once again, I scrolled further, toward the very end. I heard a weak screech and something sliding across the ground, while a set of boots followed behind. The screeches gradually became more intense but were silenced by a gunshot.

"Qi'val Quavek, the negotiations have ended in an unfortunate tragedy."

Qi'val?

"Await my arrival back at the ship and destroy this vessel. As of this moment, the humans are at war with the Zeltons. Which doesn't leave us with much time to find Valzeron's fifth child—"

The recording was cut short. I leaned forward in my seat and rubbed my chin, reflecting deeply on all that I had heard.

So . . . the invaders were . . . our allies? If this is true, then that means they came to us in peace three years ago.

"And your father truly was the one who started this war; he broke the peace, he made enemies out of the invaders, put millions of innocent lives at—"

No! I blurted, countering the argument of a sinister voice in my head. *I refuse to believe that still. It was the Diramal's doing; he manipulated my father. If it wasn't for that private conversation before the launch, things would have gone very differently between us all that day.*

"Still, it doesn't change the fact that Jinn-hid Bod Criptous pulled the trigger. It doesn't change the fact that he was the first human to draw blood on the Zeltons," said the devious voice.

Doesn't change the fact that the man who was my father died long before his physical body pulled that trigger, I replied. The voice in my head had nothing to say in reply to that. *What this recording also tells me is that the Diramal and the Cho'Zai, or . . . Qi'val are perhaps not what they seem. Yet there are still plenty of questions left unanswered. What are these . . . Zeltons doing with my kin? Where were these other settlements my kin had established across the cosmos? Why did we need them? Who is this Valzeron and what is the fifth child?*

Only time would tell.

Those who seek power often fall from it It is the humble who find and prosper from it.

Photo taken by Jingjing Huntley

About the Author

James McGettigan is a young, ambitious writer and filmmaker. He started writing this series when he was eleven years old, in early 2012. At the age of twenty-three, he's managed to put together three complete books and has dozens of others in the works, in various fictional genres. He's also gained an immense amount of experience in the domain of filmmaking, working with various artists like the Trestles, Lyndon-Enow, and Goofee Jay, producing his own original content, and is in the midst of putting together a comedy TV series. He's currently studying at the Academy of Art in San Francisco to get his BA in Video Editing and has intentions of one day converting the Altered Moon series into a film franchise, among other stories he's currently working on.

The Author would also like to express his sincerest thanks to the readers for supporting this series that has been ten-plus years in the making. He would also like to invite the readers to share their thoughts and leave reviews of his books on the online platforms on which they are sold. This would be greatly appreciated and further support the author in his ability to publish the many stories he has in store for the world. Thank you.

Author's Social Media

Instagram: @seamus_eiteagain
Twitter: @james_mcgetti22
TikTok: @james_alan_mcgettigan
LinkedIn: https://www.linkedin.com/in/james-mcgettigan-334140174/
YouTube (Stories of The Dust Cosmos): https://www.youtube.com/@StoriesofTheDustCosmos/videos

Special Acknowledgements

Jingjing Huntley
Serena Lucatero
Jason Frank Jr.
Kyle Davis
Judy McGettigan
Anthony McGettigan
Fabiana Lezama Granado
Jacqui Corn-Uys

Glossary

Änga: A deep, meditative-like state. It is a practice that only members of the faith are allowed to partake, During which, the practitioners have powerful and detailed psychological experiences, similar to that of ayahuasca. Idols of Anua's faith are taught, in enclosure, how to achieve this state of mind on command.

Cho'Zai: The most blessed soldiers on Anua's scorched Galiza. Born with natural and rare dark red irises, they are bred for war from the day they are brought into the world. They are sworn to the Diramal before country and civilian and their obedience lies solely with the one who bears the rank. Complicating their own ranking, they are considered less skilled than an Alpha but fiercer brawlers; they do not answer to any rank that is below the Diramal, but they cannot govern themselves.

Dailagon: Diamond-shaped craft, equipped with anti-gravity technology that can allow the humans to survive an aerial fight with the Zeltons, if they are hyper-aware and extremely tactical. But anti-gravity cannot match the speed of a quantum field and for most humans, aerial combat with the Zeltons is an almost assured death.

Diramal: An autocrat who holds executive authority over the Utopian people and soil. They decide whether or not to declare war, attend foreign meetings, and maintain foreign relations. There is almost no limit to their power and authority, so long as they don't get caught doing something morally or legally wrong. They have the final say on what the public is allowed to know and remain oblivious to, and thus they keep close relations with members from I.I.D. and M.I.S.T.

Dövar: Someone who has been dead for under an hour (usually a soldier) and been brought back to life via the nano-regenerators. They are often very reserved, monotone, and demonstrate a severe lack of emotion and overall feeling. They operate and come across as someone who is only half alive. But there are a few exceptions to this kind of behavior among the Dövar.

Důlabega Quadrant Incident: A documented exchange between the Diramal and the Zeltons dating back to the time of the deep space S.E.F. missions, carried out by Jinn-hid Bod Criptous and the Diramal himself. Not much can be taken from the content of the exchange, but there's a clear indication of a slaughter, somehow carried out by the Diramal himself.

E.S.P. 101 (Electric Shock-put 101): A human weapon that shoots small, concentrated globes of lightning, fired at high velocities, and held in three-by-three-inch square quartz crystals. The rounds can and will tear through any material—unless the gun is preset to "stun." The denser the material the round hits, however, the more quickly the electric entanglement of the round dissipates.

Fizer: A multipurpose, tactical device registered to Utopian militia bodies—with a few exceptions—and embedded in their forearms. Its purposes extend from presenting the user grids of their current location to communication, and more.

Ho-Jinn: A higher-end ranked official. They can serve on court-martials and hold commands of hundreds of soldiers among the ranks of Gromrolls and Krollgrums.

I.I.D. (Information of Interests Department): A Utopian government agency, responsible for tracking and filing all military operations, as well as economic and scientific data.

Jinn: A higher-end ranked official. They can lead brigades in the thousands among the Dukas and Alphas. They report directly to the Jinn-hid and they may also serve on a court martial. Their responsibilities lie mostly in overseeing battle strategy across all brigades outside their own.

Jinn-hid: The second most powerful ranked official in the Utopian military and the country. Only one may hold the rank at a time. They report directly to the Diramal and it is not usual for the Jinn-hid to command brigades or train soldiers, in addition to their standard duties. Both Amat and Bod Criptous are peculiar in this way. They are the Diramal's spokesman, advisor, and remain in close contact with the Jinns. They hold the power to reserve the Utopian armies to organize brigades overseas. For instance, if the Diramal declares war on another country, the Jinn-hid decides how many soldiers are sent off where and when, and how many remain on home soil. In theory, they know everything the Diramal does.

Io-Pac: A low-level officer rank. They ensure safety and efficiency during missions.

Karn: An Irenole term, meaning "toddler."

Koyůt: Lower air defense rank. They are responsible for piloting and manning the weaponry of the Fades.

Laquar: A durable, liquid shielding used for a variety of purposes. Formed in part by liquid oxygen, plasma, muon particle, and a high enough volume of melted magnetite that it creates a stable forcefield from liquid and gaseous elements. In addition to its being composed of liquid oxygen and plasma, in the form of a suit or domed shielding at the bottom of the ocean, the two continuously counteract one another, to provide its shelled interior with gaseous oxygen. Metals or sharp edges will break the integrity of the substance. However, the substance is incredibly durable that in the event it's torn or broken, so long as it's not totally obliterated, it will *rapidly* reform itself in a matter of microseconds.

Magplaz: A human weapon that shoots concentrated magma rounds. Contact with such a round will pierce and melt through almost any material, with the exception of a few materials and rare metals. Nano-metal specifically—which comprises the quantum suits of the humans—can offer strong resistance to a single magma round, as the nanites themselves can effectively resist the melting temperatures. Consecutive hits from magma rounds would lead to the death of any soldier wearing a quantum suit, thus a single round could kill anyone not wearing one.

M.I.S.T. (Military Investigative Sciences and Technology): A military corporation, responsible for the investigation and development of advanced technologies and weaponry, much of which is classified. They do, however, contribute to a lot of the progress of the Utopian society as a whole and the Utopian allies, creating cleaner, safer means of transportation, health care, and energy usage.

Mond: A male figure of the global faith that is kept on Galiza, surrounding the moon; Anua. Keepers of ancient knowledge surrounding the religion of Anua. They are guides and wisemen that one can look to in times of uncertainty and gloom.

Neuro-chips: A rectangular device that ranges in size depending on the code. It is installed at birth and designed to grow in part with the brain. A standard code one neuro-chip is small and takes on a thin, webbed shape, spanning over the top of the brain. Whereas a code nine can take up almost a tenth of the brain's anatomy and compensate for the functions in either hemisphere of which it is placed. Any neuro-chip upgrade is used as a means of repercussion in the Utopian society, each one further limiting an individual's freedom and control over their own biology, thoughts, and emotions.

Pac: A moderate rank for an officer. They hold command over the base armory, and oversee inventory and rations. Their responsibilities extend to ensuring that Fades are loaded with proper equipment and accessories before a launch. They can also serve as training officers among various lower ranks.

Pac-Qua: A moderate rank for an officer rank. They hold the immediate command over base troops when higher-ranking officials are not promptly available.

Rella: A female figure of the global faith that is kept on Galiza, surrounding the moon Anua. They are keepers of sacred medicines and practices that only they are allowed to partake in or those they deem deserving of them.

Reikag: The head of base security. This officer has special clearance and access to various levels of classified information. They enforce laws and can pass judgement among civilians and military personnel until a proper trial can be arranged.

Sphike: The name of the smaller Zeltonian combat craft.

Skiv: Human scavengers and the majority of humanity over the course of the war with the Zeltons, abandoned by the various militias of the world. Common people with no tie to military personnel. They spend most of their time starving, tucked away in the ruins of cities and towns, trapped in the crossfire. They're lucky if they can find a few days' worth of food at a time.

Splice: A hilted device that, when flicked, forms a short, nano-metal blade. A weapon that was developed during the rise of regenerative nano-tech, in the first year of the war of the Zelton/human war.

Qi'val: A rank shared between the Varx: Quavek, Xaizar, and Voruke—among the Diramal's best and Zothra's lieutenants. When they operate outside the immediate command of Zothra and or the Diramal, they can control fleets of Varx at a time, but never Vix.

Quantum Fade: A perilous side effect that can threaten the user of any and all quantum suits. While the suits can facilitate a quantum field for humans in a battle against the Zeltons, their biology is not equipped with the stabilizing Meceuro atoms. Found naturally throughout the anatomy of the Zeltons, the Meceuro atoms split, expand, and bounce off one another at high velocities. Not only does this allow the invaders to alter time at any depth they so desire, it holds their organs, bones, blood vessels, skin, and everything else in place, so that they may move at great speeds without the risk of harming themselves. The QS-25 allows the humans to match these speeds, most of the time, moving at speeds beyond sound. Amat himself can reach greater. But the difference between the QS-25 and the Meceuro atom itself is that the suit can only protect its users from external threats and if its limits are pushed too far, there's nothing stopping a human heart from imploding or lethal and rapid brain hypoxia.

Vi-warmigol: An organic bio-weapon in the form of an insect. They were developed by M.I.S.T. researchers during the time frame of the Utopion/Afeikita war, as a means of infecting open wounds and killing off the incapacitated Kintabú alliance. Unfortunately, production of the weapon was discontinued and its use was made illegal when the rotting corpses that had been infected spread a plague that nearly wiped out more than half the Afeikitan continent.

'Versing: An ability that allows Amat to reverse the movements of any being he directs his palm toward. So far as he knows, Amat is the only individual capable of this power.

Vorüm'Qij: The true rank of Zothra, the Diramal's second. When the Diramal is absent, he holds command of whichever Vix and Varx accompany him. He is the only bearer of the rank.

Warv: A general Utopian term for Skivs who have scavenged their own means of self-defense, taking up armor and weaponry off dead soldiers. They launch their fronts not only against the invaders but the militia as well. They despise the militia and fear the mysterious Shadow Scar, whom the Warvs have associated with the militia under some kind of twisted, secret genetic modification program. Their first priority is themselves and will rarely take on newcomers. By the third year into the war, they have become formidable in their fighting skill and are not a threat to be taken lightly.

Milton Keynes UK
Ingram Content Group UK Ltd.
UKHW020244221123
432980UK00016B/1010